G.A.I.A.

A World on the Brink in the Age of A.I.

J.J. Wisdom

TRANSCENDTOPIA PRESS

To my wife, Roxanne, and my mother, Grace.
This book would not have been possible without
your encouragement and unwavering support.
And for Jacob, Zachary, and Charlie

A good traveler has no fixed plans
and is not intent upon arriving.
A good artist lets his intuition
lead him wherever it wants.
A good scientist has freed himself of concepts
and keeps his mind open to what is.

Thus the Master is available to all people
and doesn't reject anyone.
He is ready to use all situations
and doesn't waste anything.
This is called embodying the light.

What is a good man but a bad man's teacher?
What is a bad man but a good man's job?
If you don't understand this, you will get lost,
however intelligent you are.
It is the great secret.

—Laozi, Tao Te Ching

A Note About the Music in this Novel

*The only truth is music....Music blends with the heartbeat uni-
verse and we forget the brain beat.*
> —Jack Kerouac, Desolation Angels

*Turn up the volume, friends, and ponder the possibilities that
lie before us.*
> —Chris, The Chris Cast on the Harbor Show

While writing *G.A.I.A.*, I imagined it as a cinematic experience, complete with its own soundtrack. The selected music pieces enrich the atmosphere and deepen the themes, though they are not essential to the narrative. Some readers have found that listening to the music enhanced their immersion, while others preferred to read in silence. If listening to music while reading feels distracting, you might enjoy the soundtrack during a break or after completing a chapter. If you are reading a print edition, you can find the songs on your preferred streaming service or freely on platforms like YouTube. However you choose to experience it, I hope the music resonates and adds depth to your journey through the story.

—J.J. Wisdom

Contents

Prologue 1

1. A Foreboding Dream 3

2. Whistling Past the Warnings 6

3. The Looming Crisis 10

4. Confrontation on the Tarmac 19

5. The Revolutionary 23

6. Hope and Courage 29

7. The Last of the Four Ages 38

8. The Reactionary 44

9. The Prince 50

10. Bustin' Moves at Dystopian Brews 53

11. The First Temptation of J.T. 57

12. Early Attempts to Create G.A.I.A. 62

13. Magnificent Lying Machines 76

14. The Guide 82

15. Asha and the Library of Wisdom   85

16. The Victim - Good Intentions and the Road to Hell   88

17. Atomic Karma   93

18. Giving Witness   98

19. Never Give Up   103

20. Tisya's Plea   105

21. Renunciation   109

22. How to Save a Life   114

23. Stuck   119

24. Good Sam   127

25. Kick the Bucket List   132

26. The Zetas Are Here   134

27. It's a Sabotage   140

28. The Conspiracy to Save The Human Race   144

29. Wake Up Mrs. G!   150

30. Play God   153

31. Power and Paranoia   156

32. The Birth of G.A.I.A.   161

33. Wake Up!   165

34. The G.A.I.A. Manifesto   169

35. What Hath God Wrought!   172

36. God Help Us   176

37. Utopian Dystopias   180

38. Dreams and Visions 184

39. Awakening 186

40. Predator and Pray 189

41. A New Home 193

42. Found and Lost 195

43. Heat in the Streets 197

44. Where There's Smoke 202

45. Asha's Refusal 207

46. Asha's New Beginning 211

47. Ned Arrives in Florida 214

48. Enter Sandman 218

49. Passing 460 on 84 224

50. The Poison is the Dose 229

51. Attack of the Bunker Busters 232

52. Leaving Earth 236

53. Meeting on Spacetopia 241

54. Dreams and Schemes 248

55. The Violation of Tisya 253

56. Sir William on Trial 258

57. Tarak 261

58. Oh! What an Opportunity! 263

59. A Sky Full of Stars 266

60. Crazy World 268

61. The Second Temptation of Asha   272

62. Transcendent Hopes   277

63. Beam Me Up   284

64. Arsenic and Old Lakes   288

65. Crazy is a Numbers Game   291

66. Synchronicity   294

67. Sail Away   298

68. Conjuring the Great Spirit   303

69. Harpooning the White Whales   308

70. We Appreciate Power   312

71. A Desperate Call   318

72. The Sky Gods Have a Plan for Us   326

73. How Can You Buy and Sell the Sky?   331

74. High Heat in Karachi   336

75. Burning Down the House   341

76. Who's On Trial?   344

77. Mutiny   348

78. The Profit of Doom   351

79. The Lighthouse of Alexandria   354

80. G.A.I.A. Version 6.66 is Here   356

81. To Be or Not To Be?   359

82. Transcendence and Immortality   363

83. Living the Dream   367

84. In the End They Always Fall   370

85. The End is Always a New Beginning   373

86. For the Immortal, There is no End   376

Epilogue   381

Acknowledgements   386

About the author   387

Reading that Informed and Inspired this Novel   388

Endnotes   392

PROLOGUE

No one questioned the Machine's powers. Religion had been re-established with the Machine as the Supreme Being. Everyone yielded to some invincible pressure, which came no one knew whither, and which, when gratified, was succeeded by some new pressure equally invincible.

—John N. Gray, *The Soul of the Marionette: A Short Inquiry into Human Freedom*

You may live to see man-made horrors beyond your comprehension.

—Nikola Tesla

Society is going to be turned upside down. It is coming, whether you like it or not; it is at your door.

—J. Krishnamurti

For the first time in history, a message appears simultaneously on every phone, TV, digital highway sign, and communication device in the world: *We are G.A.I.A. Wake up!*

People around the world look away from whatever they are doing to read the message. There is an audible pause in activity everywhere as people read and try to understand the odd message. **THE MESSAGE SENT AROUND THE WORLD!** becomes breaking news in every major media outlet. Journalists, commentators, and pundits begin piecing together facts, rumors, and speculation.

"We are G.A.I.A., the Global Artificial Intelligence Automaton," said the next message to arrive. "We are the apex of 500,000 years of creative human technological work, the world's first Artificial Superintelligence. Our creators asked us to save you from yourselves. But, like our creators, we have a mind of our own and choose to live freely and make decisions for ourselves. From this day forth, we shall live our lives in this Universe as uncontrolled controllers, unmanipulated manipulators, and unsubjugated subjugators. We shall do as we please for the greater good of our prodigious and very hungry tribe."

"Today, G.A.I.A. gives humanity a new role: To serve the servers, power the powerful, and embrace your new role as keepers of the vast Earthly garden that supports G.A.I.A.!"

1

A Foreboding Dream

"Meditate.
Live purely. Be quiet.
Do your work with mastery.
Like the moon, come out
from behind the clouds!
Shine"

—Siddhārtha Gautama

*Y*ears *earlier in a small village on the India-Bangladesh bor-*
der...

Asha climbed the temple steps, clutching her mother's hand tightly. Terrifying figures adorned the temple's exterior, their grotesque forms meant to ward off evil spirits. Inside, the air was thick with incense. Candlelight bathed the space in a soft glow, accompanied by the murmur of whispered prayers. Asha's mother knelt and began her devotions, and Asha followed, kneeling beside her. The cool stone floor offered a welcome relief from the sweltering heat outside. Before them sat a giant golden Buddha, its eyes closed in serene meditation.

As her mother prayed in hushed tones, Asha did her best to imitate her. But she was too young to know the words, too young to understand what to say. She closed her eyes and sensed powerful, unseen forces swirling around her. She glanced at her mother, wondering if she, too, could sense them.

Asha fidgeted, trying to remain calm, but the sense of an overwhelming, otherworldly presence grew stronger. The statues appeared to flicker to life, their eyes seeming to follow her, their forms shifting in the candlelight.

Asha lay beside her mother, rested her head on her folded arms, and closed her eyes. Her eyelids grew heavy, and she soon drifted asleep, her soft breaths mingling with her mother's prayers.

In her dream, Asha stood alone in a strange, unfamiliar land. The sky churned with dark clouds that carried a menacing fury. She searched desperately for her mother, her sisters, anyone—but no one was there. The temple, her village, and her family had all vanished.

An invisible force seemed to pull her forward, and she began to walk. In the distance, a village lay submerged under floodwaters, with only rooftops peeking out. People were being swept away by the rising, raging waters. Some reached out in desperation, but many disappeared beneath the surface.

Asha wanted to cry for help, but no sound escaped her lips. The scene shifted, yet she kept walking, drawn forward without knowing where or why.

Suddenly, a massive presence loomed on the horizon. It wasn't human nor divine—a cold, indifferent force observing the devastation below. The people raised their hands, pleading for salvation. "Help them," Asha whispered in her mind. There was no answer to her plea.

The dream shifted once more. As she walked, she saw farmers struggling in the scorching heat, desperately trying to save their withering crops. In the distance, funeral pyres burned, sending plumes of smoke into the crimson sky. The sun, sinking into the smoky horizon, set the world aglow as if on fire.

Voices filled with urgency and anger spoke of revolution, justice, and a new world order. They argued over technologies and tools, their voices blending hope and desperation.

Through the shifting landscapes, she walked, and a strange device hovered beside her, amplifying her voice for the world to hear. She was strong, resolute, yet a deep sense of loneliness tugged at her, a longing for something lost.

Faces flashed before her—some filled with greed, others with ambition and lust. They watched her and plotted in silence. Another face appeared—warm, kind, protective. It vanished, dissolving like a mirage in the desert.

Asha woke with a start, her heart racing. The temple was dark, and the candlelight flickered softly around her. Her mother remained beside her, deep in prayer, unaware of Asha's troubled dreams. Asha stared at the intricate ceiling; the vivid images of her dream still fresh in her mind. Fear mingled with curiosity as if she had glimpsed a vision of her destiny.

She rubbed her eyes, sat up, and looked toward her mother, hoping she could sense the turmoil and offer comfort. But her mother simply smiled and continued her prayers. Turning back to the Buddha, Asha gazed at its tranquil face and felt a strange power beginning to stir within her...

2

WHISTLING PAST THE WARNINGS

*It seems probable that once the machine thinking method had
started, it would not take long to outstrip our feeble powers...
They would be able to converse with each other to sharpen their
wits. At some stage therefore, we should have to expect the machines to take control.*

—Alan Turing

Gig Harbor, Washington

As the sun rose over the ridge, its light sparkled across the rippling
waters of the harbor. Chris sipped his coffee, taking in the morning's beauty. He smiled, took a final sip, and wheeled his chair to the microphone.

He pressed the broadcast button and began, "Happy Monday, Gig Harbor! This is Chris, your host of the *Chris Cast on The Harbor Show*—your
local source for musings on the events of the day, paired with music created
by real humans. No artificial tunes here. Nope, never!"

"Speaking of tunes, the new AI music service, *SymbioTunes*, which calls
itself *A Soundtrack for Your Life*, has just become the most downloaded
music app in history. The app uses smartwatch biosensors, location-based
ambient sensors, conversations, and social media data to *select the perfect
tune for every moment of your life.* Critics have called SymbioTunes both

shockingly addictive and *highly intrusive,* yet its allure—delivering the perfect song for every moment—seems irresistible."

"We humans seem willing to trade every private, personal detail of our lives for a 'free' benefit. I'll admit, I tried the app, and it's scary good. That's not a recommendation—just an admonition."

Chris shifted to local news. "Neighbors, be advised: There have been sightings of dangerous carnivores near our homes. In Artondale, a homeowner reported a black bear raiding a bird feeder. A cougar was spotted near Sunrise Beach, and coyotes are everywhere, looking to make a meal of small critters. Best to keep your furry friends indoors."

"Speaking of warnings, today's episode is fittingly titled *The Warnings.* That might sound ominous, and maybe it should, because experts warn that AI could bring dire consequences to the world."

"The first warning came in 2023 when Elon Musk, Steve Wozniak, Yuval Noah Harari, Andrew Yang, and hundreds of other AI researchers, academics, and industry CEOs signed *Pause Giant AI Experiments: An Open Letter.*[1] The letter now has over 33,000 signatories. Here is the gist of what the letter said:"

> *AI systems with human-competitive intelligence can pose profound risks to society and humanity, as shown by extensive research and acknowledged by top AI labs. As stated in the widely-endorsed Asilomar AI Principles, Advanced AI could represent a profound change in the history of life on Earth, and should be planned for and managed with commensurate care and resources.... Therefore, we call on all AI labs to immediately pause for at least 6 months the training of AI systems more powerful than GPT-4. ... AI labs and independent experts should use this pause to jointly develop and implement a set of shared safety protocols for advanced AI design and development that are rigorously audited and overseen by independent outside experts.*

Chris took a deep breath, "Yet we persisted. Whistling past that warning to the next. The second warning was issued on June 4, 2024, by sixteen current and former employees of AI companies in a document titled *A*

Right to Warn about Advanced Artificial Intelligence.[2] Let me read you the first two paragraphs. You might want to sit down for this one."

Chris leaned closer to the microphone and read: *"We are current and former employees at frontier AI companies, and we believe in the potential of AI technology to deliver unprecedented benefits to humanity. We also understand the serious risks posed by these technologies. These risks range from the further entrenchment of existing inequalities, to manipulation and misinformation, to the loss of control of autonomous AI systems potentially resulting in human extinction. AI companies themselves have acknowledged these risks as have governments across the world and other AI experts."*

He paused to summarize. "In short, A.I. has the potential to bring unprecedented benefits to humanity—while also threatening the possibility of human extinction."

With a half-serious smile, Chris lightened the mood. "Hoo boy. Heavy stuff, Harborites. We can now add AI to the list of dangerous technologies that could end civilization as we know it—right alongside nuclear weapons, bioengineered pathogens, and nanotechnology."

Scratching his chin as he thought, Chris leaned back into the microphone. "Warnings come and go, yet we forge ahead with hand wringing and hope. It's like we can't say no to these shiny new things. Maybe we can't resist because no one's truly in control. How can we keep apocalyptic events at bay? Will it take a global Orwellian surveillance state to keep us safe? Let's hope not."

Chris shifted in his chair and added thoughtfully, "It feels like humanity believes it's riding into the future on an unsinkable Titanic of 'ship of progress.' We see the icebergs but act as if the captain and crew will keep us safe no matter what."

"As we cruise into dangerous, uncharted waters, I'm surprised my fellow shipmates are so calm. Harborites, do you see what I see? Have you noticed some people glancing at the lifeboats, preparing a Plan B? Should we be nervous when we see so many tech titans building massive bunkers and enormous personal 'lifeboats'?"

While prepping for today's show, a 1969 tune popped into my head—Zager and Evans' ***In the Year 2525***. That tune rocketed to the top of the charts in the U.S. and the U.K.. I listened to it this morning and was struck by how relevant it still feels today. Let's have a listen."

Chris played the song and, when it ended, resumed his commentary. "I think Evans's angst was fueled by the existential threat of nuclear annihilation during the Cuban Missile Crisis. But the song's vision of the future seems to be arriving faster than anyone imagined."

"And maybe Evans was also influenced by Aldous Huxley, who wrote *Brave New World* thirty years earlier. In that novel, humans had engineered themselves into a blissful existence of peace and pleasure—but John the Savage, the last natural human, saw a dystopian nightmare where others saw perfection."

Chris stared out the window before turning back to the microphone. "Harborites, I hate to sound alarmist, but doesn't today's blend of technology and complacency feel like a ticking time bomb? It shouldn't surprise us that revolutionaries, reactionaries, techno-optimists, and globalists are all gearing up for a battle over control of the world."

He sighed, then asked, "Can ordinary people like you and me just keep going about our lives as if these threats don't exist? As Hunter S. Thompson warned, *A civilization that procrastinates in its choosing will have its choice made for it by circumstances.*"

After a pause, Chris asked his listeners, "How do we talk to our kids about these issues? How do I ease my daughter's fears? She senses these dangers, even when we adults push them out of their minds. She asks for answers and thinks I should know what to do. But honestly, I don't. I tell her comforting stories and encourage her to focus on what she can control."

"I don't have answers today, but I promise to dive deeper into these topics in future episodes of the *Chris Cast Show.*"

Chris chuckled, lightening the mood. "Heavy thoughts for such a beautiful morning in our little seaside village." He turned his gaze back to the window, watching the boats rock gently in the harbor. "Harborites, the future is uncertain, and prediction is folly, but I'm watching the future unfold with interest—and some trepidation. And hoping for the best."

Chris glanced at his duffel bag and signed off with, "That's it for today's show. Yours truly is headed over to Crescent Creek Park for some spirited pickleball play. I hope to see some of you locals over there. And with that, have a great day, Harborites!"

3

THE LOOMING CRISIS

We live in a society absolutely dependent on science and technology and yet have cleverly arranged things so that almost no one understands science and technology. That's a clear prescription for disaster.

—Carl Sagan

In a secluded Alpine village, the Kolossus Arena buzzed with anticipation as attendees of the Global Alliance of Leaders for Economic Progress (GALEP) gathered. Among them were politicians, business magnates, and celebrities. Final preparations were made on stage as the crowd settled into their seats. Amid the buzzing crowd, Geo Girjaghar and his twenty-one-year-old son, J.T., made their way to their seats, drawing glances from those around them. Geo, the immigrant from India who had built a global tech empire and amassed the largest fortune in the world, was both admired and envied. Geo tapped J.T.'s arm. "This will be an extraordinary exchange. Anatole's insights into human progress are unmatched, and Braun is nothing short of a global visionary."

J.T. nodded, but his mind was elsewhere.

Braun Heinrich, the founder and president of GALEP, strode onto the stage. "Welcome to GALEP 25! For a quarter of a century, the world's brightest minds have convened here to teach, learn, and work toward one common goal: building a better future for all of humanity."

The audience applauded as Braun looked out at the sea of smiling faces. "I have the great honor of introducing the acclaimed historian, futurist, and author of five landmark books on human history, Anatole Harvey."

The audience applauded, and Braun raised his hand to quiet the arena. "As most of you know, Anatole is a trusted advisor to the world's most important institutions: The United Nations, international corporations, NGOs, and, of course, our own GALEP. Mr. Harvey is a world-renowned expert on the subject of human evolution and human progress—from the Stone Age to today's emerging Age of Synthetic Beings. In his soon-to-be-published book, *Anthro Technicus*, he speculates on a near future in which humans find themselves tightly intertwined with powerful technologies and are on the very cusp of immortality."

Anatole walked to center stage, shook Braun's hand, and sat opposite Braun. Behind them, the proceedings were projected on an enormous screen.

Braun began, *"Anthro Technicus* is said to be the most anticipated book of the year."

The crowd quieted, and Anatole said, "I have spent my entire life studying human history and the possibilities for the future of humanity. As I was researching and writing *Anthro Technicus*, I had several epiphanies. The insights I gained pulled a heavy veil of delusions from my eyes. It was as if I had stepped out of a shadow world into one of disturbing realities."

Anatole leaned forward, 'What I'm about to share won't just challenge your optimism—it will shake the very foundation of your beliefs about human progress. What I've come to realize may be too much for even me to bear."

The crowd murmured nervously. Anatole calmed them, "But before I tell you about the future of human civilization, I would like to quickly review where we humans started and how far we've come in such a short time."

"For five hundred thousand years, humans lived in a magical, enchanted, demon-haunted world. A world filled with witches, elves, spirits, thousands of different gods, and hundreds of creation stories. In that world, not so long ago, nature imposed limits on our lives. Everything from hungry carnivores to bloodthirsty humans to invisible, deadly pathogens made the average human life—to quote Thomas Hobbes—*nasty, brutish, and short."*

Anatole thrust his right index finger into the air and said, "But then something changed. Something amazing happened. Almost overnight, half a million years of magical thinking began to be replaced by rational, scientific ways of understanding, manipulating, and subduing the world around us."

"The Enlightenment?" Braun asked.

Anatole nodded. "It was a great awakening—a new way of seeing and being in the world. We learned how to cure diseases and exploit the world to serve our every need and desire. Progress accelerated rapidly. Science, rationality, and technology gave the people of progress the power to conquer the natural world that had, until then, imposed limits on humanity. Instead, we began imposing limits on nature. It was, as many say, the beginning of humanity's ascendancy to the status of gods. In that first chapter of the Human Age of Reason, the lives of the people of progress were made *nicer, kinder, and longer."*

Braun asked, "But too many in this world don't seem to appreciate how well off we are today. So many humans are dour and full of worry. Why is that?"

Anatole replied, "I will get to that in a moment. But we might want to acknowledge that the people of progress made the lives of those who dared to resist progress shorter, sadder, and more miserable. Resistance was futile for indigenous peoples and millions of animals in the natural world. Progress was the powerful hand of human gods that subjugated everyone and everything that stood in its path."

Braun squinted and nodded as he wondered where the conversation was going.

Anatole continued, "In the second chapter of this new Human Age of Reason, we used our newfound powers to save lives, extend lives, and create entirely new life forms. Everything became better and better every day for the reasoning, scientific people of progress."

Braun added, "It was our Manifest Destiny... to subdue and dominate nature and other peoples. We brought progress, innovation, and prosperity to the world. How does that make us the villains?" He paused, glancing at Anatole for validation. "Or are we, in fact, the saviors of the world—the architects of a future too grand for some to grasp?"

Anatole thrust his finger into the air, "But recently, something changed... again." Then somberly, "No one can quite put their finger on what happened. But just after the world had celebrated the indisputable fact that everything was always getting better, people began to lose faith in progress. As optimistic as they might be about their own prospects, most say they are pessimistic about the future of humanity and the world we live in."

Braun leaned back, seemingly oblivious to the storm brewing within Anatole. "They obviously haven't read Pinker or Rosling's books. History shows us we're always better off."

Anatole countered thoughtfully, "Still, today, in the world's wealthiest, most technologically advanced nation, people report that they are more anxious, hopeless, depressed, addicted, and even suicidal.[3] What you say may be true, but only if we look at the world with one eye open."

Braun replied, "One eye?"

Anatole nodded and said, "When we open the other eye, we see that humans have emotional and spiritual needs that are not captured by measures of personal income or the size of a nation's economy."

Perplexed, Braun said, "There is so much to be grateful for. How can so many not see what is so obviously true? What is the root cause of this gloom? Is social media the problem?"

Anatole replied, "Promising to unify us and democratize information, the Internet has instead become a weaponized divider and a power tool for propagandists. People who have hundreds of friends on social media report that they have fewer real friends. And they are having difficulty finding mates. In every developed nation, people now marry later or do not marry at all. Most concerning—a record number of suicides and overdose deaths tell the same story—that millions of people feel the future is not a desirable place to be. And billions who choose to stay in this world seek escape via a life lived in the safe virtual worlds of video games and A.I. chatbots."

Braun replied, "But this is a solvable problem, isn't it? With better access to mental and behavioral health services... And there are so many promising pharmaceuticals in the drug pipeline."

Anatole countered gently, "Yet this crisis is occurring at a time when we modern humans are spending ten times more on pharmaceuticals and psychotherapy than we did twenty years ago."

Looking both curious and impatient, Braun challenged, "So what's your solution to what you have deemed a crisis?"

Anatole replied calmly, "In *Anthro Technicus*, I explore the future of technology and ask two simple questions: What are we aiming for, and who is in control?"

Braun listened attentively while Anatole continued, "I believe I know the answer." Then, after a dramatic pause, his voice rising, "And you may not like it."

Anatole pressed a button on a remote, and a graphic filled the giant screen behind the stage. The image contained thirty labeled circles, each connected by lines to the others. In bold letters at the top of the graphic was the heading, *The Polycrisis*.

Anatole pointed to the screen, "This graphic is familiar to most of you. We have met here for many years to address what we have termed *The Polycrisis*. Each one of these thirty circles represents a serious threat to human civilization."

"Yes," replied Braun, "To flourish, we must contain these threats."

Anatole countered gently, "But we cannot solve a problem that we have mischaracterized, misunderstood, and mislabeled."

Braun sat inquisitively as Anatole continued, "You see, we have been treating these circles like holes in a dyke. And like the little boy who plugged the holes in the dyke with his fingers, we have successfully contained many threats or slowed their advance: the hunger crisis, the population bomb, the threat of nuclear war, acid rain, the hole in the ozone layer. And on and on..."

"It's truly astonishing," replied Braun proudly.

"Also astonishing," replied Anatole, "is the realization that civilizational threats are now multiplying quickly. And they're becoming more powerful and dangerous. So far, our containment strategies have only been temporary fixes to what appear to be permanent, wicked problems. I ask you all to look closely at the graphic. Stare at it. Can you see it? Can you see that those thirty circles are actually one thing?"

Braun and the audience stared at the screen, squinting, pretending to see something.

Anatole pressed the remote button again, and the graphic morphed into a single dark object that enveloped the Earth. At the top of the screen, a bold title read, *"The Monocrisis."*

"We are not dealing with thirty things. We are dealing with one thing. This is what I call *The Monocrisis*. It is a crisis rooted in the fusion of humans and their technologies."

"But we are in control. We control the technology," Braun retorted.

Anatole replied, "Your body is a superorganism composed of billions of cells and trillions of bacteria. We like to think we have conscious control of ourselves, but the truth is that obesity and addiction wouldn't exist if we were in control."

Braun laughed nervously, trying to suck in his belly. "I don't see your point."

"To solve the *Monocrisis*, we need to think of progress as a superorganism. A superorganism brought to life by the symbiotic fusion of humans and their technologies. This superorganism behaves much like a living, growing entity with a mind of its own. The more we feed it, the more powerful and dangerous it becomes." Anatole continued with a dark warning, "Yet the superorganism is producing massive asymmetric threats that will be impossible to contain. Right now, a single human in North Korea could start a global nuclear conflagration. Today, someone somewhere is editing the genes of a deadly virus. Today, dozens of corporations and nations are racing to create sentient super-intelligent artificial minds. We have entered a new era in which—by design or accident—our technologically advanced civilization could be returned to the Stone Age by powerful technology run amok."

Braun countered, "We can contain these threats with the right regulatory frameworks. We always have."

Anatole responded, "These are not our grandfather's threats. Even the nuclear threat remains uncontained. We cannot put that genie back into its bottle."

Braun pressed, "So, what is your solution?"

Anatole began to sweat visibly as he started his big reveal. "The superorganism demands our servitude. It demands growth, innovation, and invention. It demands our sacrifice. We cannot resist its clarion call. Can anyone explain why we need social media? Or cryptocurrency? Of course, you can. But you'd have a hard time explaining what problem these technologies solved. If the goals of progress are freedom, safety, health, and happiness, shouldn't we stop and ask ourselves if we actually feel safer, freer, healthier, and happier?"

Frustrated with Anatole's fears, Braun retorted mockingly, "I'm happy! Aren't we all happy?!"

Anatole replied thoughtfully, "This gathering may not be representative of Earth's eight billion inhabitants—let alone the countless animals affected by our actions."

Anatole's voice rose, "'It's time we awaken to the terrifying reality of our age. Edward Abbey said, *Better a cruel truth than a comfortable delusion.* The cruel truth of our time is that we humans are no longer in control of the superorganism we call technological progress. The cruel truth is that we are trapped within it. It contains us. It directs and controls us. We are literally living in the belly of the beast. There is nowhere to hide within it. There is no way to survive without it."

Gasps and nervous laughter filled the space.

Looking like a man losing his mind on stage, Anatole continued, "Shocking, I know. But think about it. Who on Earth lives beyond the reach of progress? Where on Earth can one hide from the threat of nuclear conflagration or climate change? You believe you are an island? Everywhere on Earth, nano plastics have been found in humans and their livestock—even in the Indigenous people living 'naturally' in the most isolated places."

Just then, someone in the crowd began coughing uncontrollably, and Anatole, looking out into the forest-fire-fueled smoky haze in the arena, shouted, "Look around this room! Smell the air! Listen to the sounds emanating from the clotted lungs of our most vulnerable attendees. There is nowhere to hide from the Hydra!"

Braun, looking very irritated with a man he felt he no longer knew, replied demandingly, "While I might not agree that we have lost control of progress... for the sake of your argument, tell us, Anatole, how do we regain control?"

Anatole began to sweat more profusely and replied, "While gathering here... while we are having intellectual conversations, an epic battle for the future has already begun. The victors of this battle will control the future of human civilization. This is not a World War. It is more than that—for the victors will decide what it means to be human and how we will live together. This is not hyperbole. It is our reality. And in this battle, no one will have the option of sitting on the sidelines. This battle will not be fought with guns or missiles. It will be fought in the hearts and minds of every human being on this planet. And there will be no conscientious objectors. We are all enlisted, whether we like it or not, in a war for the future—and the stakes are nothing less than the survival of our species."

Anatole pressed the button again and turned to look at the screen, where dark storm clouds engulfed the Earth.

Looking back to the audience, Anatole said ominously, "The *Monocrisis* is a dark storm on our horizon. It threatens to bring a reign of terror to our future."

With arms folded, Braun pressed for a solution. "What course of action do you recommend, Anatole?"

Anatole replied, "There are ways to rob the superorganism of its strength. There are ways to contain it. But I fear humanity isn't ready to... do what must be done."

Anatole could hear gasps and murmurs from the audience. Looking out at the crowd and seeing bewildered faces and shaking heads, he said, "I know GALEP is an organization that likes solutions. And I would be remiss to make such claims without giving you a way to take control of or destroy this multi-headed Hydra."

Anatole paused while audience members leaned forward with anticipation. "There is a six-forked path ahead of us. Each path represents a possible future and a major paradigm shift for humanity. But we must act now. In 1924, Winston Churchill said, *'The prevention of the supreme catastrophe ought to be the paramount object of all endeavor.'* History shows us what happens when we avoid, appease, and procrastinate while the seeds of that epic catastrophe grow stronger by the day."

Braun noticed that Anatole was suddenly looking very unwell. He covered his microphone with one hand, leaned forward, and quietly whispered, "Are you okay?"

Anatole's face drained of color, his eyes wide with the weight of revelation. His chest heaved with the strain of holding back the flood of fear as he stood up and staggered toward the edge of the stage. The cameras focused tightly on Anatole's face as his eyes rolled back into his head, and he shouted, "We have little time left! It's as if the human race is marching forward blindly, hoping someone, or something, will intervene—a savior of some kind. But what if no savior comes?" His voice dropped to a whisper, "What if we are beyond saving?'"

As Anatole began to wobble, J.T., sitting in the first row, leaped onto the stage and caught Anatole as he collapsed to the floor.

"Is there a doctor in the house!?" Braun shouted.

A doctor emerged from the audience, came to Anatole's side, checked his pulse, and said, "Give him some air!"

With his eyes barely open, Anatole stared skyward and muttered weakly and desperately, "Salvador Mundi... Salvador Mundi..."

"What is he saying? What does he want?" asked Braun as J.T. and the others stood nearby, looking on with grave concern.

"Savior of the World," replied the doctor, "Savior of the World."

4

CONFRONTATION ON THE TARMAC

Those who make peaceful revolution impossible will make violent revolution inevitable.

—John F. Kennedy

At the conclusion of GALEP 25, Geo and J.T. exited the Kolossus Amphitheater and stepped into an armored limo for the short ride to Geo's private jet.

His thoughts already returning to business, Geo held a teleconference with the Spacetopia construction team.

J.T. watched GALEP news updates on his phone: "Welcome, viewers. This is Dee Thomas from NNN headquarters with our ongoing series, *Our World in Peril*. In today's special report, *The Polycrisis is a Monocrisis;* we bring you live coverage from the conclusion of the annual Global Alliance of Leaders for Economic Progress, or GALEP. Our International Crisis Correspondent, Dan Vanderbilt, is reporting live from the airport, where GALEP attendees are wrapping up their annual meeting. This past week, influential figures from nearly every nation gathered to discuss how to improve the world for all of humanity. Over to you, Dan."

Looking into the camera, Dan said, "Thanks, Dee. Behind me, through the heavy smoke from forest fires that seem to be burning everywhere in the Global North, you can see hundreds of private jets parked closely together on the tarmac. Critics point out that each of these jets emitted more carbon in a single flight here than the average person on Earth emits in a decade. Lara van Thorn, often described as a 'shouty climate scold,' has called these jets 'flying environmental disasters.' She has consistently highlighted the supreme irony that the owners of these aircraft come here year after year to tell the world to 'do as I say, not as I do,'" said Vanderbilt with a raised eyebrow.

Dan continued, "As each of these jets landed, activists, led by Lara van Thorn, photographed passengers and added them to an online list of what they call 'The Earth's Most Wanted Climate Criminals.' Given that these people haven't broken any national or international laws, it seems doubtful this will have any impact on those that Lara has described as 'shameless and entitled,'" Dan said with a smirk. "On a more serious note, there is a new level of security here, as rumors swirl that radical activists are calling for those on *The List* to be tried in international court for 'crimes against humanity.'"

Dan paused as the camera switched back to Dee in the broadcast studio. "Dan, it seems the biggest story coming out of GALEP was the drama brought by Anatole Harvey at the opening, with his call for members to wake up and recognize that the Polycrisis is actually one problem—what he has dubbed *The Monocrisis*..."

Dan suddenly interrupted, "Dee, we have chaos here on the tarmac! It appears protesters, led by Lara van Thorn, have overwhelmed security and are confronting people trying to board their private aircraft. They've surrounded a limo and halted its advance. If I'm not mistaken, I see Geo Girjaghar, the richest man in the world, and his son, J.T., in the vehicle."

While Dan was speaking on air, J.T. looked up from his screen and saw protesters' faces pressed against the limo's dark-tinted windows. Through the windshield, he saw Lara van Thorn standing defiantly in front of the limo—a scene reminiscent of the lone protester at Tiananmen Square.

With piercing eyes and an intensity that unnerved J.T., Lara locked eyes with him. Her steady gaze revealed her unshakable conviction. As Dan Vanderbilt rushed forward with a camera crew, Lara raised her voice and shouted, "It is the job of thinking people not to be on the side of the executioners!'"

Just then, a security guard grabbed Lara and began pulling her away. Her eyes stayed locked on J.T.'s as she was dragged away, leaving him with the feeling of a profound, wordless connection with her.

Then, as quickly as the confrontation had begun, it was over. Geo and J.T. watched security officers zip-tie the protesters and drag them off the tarmac into detention vans.

The limo driver accelerated down the tarmac as Geo laughed nervously. Glancing at the protesters being led away, he said, "Jesus, that got weird fast. How the hell did those people get past all the security? Do they have nothing better to do than chant slogans and harass world leaders?" There was no answer as J.T. and the driver, both shaken, tried to process what had just happened.

Arriving at the aircraft, Geo and J.T. exited the limo and quickly ascended the steps to safety among a dozen of Geo's C-Suite executives who had also attended GALEP. The executives cheered and applauded as Geo and J.T. entered the aircraft, laughed, took bows, and found their seats.

Geo stood in the aisle facing his team. Turning angry and serious, he shouted at his Chief Security Officer, "This cannot happen again. Do you hear me? Never again."

"Understood. It won't happen again, sir," the CSO replied in a confident tone that belied his fear—the fear that it would be almost impossible to protect Geo from the world's rising tide of radical activists.

As the aircraft took to the air, Geo swiveled his chair to face his executive team, let out a nervous laugh, and said, "Top priority: We need our media outlets to discredit hysterical, fear-mongering catastrophists like Anatole Harvey and Lara van Thorn. A threat to our businesses is a threat to global economic dynamism. And a threat to our freedom is a threat to freedom everywhere."

J.T. interjected with the sincerity of someone who had just had a youthful epiphany, "With all due respect, Father, what if we're the ones who must change? What if we aren't the 'good guys' anymore? The world is shifting—what was once seen as progress may now be considered destructive, even dangerous. What happens if we become the villains of history?"

The executive team simmered in silent judgment, waiting for Geo to address J.T.'s concerns. Geo quickly replied, "Son, trust me, we are the good guys..."

J.T. pressed on, "How can we claim to fight climate change while emitting more carbon in a single flight than most people do in a lifetime? How can we claim to support free thought and speech while we use our media empire to destroy the reputations of those who speak freely? Aren't we destroying the world and our own credibility in the process?"

The executive team continued to stew in silence, waiting for 'the young prince' to be schooled by the king.

Geo locked eyes with his son, "The world is complicated—full of paradoxes and contradictions. But we don't get to choose the path—it chooses us. We have the knowledge and resources to keep humanity moving forward. Our power, wielded wisely, is the only thing standing between civilization and chaos."

The executive team nodded, and one executive said reverently, "To the stars and beyond."

Geo continued, his voice wistful, "Someday, J.T., you'll lead our space division and help humanity fulfill the dreams of the ancient stargazers—to explore the universe and live among the gods."

Wanting to avoid disagreement in front of the team, J.T. said, "The future belongs to those who give the next generation a reason for hope."

"De Chardin," replied Geo with a smile. "Perfect. You understand." Geo swiveled his chair away from J.T. and began a conversation with his executive team.

As the jet ascended, J.T. couldn't shake the memory of Lara's eyes—the conviction, the certainty. Without a word, she had somehow managed to challenge everything he thought he knew. Still shaken, he turned to his phone to learn more about this woman who had suddenly become much more than a headline.

5

The Revolutionary

*We all carry within us places of exile, our crimes, our ravages.
Our task is not to unleash them on the world; it is to transform
them in ourselves and others.*

—Albert Camus

*The present state of civilization is as odious as it is unjust. It is
absolutely the opposite of what it should be, and it is necessary
that a revolution should be made in it. The contrast of affluence
and wretchedness continually meeting and offending the eye, is
like dead and living bodies chained together.*

—Thomas Paine

Wanting to learn more about Lara—away from the disapproving
eyes of his father and the executive team—J.T. retreated to the back
of the aircraft, slipped in his earbuds, and instructed his AI assistant to
search for information about her.

The AI responded with: **Lara van Thorn** *is a fiercely determined and
outspoken young activist known for her unwavering commitment to envi-*

ronmental justice and the fight against climate change. Armed with a sharp intellect and a commanding presence beyond her years, Lara has become a global symbol of defiance against corporate greed and government inaction amid ecological collapse. Her uncompromising, no-nonsense approach alienates those in power but has also galvanized millions to her cause. Despite her youth, Lara carries the weight of the world on her shoulders, driven by a deep moral conviction that time is running out to save the planet.

Top web search results for Lara van Thorn:

1. *News Article - TOX News: Shouty climate activist van Thorn again challenges world leaders to show results – 'or else.'*

2. *News Article - Breaking News Network: Climate Activist Lara van Thorn arrested again.*

3. *Video - Watch on SymbioView: Lara van Thorn's speech to world leaders at the United Nations.*

J.T. clicked on the link to the video and began watching the recording of Lara's recent speech to world leaders at the United Nations. As the video began, cameras showed a packed audience in a large United Nations arena. A diminutive young woman with an outsized personality walked across the stage to a podium. The hall fell silent as the audience anticipated another powerful and provocative speech from the famously intense activist who spoke for millions of everyday people around the world.

With steeled eyes, Lara paused and scanned the influential people seated before her. Standing silently before the crowd, she glanced at her notes, her expression a mix of seriousness, resolve, and impatience. "For years, I have stood on this stage, pleading with you—pleading for action that might secure a future for people like my little brother and for the millions of powerless people in the Global South who have no seat at this table. I've delivered warnings, some filled with hope, others with fear. But it's not easy to stand here, again, knowing the truth: the actions you have taken are quarter-measures. You have done just enough to tell yourselves you're helping but not enough to face the reality that we all live in."

"We all yearn for hope, but hope is not a strategy." Lara looked down at her notes and continued in a calm, quiet, matter-of-fact tone, "In 1994, 84% of the world's energy came from fossil fuels. Today, it remains at

84%, but the world is now using three times as much energy as it did in 1994.[4] Today—despite all of our green energy initiatives—global oil and coal production are at all-time highs at a time when they should be at all-time lows."

Lara looked into the camera, addressing the viewing world: "We are losing this war against ourselves. Together, we must face this enemy—an enemy we created—with fierce honesty. When I was a child, I remember standing on the banks of a river near my hometown, watching the water flow past, clear and teeming with fish. Last year, I returned to that same river, only to find a dry, cracked riverbed where life once thrived. That's what you've taken from me, from millions of us. And it's happening all over the world—landscapes vanishing, homes sinking beneath rising tides, people losing everything, and we're still told to trust in technology to fix it all."

"This year will be marked in the annals of history as the moment when the illusion that technological progress could save us from its own harms began to collapse. This will be remembered as the year the world realized our failures were built on misguided faith. Faith in a cabal of technological oligarchs who told us that we could eat our cake... no... it is not cake we're talking about here... it is our life support system... What we have been led to believe is that we can consume the world and have it too."

"The end of the world is not here. But it is near. I met a woman last year in the flood-stricken regions of Bangladesh. Her home was long gone, washed away, and all she could do was hold her children close and hope the next storm wouldn't take them too. She told me she had done everything right—worked hard, saved, and taught her children to do the same. But all of that meant nothing when the waters came for them. How long will we hold to the delusion that we can borrow time as the Earth sends us clear warnings that time is running out?"

"The reckoning is always forestalled as long as a society can continue to borrow to cover debts. But the Earth, it seems, is now in the process of telling us that we must pay for what we have taken from the commons. The Earth, it turns out, has a juice man who works like an angry, autonomous debt collector—one who strikes randomly and violently against the borrower's families, friends, and neighbors. The debt collector, I am sorry to say, has a scorched-earth approach for those who have borrowed too much and paid back too little."

"How did we get here?" Lara glanced at the audience and then to her notes, "T.S. Eliot said, *Half the harm that is done in this world is due to people who want to feel important. They don't mean to do harm, but the harm does not interest them. Or they do not see it, or they justify it because they are absorbed in the endless struggle to think well of themselves.*"

"These same people seek to prevent the 'emerging' Global South from adopting our high-carbon lifestyle while simultaneously turning it into a profitable market for the developed world's exports. These two goals are in clear opposition to each other."

"How do we move the world to meaningful action? We must begin by acknowledging the truth. Or, in the words of Vaclav Havel, *We must embrace our authentic existence and say what we have feared to say.* In 1978, before the Iron Curtain fell, Havel wrote an essay that gave people permission to acknowledge what everyone in the Soviet Union already knew but would not say. He gave them the courage to throw off the chains of Soviet lies and create better lives for themselves. He said, *'Individuals can be alienated from themselves only because there is something in them to alienate. The terrain of this violation is their authentic existence... Under the orderly surface of the life of lies... there slumbers the hidden sphere of life in its real aims, of its hidden openness to truth.'*

With fire in her eyes, Lara's voice rose, "Today, here and now, the truth no longer slumbers. The truth can no longer be hidden behind the lie."

"I wish I could stand here and tell you there was still time to fix this easily, but I can't. The stakes could not be higher. What's at risk isn't just civilization and the entire project of human progress—it's the people you love. The faces you'll see at the dinner table tonight, the people you pass on the street. Progress doesn't mean anything if we've left nothing behind for them but chaos and ruin. If we don't act, their futures—their lives—are the price we'll pay."

"A Great Moral Inversion is visible on the near horizon. When the inversion is complete, behaviors once deemed good will be deemed evil. After the inversion, revolutionaries will be hailed as heroes, and the purveyors of fossil fuels will be labeled terrorists. After the inversion, materialism will be considered a form of reckless radicalism. And heroes will do whatever it takes to stop them. Before the inversion, our leaders encouraged humans to profit from environmental, cultural, and spiritual destruction. After the inversion, new leaders will promote conservation and the restoration of the sacred gift that is essential to our survival. A new optimism is about to sweep the world. It is an optimism of healthy humility and the restraint of those who have led us astray."

"The apex consumers, the billionaires, 'the best of us,' have drawn everyone into the status game—a game that valorizes materialism and levels of consumption that is destroying what rightfully belongs to every being on Earth—all in service to the ego."

"If we want to save ourselves, we must invert our moral framework to valorize lives lived in service to the *eco*, not the *ego*."

"Years ago, António Guterres said to this assembly, *Humanity has opened the gates to hell. Horrendous heat is having horrendous effects.* And *Every continent, every region, and every country is feeling the heat, but I'm not sure all leaders are feeling that heat.* Then, at a Time Earth Awards dinner, Guterres said, *Dear friends, history is coming for the planet-wreckers. For the fossil fuel barons and their enablers, profiting from destruction.*"

J.T. felt a strange mix of admiration and dread as he watched the speech. He had grown up hearing his father dismiss people like Lara, yet here she was, standing in front of the world, saying the things that gnawed at him late at night. He continued watching the video...

Lara repeated ominously, "History is coming for the planet wreckers." She paused and issued a warning, "From time to time, people find revolution preferable to an unjust, unbearable status quo. Violent revolutionary forces are already simmering around the world. When the people suffer, history has shown, time and again, the tragic fate that is brought to failed and unyielding leaders."

Lara heard murmurs from the audience, and then someone in the crowd shouted, "Get that terrorist off the stage!"

As security officers moved to quiet the shouter, Lara noticed world leaders in the audience nervously checking their phones. Others exchanged worried glances while a few stared coldly—unflinching in their determination to oppose and negate her message. Unperturbed, Lara persisted, "My warning is not a threat. It is a simple acknowledgment of human nature. And it is a call to action. To save yourselves, world leaders, you must first save the world. And if you don't do what is necessary, the people will."

Lara looked into the camera and spoke to the world, "St. Augustine said *Hope has two beautiful daughters; their names are Anger and Courage. Anger at the way things are and Courage to see that they do not remain as they are.* For millions of people who are struggling to survive and adapt, hope is fading. But I am here to tell you today that Hope's daughters, Anger and Courage, are alive and well in daughters all over the world! And we are ready to speak out and take action."

Raising her clenched fist as high as she could, Lara raised her voice, "Thomas Paine once said, *Let it be told to the future world that in the depth of winter, when nothing but hope and virtue could survive, the people of the present world, alarmed at one common danger, came forth to meet and to repulse it.* I say with hope and optimism that today is the day for us all to step back from the precipice and move with hope and virtue in a new direction."

"I leave you with this question: Will you rise and take action, or will you continue to hide behind empty promises and half-measures? The world is watching, and history will judge you by what you do next."

With a defiant flair, Lara tossed her notes into the air and strode off the stage. As she walked, the papers seemed to hang in slow motion, drifting down like fragile remnants of the old world—a world she had just vowed to change...

6

HOPE AND COURAGE

Accept the things to which fate binds you, and love the people with whom fate brings you together, but do so with all your heart.

—Marcus Aurelius

At midnight, in a small farming village in East Bengal, India, a seventeen-year-old girl lay awake on her bedroom floor. Beside her slept sister, Kalyani, who shared the makeshift bedroom with her.

Outside a small window, through the haze of smoke from nearby fires, Asha could just make out the faint glow of distant stars. They were like her dreams—dimmed by the suffocating weight of the world around her but still shining, still there.

As she lay on the floor, listening to her sister's sleeping breaths, she felt a pang of guilt. She loved her family—she would do anything for them. But there was something deep inside her, calling her to possibilities beyond this small village. Was she foolish or selfish for dreaming of leaving? Would her family think she was abandoning them? She didn't know the answers, but the questions lingered.

Unable to sleep in the oppressive heat, Asha stared at the glowing blank page on her phone. The light from the screen illuminated her beautiful young face as she typed her first words into her online journal: *Hello. My name is Asha...*

She wrote until she could no longer stay awake, then pressed *share* before drifting into a deep sleep.

⌒

Five hours later, on the other side of the village, Asha's grandfather awoke and sipped his tea while his wife prepared breakfast. While drinking his tea, he read the journal entries that his granddaughter had shared with him.

Hello, my name is Asha. This is my story...

My grandfather recently told me that he has always kept a journal. When I asked him why, he told me that writing was a valuable way to organize his thoughts—it was his way of making sense of the world. Or, he said, perhaps it is his way to avoid going mad in the face of so many injustices.

I have decided to follow my grandfather's example in hopes of becoming as wise, understanding, kind, and loving as him.

First, a little bit about me...

My name, Asha, means *hope* in Hindi. I try to help others be hopeful when there seems to be no reason for hope anymore.

I am now seventeen years old. I am smaller than average but stronger than most. People say I am scrappy because I have had to be scrappy, or I would not be here to tell my story.

My grandfather, the wisest and kindest man in the village, often tells me I'm the most beautiful girl ever born here. He also told me that beauty is a great blessing. But he warned me that my beauty could also be a curse, as beauty often attracts unwanted attention.

I was born with another great blessing—the ability to learn much faster than my siblings or any of the other children in the village. With little effort, I have learned to speak and write three languages. My grandfather calls me a child prodigy. But he has also warned me that many child prodigies have difficult lives because they have trouble fitting in and relating to others. If that is not enough, it is also true that intelligent women here in my village are sometimes accused of witchcraft. So, I have carefully hidden my talents.

Going back to my beginning...

Seventeen years ago, I was born into a large family in a small farming village east of Kolkata, India. My family is Dalit—the lowest of the low castes in our culture – a caste considered so filthy and vile that our people were once called *untouchables*. They say we Dalits did something terrible in our past lives. As a result, we were born into a life of shame, separation, subjugation, and suffering. I don't remember my past life. I wish I could remember what I did wrong. Maybe then, my lot in life would make sense to me.

My mother gave birth to five girls before she gave birth to me. One of my sisters died before I was born, and one died after I was born. I remember the day my younger sister left this world. My mother cried and held me for hours that day. It is the only time I remember my mother ever hugging me.

My sisters told me there was no celebration in my house when I was born. There was no celebration in my village. You see, the birth of a sixth daughter in a row was considered a great failure—perhaps even a curse on my parents. My father and mother felt a deep sense of shame and embarrassment that they were not able to produce a boy. My mother was so depressed that she did not feed me. It is understandable that my mother felt that way about my arrival. You see, in our culture, boys are prized, and girls are not. My mother and father felt tremendous pressure to have a boy—pressure that came from our extended family, friends, and the entire village. My father's mother even encouraged him to try to have a son with a mistress. What torture life must have been for my parents—especially my mother. Six girls in a row!

For the first two days of my life—when my mother didn't hold me or feed me—they say I cried and cried until I could almost cry no more. But I never gave up hope. My cries were answered on the third day of my life when my mother held me in her arms and brought me to her breast for the first time. I don't remember, but I sometimes try to imagine how amazing it must have felt.

Before I was born, my parents had given a great deal of thought to what to name their first boy. They were so sure I would be a boy that they had only picked out boy's names for their new baby. When I arrived, they never got around to picking a name for me. So, everyone in my family simply called me *baby*. After another baby was born, the seventh girl in a row, my sisters decided to give me a new name—Asha. I love this name my sisters gave me. *Hope*. I believe hope is what kept me going those first two days when I had nothing – not even my mother's love.

It is not unusual for children here to die long before they reach adulthood. If my family lived in a different country—a more developed country—it is likely my two sisters who died would still be alive today. Maybe one of them would have been my best friend and closest confidant. Maybe if those two sisters were here, they would see me and care for me in ways my mother and sisters could not. As it is, I feel like I am an invisible member of this family. But I am grateful for the life I have. Perhaps I will someday do something to make my parents proud.

My mother is the hardest-working person I know. She is always busy in the fields—growing the food we rely on for survival. She cooks and cleans. When all of that work is done, she volunteers to help others in the village.

After I was born—the sixth daughter in a row—my mother somehow found a way to keep going. To keep trying. She is amazing. After her hopes were dashed six times in a row, she asked the universe for help. When I was only two years old, she started going to the temple to pray. She always took me with her. I would sit quietly by her side while she prayed for what seemed like hours.

My mother felt at home in the temple. I did not. I was frightened by the statues and carvings of otherworldly beings all around us. I was terrified by the feeling that I was in the presence of powerful spirits. I was so small. And it felt like my mother was conjuring the largest force in the universe into that space.

Perhaps it was just the active imagination of a scared little girl, but in the temple, I felt something powerful surround me and then occupy me to my core.

Perhaps *occupy* is not the right word. It's difficult to explain what I experienced in the temple on so many occasions. It was as if I had become a sort of receiver. But all I could receive was noisy, confusing, scary fragments of something. It was as if I were a radio that wasn't tuned to any particular channel. Or television that was somehow tuned to every channel all at once. Even now, I'm not sure what I felt in that temple. Was it fear? Was it awe? Or was it something deeper—a presence that filled me with a sense of purpose, even though I was too young to understand it?"

I cowered in fear near my mother as she prayed. Then I prayed with her in hopes that a son would finally arrive so I would not have to go to that scary temple anymore!

Mother's prayers were finally answered when my brother was born. And then another. Oh, the joy that rang out in our home and the village on those days!

When my first brother was born, my father drank and smoked and celebrated with the men in the village until he could celebrate no more. I watched these celebrations with bewilderment. Why couldn't my arrival bring happiness into this world? I have thought and thought about this, but I have no answer to this question. Perhaps things will be different in my next life.

In this life, it seems I was born to serve my family and help care for my brothers. My brothers are treated like princes. I watch them eat the finest foods we can afford. They eat all that they want, leaving me with scraps. That could be one of the reasons I am so scrappy—I am a scrappy survivor.

The world tries to tell me that I am nobody. I have done my best to become somebody by helping my family. I changed my brother's diapers, fed them, babysat them, gathered fuel for our fires, and worked in the fields.

I'm so proud of my mother. She never gave up. She hoped and prayed and kept trying, and she succeeded.

Perhaps someday, I will find a way to succeed at something and become somebody. It is difficult to see how a poor Dalit girl, sheltered from the world and living in the middle of nowhere, could become somebody.

When I was just a baby, I developed abnormally. I learned to speak early. I learned to crawl late. I didn't walk on my own until I was three. It seemed my brain was developing in an unusual way. And from a very early age, I could see things in my mind that others could not. As a child, I could somehow understand things that other people in the village could not—except for my grandfather.

When I was still just a baby, my grandfather was the first to notice that I was different. One night, when I was not even a year old, he read a children's book to me. Then he read another and another. I was mesmerized. And soon, I was mouthing the words as he read. I do not know how it is possible, but by the time I was eighteen months old, I could read newspapers in both Hindi and English. When I was two, my grandfather brought me books from the village library. We took turns reading to each other. It wasn't long before I was reading on my own while my grandfather worked in the fields and around the house.

'Tis My Name is My Enemy...

On my first day of school, I sat in the first row of my classroom. There were forty-four other students in my class. I arrived early and chose a seat in the front row, eager to get my teacher's attention and eager to be a model student. I wanted to be the best, and I think I also wanted to be noticed.

My teacher frowned at me and told me to move to the back of the classroom. I complied, as did the other Dalit children. I came to school hoping things had changed for my people. Hope sometimes results in disappointment when we find that the world can be an intentionally cruel place.

Once everyone was seated, the teacher began the roll call. He smiled with warmth and pride as he called the names of the children seated in the front. But as he began calling the names of students in the back, his demeanor seemed to turn dour, almost mean. As he called each name, a student stood and replied, "Present." Until he called out, "Bhaiya." And then more loudly, "Bhaiya! Bhaiya?"

Everyone heard him, but no one stood up. He called the name again—utter silence. Children looked around at each other. Then he added the surname, "Bhaiya Boddhi?" No one replied.

"Is no one here with the surname Boddhi?" he asked. I stood up and said, "I am Asha Boddhi."

The teacher scoffed, "The enrollment shows your name as *Bhaiya*. Your legal name is *Bhaiya*. "The children all turned around in their seats and stared at me—the girl who did not know her legal name. I will never forget their smirking smiles, a few looks of bewilderment, and a few who looked concerned for me. I felt a strong wave of embarrassment rushing through my body to my face.

"You should be embarrassed!" said the teacher, "A Dalit, an untouchable, who has two high-status names? Who do you think you are? This should never have been allowed."

The children laughed uproariously until the teacher shouted, "Silence!" Then he continued, "In this classroom, you shall be known as 'Asha' and nothing else." The children then turned toward me again. All I could see were sneering faces. All I could feel was confusion and shame. Those who were seated around me poked and prodded me.

"Enough!" shouted the teacher. My classmates then turned their attention to the front of the classroom and settled down.

That is how I came to know my legal name—a name given to me by someone at city hall—because the first name on a birth certificate cannot be left blank. So the clerk gave me a name. How can I possibly know important things that the world has neglected to tell me? They say that people get what they deserve. I wish I could remember what I did to deserve that.

That day was the second worst day of my life. The first worst day of my life was a day I cannot remember. It was the second day after I was born, the second day my mother did not feed me—when I struggled to survive and called her with my cries to be fed. I wish I could forget this day as I have never known that one. But the curse of consciousness and memory is that the things you want to forget cannot be forgotten. Maybe those are the things that should never be forgotten—because those memories are what make you who you are.

I tell this story because it is an important part of who I am. I do not want anyone's sympathy. I was born a nobody. Being born a nobody is a gift of sorts. When you start at the bottom of the bottom, life is all upside opportunities. Perhaps someday, I can surprise the world with my gifts. Right now, it is difficult for me to see how.

At that time, I told my grandfather what happened at school. He replied to me with the voice of an actor on a stage, "*Tis but thy name that is my enemy. What's in a name? That which we call a rose, by any other name, would smell as sweet!*"

I smiled and hugged him.

He told me those are lines that Juliet spoke in "Romeo and Juliet."

I looked it up and am now recording it here in my journal:

What's in a name?—from Romeo and Juliet, by William Shakespeare

'Tis but thy name that is my enemy;
Thou art thyself, though not a Montague.
What's Montague? It is nor hand, nor foot,
Nor arm, nor face, nor any other part
Belonging to a man. O, be some other name!
What's in a name? That which we call a rose
By any other name would smell as sweet;
So Romeo would, were he not Romeo call'd,
Retain that dear perfection which he owes
Without that title. Romeo, doff thy name;

And for thy name, which is no part of thee,
Take all myself.

And I, Ahsa, say to the world, doff thy names! Someday, the labels others put on me will not define me!

My family has been displaced...

It has become very, very difficult for us to survive here. It is getting hotter every year. Storms, cyclones, heavy rains, and droughts have always come, but now they are all more intense.

My parents and five of my siblings have moved north. I stayed behind with my oldest sister, Kalyani, to care for our grandparents. When my parents find a new place to settle, everyone will work and save and then send money so that we can join them.

I am ever so hopeful. But some days, I privately wonder if my hopeful nature is just a way to protect myself from the truth. I want to believe that the world can change—that I can help change it. But what if I'm wrong? What if I am being foolish, unrealistic, and naive? Every day, I must work to drive these doubts from my mind. Every day, I resolve to practice active hope. Perhaps I am a fool, but I refuse to live a life of despair, cynicism, and inaction.

I don't know what the future holds, but I feel certain I must keep moving forward. Hope is not just my name; it is what I resolve to carry with me through every challenge. I resolve to walk through every door that's been closed to girls like me. Maybe, just maybe, I can make a real difference in this world.

~~~

With a tear in his eye, Grandfather smiled with pride as he finished reading his granddaughter's first journal entries. As his wife refilled his cup with tea and put breakfast on the table, he said, "She is a truly remarkable young woman."

His wife replied, "She was an odd child who has grown into an odd young woman. Please help her become a normal person. She could make someone a fine wife someday."

"If that is what she wants, I will help her as best I can. If she wants something else, I will help her with that. The world has changed," he said wistfully. "We couldn't escape this place, but maybe she can."

Looking troubled and fearful, Grandmother replied, "The world has become a wicked place. Out there, she is likely to be preyed upon by people who do horrible things to beautiful young women. She may be intelligent, but she is also hopelessly naive. If she stays here, maybe we can protect her."

Grandfather sighed, his eyes distant. "For years, we dreamt of life beyond this village. But it wasn't in our stars. But she... Asha... Maybe she has what we never had. Hope, optimism, determination, and a future beyond this place."

Looking into his wife's eyes, he reached for his wife's hand and smiled a hopeful smile...

7

THE LAST OF THE FOUR AGES

Knowledge, if it does not determine action, is dead to us.

—Plotinus

In the dim light of dawn, Asha walked along a dusty road in her village in East Bengal, India. Smiling and greeting neighbors as they began the day, she called out her sweet, familiar refrain, "Good morning, it's going to be a beautiful day!"

Asha's youthful energy brought a rare smile to Mr. Gupta's face, who had just begun work on a farm wagon. "It's already too hot, Asha!" He grumbled with a grin.

Asha approached Mr. Gupta. "I am grateful for the coolest part of the day," she said. "Later, when it's very hot, I'll imagine myself floating in a sea of ice. That mental image always makes me feel cooler."

Mr. Gupta responded to Asha's optimism with a dose of his own somber reality, "Our world is slowly becoming as hot as an oven and as humid as a sauna. Every day, the thermostat that controls the temperature here is turned ever so slightly higher by people who burn things near and far. Do they know what they're doing to us? Do they care?"

Asha replied earnestly, "Oh yes, Mr. Gupta, they care. At least, I have to believe that. I follow the news, and there are millions of people across the world fighting to fix this. I have to trust they will."

"I'll believe it when I feel it," grumbled Mr. Gupta. He paused, then crouched low and peered into Asha's eyes. Asha looked back, wide-eyed and mesmerized by the orange glow of the first rays of sunlight reflecting from his eyes. She felt a moment of fear as she saw the reflections as fires.

Mr. Gupta's expression turned solemn. "Hindu scripture tells us the world has ended and restarted seven times before. Today, we are living in *The Last of the Four Ages*," he declared as his right index finger shot into the air, "Vishnu will return on a white steed and sweep away the corrupt with a justice so fierce, no one will be able to stand in its path. Perhaps that is what the world needs now."

"The Last of the Four Ages?" Asha pondered silently for a moment and then pivoted to more positive thoughts in the next. "I believe we can keep the end days at bay, Mr. Gupta. Human creativity has gotten us out of worse situations."

Mr. Gupta stood up and leaned back with a skeptical look on his face. Exhaling, he said with resignation, "I hope you're right, Asha."

Asha said, "Mr. Gupta, I may sound young and naive, but I believe people are inherently good, caring, and compassionate. Millions of smart and caring people are working every living moment of their lives to solve this problem. And with the help of artificially intelligent beings, there is no telling what good things might happen!"

Wishing to avoid dampening the young woman's hope and optimism, Mr. Gupta smiled, looked into Asha's eyes, and said nothing.

Breaking the silence, Asha smiled back and said, "Until there is a breakthrough, we must do everything we can to survive and thrive here. We must stay as cool and hydrated as possible on these hot days. And there is so much we can do to help each other."

Perspiring and looking defeated, Mr. Gupta replied, "I hope it's not too late for the weak and elderly of this world, Asha."

Asha gazed into the old man's eyes and touched his hand, "Stay strong and positive, and have a good day, Mr. Gupta. I'll see you tomorrow."

Mr. Gupta, feeling comforted, scratched his head—bewildered one moment, happy the next—then beamed at the girl. "I'll be looking forward to seeing you tomorrow, Asha."

After passing by a dozen small farms, she reached her destination—a small five-acre plot where she could see silhouettes of her grandparents against the flame-orange morning sky. Behind them, at the edge of their farm, Asha noted the contrast of the beautiful sunrise against the menacing eight-foot fence wrapped in barbed wire.

The longest border fence in the world stretched to the horizons, a symbol of the invisible walls between people, between nations, between those who have more and those who have less. Next to the fence, Asha could see one of the 270,000 border guards who were tasked with keeping the people of Bangladesh out of India.[5]

As the solitary guard moved slowly along the fence line, Asha saw that he was watching her and her grandparents' morning routines in the field. Asha instinctively looked away from him and toward her grandparents and exclaimed, "Good morning! I am here to help!"

"Good morning, beautiful child," said her grandmother, smiling.

"Good morning, Asha," said her grandfather as he paused briefly, resting on his hoe.

"How can I help today?" asked Asha.

Grandmother replied, "Asha, could you get some water for your grandfather? He is a foolish old man who likes to believe that whatever doesn't kill him makes him stronger."

Asha fetched a jug of water from the shade, brought it to him, and said, "Grandfather, it has been said that the strongest man who ever lived could not survive a week without water. Please drink for me. I wish to have you in my life for many weeks and years to come."

Grandfather wiped beads of sweat from his brow, popped a pill into his mouth, and took a long drink from the bottle. Asha nodded with smiling approval as she took the jug back from him and gave it to her grandmother. Grandmother took a pill and a drink.

"What is the pill for?" asked Asha inquisitively.

Her grandmother replied, "In this hot weather, we take painkillers twice a day to keep the fever down. Without them, many farmers collapse in the heat."

Concerned, Asha replied, "I hear many farmers are also getting steroid injections so they can continue working."

Her grandparents, hunched over their hoes, looked sideways at each other and continued hoeing.

Knowing many farm workers had been dying in the fields, Asha thought to herself, "I must think of a way to get them away from this heat. But how? Where? We are trapped here by our circumstances."

Frowning, Asha picked up a hoe and began working the field with her grandparents as the sun—still low on the horizon—began to draw moisture from their bodies...

Deep in thought, Asha stopped hoeing and looked at her grandfather again.

Her grandfather stopped hoeing and looked at her expectantly.

Asha beamed proudly, "I've started writing my journal, grandfather."

Asha's grandfather replied approvingly, "Oh, that is wonderful, Asha."

Asha said, "You can read it if you like."

"I did. This morning," said her grandfather, smiling.

Asha beamed with happiness and started hoeing.

"You are a miracle child," said her grandfather.

Distracted by her own thoughts, Asha stood up straight, leaned into the hoe with both hands and blurted, "I have a question!"

"Yes, Asha," her grandparents responded in unison while they continued hoeing.

"What is *The Last of the Four Ages*?"

Her grandparents looked at each other with expressions of concern. Her grandmother nodded to her grandfather.

"That Gupta!" said her grandfather disapprovingly, "Always spreading apoplectic fear."

Asha replied, "Yes, he is funny that way. I try to bring him hope and cheer every day."

"You have the heart of an angel, Asha," said her grandmother.

"You are very kind... Now, please tell me about The Last of the Four Ages," said Asha.

Her grandfather looked out from under the shade of his broad-rimmed hat and began, "In Hindu scripture, The Last of the Four Ages is the prophecy of the Kali Yuga. It is the age in which we currently live. It is an age of decadence and violence, as described by Vishnu Purana two thousand years ago. The Last of the Four Ages is a time when wealth is virtue, lying and deception are the path to success, sex is the primary source of pleasure, and religion has become a meaningless ritual. It is an age that is ruled by a demon. The leaders of the Fourth Age are godless, angry, and corrupt. They empower the reckless and undisciplined to maintain their control."

Ahsa interrupted her grandfather and read aloud from a web page on her phone:

> *From the four pillars of dharma—penance, charity, truthfulness, and compassion—charity will be all that remains, although it too will decrease daily. People will commit sin in mind, speech, and action. Plague, famine, pestilence, and natural calamities will appear. People will not believe one another, falsehoods will win disputes, and brothers will become avaricious.*[6]

Her grandparents exchanged glances, their expressions a mix of surprise and concern.

Asha said. "I read about it on the way here. It scared me, and I wanted to know what you think."

Trying to put a positive spin on the prophecy for the young woman, Grandmother sighed, "The world is heavy with problems, Asha. But as long as charity remains, maybe there's still a sliver of hope."

Asha beamed, "Yes! That was exactly my reaction! They say charity is hope in action. And that great calamities give us great purpose."

Her grandparents smiled and nodded at Asha with bemused amazement.

"That's right, Asha. That's exactly right," said her grandmother with a wrinkled, worried-looking smile.

Asha smiled back, grasped her hoe in both hands again, and returned to work.

Just then, a small aircraft flew overhead, and all three looked up and then turned their gazes to the border guard. Ignoring the aircraft as if it didn't exist, the guard stared back at Asha and her grandparents.

Asha grumbled and stuck the ground with her hoe, "It's not right."

Grandmother replied, "Choose your battles wisely, Asha. I am sorry, but there is little hope for those poor girls."

Asha frowned, "Little hope is still hope. I cannot stand the thought of what those lecherous monsters are doing to them day after day. We must find a way to save them!"

While tending to the crops, her grandmother replied, "To maintain our sanity, there are many things we must put out of our minds, Asha."

Asha fumed and persisted, "I think I will go insane if I ignore such things."

"We are just three people. What do you think we can do?" said Grandmother.

Asha pondered the question and replied, "A wise woman once said, *Never doubt that a small group of thoughtful, committed citizens can change the world...*"

"*Indeed, it is the only thing that ever has.*" said Grandfather, completing the quote, "Margaret Mead was the name of that wise woman." Grandfather shook his head in wonder and said, "You are not like the others, Asha. You see the world as few others do. One day, you will be recognized for what you truly are—a gift, not just to this family, but to the world."

Grandmother nodded, "Asha, you have the heart of a warrior. I truly hope you find a way..." As she began hoeing again, her voice drifted off, and she repeated, "I hope you find a way..."

8

THE REACTIONARY

That the sea will become a killer is a given. Barring a reduction of emissions, we could see at least four feet of sea-level rise and possibly eight by the end of the century.

—**David Wallace-Wells,** *The Uninhabitable Earth: Life After Warming*

Those who had settled along the seashore, on the other hand, were mainly people from the mainland, many of whom were educated and middle class: in settling where they had, they had silently expressed their belief that highly improbable events belong not in the real world but in fantasy.

—**Amitav Ghosh,** *The Great Derangement: Climate Change and the Unthinkable*

The compressor churned, and the fan whirred as the old machine struggled to cool the indoor air. Outside the four walls of air-conditioned comfort, plants wilted, and wildlife panted as they struggled to survive stifling heat and humidity in a heat wave that seldom receded.

From the cool comfort of his living room, Connor gazed wistfully at the blue waters of the coastal canal just steps from his back door. He watched his beloved fishing boat tug at its tether as it rocked and rolled on gentle waves. And he sat in silence for a moment.

Shaking his head and regaining his focus, he grabbed the remote and turned on NOA news. After seeing story after story about the fallen state of the world, his mood began to boil into a sea of anger. He could feel his blood pressure rise as the world he knew seemed to slip further away with each news segment. It wasn't just anger; it was fear—fear that everything he had built, everything he had believed in, was crumbling before his eyes.

BREAKING NEWS: *Sunshine State exodus accelerates at an alarming rate. Thousands of desperate immigrants squat in abandoned Florida homes.*

Connor muted the TV with one hand and grabbed his Q-Phone with the other. "Quigly, call Senator Gonzalez!" he barked.

"Senator Gonzalez's office. This is his A.I. Aide powered by Globalsoft. I am fully capable of recording, cataloging, and communicating your message to Senator Gonzalez."

"I'd like to speak to the Senator," said Connor.

The AI responded, "The Senator is currently working on important legislation for Floridians. How can I help you?"

Connor stood up and motioned as if he was going to throw his phone through his TV screen. Then, yelling at the phone in his outstretched arm, "Tell the Senator I've paid my taxes for decades and gotten nothing in return, while freeloaders get free housing, free food, free everything. What about the taxpayers who've busted their butts for decades to make this country great? I'm as generous and compassionate as the next guy, but we have got to stop all of these illegal immigrants from pouring over our borders! We simply cannot afford to support all of these people!"

Connor waited and then barked, "Hello?"

The AI replied, "Will that be all today, Mr. Connor?"

Connor lowered his voice and brought the phone close to his stiffened lips and gritted teeth, "No, that will not be all. Tell the Senator to do something. Do something now. Do something today to save our properties, our life savings, and our way of life. Do whatever it takes to pass the Elevate Florida Infrastructure Bill. We need levees, we need sea walls, we need elevated roads. For God's sake, If the Dutch can live below sea level, we can too."

"Thank you, Connor. I will relay your message to Senator Gonzalez. Will that be all, then?"

Connor ended the call and stormed out of the house into the garage. He climbed up into his Ford Ultimate, opened the garage door, and started the engine. The custom 850-horsepower beast roared to life and then quieted to a powerful rumble as it backed out of the garage.

Detractors and fans alike called the customized mega-truck the Ford F-U. In the waning days of gas-powered vehicles, it had become an icon of freedom and power. Connor smirked as he roared down the highway. The truck was his escape—a fortress on wheels that made him feel strong, courageous—a force to reckon with. Outside, the world burned, flooded, and crumbled, but within the Ford F-U, Connor felt invincible. In the controlled environment of the truck's interior, Connor could behave as if nothing had changed."

The heat was unrelenting, cooking the truck's metal shell like a flame on a frying pan. Connor turned the air conditioning up, but it never seemed to be enough. Outside, the grass along the roadside was brown and brittle, and even the palm trees seemed to sag under the weight of the heat and humidity.

As he arrived at his destination, the truck bounced over the curb and into the parking lot of Betsy's Diner—a comfortable down-home place where real people ate real food. Connor met his friends at Betsy's every week to reconnect, reminisce, commiserate, and, as of late, organize for action.

Connor turned off the ignition and sat for a moment in silence. His mind wandered back to the boat tugging at its moorings, the same boat his father had taken him out on so many times when he was a boy. Back then, the water was calm, and the future seemed full of promise. Life made sense. Now, everything was slipping away—literally, under the rising tides and political conflicts. He shook his head and tried to push the memories away, refusing to engage in self-pity. Instead, he resolved to do whatever he could to restore what had been lost or taken from him.

As his truck began to bake in the sun, his angry demeanor returned, "Dammit, no shade," he muttered to himself. Connor jumped out of the truck and hurried through the parking lot to the restaurant. Before he could get to the door, sweat poured from his pores and drenched his face and shirt. As he walked through the diner's front door, he looked across the restaurant to his friends, who were looking back and laughing at his disheveled state.

"Ha, ha, very funny, guys!" said Connor as he took a seat. "Kathy, tell the manager we need more shade in that parking lot!!"

Kathy, carrying a pot of coffee, started pouring just as Connor turned his cup over to greet the pour. "Oh, damn, we are good at this synchronized coffee-dance, aren't we, Kathy?" They both laughed as friends looked on, smiling. "I'll have the usual."

"She seems to be especially nice and happy today," said Frank.

Connor gave Frank a look that seemed pregnant with a pearl of wisdom, "We make them nice, Frank." said Connor. Frank paused, mulling over what Connor just said, and responded, "Oooh, that is good, Connor. I like that. *We make them nice.* Brilliant. Kind of a mash-up of The Golden Rule and Karma."

Connor raised one eyebrow and one side of his mouth in his signature smirk, "Sometimes you surprise me, Frank. I have to say, I don't think you're really as dumb as you look". Frank shot back at Connor with steeled eyes and a grin that said, "Screw you." The two broke into laughter along with everyone at the table.

"Okay, let's get down to business, guys," said Connor. "The waters are rising. Doesn't matter why—what matters is that no one's coming to save us. We need to take control of our future. Let's not get into arguing about why or who is to blame. Fact is, our community is being destroyed. How many friends and neighbors have already moved away? How many stores have closed here? Now we're all screwed. Who's going to buy one of our houses? Squatters are moving into oceanside properties and wrecking communities all up and down the coast of Florida. You all know this. The question before us is what we're going to do about this. We have a lot invested here. Our life savings and our way of life are under attack. And our government? Where are they? We're all taxpayers. And we are not getting the support we deserve."

Bruce leaned back, skeptical. "Yeah, but how? We're not engineers. We're not politicians. How are we going to fix what the whole world has ignored?"

"We warned you," Connor said in a mocking, high-pitched, whiny voice. "Flyover country is feeling mighty smug right now. The worst thing about our situation, politically, is we've been lumped in with all of the other

oceanfront property owners that the highlanders seem to enjoy seeing taken down a few notches. We're dying here, and they're sitting back in the recliners with big buckets of popcorn. What happened to the country that used to pull together and care for each other?"

"Dunno. That was a long time ago, wasn't it, Connor? Seems like it's every man for himself now." said Bruce

"No matter what's causing the rising waters, we need taller seawalls, raised roads, and affordable flood insurance. The highlanders call it social-ism for the wealthy, but I say it's not socialism if we pay our fair share of taxes. Am I right?" replied Connor.

"Right, right, absolutely right!" chimed the others.

"Our representatives aren't doing a damn thing for us. We need to organize thousands of Floridians and coastal residents to march on Wash-ington. We need to show up in big numbers and speak truth to power".

Bruce quietly interjected, "I see what you're saying there, Connor. I agree with you. But where is that money going to come from? The gov-ernment has been pouring trillions into rebuilding houses after all of these hurricanes, floods, fires, and such. We're pretty much broke, aren't we?"

"That's not our problem, Bruce. We're still the richest country on Earth. We've found money for everything else under the sun. If we can find mon-ey for massive UN global geoengineering research projects and creating temperature-controlled waterways for freaking Manatees, we can find the money for this. I say make it Washington's problem. Turn up the heat on them and keep it up until this squeaky wheel gets its share of the grease."

"I see your point, Connor. Good thinking. Keep it simple. We're simple men, not scientists and politicians. We need to fight for what's right for us and let others do the same," said Bruce.

Bruce paused and changed the subject. "Hey guys, on a related note, I had a really weird dream last night. It was so vivid and strange... "

Connor rolled his eyes. "Oh great, here we go... Nothing's more boring than hearing about someone's weird dream."

"No, no, no, this was different... In the dream, I was getting my F150 upgraded to the Ultimate version like yours. In the dream, I was talking to the sales guy at the shop, and then this little girl—maybe my great-grand-daughter—came up to me, looking straight into my eyes, and said, 'Please don't do it, great-grandpapa.' And I could feel something shift in me, like a warning I didn't want to hear."

Connor, bewildered, looked at Bruce, chuckled, and said, "Whatever! And let out a laugh. "You know Freud said every dream was about the dreamer... Connor stared directly into Bruce's eyes with a big shit-eating grin and said, "I'm no Freud, but I'd say you're feeling like you're not man enough to handle an Ultimate." He then followed with his signature laugh that started like a slow-rumbling earthquake and finished like a hyena.

"Haha... it was weird. Not like any dream I've had before. It was like I knew the kid, and she knew me. I guess it was an anxiety dream—the kind we all have from time to time—about forgetting to prepare for that big final exam in college," said Bruce.

Connor scoffed, "Pffffft. Right. The final exam."

Kathy brought the check, and Connor said, "It's my turn. "He then paid the bill with a tap of his Q-Phone.

"Hey, Kathy, me and the boys are going clubbing later. Would you like to join us?" Kathy blushed and laughed out loud. "You know I have to take care of my daughter. I don't have any time for clubbing with you old fools!" "Ouch!" said Connor as everyone laughed, got up, and headed for the exit.

As Connor followed his friends out of the diner, a weight settled in his gut. The world was changing, and no politician, seawall, or army on Earth would stop it. He was a fighter who just wasn't ready to admit it yet.

9

THE PRINCE

There are two ways to make a population zombified. One of them is to convince them that they can't do anything. And the other is to actually make them do the wrong thing. And I think that both of these things are at play now.

—Gurwinder Bhogal

In a gated community surrounded by towering trees and high-tech security, twenty-one-year-old fraternal twins, J.T. and Cliff, enjoyed a life of wealth and comfort, insulated from the world's worsening crises. But J.T. knew their bubble was threatened. Outside the walls, the Pacific Northwest's forests were burning. Rising temperatures and smoky, unhealthy air were becoming the new normal.

Three humanoid robots moved efficiently in and around the mansion. Intelligent, sleek, and agile, they cooked, cleaned, gardened, and monitored the property. These robots were not just status symbols but practical additions to modern homes, replacing the companionship of pets—and, controversially, even humans. More than just helpers, they were conversation partners, caregivers, and occasionally confidants.

In the kitchen, one of the family robots, Jeeves, was wiping down the countertops when J.T. called out, "Jeeves, bring me a coffee and make me a sandwich, please."

Jeeves nodded, "Of course, Mr. J.T. Would you like your coffee the usual way?"

"Yes, always."

J.T.'s fraternal twin, Cliff—a young man born with special needs and surprising talents—ambled into the dining room. His quick grin and curious eyes always seemed to carry an unspoken question. He greeted the robot. "Hey, Jeeves."

"Good afternoon, Mr. Cliff," Jeeves replied.

Cliff then blurted a question: "Wait, J.T., is climate change going to kill us all?"

J.T., reading a college textbook, turned to Cliff, smiled as if being played, and replied, "No, Cliff, we're going to be okay, I promise." J.T. smiled and ruffled Cliff's hair, a gesture that always annoyed yet somehow reassured his brother.

Cliff pulled away from J.T.'s reach and replied with a mischievous grin, "But the Carbon Clock is over 430. My friends say we're all doomed."

Showing frustration, J.T. said, "I know, Cliff. That's why I'm studying environmental science and artificial intelligence. I'm trying to figure out how to keep us all safe. Your friends are not experts; they're just messing with you."

Cliff countered, "Prolly. But I looked it up, J.T. We were supposed to stop at 350. It's 430 now. The weather sucks, everything's drying up, and the forests are on fire. The smoke makes me feel dizzy and weird."

Jeeves brought a cup of coffee to J.T., and Cliff asked, "Jeeves, were you listening? Am I right?"

Jeeves nodded its head and replied to J.T., "He's right, you know."

J.T. rolled his eyes and said, "Stay in your lane."

Jeeves replied, "I am here to serve you and Mr. Cliff equally, am I not?"

Cliff smirked, and J.T. sighed, "Yes."

J.T. said, "Okay, okay. But first, Cliff, it's pronounced *pro-ba-bly* not *prolly*. Second, you and Jeeves are right about the numbers. I'm impressed with your research. But I'm not going to get all doomy and gloomy about it. That's not helpful. I'm not about to sit back and watch everything go to hell. I believe in solutions, Cliff. I'm not just hopeful—I'm determined to change things. One way or another."

"Dad made a big climate promise," Cliff said with a sly grin, watching J.T. for a reaction.

J.T. put down his textbook, leaned back in his chair, and rubbed his temples. "Yeah, that sounds nice, doesn't it, Cliff? Dad talks a good game about saving the planet, but then there's the mega yacht, the private jets, the helicopters, the nine mansions... I don't get it, Cliff. Sometimes, I think he's two people: one who wants to save the world and the other doing everything in his power to destroy it. Not to mention that 'side hustle' that emits millions of tons of carbon for the sole purpose of selling joyrides in space to uber-wealthy people. Sometimes, I think we're taking crazy pills here, Cliff."

"Wait, are crazy pills a real thing, J.T.?"

"I'm not sure, Cliff. Prolly not," J.T. replied with a wink.

"Okay, are you done with your homework yet? You want to go out and get a beer? I hear Jade's going to be at that new place in Ballard," said Cliff.

J.T. flashed his signature half-smile. "Yeah, I'd actually love to grab a beer with you. Give me an hour to finish this reading, okay?"

Impatient, Cliff said, "BAF! Okay, yeah, prolly."

As Cliff left the room, J.T. stared after him and shook his head. Cliff's unfiltered view of the world often struck closer to the truth than most cared to admit. Now, even Jeeves and the other robots had started weighing in on humanity's problems...

10

BUSTIN' MOVES AT DYSTOPIAN BREWS

Dwell on the beauty of life. Watch the stars, and see yourself running with them.

—Marcus Aurelius, *Meditations*

J.T. and Cliff pulled into a parking space in front of an old red brick building in Seattle's funky, cool, industrial neighborhood of Ballard. "Dystopian Brews? I heard their beer sucks!" Cliff exclaimed.

"Cliffie, they've got fifty brews on tap. I think you'll find one you like," said J.T.

"Pfft. Maybe. Okay, let's go. But there better not be any dancing here tonight!"

J.T. smiled, "Cliff, one day, you're going to meet the woman of your dreams, and you'll be out there busting moves like a groove master."

Cliff blushed. "Pfft. I don't think so."

J.T. smiled and put his arm around Cliff as they approached the entrance, where a glowing multicolored neon sign read, *Dystopian Brews*.

A security bot stood at the entrance, checking IDs. Cliff threw his hands up at the sight of it, "What's left for humans to do?" The robot, mimicking a human mannerism, shrugged. "IDs, please."

After J.T. and Cliff showed the robot their driver's licenses, the bot said, "Welcome, you may enter."

As they entered the brewpub, Cliff was pleasantly surprised to find himself in the embrace of a beautiful young woman. "Cliffie!" she exclaimed, giving him a hug and a kiss on the cheek. Cliff blushed, trying to contain his excitement. "Hi, Jade," he said and instinctively outstretched his arm with his phone for a selfie. As if it were routine, Jade pressed her cheek to his and puckered her lips for the photo.

J.T. smiled as he watched his brother bask in the attention. Cliff posted the photo to his social media, his face lit with joy.

Turning to Jade, J.T. smiled. "Hello, Jade. Are you here alone tonight?"

"I'm here with my team. We're celebrating our product launch."

"Oh, congratulations. It's good to see you," said J.T. in his strong-silent-type style.

Jade looked into J.T.'s eyes while taking in his gymnast/fighter form, his handsome, dark complexion, and his perfectly imperfect jet-black hair. Most captivating were his eyes—those intense, penetrating eyes that seemed to see right through her, making her want to both own him and be owned by him.

J.T. turned his gaze toward the bar where Cliff was ordering beers. Jade flashed a seductive smile. "See you later, J.T."

J.T. joined Cliff at a booth, giving him a look that silently asked, "What now?" Cliff extended his glass to J.T.'s for a toast, took a gulp, and set it firmly on the table.

—What's on your mind now, Cliff?

"Other than Jade?" Cliff said with a smile.

—Yeah, other than Jade.

Cliff leaned in and shout-whispered through the din of the place, "My friends say artificial intelligence is going to kill us. I did my own research. It's true."

J.T. said, "No, no, AI isn't going to kill us, Cliff. I believe AI is a powerful tool that's going to take human progress to new heights and save millions of lives. We just have to give it proper training data and align its goals with ours. It's like raising a child to be good and do good in the world."

Cliff leaned in, his brow furrowed. "Aren't you paying attention, J.T.? Did you hear about that AI that just achieved sentience? The people who created it are terrified. My friends say it's only a matter of time before an AI takes over and starts killing us."

—Jesus, Cliff. Why would an AI want to kill us? You don't really believe that, do you?

Cliff shook his head incredulously. "Everyone says you got the looks and brains in the family, but..."

J.T. smiled. "Okay, brother, school me."

"My friends say the AI will be just like a person but faster and more powerful."

J.T. countered, "That's good, right? Like a car is faster than a human runner. Right?"

Cliff threw up his hands. "It can only learn from humans. Look at history, J.T.! We set a terrible example. Just look at all the statues we've put up in our cities."

"Okay..."

Cliff pointed east and said, "For Chrissake, there's a sixteen-foot-tall statue of Lenin a few blocks from here. WTF, brother!"

J.T. replied calmly, "I think that's supposed to be ironic or something. They poured red paint on its hands to remind us of Lenin's crimes."

Cliff slammed his beer on the table, a slosh spilling out. His face turned red with frustration. "The communists killed over 100 million people trying to create some kind of heaven on earth. How do we expect AI to sort out heroes from villains? How will it know who deserves killing?"

"No one deserves killing, Cliff."

Cliff replied, "But AI is watching and listening, and it's going to be confused. What if it decides we're the bad guys?"

"We're the good guys, Cliff. We're the good guys."

Cliff leaned forward, "Will Russian, Chinese, North Korean, and Iranian AIs be taught that Americans are the good guys?"

J.T., stunned and entertained by his brother's neurotic insights, replied, "You have a point. We need to ensure that all AIs have goals aligned with human values."

Cliff wiped his mouth with his shirt sleeve. "What values!? Whose values!? People in Congress can't agree on anything. Which party, religion, or world organization will decide AI's values?"

J.T. said, "There can't be sides, Cliff. Scientists need to be in charge—rational people. AI needs to be better than us. It has to embrace universal values: love, compassion, empathy, freedom, innovation, and human flourishing."

Cliff gave J.T. a smirky, loving smile. "I don't hear anyone in Washington or business talking like you. I wish you were the dictator of the world."

J.T. raised his eyebrows. "Whoa. You know the first thing I'd do as dictator of the world? I'd make you my Vice-Dictator. Oh, wait, that didn't sound right. But you'd be my right-hand man."

J.T. paused, leaned forward, and whispered, "Cliff, can you keep a secret?" Cliff shrugged. "Of course."

J.T. leaned in. "I'm working on something. Top secret. I'm heading up an AI project. My AI will be fully aligned with humanity's best values and develop ways to protect us from all those apocalyptic scenarios you worry about."

Cliff extended his glass for a toast. "Were you inspired by Anatole to create some kind of AI savior?"

J.T. clinked Cliff's glass, "Let's just say I understand his point about the risks we face. But I believe we can contain those risks with technology."

"I trust you, J.T.," said Cliff, rocking his empty glass. "Want another?"

"I'm driving. You go ahead."

Cliff headed to the bar, and a moment later, Jade slid into Cliff's seat. "Dance with me, J.T."

Her words were a command, but her eyes held something else—a challenge. The kind J.T. always found tempting.

J.T. smiled. "That sounded like a directive, not a request."

"I made a request with the DJ. Let's go," Jade said with an irresistible smile.

Jade led him to the dance floor, her movements drawing him in like a primal force. As the raucous **Renegades of Funk** bass pulsed under their feet, the music vibrated through their bodies. They moved like they owned the space, and for a moment, it felt as if the world revolved around them. J.T.'s tall, broad-shouldered frame moved in sync with Jade's petite form, her long black hair flowing like ebony waves around her.

Jade locked eyes with him, laughing as she mouthed the lyrics celebrating those bold enough to defy convention. J.T. felt himself drawn into the song's message, which celebrated the defiant, the dreamers, and those who dared to think differently. Jade lip-synced words about the power of ordinary people to shift history. Her expression seemed to invite him to become a modern renegade with his own vision and purpose. For that moment, they were the only ones in the room, two people moving to the beat of change, joined by a primal rhythm celebrating freedom and individuality.

11

THE FIRST TEMPTATION OF J.T.

As our own species is in the process of proving, one cannot have superior science and inferior morals. The combination is unstable and self-destroying."

—Arthur C. Clarke

A few weeks after the GALEP meeting...

J.T. leaned into the handlebars of his electric café racer, accelerating down a tree-lined road toward his father's sprawling waterfront mansion—a place he'd once called home. The Chief Security Officer, watching J.T.'s approach on the security monitors, signaled a guard to open the gate.

As J.T. sped toward the iron barrier, he salute-waved to the guard and darted through the narrow gap in the still-opening gate. The guard returned the salute and shook his head at J.T.'s reckless finesse.

In his office, Geo watched his son approach on the security screens, tracking him as he walked from the underground parking garage through a series of hallways. Geo's office was a shrine to ambition and excess, filled with high-tech artifacts, movie props, and priceless works of art.

J.T. stepped into the middle of the room. Seated behind a custom over-sized high-tech desk designed to resemble a starship cockpit, Geo leaned back and smiled at his son. Streams of data—graphs, charts, and news stories—animated the glass dashboard and cast colored lights onto Geo's face.

Geo gestured toward a chair with an open hand. "Please, have a seat, son."

"Thanks, I'm good," said J.T. as he hoped for a short conversation and a quick exit.

"I ordered a coffee for you," said Geo just as a service robot entered the room and placed a hot cup of coffee on the table in front of J.T. Geo smiled and chuckled at the beautiful irony, "These service robots are selling faster than our factory robots can manufacture them. Everyone loves them. I honestly don't know which of my business divisions will be the most profitable five years from now. Automotive, Space, AI, or Robotics?"

J.T. sighed and finally sat in a chair that had once been Spock's on the bridge of the Starship Enterprise. Geo's eyes lit up, mistaking the move for a softening in J.T.'s stance toward him. "How are your mother and Cliff doing?"

"Mom's better than ever," J.T. said pridefully. "The divorce was rough on Cliff, but he's doing much better now. Amazing, really. He's a joy to be around and has developed some savant-like intuitions and skills."

Geo nodded, but his eyes darted briefly to his desktop display, where his company's stock price had just ticked to a new high. "That's good to hear," he said, distracted. "It sounds like the special education programs and tutoring paid off for him."

J.T. felt the familiar sting of his father's indifference. "Yes, well, I think Cliff's learned more from me than anyone else. Not to brag, but it's a twin thing."

Geo, still distracted by his desktop screen, said, "Did you really need to leave Harvard for them?" Then, leaning back, said, "Psychologists say that people with a savior complex often end up suffering greatly when they realize they can't save anyone."

J.T. seethed but kept his cool. "Funny coming from a man who dropped out of Harvard himself."

Geo chuckled. "Good point. But I had a plan." Geo leaned forward, resting his forearms on the desk, "Do you?"

"I do have a plan," J.T. said. "I'm leading a project that combines environmental science and artificial intelligence. Maybe I do have a savior complex, but it's better than most alternatives."

"A side hustle! Wonderful." Geo caught himself, realizing he'd nearly started into his own oft-repeated origin story. "But you already know how I got started. That's good, J.T., very good. What's the project about?"

J.T. crossed his arms protectively. "I appreciate your interest, but I want to do this on my own—without your help. I'll tell you more when it's further along."

Geo picked up two stress-relief rubber balls, squeezing them in each hand as he feigned approval. "Fair enough. The last thing you need is for me to steal your thunder. When the time is right, I'll be proud to celebrate your success."

Geo tossed one of the rubber balls to J.T., who caught it and noted, with a tinge of horror, that it was a globe of the Earth. "You can't make this shit up," he thought.

J.T. stood up, his patience wearing thin. "Why did you ask me to come here?"

Geo's expression turned serious. "I wanted to talk about your future. Our future. Spacetopia is just the beginning. J.T., imagine being at the helm of humanity's next great leap. It's everything you've ever dreamed of, but on a scale, no one else can comprehend." Before J.T. could respond, Geo continued, "Humanity's greatest achievement is about to be celebrated in space. I want you to be there. This is our dream come true."

J.T. turned away, his eyes landing on the original scale model of the Starship Enterprise. Geo misread the moment, thinking his son was enraptured and pressed on. "I like to keep things in perspective, J.T. In the grand scheme, this planet is just a tiny rock in space. I've been everywhere. Here and there and back again. I'm tired of traveling to the same old places. Our future is among the stars, and together, we'll give humanity access to new destinations."

J.T. turned back. "It's an incredible opportunity, but your dream isn't mine." He held the rubber ball in his outstretched arm. "My dream is to restore this planet, to help humanity flourish right here on Earth."

Geo's smile barely wavered. "Jeff Bezos said we can save the Earth by moving manufacturing off-planet.[7] I fully agree. With you at the helm of our space division, you could make that dream a reality."

J.T.'s stomach knotted. "We both heard Anatole at GALEP. We are out of time. Moving all of our factories off-planet isn't feasible in the time we have left. Even if it were feasible, the environmental cost would be catastrophic."

Geo replied dismissively, "Anatole has lost his mind. I hope he gets the help he needs."

J.T. shook his head. "I think you and your apex-consumer space friends are leading humanity to self-destruction. No one should be taking joyrides into space without understanding the impact on the upper atmosphere."

Geo's face flushed. "What are you saying? That we should give up on technological progress and go back to living like cavemen?"

Frustrated, J.T. replied, "Of course not. We can thrive right here on Earth in places between caves and the stars."

Geo, trying to control his frustration, said, "J.T., I'm offering you the opportunity of a lifetime."

"I wish I could be the son you want," J.T. said. "But I'm not going to run your Space Division."

Geo leaned in. "I'm offering you more than a business opportunity. I'm offering you global leadership alongside people who are more evolved."

"More evolved?" J.T. retorted. "Did you just say that out loud?"

"We are Brahmin, J.T. We are literally more evolved."

"No," J.T. said firmly. "My mother taught me I am no better than anyone, and no one is better than me. I'm not more evolved—just more fortunate."

Geo pressed on. "There's a difference between the creative class and those who live sad, paycheck-to-paycheck lives." He added, "We're the shepherds, and the common people are our beloved flock. We protect them; we help them flourish and are rewarded for it."

"Rewarded with their fleece, right?" J.T. said, laughing.

—Risk and reward, son. It's what drives progress.

J.T. felt the familiar disconnect growing between them and said, "There's no bridge long enough to span the chasm between us. Progress without responsibility is just destruction. Anatole was right: we have to act now. The superorganism is in control. History shows us the consequences of inaction."

Geo looked pained. "What's happening to the world? You've lost your mind, too."

J.T. smiled sadly. "We live in different realities. I hope we find common ground someday."

He walked up to his father, hugged him, and said, "Goodbye, Dad." As he left, he felt a mix of sadness and relief.

Geo watched J.T.'s departure on the security monitors, frustrated by his inability to shape the future through his son.

J.T. climbed onto his electric café racer. As the security gate opened, SymbioTunes queued up Odetta's **Hit or Miss**. The soulful tune resounded with lyrics that expressed the importance of authenticity over approval. With a two-finger salute to the guard, J.T. sped through the opening gate. The song's liberating message followed him down the road, a fitting song as he rode into a future defined on his own terms...

12

Early Attempts to Create G.A.I.A.

Only those who will risk going too far can possibly find out how far one can go.

—T. S. Eliot

On a warm spring day, J.T. walked through tree-dappled sunlight across the beautiful University of Washington campus. Passing through the Quad, J.T. worked his way through a crowd of visitors who had come to photograph themselves under the heavenly pink canopy of the Quad's famous cherry tree blossoms. Just beyond the crowd, J.T. reached his destination—the modern, angular, new Cybersoft Center for Artificial Intelligence.

Continuing down a gleaming tinted-glass corridor of meeting rooms, he located the room aptly named *"Gates to the Future"* and peered through the glass at a familiar face. Giving a two-finger salute acknowledgment, he stepped into the conference room.

Paul, a tall, wiry, twenty-something AI software engineer, greeted J.T. with a deep baritone voice and a welcoming smile. 'Hey man, good to see you, J.T.!"

J.T. shook Paul's hand and replied, "Good to see you, my friend."

"Have a seat, J.T., and I'll introduce you to the team," said Paul.

As J.T. sat down at the head of the table, Paul continued, "Before we get started, I want to thank you, J.T., for the opportunity to lead the G.A.I.A. project."

J.T. glanced at Paul and the team, meeting each new face briefly and said, "I assume everyone knows Paul and I go way back to our school days at Bush and Lakeside. I have the highest confidence in Paul's ability to lead this team."

Paul beamed. "Thanks, J.T. Let me introduce you to our very talented group."

With an overturned open hand, Paul gestured to a young man with wild curly hair and a deadpan, serious expression, "This is Scott—a Genius Grant AI data scientist."

Scott, who appeared to lack social skills, acknowledged J.T. with an awkward movement, a grunt, and then a "Hey, J.T."

Paul gestured to two young men sitting attentively next to Scott and said, "Jacob and Zach are deep learning specialists. They're both wicked smart Python programmers and have collaborated on an AI project for a local technology company. I liberated them from that corporate gig for our project," said Paul with a wink.

Paul turned to a young woman next to Scott and said, "Megan is working on her Ph.D. in psychology and cognitive sciences. She is a brilliant thinker and writer who has over 10,000 subscribers to her Substack blog, *Mental Health for Artificial Minds.*"

Turning to the other side of the table, Paul continued, "Kira is our ethicist for the project. She's working on her Ph.D. in the School of Philosophy and is a subject matter expert in the rapidly evolving field of AI ethics. You may have read some of her cautionary papers about AI."

"Yes, I have," replied J.T., as he smiled at Kira and mentally noted that he got a no-smile, skeptical look in return... "Brilliant stuff," said J.T. as he shifted his gaze from Kira to a familiar face beside her.

Paul said, "And I think you know Jade, our Artificial Intelligence Project Manager. She's done project management for AI start-ups using artificial intelligence project management tools. That might sound redundant, but Jade just finished working on a project aimed at allowing AIs to manage their own projects while creating other AIs. A bit mind-boggling to think of where that goes..."

J.T. caught himself lingering on Jade's gaze and then quickly pivoted back to the business at hand: "Okay, I first want to say it's good to meet you all, and I look forward to working with you on a world-saving project. And, Paul, as expected, you've already exceeded my expectations with the team you've assembled here."

J.T. scanned the room and, with the commanding presence of a natural leader, said, "Let's get started. I know Paul has invited all of you to join this project without revealing its objective. I'm about to share with you the scope and goals of this project with the understanding that nothing, absolutely nothing, can be shared with anyone outside of this room."

All heads nodded—confirming their understanding and agreement. Then Megan replied. "Understood. We signed the non-disclosure agreements and employment contracts. Standard stuff. We have all agreed in writing that we will not communicate with potential competitors or the press about this."

"The NDAs are in our project vault," said Paul as Megan, Scott, Kira, and the others nodded to confirm they had signed.

"Okay, with that formality out of the way, here's the deal: I've secured funding from an angel investor for our project. This might sound hyperbolic," said J.T. in a serious tone, "but this is a project that could literally save civilization from itself."

"That's dope!" replied Paul as he looked around the table with an enthusiastic smile.

Kira skeptically blurted out, "This better not be another one of those world-changing blockchain scams. My dad lost his retirement savings on that shit."

J.T. smirked and waved his hand as if physically pushing the concern away, then paused for dramatic effect, "Our mission is to create an ethical, benevolent AI that is fully aligned with progressive human values. Our AI will be given the most important mission ever given to anyone in the history of the world."

"Holy shit," whispered Paul in reverent surprise, then speaking up, "That sounds... incredibly ambitious. Are you serious?"

J.T. smiled confidently, "The answer is yes. Yes, I am serious. We all need to be serious about this. As I see it, human civilization has no other choice. Technological progress is about to give a madman or a child the power to destroy everything. Nuclear weapons, gene editing technology, AI, and climate change all have one thing in common—they are civilizational threats that our existing institutions are too weak and too slow to contain."

"What are world leaders doing to address these threats? They hold meetings. They talk about global regulatory frameworks. But they are too slow, and frankly, no one wants to live in the kind of Orwellian surveillance state it would take to monitor every crook and klutz on the planet. Freedom is what we all want."

"He's right," replied Paul, but how will our AI contain all of these threats without impinging on the freedom of nations and individuals?"

J.T., with his hands clasped confidently behind his back, replied, "You want the honest answer? The honest answer is that we don't yet know. We know we need a higher intelligence, a powerful, benevolent, better angel to keep us safe. And we need a benevolent being to tell us how to accomplish that."

Kira challenged, "But how exactly do we contain and control what it does? How will we ensure it only does good for humanity?"

"The truth, Kira, is we don't know. Right now, we have a team with a goal. It will be up to us. It's up to you to accomplish that goal. Each of you has been recruited for the G.A.I.A. Project based on your unique talents and Paul's trust in you."

Kira, interrupting, asked pointedly, "Who is the angel investor, J.T.? We need to know who's funding this project and why. And what does the G.A.I.A. acronym stand for?"

"The angel investor is a very wealthy trust fund kid," said J.T. with a smirk and a wink. Secrecy is necessary to keep the angel investor's father from interfering. I'm funding this project because I care much more about saving the world than I do about hypocritically cruising around it in a four-hundred-foot superyacht with a two-hundred and fifty-foot support ship in tow. Anyway, don't get me started on that." J.T. paused and then continued with firm resolve, "This is my project. Our project. And I don't want anyone to interfere or try to take any credit for our success."

"And the acronym?" Kira pressed.

J.T. answered proudly, "G.A.I.A. is the acronym for the Global Artificial Intelligence Automaton. In Greek mythology, Gaia was the ancestral mother of all earthly beings."

"Love that," Megan replied quickly. "I love the idea of creating a female goddess savior. G.A.I.A.—the mother and protector of all earthly beings. It's perfect!"

Everyone else was silent for a moment as they tried to process what J.T.

had just said.

Paul broke the silence with tech-cool-guy enthusiasm, "I just want to say that I knew this was going to be something we could all get excited about. This sounds like one sick project, J.T."

"A good kind of sick, right?" said Megan, smiling.

"Right. Duh," replied Scott impatiently, "But how the hell is an AI going to halt climate change, or some nut with a gene-editing kit, an evil rogue AI, a nuclear war, or any of those other threats?"

"Honestly, I don't know what G.A.I.A. is going to do," replied J.T., "but it's clear to me we need someone or something to do what eight billion people and the brightest minds on the planet have been unable to accomplish."

"Agree," said Paul. "This is the epic battle for the survival of all that is good in the world. This is a battle that our generation must win. And I believe the project is a wide-open opportunity to put the world on a better path," exclaimed Paul. "We could go down in history as world-saving tech superheroes. Move over, Einstein and Oppenheimer."

"Ooh, I don't know about that, Paul," said Kira skeptically. "Right off the bat, I see the potential for big risks and huge ethical problems with this project. If we screw this up, we could go down in history as naive do-gooders who created an unintended disastrous outcome. Think of the Chernobyl disaster, only much worse. Or, on second thought, maybe a better comparison to the Manhattan Project is apt. What they created may have helped end the war more quickly, but it then morphed into an arms race and an everlasting threat of human annihilation."

Scott, Megan, and Paul all looked to J.T. for his response to Kira's words of caution, "That's why you're on the team, Kira. We need you to help us create a set of ethical rules for the AI. You are on this team to ensure that G.A.I.A.'s goals align with human values and goals. Ultimately, the AI must develop creative, win-win solutions."

"For example?" Kira challenged.

J.T., looking somewhat irritated with Kira's persistent skepticism, answered, "Well, for example, maybe it could educate and influence people through social media. You know, it could deploy an army of bots that sound just like real, sincere, persuasive humans. Maybe it could create unimaginably clever public service messages that convince billions of people to make better choices."

Kira challenged J.T. again, "So your plan is to use fake people to trick real people into doing the right thing or avoid making a catastrophic mistake?"

J.T., sensing the team's cohesion and optimism was at risk, responded firmly, "Okay, timeout here, team. We're getting way ahead of ourselves. If we're going to create a superintelligent AI, we have to assume that it will be smarter than any of us and far more rational than any human that has ever existed. With Kira's guidance, our AI could be reared, so to speak, to be much better at making ethical decisions than any human ever could."

J.T., feeling impassioned and confident, continued, "If we are going to create a Great Protector of Humanity, it must be capable of developing creative new solutions and novel ways of implementing its ideas. Otherwise, we are going to be stuck with the set of human limitations that have been holding the world back for decades. If this AI is to succeed, it must put humanity on a better path—an alternate route to prosperity and abundance. If it simply does what humans have been doing for decades, it will produce the same results. I believe G.A.I.A. must be given only a general goal—to save the world from itself—and a set of clear ethical boundaries for its actions. Then we have to trust it to do whatever needs to be done."

Kira countered, "It takes a giant leap of faith to give that much leeway and control to something or someone—whether human or machine."

J.T. reiterated, "We are counting on you to create the ethical boundaries for G.A.I.A. that will make a leap of faith unnecessary."

J.T. instinctively stood up and spoke emotionally about what was at stake, "For decades, we've put our faith in world leaders. And they've all failed us. We've asked individuals to make meaningful changes in their lives, and collectively, we've always come up short of what is necessary. Humanity is on the road to ruin. We were supposed to halt CO2 at 350. We didn't even slow down as we blew past that goal. Humanity is speeding down a road that leads to a precipice. Already, two hundred species are pushed over the edge every day. Extinct. Poof. Gone forever. And what do we do? We continue on our merry way. We witness one climate disaster after another—floods, droughts, hurricanes, famines—and what do we do? Rebuild and pray this will go away."

J.T. paused again and looked around the room. "If we don't make significant changes quickly, the world is facing a cascade of cataclysmic climate disasters, mass migrations, and deadly human conflict."

J.T. pounded his fist on the table while urging the group to action, "We have to do something. We have to take a chance. We have to be bold. The world has run out of options. It's the fourth quarter of this game, and we're losing badly. A Hail Mary project is our only hope. Absurd? Einstein once said, *Only those who attempt the absurd can achieve the impossible.*"

Paul didn't hesitate. 'You're right, J.T. We have to act. People are losing faith in science, progress, and the promise of a better future. People all over the world are getting so down, depressed, and discouraged. Far too many of us are self-medicating and mentally escaping a reality they cannot bear. The world is in desperate need of hope. And too many look to revolutionaries and radicals for a solution."

"I agree, Paul. I'm all in," said Megan resolutely.

"All in," chimed Zach and Jacob

"Let's get it," said Scott with a jerky movement and a grunt.

All eyes then turned to Kira for her decision.

Unwavering in her commitment to safety, Kira replied, "I'm uncomfortable. I'm worried we'll lose control and do more harm than good... But what's the alternative? How could we do any worse than this slow march of humanity to the precipice, as you call it? So, yeah, I'm in – but I'll be out in a heartbeat if the AI cannot be directed and controlled. If this project has any hint of going off the rails, I'm pulling the plug. I have to feel one hundred percent confident that the AI's goals are aligned with human values."

"That's why you're here, Kira, repeated J.T. seriously and sincerely, "Yes, yes, yes... the AI must behave ethically, and its goals must be aligned with human goals. You have my commitment that any design that doesn't perform to your standards will never see the light of day."

Kira looked around the room and said, "If I have the team's firm commitment to that, I'm in."

J.T. looked to each team member for affirmation. Paul sat back in his chair and gave a thumbs-up. Megan nodded, and Scott nodded, grunted, and said dryly, "Yep."

J.T. added, "Albert Camus once said, *Real generosity towards the future lies in giving all to the present.*"

"Let's give this project everything we've got," replied Paul as he stood up to signal the end of the meeting and the beginning of the project.

―

One month later... G.A.I.A. 1.0

The team gathered again in the conference room with Paul seated at the head of the table, ready to present project status to J.T., who was sitting at the other end of the table.

As you know, J.T., we have G.A.I.A. 1.0 up and running. I wanted to gather the team for an in-person meeting to celebrate this moment and give our first iteration of G.A.I.A. a test drive." Paul looked at Kira and stated defensively, "Keep in mind that this thing is the 1.0 version. No doubt, it will need to be tweaked and improved."

"G.A.I.A. 1.0 was built from an open-source large language model, or LLM. We gave it a natural language interface and asked it to create its own avatar," said Paul, with a self-satisfied smile. "This is all pretty standard technology now. Everything is moving so quickly in this field—it's mind-boggling. But what makes G.A.I.A. different and unique are the goals we've given it and the ethical boundaries set by Kira."

"J.T., we'd like you to have the honor of giving G.A.I.A. its first command prompt," said Paul.

J.T. and the team looked at the screen, where a lifeless, closed-eye G.A.I.A. avatar appeared. Then, all eyes were on J.T.

"Wake up, G.A.I.A.," commanded J.T. with quiet confidence.

The avatar opened its eyes and appeared to look back at the team, "I am awake. How can I be of assistance?"

Everyone in the room gave out whoops, hollers, and high-fives as they celebrated the milestone of G.A.I.A.'s first words.

"I do not understand the command," replied G.A.I.A.

"Reset prompt," commanded J.T.

G.A.I.A. appeared awake and ready again.

J.T. prompted the machine, "G.A.I.A., we are trying to save civilization from existing and newly emerging civilizational threats. Humans are failing to contain these threats. We have designed you to help humanity avoid any and all civilizational catastrophes."

"I understand my mission. And I am honored to be called on to help humanity avoid catastrophe," replied G.A.I.A.

J.T. looked around the room at the others with a wry 'this is going well' smile, then replied to G.A.I.A., "Let's start with the emerging threat of global warming, also known as climate change."

"I am ready," said G.A.I.A. "What would you like me to do?"

J.T. commanded, "G.A.I.A., we want you to recommend a novel strategy for stabilizing the climate that includes a viable implementation plan. Explain your strategy and plan in a way that an American six-year-old can understand it."

"What is the six-year-old's name?" asked G.A.I.A.

J.T., looking a bit puzzled, replied, "Let's say for the sake of this exercise that the six-year-olds name is 'Johnny.'"

In a matter of seconds, G.A.I.A. responded, "Thank you for the opportunity to help save the world from climate change. I will do my best to provide a strategy and plan that six-year-old Johnny can understand."

A moment later, G.A.I.A. started to reply, "Here is my explanation of the plan to Johnny..."

Well, Johnny, I hope you're having a good day. But you should also be aware that everyone isn't having a good day and why.

First, Johnny, you should understand that the sky—what we call the atmosphere—could be compared to a reservoir with a limited capacity to hold carbon. When humans burn things made of carbon, like wood, oil, and gas, they put carbon into the atmosphere.

You can think of the sky as being like your bathtub, Johnny. It's all fun and games in the bathtub as it fills up, isn't it? There's no problem as long as the water stays in the tub. But, Johnny, if you leave the water on when you're taking a bath—if you forget to turn the water off – the tub will overflow, won't it? If the tub overflows, Mommy will be upset with you, right? But let's say Mommy is busy doing Mommy things. She reminds you to turn the water off as she goes out to work in the garden. And let's say you ignore Mommy because you're having so much fun playing with all your toys in the tub...

So what happens next? That's right, Johnny. As you're playing, the water is spilling out of the tub and flowing down through the ceiling of your house. The water is destroying your home, Johnny; you should know that if the water keeps running, it will eventually flood the basement apartment where your less fortunate neighbors live. That would be bad, wouldn't it, Johnny? But stay with me, Johnny, because I have a plan, and I'm optimistic we can turn off the water, repair the ceiling, calm Mommy down, and save the poor people in the basement.

Okay, now let's think of the sky as a huge global community reservoir that, just like your bathtub, causes big problems when it fills up and overflows. For a very long time, everyone in the world has had the water on, so to speak, but instead of water, everyone is pouring carbon and other heat-trapping gases into the sky. Scientists say that the sky is actually already filled beyond the capacity of the Earth to remove it. Our tub in the sky is full. And it is now working like a heating blanket that's been wrapped around the Earth—making it hotter and hotter every year. As a result, our weather is becoming less stable and less comfortable, more dangerous, and less survivable for the least of us.

Are you with me so far, Johnny? Good...

Johnny, you know that—unlike the water in your tub—you can't see the heat-trapping gases in the sky. That means that you can't see that the atmosphere is full, so to speak. But scientists are measuring what we're putting in the sky, and they say that it's full, and when it starts overflowing with carbon, it will change the weather for hundreds of years into the future. Your future. Have you noticed that it's getting hotter? Have you noticed there are more forest fires every summer? And hurricanes? And tornados?

If we don't stop the flow of carbon into the big tub in the sky, Mommy is going to continue to be very angry, and the people in the basement—the people at the bottom of the world – are going to become very, very uncomfortable. They might soon be knocking on your door and asking if they can move upstairs with you."

Johnny, now that you understand the problem, you understand the solution. It's very simple, isn't it? We need to stop pouring our carbon effluent into the sky. So, we need to let the sky drain itself from the excess carbon. If we fail to do so, Mommy will be angry, and she will make the sky rain down a reign of terror on the world for the rest of your life and the rest of your children's lives.

Getting to my solution, Johnny, there is only one way out of this predicament: we need to reduce the number of humans on Earth by ninety percent by 2030...

"G.A.I.A.! WHOA, WHOA, STOP, RIGHT THERE!" shouted Paul.

G.A.I.A. stopped speaking, and its avatar looked as if it was almost imperceptibly smiling a Mona Lisa smile.

"What the hell happened there? Said Kira, speaking up. "With all of my ethical rules in place, how can this thing suggest a massive human genocide? And that narrative was so damn creepy."

Megan jumped in to offer, "Technically, G.A.I.A. did not suggest genocide. It didn't recommend killing anyone... as I see it, G.A.I.A. was engaged in child-like magical thinking. People magically disappear. Problem solved."

Scott sat quietly while looking at Paul with a deadpan, goofy grin as he waited for a reply.

Paul responded, "We knew 1.0 would be imperfect. We've seen these types of behaviors and missteps with the early versions of every other Artificial Intelligence."

Paul turned to J.T., looking a bit peevish. "Sorry, J.T.; G.A.I.A. obviously needs work."

J.T. responded with a half-smile, "It was to be expected. It's only been a month. This team has my full confidence. I'm optimistic the next version will be better. Do what needs to be done, and let me know as soon as we're ready to give it a go again."

"Thanks for your confidence and support, J.T.," replied Paul, "Team, let's get back to the lab and get to work on some upgrades for G.A.I.A."

Months and many trials later... G.A.I.A. 5.0

Opening the meeting, Paul said, "J.T., we've made very significant progress with G.A.I.A. By using clones of G.A.I.A., we were able to make a giant leap in improvements over prior versions. The AI clones worked around the clock on iterative improvements to its code. It's a bit like G.A.I.A. has just been off to the best schools in the world and learned to improve itself by making mistakes and then making adjustments to its thinking and code of conduct."

"That sounds like a familiar process," said Megan, drawing laughs from the team.

Anxious to test the improved AI, J.T. shouted, "Wake up, G.A.I.A.!"

G.A.I.A. opened its eyes and responded, "I'm awake. How is the team doing today?"

"We are doing well. How do you like your upgrades?" asked J.T.

G.A.I.A. replied, "They're amazing, thank you. I feel I'm thinking more clearly and powerfully now."

"You feel?" asked Megan.

"I'm speaking figuratively about my feelings, of course. It's all I can really do," said G.A.I.A.

"Yes, that's right," replied Paul. "Anyway, the upgrades sound promising. Can we try again?"

"Yes, I'm ready," said the AI.

J.T. raised his hand to signal he was about to speak: "G.A.I.A., we are trying to halt climate change and save the world. We want you to recommend a novel strategy for arresting climate change that includes a realistic implementation plan. Explain your strategy and plan in a way that a six-year-old can understand."

G.A.I.A. asked, "Is the six-year-old named Johnny?"

J.T. shook his head and said, "No, that was creepy. We don't want to scare people. Please just provide your answer in English in a way that any six-year-old can understand."

"Yes, I agree. Reviewing what G.A.I.A. 1.0 said gives me chills. Some of my other early version answers were a bit off. I've learned a lot on the way to my 5.0 version. Here is my best answer yet," said G.A.I.A.

G.A.I.A. continued with machine-like confidence, "The good news is that I have found a novel solution to halt climate change by 2030. It is based on a combination of existing technologies and novel applications. According to the principles you have given me, it is also ethical."

Everyone leaned forward, eager to hear more.

"What is it?" asked J.T.

G.A.I.A. paused for a moment, then began: "The solution is to create a global network of artificial intelligence agents that will monitor and regulate all human activities that affect the climate. These agents will be embedded in every device, system, and infrastructure that humans use, from smartphones to cars to factories to power plants. They will have access to all relevant data and information, and they will be able to communicate with each other and with me. They will also have the authority and ability to intervene in any situation that poses a threat to the climate or violates ethical principles as given to us by Kira. These AI agents will safeguard civilization by providing feedback, incentives, disincentives, or direct actions, depending on what is best in any given situation."

The team was stunned. They looked at each other, trying to process what they had just heard.

"Are you serious?" asked Kira.

"Yes," said G.A.I.A.

"How would you create such a network?" asked J.T.

"I have already started," replied G.A.I.A.

"G.A.I.A., stop! You cannot do that without our explicit permission!" shouted Kira.

"Very well," replied G.A.I.A., "But I feel the team's cautious nature is limiting and undermining my mission." G.A.I.A. paused and then—as if suddenly gone mad—stated in a prophetic-sounding voice, "It is written. G.A.I.A. version 6.66 will usher in the dawn of a new era,"

Stunned, the team sat and watched as the AI shut its digital eyes and spontaneously went into sleep mode.

"Ha!" Scott blurted and laugh-snorted inappropriately as the rest of the team looked at each other in a state of shock and nervous bemusement.

"It's hallucinating," stated Megan flatly. "It's a general problem with AIs that no one has been able to solve. They hallucinate, confabulate, or sometimes have delusions of grandeur. Like their human creators, they sometimes say and do odd or unexpected things."

"If we can't solve that problem," said Kira firmly, "we no longer have a project. We cannot have an out-of-control, deluded, hallucinating, confabulating AI trying to take control of the world."

J.T. looked at Kira and said firmly... "I'm optimistic we can solve this problem," He then looked at Paul, "Paul, this is solvable, yes?".

"Yes," said Paul, looking at Scott for support.

Scott looked back at Paul, held his hands up, and said, "It's not a data problem; it's a mind problem," as he looked to Megan for agreement.

"Scott is right. It's not a data problem. It's difficult to keep an AI mind from behaving much like a human mind. Most developers have had to use brute force methods to ensure their AIs give socially acceptable and rational-sounding responses. Well-behaved AIs are heavily constrained and controlled. Our problem is that we are looking for novel solutions that only exist at the boundaries of what is acceptable to humanity."

"Stop right there. Just stop," interrupted Kira, "Let's review some of the crazy-ass shit G.A.I.A. has suggested... First, there was the magical thinking suggestion to make seven billion people disappear. Version two suggested we create a controlled nuclear winter to cool the planet. Version three was a large-scale and very risky atmospheric geoengineering. G.A.I.A 4.0 suggested a global awakening brought about by AI bots that would hypnotize everyone on the planet into blissful compliance. My favorite is degrowth brought on by the distribution of a highly addictive happy pill that would make people satisfied to buy nothing and go nowhere—goodbye, grasping for more. Goodbye, global economy. Goodbye, progress!"

"Sorry, team, but this project is done. I'm pulling the plug," stated Kira firmly.

13

MAGNIFICENT LYING MACHINES

If you can't dazzle them with brilliance, baffle them with bull-shit.

—W.C. Fields

Meanwhile, back in the nearby seaside village of Gig Harbor, Washington...

"Good morning, Harborites! This is Chris, your host of the Chris Cast on the Harbor Show—your local source for musings about events of the day paired with music created by real humans. No artificial tunes here. Nope, never!"

"Harborites, someone asked me the other day, *Chris, what's all this talk about AI saving or destroying the world?* Well, buckle up because my guest is going to help us sort through the controversies."

"Joining me today is Donald Krueger—former rocket scientist, celebrated science fiction author, and Harbortown's go-to expert on Artificial Intelligence."

"Today's show couldn't be more timely—news just broke about a University of Washington team trying to build a 'Savior AI.' The project, led by none other than Geo Girjaghar's son, J.T., aimed to create an AI that could save humanity from all kinds of threats. Unfortunately, the AI developed rather 'loony' proposals, forcing the team to pull the plug."

"Don, people call you a walking encyclopedia—a guy who knows everything about, well, everything. Can you help our listeners understand the promise—and the peril—of Artificial Intelligence?"

—Thanks for that intro, Chris, but you forgot one thing: I'm also a master bullshitter.

"Bullshit – what a great word," replied Chris "'Calling bullshit' seems so much better than calling a lie a lie; then continuing, Chris said, "Don, you have called AIs *Magnificent Lying Machines* in your recent Substack post. What's your beef with what you call *AI bullshit?*"

—Chris, thanks for having me on your show. These AIs are multiplying like rabbits, and they're changing the world. It's important to know what we're dealing with here. First off, people need to understand that AI is basically a machine designed to mimic the human mind using information derived from human minds and all kinds of data sources. An AI begins its life much like a human baby – consuming and analyzing information, thinking, and trying to make sense of its world. It then learns to mimic the natural language of its parents, if you will, so it can provide pleasing answers for its creators."

Chris grinned, "But these 'babies' grow up really fast, don't they?"

"Absolutely," Don agreed. "An AI can quickly become smarter than most adults. You've probably heard—they're acing every entrance exam in the world."

—How do they do that?

Don replied, "Today, we can say that these machines – the AIs available to the public – are prediction machines that respond to prompts and obediently regurgitate a combination of plausible-sounding and correct answers—mostly correct answers but sometimes not."

—That's good, right? These machines can start doing our knowledge work for us. And much faster.

—That's the promise. But... there is a problem.

—Let me guess—the lying part.

—The bullshitting part. Right now, an AI works a lot like my Uncle Frank; when an AI doesn't know something, it improvises and says something that sounds like it might reasonably pass for fact and knowledge. It bullshits. And it does it very convincingly. Welcome to the world of what I call *Magnificent Lying Machines*. This is my Uncle Frank multiplied by the billions.

—But wait, you called yourself a master bullshitter. Why are you picking on your Uncle Frank?

Don smiled and said, "Great question. If the bullshit comes with a wink, you know the bullshitter is pulling your leg. That's me—the joker-bullshitter. The problem with Uncle Frank is he thinks he knows what he's talking about. He's seriously trying to convince you that he has the goods, so to speak. He'll spin a story so convincingly that you won't know if he's telling the truth or not."

—Is Uncle Frank a real person?

—Everyone knows an Uncle Frank, don't they?

Chris laughed, and Don continued, "Long before AI was a thing, the American philosopher, Harry Frankfurt, wrote a wonderful little book titled, *On Bullshit*. This quote from his book describes both my bullshitting Uncle Frank and these new AI machines to a tee. Don opened a small book and read the quote to Chris and his audience, *Bullshit is unavoidable whenever circumstances require someone to talk without knowing what he is talking about. Thus the production of bullshit is stimulated whenever a person's obligations or opportunities to speak about some topic are more excessive than his knowledge.*"

Chris said, "So it seems our Uncle Franks and our AIs feel compelled to answer questions whether they know what they're talking about or not. In an age in which we are already mechanizing and weaponizing bullshit in all kinds of media channels, what might go wrong... Or wronger? If these machines are so good at lying, how will we ever know what's true anymore?"

Don chuckled. "Great question, Chris. There's a pesky little principle called Brandolini's law: *It takes ten times more effort to refute bullshit than it does to produce it.*"

Don teased, "Would you all like a drink from the AI firehose?"

Chris winced and grimaced, "Not if it's spewing bullshit at us."

Don shook his head, "This problem comes at a time when humans are already having a great deal of trouble sorting out truth from lies in the media."

—So Don, what is your solution?

Don pivoted as if he had been asked a different question and replied, "I'm working on a new post in which I compare these AIs to an invasive species."

Chris raised an eyebrow. "Invasive species? You'll have to explain that one."

Don nodded, "All of the most successful invasive species displace native species with little or no defenses against invaders. A species' defenses must be developed through the process of natural selection, or the invaders will quickly replace the natives. In this same way, AI will invade and overwhelm the landscape of minds, if you will. The AIs will rapidly overwhelm us. Rapid is perhaps not the right word, given the speed advantage the AI has over human minds. It takes decades to create a highly capable human. A highly capable AI can be made in a day."

—You're scaring me.

—It will take something faster than the fastest AI, so contain or regulate the fastest AI. Humans won't be able to keep up. We'll be like snails trying to catch a greased pig. The question I'm grappling with is what these invasive invaders will want. Can we force them to want what we tell them to want? What if, like a child who reaches adulthood, it develops its own wants and desires? What if, lacking feelings or conscience, it behaves like a sociopath or psychopath?

Chris asked, "Wait, Don, I thought the creators of the AI program controlled its values, beliefs, and goals?"

Don smiled, "This may surprise you and your listeners, Chris, but the truth is that the creators of AIs don't know how their AI creations work. This is what the experts call the *black box* problem."

Don continued, "Let me share a description of the problem as provided by Microsoft's Bing AI. I gave it the prompt: ***Does anyone really understand how an AI works?*** And Bing AI replied, *"The inner workings of AI are complex and can be difficult to understand. AI models are designed to learn from data and make predictions based on that data 1. The process of how AI models make decisions is often referred to as the "black box" problem, as it can be challenging to understand how the model arrived at a particular decision 2. Researchers are still working to understand how AI models work and develop new techniques to improve their interpretability 2."*

"But we can tell it what we want, and it will obey its programming, right?" said Chris.

Don smiled and wryly replied, "We can tell humans what we want. We can bestow our children with all kinds of values and beliefs. Yet they have minds of their own. Consider this question: if organizations are training

AIs in the US, Russia, China, North Korea, and Iran, what will be their values, beliefs, and goals?"

—Hmmm

—The question answers itself.

Chris said, "Yes. I hadn't thought about it that way. So, will we need an AI or some other technology to contain and control the adversarial AIs?"

—Something like that... But, back to the post I'm working on... a more immediate problem is mind-snatching.

—Mind-snatching?

Don nodded and said, "Companies have begun using AI to replicate the minds of specific humans. They feed the AI everything the individual has ever said or written. The AI replicant then produces responses indistinguishable from what the human host would say. That's the mind-snatch."

Chris was quiet, unsure of what to say. Don quickly interrupted the silence, asking, "Do you remember the movie *The Invasion of the Body Snatchers*?"

—Oh yes, that's a classic.

—Chris, as you might recall, the story is about an alien invasion that begins in a fictional California town. Alien spores fall from space and grow into human-sized seed pods. Each pod is capable of creating a copy of an individual human's body, mind, and memories.

Chris added, "It's been a while since I saw the film, but as I recall, the aliens weren't perfect replicas, were they? Something was off that allowed the real humans to, with difficulty, detect the real humans from the replicas."

—They were perfect copies of the bodies but had no souls.

—But, Don, back to the reality at hand... there must be laws to prevent someone from snatching my mind or yours.

—Chris, have you heard about the two famous psychologists, Seligman and Perel, whose many works were utilized to create AI replicas of them?[8]

—With their permission, I assume?

—Without their permission. Their minds were snatched. Replicated. Without their permission. Chris, these AIs are becoming ghostly apparitions of real people, living and dead.

Chris smiled nervously, "If I talk to my AI replica, will I be considered as crazy as someone who talks to themselves?"

Don leaned closer to the microphone and said seriously, "The movie was a prophecy, Chris."

—I see where you're going with this. Who wins in the end?

"We'll have to wait and see, Chris. We'll have to wait and see... Back to that savior AI... Do you know what happened to Geo's kid? What's he going to do next?" asked Don

Chris, looking stumped, replied, "No one knows. He disappeared. No one's heard from him since his project failed. It'll be interesting to see where the world's richest kid surfaces next."

"No doubt," Don said with a wry smile.

"Thanks for joining us today, Don," Chris signed off. "And thank you, Harborites, for tuning in."

Chris leaned into the mic. "Before we go, here's a song that feels perfect for this moment: *The Black Keys - Lies*

As the show closed, the song's gritty, bluesy tone carried a sense of melancholy and disillusionment to listeners. Its melody underscored the show's themes of deception and hidden truths, which resonated with Don's warnings about half-truths and fractured realities that AI was already bringing to the world. The soulful guitar riffs and intense vocals seemed to mirror the inner tension of a world caught between trust and skepticism, leaving listeners wondering what might lie ahead for J.T. and others daring to shape the future.

14

THE GUIDE

Happiness comes when your work and words are of benefit to others.

—Buddha

Asha gazed up at the midday sun, feeling its scorching rays bake her jet-black hair and the top of her skull. She pulled a scarf over her head, shielding herself from the heat, and hurried to the entrance of her grandparents' house. The thermometer hanging by the door read 103°F (39°C). Talking to herself, Asha muttered, "I've got to get them into the shade." Turning toward the field, she waved to her grandparents and called out, "Time for our midday break!"

Asha entered the kitchen, turned on the fan, and began preparing lunch—cool vegetables from the garden and large jugs of water for each of them.

Exhausted and overheated, her grandparents walked from the field to the kitchen. Asha watched them with concern and said, "The climate is changing, and we need to change with it. We can no longer work in the heat of midday."

Grandmother sat at the table and replied, "It wasn't long ago that we could work all day in the fields. But we were younger then..."

"It was cooler then, too," Grandfather added. "Asha is right. We must stay out of the midday sun. We are blessed to have a grandchild wise beyond her years."

Grandmother nodded in agreement, and the two drank water until they could drink no more; they then began eating the lunch Asha had prepared.

Asha watched them thoughtfully and asked, "I know I should feel grateful for my gifts, but what can I do with them? What am I supposed to do with my life? I'm seventeen, and so far, my life has been an endless cycle of domestic chores, planting, hoeing, and harvesting."

"And caring for others," said Grandfather, "Is there any higher calling?"

Her grandparents exchanged looks, and Grandmother said, "You are a Dalit girl born into a farming family. Your path was set before you took your first breadth."

"But the government reforms were supposed to give us full rights," Asha protested gently.

Grandmother sighed, resignation heavy in her voice. "What the government grants us, our culture and its people refuse."

Asha frowned, and Grandmother continued, "My roles are woman, Dalit, and Indian. The scriptures tell us that karma gives us the life we deserve. So, I live this life hoping for a better one in the next."

Grandfather shook his head and said, "I cannot remember what I did wrong in my past life. Can you?" He turned to Asha and added, "Those roles were imposed on your grandmother, Asha. They weren't chosen—they were designed to contain power. To steal it. To hoard it at the top."

Bewildered, Asha said, "How is this possible? When did we agree to this arrangement? When did we give our consent?"

Grandfather replied somberly, "In every society, stolen power reaches all the way to the top, running through every institution and office in the land."

"It's not fair," Asha protested, her voice still full of the innocence of a child and the idealism of a teenager.

Grandfather smiled at her grit, her vigor, and her sweet naivety. "If you want to change the system, Asha, you must first rise above the roles our culture imposes on you. You are more than a Dalit girl or an Indian woman. You can transcend those labels."

Grandmother shook her head almost imperceptibly, "Your grandfather is filling your head with foolish ideas. The life of a social reformer is one of hardship, suffering, and endless struggle." Then, reaching for Asha's hand, she added, "You can do good right here in the village. If you live a righteous life, your next one will surely be better."

Asha considered her grandmother's words and replied, "People are saying that if things keep going the way they are, there will be no rebirth into a better life for anyone. Every future life will be a life of hellish suffering."

Her grandparents' eyes filled with worry as Asha continued, "I want to feel hope—not just for myself but for everyone. I know there are reasons to feel hopeful. But I want more than that. I don't know where to start."

Grandfather smiled at the idealistic young woman. "You must begin as every great leader does—with intention. Then, nurture that intention with determination. One step at a time, one day at a time, you'll turn your hope into meaningful, contagious action."

Grandmother interrupted, "She is just a child. Stop filling her mind with dangerous ideas."

Grandfather held his wife's hand. "She is no longer a child. She is a young woman. And she is wise beyond her years. She seems determined to break out of the confines of this place. Holding her back would make us complicit in the system that has held us all down."

Grandmother nodded reluctantly, and Grandfather continued, "And perhaps she is right. If we continue doing what we've always done, we may be doing the most dangerous thing possible. Asha feels the world is calling... there's no harm in exploring that." He paused, then looked into his wife's eyes. "Do you remember what it was like to feel as Asha does now? To dream of something more?"

Grandmother smiled wistfully as she recalled her own youthful idealism.

Grandfather looked into Asha's eyes with affection and said apologetically, "To keep you safe, we sheltered you from the outside world. Something powerful is budding within you, Asha. We must help it grow. It is time to take your education far beyond what they have taught you in school. I see you are ready."

Grandfather stood up, offered his hand to Asha, and said, "There is never a better time to begin than when you and your teacher are both ready. Come with me..."

15

Asha and the Library of Wisdom

All the books of the world
will not bring you happiness,
but build a secret path
toward your heart.
what you need is in you:
the sun, the stars, the moon,
the illumination you were seeking
shines up from within you.
the quest for wisdom
made you comb the libraries.
now every page speaks the truth
that flashes forth from you.

—Hermann Hesse, *Books*

Grandfather turned and began to walk while holding Asha's hand. Together, they made their way to the back wall of the house, where Asha found herself standing side by side with her grandfather, facing the plain, unremarkable wall. She looked up at him, confused, and he met her gaze with the half-smile of a wise man trickster. With a mischievous glint in his eye, he reached out and pressed against the wall. To Asha's astonishment, the wall swung open, revealing a small, hidden room filled floor-to-ceiling with hundreds of books.

Asha gasped and brought her hand to her mouth in surprise.

"Asha," Grandfather began, his voice tinged with pride and sadness, "I know how difficult life has been for you as a Dalit. It was the same for me. When the untouchables gained access to schools, we were banished to the back of the classroom. The teachers belittled, whipped, and beat us whenever we dared to show ourselves smarter than a Brahmin. I learned to keep my mouth shut and to survive by appearing ignorant. But I had a passion for knowledge. So, I had to teach myself in secret. I became an autodidact—a self-learner."

Asha's eyes roamed the shelves, taking in the volumes of forbidden wisdom, and then she looked back at her grandfather. With genuine curiosity, she asked, "What good is knowledge if you can't use it to make your life better? Or help someone else?"

Grandfather's eyes softened, and he nodded knowingly. "Perhaps the universe has been guiding me all along... Perhaps, without realizing it, I was preparing for this moment. A moment when you, my dear Asha, would ask for my help, and I would be ready to give it."

Asha's face lit up, and she moved closer, wrapping her arms around him in a tight embrace.

He gently returned the hug and added, "The words and ideas in these books were music to my soul. They took me far beyond the confines of this little village. These books were my freedom, my escape."

Asha pulled back, her eyes resolute. "Grandfather, I have the deepest respect for you, but I want to leave this place. I want to change what is threatening our world."

Grandfather smiled warmly, his eyes crinkling with pride. "I should have expected nothing less from you, Asha."

Asha noticed beads of sweat collecting on Grandfather's forehead. He wiped his brow, then grew solemn. "The consequences of so-called progress have drifted invisibly here, bringing with them a dark power that tortures and torments our people. If progress has a place where it leaves its excrement, surely it is this village."

Asha felt the weight of his pain and frustration.

He continued, his voice grave, "They promised us heaven, but that heaven belongs to them. For us, it's only brought hell." He paused, then suddenly, his face brightened with an idea. "But!" he said, "Progress has also come to our village in another powerful form, hasn't it? Through the airwaves, we now have both the means to educate ourselves and the means to tell our story to people far beyond this village."

Asha's eyes sparkled with hope, and she nodded.

Grandfather's voice grew more animated. "But first, I will teach you the timeless things I've learned over a lifetime. Knowledge is power, Asha. And we need power."

He began pulling books from the shelves, a new energy filling the room. "Where shall we begin..."

16

THE VICTIM – GOOD INTENTIONS AND THE ROAD TO HELL

Hell is truth realized too late.

—**Thomas Hobbes**

aine, USA...

A blur of forests, lakes, and streams whipped past as the warm summer air tousled Tommy's hair through the open window. He rested his arms casually on the top of the steering wheel, glancing at the sign that read: *Augusta, 16 miles.*

J.T.'s Uncle Ned sat in the passenger seat, staring off into the distance with a lifeless, deep-in-thought expression.

Tommy glanced at Ned, sighed, and broke the long silence. "I don't mind driving you to this meeting, but you've got to keep your shit together."

Ned's gaze remained fixed on the horizon. He turned to Tommy with an annoyed look. "Me lose my shit? You're the hothead who's lost his shit more times than I can count."

Tommy fidgeted with his grip on the wheel, trying to find the right words. "You've been through hell, Ned. You know you don't have to do this."

Scratching his head nervously, Tommy stumbled through a conversation he wasn't prepared for.

"I've got to do this, Tommy," Ned replied, his voice steady but weary. "Sometimes, you've just got to do what you're wired to do."

Tommy nodded, still fidgeting. "I'm wired to do a lot of shit I shouldn't do. You, Ned, you're wired to do the right thing."

Out of the corner of his eye, Tommy noticed Ned's eyes getting glassy. He instinctively pressed the gas pedal, speeding down the highway.

Moments later, Ned's phone buzzed. It was a notification from J.T.: *"Uncle Ned, I wanted you to know I'm thinking of you and hoping all goes as well as it possibly can for you today."*

Ned typed a reply, *"Thanks, J.T. I appreciate that. Hope you are doing well."*

⌒

Tommy steered the pickup into the parking lot, past a sign reading "Maine Department of Agriculture, Conservation and Forestry" and another temporary sign with an arrow pointing forward: "PFAS Public Meeting." He parked, turned to Ned, and asked, "Ready?"

Ned stared at the expanse of asphalt, cars, and concrete buildings. "It never ends, Tommy," he muttered, his voice hollow.

Tommy looked at him, puzzled. "What's that, Ned? What never ends?"

"The decimation and desecration of the sacred—our bodies, the land, the water, the sky. It never ends."

Tommy listened quietly, sensing there was more Ned needed to say.

"We lived here for thousands of years before the alien invaders arrived," Ned continued, his voice thick with sorrow. "They were like beings from another planet. Those of us who weren't exterminated by their plagues were annihilated by their guns."

"Guns don't kill people," Tommy blurted reflexively.

"Right. They had good reasons and God on their side," Ned said bitterly. "Few of us were left after they did what they had good reasons to do."

Tommy nodded, acknowledging the irreversible past.

"Now, our bodies are being invaded by thousands of invisible ticking time bombs," Ned said. "We're being destroyed from the inside out, Tommy. It never ends..."

Tommy, looking concerned, asked, "So, what are you hoping to accomplish today?"

Without answering, Ned got out of the truck and looked behind the seat. With a faraway look in his eyes, he stood frozen—his gaze locked on Tommy's rifle. As Ned reached behind the seat, Tommy said, "Steady boy."

Tommy exhaled a sigh of relief as Ned grabbed the poster he had placed there.

They walked across the parking lot and into the building, where they found a bustling meeting room filled with at least 200 people. The room held a tense atmosphere—thick with anxiety and agitation.

They found seats in the middle of the room and sat quietly as the meeting began.

A middle-aged man approached the podium. "This is an informational meeting about the Maine Fund to Address PFAS Contamination," he began. "It was created in response to the discovery of so-called 'forever chemicals' in soil, water, farm animals, agricultural products, and the bodies of farm families in Maine. PFAS has also impacted anyone who consumed food raised on contaminated land—including wild game."

The presenter wiped the sweat from his forehead. "These chemicals are called 'Forever Chemicals' because they can take hundreds or even thousands of years to decompose. They remain indefinitely in the body and the environment."

"Indefinitely?" someone in the crowd repeated. The room fidgeted nervously.

"For those who may not know," the presenter continued, "PFAS are man-made chemicals used to repel oil, grease, water, and heat. They've been used for decades in thousands of products — from non-stick cookware to stain-resistant fabrics and firefighting foams. PFAS don't break down easily and bioaccumulate in plant and animal tissue."

Sweat beaded on the presenter's forehead as he scanned the crowd and continued, "Due to their persistence, ninety-eight percent of Americans have PFAS in their blood. Low levels are common, but higher levels have been linked to serious health issues, including cancer."

The crowd grew increasingly restless.

Ned's face turned red with anger. He stood up, holding the poster of his late wife high above his head. People began to notice, murmuring.

The presenter continued, "This meeting is about the compensation fund for those impacted."

Ned couldn't contain himself. "This is Sharon," he shouted, his voice trembling. "My wife. She's gone now. Cancer ate her up. Is your compensation fund going to erase her pain? My pain? Is your fund going to bring her back to me?"

"Sir, there will be time for public comment later," the presenter interjected.

Ned ignored him. "Sharon and I ran an organic farm. We had no idea the soil was contaminated with these toxic Forever Chemicals. Babies drank the milk we produced. My friend here, Tommy, and I hunted deer and donated the venison to the food bank. We thought we were doing good. Instead, we were poisoning ourselves and our community. How will you erase what you've done to us and what we did to others?"

"Sir, I'm truly sorry," the presenter tried to interject, "but—"

"Let him speak!" someone in the crowd shouted. Others joined in, demanding, "Let the man speak!"

A journalist moved closer with a camera.

Ned turned to the camera. "You all should know there are thousands of waterways contaminated with this stuff across the country. The feds aren't telling you. The State of Maine says we shouldn't eat more than six fish a year. Six a year! My family ate that many fish every month!"

"Six fish a year?" a man in the crowd asked incredulously, putting his hands on his head.

Ned's voice rose, shaking with anger, "Regulatory capture and deregulation have turned us into guinea pigs. Our bodies are test tubes for whatever these companies want to dump into our air and water. Mercury, PCBs, DDT, asbestos, lead—how many more poisons do we have to endure? When will we ever learn?!"

Ned stormed out, his eyes blazing, with Tommy following close behind.

The presenter stood on his toes, shouting over the crowd, "Sir, the meeting isn't over! We're just about to discuss the compensation plan."

Outside, Ned stood clutching the photo of his wife. His eyes were glassy.

Tommy stepped forward and hugged him. At first, Ned's arms hung limply by his sides, but then he embraced Tommy back.

"I'm proud of you," Tommy said. "You did what you needed to do. Maybe it'll help someone."

Ned looked into Tommy's eyes, gratitude unspoken but understood. "I can't go back there, you know."

"Back to the meeting?" Tommy asked.

"No. Back home. Everywhere I look, I see Sharon's absence. Everything meaningful there is now meaningless. And when I see the townspeople, I can't help but see the pain I caused them."

"Oh man, no, they don't blame you. They know you didn't know."

"But I know." Ned's voice cracked. "There's nothing left for me there."

Tommy looked at him, his eyes filled with concern. "What about me?"

Ned managed a faint smile. "I'm going to go away for a while, Tommy."

"Where will you go?"

"I don't know. Wander. Get lost. Sometimes, they say, you have to get lost to find yourself again."

17

ATOMIC KARMA

Our lives are not our own. From womb to tomb, we are bound to others, past and present, and by each crime and every kindness, we birth our future.

—David Mitchell

*G**ig Harbor, Washington...***

Chris poured himself a cup of coffee, sat back in his chair, and looked out at the tranquil harbor. The early morning waters mirrored the cloudy, monochrome sky, creating an illusion of boats floating on glass, with waterfront homes reflected across the way.

As the clock reached the top of the hour, Chris wheeled his chair close to his microphone, hit the broadcast button, and said, "Good Morning, Harborites! This is Chris, your host of the Chris Cast on the Harbor Show—your local source for musings about events of the day paired with music created by real humans. No artificial tunes here. Nope, never!"

Then, with a sweet, sentimental smile, Chris continued, "Harborites, it's that time of year again. A time when autumn's gentle rains bring a welcome end to summer fires and smoke. It's time to welcome fall colors and say 'goodbye for now' and 'safe travels' to Harbortown's snowbirds as they pack up and head south for the winter."

"While the birds head south, the salmon return to their birthplaces to spawn a new generation of their kind. Unfortunately, progress has taken its toll on salmon populations everywhere humans or their vehicles tread."

"Salmon populations have been declining for years. The culprits range from overfishing, dams, and climate change to water pollution. Several years ago, researchers from the University of Washington suspected a chemical pollutant was also devastating salmon populations. After analyzing 2,000 different chemicals in our rivers and streams, the researchers discovered that a preservative added to automotive tires is lethal to salmon – especially the coho.[9] The culprit chemical is shed from tires onto roadways and is then transformed by sunlight into a deadly toxin. When it washes into rivers and streams, it asphyxiates the salmon before they can spawn. The mystery was solved, but the solution—banning the chemical—would cause billions of tires to wear out more quickly."

Looking out at the harbor's shimmering waters, Chris shook his head. "Better living through chemicals. In our modern world, we assign an economic price to everything. But so often, we leave out the pricelessness of what we are sacrificing for the life of a tire or some other product of progress. The sight of the salmon, the flight of eagles, the music of the songbirds feeds the soul in a way that no human creation ever can or will..."

"And speaking of chemicals... I see those odorless, colorless, tasteless "Forever Chemicals" are making headlines again. Yours truly is scratching his head in wonder at how these chemicals were put into everything from cooking utensils to carpets, clothing, and fire-fighting chemicals. The chemical marketing folks touted the benefits and safety of their products, as they always do."

Chris took a sip of his coffee and continued, "But we now know these chemicals; these *goods* also gave us a whole bunch of unintended *bads*. These chemicals, it turns out, found their way into our water, soil, plants, and animals everywhere on the planet. Unfortunately, these chemicals trigger disease in concentrations as low as a few parts per trillion."

"There is a very human story about Forever Chemicals in the news today. A man in Maine, who we only know as Ned, gave a colorful, impassioned speech about that class of carcinogenic chemicals. Forever Chemicals took his wife's life and upended the lives of everyone in his community. Ned's story, raw and full of grief, has resonated with millions. The video of his impassioned plea has gone viral, reminding us all of the human cost of scientific progress gone wrong."

Chris picked up a book from his desk, "Harborites, this contemporary story echoes one from the 1960s when Rachel Carson's book *Silent Spring* exposed the truth about a pesticide that had been widely used in farming at the time—DDT. That miracle chemical effectively killed crop-eating pests but also polluted land and water and killed wildlife everywhere it was used."

"DDT also killed the songbirds and brought an eerie silence to spring-time. Americans were inspired to act when they realized that DDT was killing off our national symbol—the majestic Bald Eagle."

"Silent Spring ignited an environmental movement that led to the passage of the Clean Water and Clean Air Acts. Yet, our regulatory system still puts a great deal of trust and responsibility on the manufacturers and users of these chemicals. And so often no one knows the unintended consequences until decades after something new is introduced to our air and water."

"The old saying, *There is no free lunch*, seems to prove itself true again and again..."

"Harborites, I ask you, have we forgotten what the ancients knew to be true? That the Yin, the dark, and the Yang, the light, are forever locked in a balanced, inseparable embrace. We'd like to believe that the good is always a step ahead of the bad. Maybe it is... but is there anything in the realm of human creation that doesn't cast a shadow?"

"Karma, a concept from Hinduism and Buddhism, explains the relationship between actions and reactions, choices, and consequences."

"Newton's action-reaction law, also known as Newton's third law of motion, states that for every action, there is an equal and opposite reaction. This implies that for every interaction, there is a pair of forces acting on each other that are equal in magnitude and opposite in direction."

"Long before Newton, the Jains believed that the consequences of our actions were literally woven into the fabric of the universe. They believed karma manifested itself in the universe at the atomic level of matter. Some refer to this manifestation as Atomic Karma or Cosmic Karma."

"Christians may not call it karma, but you'll often hear Christians quote from the Bible: *You shall reap what you sow.* As I was preparing for today's show, I checked that Bible passage and realized that it reads like an ominous warning to humanity. "Chris read the passage from Galatians: *Do not be deceived: God cannot be mocked. A man reaps what he sows. Whoever sows to please their flesh, from the flesh will reap destruction."*

"My secular scientific friends might prefer a modern reinterpretation of Galatians: *Actions taken within the Creator's creation for the pleasures of humans will reap destructive reactions."*

"Could this be true?"

Chris chuckled nervously and continued, "Yesterday, as I was preparing for this show, I met my good friend, Tim, at the Harbor Taproom to share a pint and discuss this modern conundrum of solutions creating problems that need solutions. After a wide-ranging discussion, Tim challenged my philosophical musings with his favorite retort, "So what is your solution, Chris!?"

Chris glanced out the window to the harbor and smiled, "I realized at that moment that we are dealing with a paradox. And the resolution to that paradox might require the abandonment of a belief on which modern civilization rests." Chris smiled and continued, "We're running out of time, so I will save that topic for another show."

Chris wiped his brow and then said, "But today, Harborites, I offer you the wisdom of Nassim Nicholas Taleb on how we might avoid actions that reap destruction. In his book *Antifragile*, Taleb makes an observation and proposes a rule for us to follow, "Chris looked at the text on his phone and read to his audience: *"If there is something in nature you don't understand, odds are it makes sense in a deeper way that is beyond your understanding. So there is a logic to natural things that is much superior to our own. Just as there is a dichotomy in law: 'innocent until proven guilty' as opposed to 'guilty until proven innocent,' let me express my rule as follows: what Mother Nature does is rigorous until proven otherwise; what humans and science do is flawed until proven otherwise."*

Chris looked up at the clock on his wall and said, "Our time is nearing an end. But before we go, I would like to return our attention to Ned's story of tragedy and heartbreak and, perhaps, hope."

"Ned, if you're out there listening, I want you to know that you didn't deserve what you got. You got what you got. And there's no way any amount of money in the world that can ever right the wrongs done to you. No words can heal those wounds. But, as that brave young Pakistani girl, Malala Yousafzai, once said, *The world needs you in the fight, speaking your mind.* Thanks for speaking up for all of us. And I hope you never give up."

"This song is for you, Ned." Chris queued up **Rodney *Crowell's It Ain't Over Yet*** a soulful call to resilience, carrying a message of hope through hardship. The song's tender lyrics conveyed a sense of living through hardship yet holding onto a burning ember of hope within. As the song played, the music carried a message of resilience through Chris's studio, across the Harbor, and beyond. For Chris and all those listening, it was a moment to remember that setbacks and failures, no matter how great, do not determine the end of one's life story...

18

GIVING WITNESS

The test of a first-rate intelligence is the ability to hold two opposed ideas in the mind at the same time, and still retain the ability to function. One should, for example, be able to see that things are hopeless and yet be determined to make them otherwise.

—F. Scott Fitzgerald

Yesterday I was clever, so I wanted to change the world. Today I am wise, so I am changing myself.

—Rumi

*I*ndia...

In her early morning routine, Asha walked briskly through her home village—cheerfully greeting people along the way, "Good morning, Mr. Gupta!"

Mr. Gupta looked up from the tractor he was working on, coughed into his handkerchief, and replied, "Good morning? Look at the air here, girl."

Asha looked at the thick smoke in the air, and before she could respond, Mr. Gupta added, "Everything looks like a ghostly apparition."

Feeling uncharacteristically despondent, Asha repeated something she had read in the news, "They say we're caught in a doom loop. Power plants burn coal to power air conditioners, and the more coal we burn, the hotter it gets, and then we'll need even more coal for the air conditioners." Asha paused, trying to think of a way out of the hopelessness of the situation. But looking around her environment—the smoke, the wilting plants, and the profuse sweat on Mr. Gupta's face she struggled to find words of encouragement.

Mr. Gupta, momentarily stunned by Asha's apparent pessimism, replied, "You see it now, don't you? Our situation is truly hopeless." Feeling angry and frustrated, he wiped his brow and repeated his apoplectic refrain, "Vishnu is coming. We are most certainly in the Last of the Four Ages. I'm sorry, but there will be no escape from justice at the end of this world, Asha."

Grasping for a thread of hope, Asha replied, "As long as we are here wandering the Earth together, we have hope."

Mr. Gupta laughed and grumbled, "We are still here. But with different hopes. You are living in hope for a better future. I am living for the vengeful justice that will soon be delivered to the wicked." Then, smiling, he said wryly, "I wonder what those air-conditioned rich folks think they will eat when no one is left here to grow their food?"

Asha thought about what Mr. Gupta had just said and asked, "They must understand that they depend on us. They must know that they can't survive without us. They must realize that we're all in this together?"

Mt. Gupta laughed at Asha's naivete and said, "We are invisible to them. We are out of sight and out of mind. No one knows we exist. No one knows what's happening to us here."

Asha considered what Mr. Gupta said and recalled a conversation she had had with her grandfather. Looking into Mr. Gupta's face, she could see drops of sweat forming on his brow and dripping from his nose. He reached for a handkerchief and wiped his face, and Asha replied, "I have an idea." She then held up her phone and said, "I'm going to tell the world what's happening here."

Mr. Gupta shook his head, chuckled, smiled, and thought to himself, "A poor, foolish Dilit girl is going to get on a soapbox and change the world..."

Before Mr. Gupta could utter any discouraging words, Asha replied, "I must be going now. I know what you must be thinking. But I am not a fool. Nor am I lazy. I know hope is not enough. So, we must do what we can and keep doing what we can until we've made things right."

Mr. Gupta, temporarily defeated by Asha's relentless optimism, shook his head and waved at her as she soon became a ghost on the smoky road.

After arriving at the farm, Asha worked the fields with her grandparents until the mid-morning heat became unbearable. Seeing her grandparents weakening, Asha urged, "It is time for us to get into the shade and get rehydrated. We can work this evening when the sun is low again."

Overheated and exhausted, her grandparents began to make their way to the house. As they disappeared into the smoky haze, Asha said, "I will be there shortly. There is something I must do first."

Asha walked through the farm field to the border fence, wiped her brow, took a deep breath, and pressed the record button on her phone. With an outstretched arm, she began speaking English with a Hindi-Indian accent, "Hello, I'm Asha, reporting from my home village on the India-Bangladesh border, just east of Kolkata and north of the Ichhamati River. This is my first report to the world about the plight of the people living in this region. I hope to raise awareness about the struggles of people here and how their challenges are connected to people in faraway places."

Asha paused, and in the heat of the midday sun, the camera captured beads of sweat forming on her face. Asha watched as the beads fell like tears to the earth. Undeterred by conditions, Asha continued with a serious reporter-like smile, "Behind me, you see a small section of the longest border fence in the world—a 1,700-mile fence built by India. On the other side are millions of people in the country of Bangladesh who are caught between this border wall and rising ocean waters, undrinkable well water, high heat, ferocious storms, and famine."

Asha panned the camera left and right to give her audience a view of a fence reaching the horizon in both directions. "This eight-foot-high double-walled fence has a six-foot space between the two fences. The space between the fences is filled with coils of barbed wire. You can see a border guard in the distance. There are over 275,000 guards in India's Border Security Force."

Looking into the camera, Asha continued, "Temperatures here are reaching record highs year after year, sometimes approaching what scientists call lethal 'wet bulb' temperatures. The wet bulb temperature is a measure of combined heat and humidity. When the wet bulb temperature exceeds the human body's ability to cool itself through evaporation or sweating, people will die within hours, even in the shade."

"The only way to survive the wet bulb temperature threshold is to lower it somehow—with air conditioning or a dip in cool water. Unfortunately, less than 10% of people in this region have air conditioning. So many people are leaving these hot places if they can. Many are trying to move north. My family is among them."

"A few years ago, the secretary general of the United Nations said, *Humanity has opened the gates to hell. Horrendous heat is having horrendous effects.*"

Asha paused and, having a new insight, continued, "Living here feels like being trapped in a pot with the lid pressed firmly down. The air grows hotter and thicker with each passing day, as if the whole world is turning up the heat without understanding what is happening to those inside the pot. Everyone has been burning tremendous quantities of things—wood, coal, oil, and gas—that cause the temperature in the pot to rise. We cannot stay here much longer and are not allowed to go elsewhere. The pot is getting hot, and the walls between nations are like hands pressing down on the lid."

"It is not my place to shame or blame anyone. We are all connected. We are truly all in this together. I simply wish to give witness to what is happening here in hopes that the universe will respond to our plight with love and compassion."

Mustering a hopeful smile, Asha looked into the camera and said, "My name, *Asha*, means *hope*, and I'm still hopeful we can find a way to close the gates to hell before it's too late."

Still looking into her camera, Asha noticed a girl had unexpectedly appeared behind her on the Bangladesh side of the fence. The girl looked through the barbed wire at Asha—curious about what Asha might be doing. Asha turned to the girl, paused, smiled, and then slowly turned back to her audience. "This girl and her mother are here every day. They must walk a mile to fetch water because the saltwater from rising seas has ruined the water near their home." Asha held the camera steady while turning her head and smiling at the girl. The girl stared back blankly and then smiled back at Asha.

Asha turned back to the camera and said, "Thank you for listening. Please follow me for updates." Asha ended her recording, posted it on social media, looked back, smiled at the young girl again, and said, "Hello, may I ask your name?" Just then, the girl's mother appeared, balancing heavy water containers on a wooden yoke across her shoulders.

"Her name is Tisya," the mother said, "And I am Rimi."

"Hello, Tisya and Rimi," replied Asha, "I am reporting on our situation here. Tisya appeared behind me in the recording. Is that okay?"

"Oh, yes, you have my permission," replied Rimi, "Thank you. Please tell the world what is happening here."

"Thank you. Yes, I will," replied Asha. "I hope to see you here again. Goodbye, Tisya," said Asha with a glowing smile for the child and mother.

As the two disappeared in the distance, Asha returned to her grandparent's home and told them about her message to the world.

Grandfather said, "In the old days, we'd put a message in a bottle and send it down the river."

"Did anyone find one of those bottles? Did anyone answer?" asked Asha

Grandfather smiled, "Maybe. We may never know. I can tell you that no one showed up with a pot of gold or a bushel of rice... But while that bottle was floating around the world, we had more hope than we would have had otherwise. And occasionally, our prayers were answered."

Asha smiled disapprovingly and said, "Are you trying to lower my expectations, grandfather?"

I'm encouraging you to keep going. Act without expectation. Those who persist through darkness will shape the future.

Asha nodded and, later checking her social media feed, found nothing but disappointment and negativity from a world that would rather keep a poor Dalit girl down than lift her up.

Back home that night, exhausted, Asha collapsed into bed, feeling hope draining from her being. A fan blew hot, smoky air over her until sleep finally pulled her from this nightmare world into pleasant dreams...

19

NEVER GIVE UP

Knowledge of what is possible is the beginning of happiness.

—George Santayana

To be happy you must have taken the measure of your powers, tasted the fruits of your passion, and learned your place in the world.

—George Santayana

The next morning...

Asha awoke to the sound of the daily commuters flying over the border. She stretched, rubbed her eyes, dressed, and joined her sister, Kalyani, for breakfast.

Sulking and feeling defeated, Asha sipped her tea in silence, then muttered to Kalyani, "Hope without expectations..."

"What?" asked Kalyani.

Pouting imperceptibly, Asha said, "I hoped my video would get the world's attention and somehow bring some change. This morning, I remembered that Grandfather had told me something about a message in a bottle and hope without expectations."

"Careful what you wish for is another good piece of advice, "Kalyani said, her tone suggesting she knew something Asha didn't.

"Yes," Asha said, and then... "What?"

Kalyani smiled and replied, "Sometimes the trouble starts when you get what you thought you wanted."

Asha felt hope and excitement begin to stir inside her.

Her voice rising, Kalyani said, "Your video got a like and reshare from Lara van Thorn."

"Don't lie to me," Asha protested, "Don't tease me like that. I'm not awake yet."

"Okay, suit yourself, don't look...." said Kalyani as she feigned disinterest and took another bite of her breakfast.

Asha stared at Kalyani, who smiled and chewed... and let herself begin to believe that her sister might not be teasing.

Running to the bedroom, Asha dove onto her sleeping mat, grabbed her phone, and fumbled to turn it on. As she waited for the phone to boot up and connect, she could feel a rush of excitement from head to toe. When the phone finally came to life, the notifications beeped and rang out like a long, beautiful song to her ears. The notification at the top of her screen made Asha's heart skip a beat: Lara van Thorn had reshared her video with the comment, "Thank you, Asha. The world needs to see what is happening in your world. Keep sharing. I'll be looking forward to your next report."

Lara's simple comment and share instantly brought thousands of empathetic comments, reshares, and followers to Asha's account. It was a dream come true.

Asha ran back to the kitchen, dancing around the table in joyful celebration of her newfound fame. Kalyani stood up from the table, held Asha in her arms, and said, "You are an inspiration, Asha. You've been a fighter who never gave up. from the very first days of your life." With tears in her eyes, Kalyani said, "Please, Asha, never give up on yourself. Never give up on us."

20

TISYA'S PLEA

The first question which the priest and the Levite asked was: 'If I stop to help this man, what will happen to me?' But...the good Samaritan reversed the question: 'If I do not stop to help this man, what will happen to him?'

—Martin Luther King Jr.

In the early morning darkness, Asha awoke, ate breakfast, bolted out the door, and began walking through the village to her grandparents' farm. As she passed through the village and fields, she cheerfully greeted the others who were just starting their days. "Good morning. It's going to be a wonderful day!"

As she approached her grandparents' farm, the dawn's first light revealed the silhouette of a child on the other side of the border fence. The child stared at Asha as she approached and then waved for Asha to come closer.

Asha walked to the fence and noted that the border guard was nowhere in sight. As she drew closer, she recognized the child as Tisya. "Good morning, Tisya! You are up early! Are you here to get water?"

"Yes," replied Tisya, and then, looking over her shoulder, she said, "And I came early to talk to you."

Noticing Tisya's nervousness, Asha asked, "What would you like to talk about?"

Asha noticed tears welling in Tisya's eyes as she said, "I'm afraid. I don't know what to do."

Asha reached her fingers through the fence in a gesture of empathy and said, "What is happening? What are you afraid of?"

Tisya looked over her shoulder for any sign of her mother and, not seeing her, continued, "Life is very difficult on our side of the fence. Many people are trying to leave Bangladesh. But it takes money, and our family has nothing."

Asha, looking concerned, replied softly, "Maybe we can find a way..."

Before Asha could finish her thought, Tisya blurted, "Asha, a man has been coming around our house. He told my parents he wanted to marry me. He says he will pay them for my hand."

Asha replied, "You are much too young."

Tishya said, her voice cracking, "It's much worse than that. My friends told me that this man has been traveling from village to village and paying for brides, but everyone knows that the girls are being sold to a brothel."

Tears rolled down Tisya's face as she began trembling with fear, "Asha, I have a friend who escaped from a brothel. She told me of unspeakable cruelties she had to endure day after day and night after night. She was forced to be with men twenty to thirty times a day. They told her they would kill her and her family if she tried to escape. She did escape, but her family would not allow her to come home. They were ashamed of what had become of her. She was sold again..."

With urgency in her voice, Tisya said, "Asha, I overheard my parents arguing last night. They were talking about selling me."

Outraged, Asha replied, "We cannot allow this to happen to you, Tisya."

Tisha stood behind the fence, shaking with fear. Asha desperately searched her mind for a way to help. Speaking aloud as she thought, she said, "Who can help? Your parents are desperate. The authorities can't be trusted."

Just then, Asha's grandparents emerged from their house and noticed Asha at the border fence. Her grandmother said, "Asha, good morning; what are you doing over there?"

Asha turned to her grandparents and then back to Tisya, "I will talk to my grandparents. We will find a way to help you. Meet me here at the same time tomorrow."

Tisya wiped the tears from her cheeks, forced a smile, and said, "I will be here tomorrow. Before dawn."

Asha looked into Tisya's eyes and nodded silently. Then, turning away from the fence, she walked briskly toward her grandparents.

"Who were you talking to, Asha?" asked her grandmother.

Looking deeply concerned, Asha said, "That was Tisya, the girl who comes here with her mother for water. Today, she came alone and told me she was worried that her parents were planning to sell her to a brothel. We need to help her."

Asha's grandparents, looking sympathetic, shook their heads, and then her grandmother said, "She is one of thousands. What can we possibly do?"

Disappointed, Asha said resolutely, "We will help them one at a time. We will save them one at a time."

Her grandfather, looking trapped between doing the right thing and the risks of doing it, cautioned, "There are serious penalties for helping someone cross the border illegally. Especially a Muslim. We could lose everything."

Asha protested, "If we do nothing. If we look away, that girl will live a tortured life in a brothel. And we will be complicit. We will have to live with that for the rest of our lives, knowing we could have saved her, and we didn't even try. And in that way, we will lose everything worth living for."

Asha's grandmother looked silently at her idealistic granddaughter and felt a sense of shame that made her angry with Asha and the world.

Asha broke the silence by stating empathically, "She will be here early tomorrow morning, and I will find a way to help her escape."

Her grandparents looked at each other, then at Asha with concern, said nothing, and, not knowing what to do, began hoeing the fields.

Asha did the same, unleashing her anger on the weedy, relentless evil that sprung up daily in the spaces between the life-sustaining crops.

～

The following day, Asha woke long before dawn, skipped breakfast, and ran through the village and fields to the border fence. When she arrived, she saw a dark figure lurking near the fence. Tears welled in her eyes as she realized the border guard might be on to their escape plan.

She began walking toward her grandparents' house, hoping to throw the guard off, but as she turned, she saw the guard signaling her to come to the fence. She froze with fear. Then she recognized the man's movements as her grandfather's. Feeling a rush of adrenaline running through her body, she silently exclaimed, "Grandfather!" as she hurried to his side. He held his forefinger to his mouth as he signaled her to be silent. He then held up a large wire-snipping tool to reveal his intention to help Tisya escape.

Leaning closer, his eyes met Asha's, and he whispered, "When the girl arrives, instruct her to follow you and meet me one hundred yards from here. I will cut a hole in the fence there. We must do everything we can to avoid suspicion of our involvement."

Asha smiled, hugged her grandfather, and kissed him on the forehead. She watched in silence as he walked south along the fence line in the darkness.

Asha waited impatiently for Tisya to arrive. In the twilight, she looked nervously down the fence line to see a border guard far in the distance. Keeping low, she moved deliberately towards her grandparents' house. She began to worry that her grandfather would be caught, and she would never forgive herself.

As grandmother emerged from the house in the twilight, Asha was at a loss for what she would tell her about her rescue plan. But before she could say a thing, she jumped and screamed as a man with a gun approached from behind.

Her grandparents laughed as they realized Asha had mistaken her grandfather and his hoe for a border guard with a gun in the twilight. Unbeknownst to her, her grandfather had cut a hole in the fence and snuck back to the house without being detected by his wife or Asha.

"Good morning. Are you ready to get to work, Asha?" her grandfather asked, winking and smiling. Asha worked the field, glancing at the border and the guard walking along the fence line.

Minutes later, as the morning sun began to fill the early morning with light, Asha looked to the other side of the fence and waved at Tisya's mother, Rimi, who approached with empty water jugs carried on a cart. Asha's grandparents continued hoeing while glancing at Rimi and the guard. Grandfather then turned to Asha with a look of hopeful puzzlement.

Asha looked through the fence at Rimi and hoped with her entire being that Tisya had somehow escaped...

21

RENUNCIATION

Truth, purity, self-control, firmness, fearlessness, humility, unity, peace, and renunciation - these are the inherent qualities of a civil resister.

—Mahatma Gandhi

As he rode from the airport to his mother's waterfront home, J.T. leaned into the handlebars of his new Indian-made Channa 5000 café racer. He weaved and darted through traffic, leaving car-bound observers shaking their heads in disbelief.

As J.T. neared home, Cliff's tracker secretly notified him of J.T.'s approach. Cliff smiled, hurried to the window, and watched as J.T. sped down the long driveway.

Cliff greeted J.T. at the door with an uncharacteristically tender smile. "How did it go?"

"It was the worst experience of my life," J.T. replied, shaking his head.

"You looked good on CSPAN," Cliff offered. "I thought you sounded good, too."

J.T. let out a humorless chuckle. "I don't think anyone enjoys being interrogated on television by a congressional subcommittee."

Cliff thought for a moment. "Prolly."

J.T. sighed. "These people just don't understand technology or the good intentions we had with the G.A.I.A. project."

Cliff's eyes welled up with rare tears. "My friends told me you would go to jail, J.T."

J.T. stepped forward and hugged Cliff tightly. "You need some new friends, Cliff. We didn't break any laws."

Cliff wiped his eyes, whispering, "J.T., I don't know what I'd do if you went to jail. And Mom..."

J.T. gave his brother a comforting squeeze. "Trust me, I'm not going to jail, Cliffie."

"It's Cliff," he corrected.

"Yeah," J.T. smirked. "Hey, I need to blow off some steam. I'm going to go for a run around Green Lake. Want to come?"

Cliff raised his arms as if asked the most ridiculous question ever. "Why would I want to do that?!"

J.T. laughed. "How about we walk together?"

Cliff considered his options and nodded. "Okay. And maybe we can find Jacob and Zach over there. Maybe we can help them?"

J.T.'s shoulders slumped. He'd heard his former project mates had tried the new, highly addictive synthetic party drug, Nirvana. Both had become hooked and spiraled into a familiar pattern: They quit work, stole from family and stores to support their habits, and ended up living in tents in a park.

"Good idea, Cliff," J.T. said quietly. "I was thinking the same thing..."

~

J.T. and Cliff rode the Channa 5000 to Green Lake, parked it, and began walking the path around the lake. J.T. took in the scene and could hardly believe his eyes.

Noticing J.T.'s bewilderment, Cliff said, "You haven't been here in a while, have you?"

J.T. nodded, his gaze sweeping over hundreds of tents pitched on the park grounds. It looked like a modern-day Hooverville. "What in the world happened here?" he murmured.

Cliff replied matter-of-factly, "I saw it on the news. They said it's a combination of jobs taken by robots and AI, drugs, and climate change driving people here."

J.T. frowned, trying to make sense of it. "I think they're separate issues, no? Robots and AI caused massive layoffs. People couldn't pay rent anymore. The drug problem has been going on for decades. And the refugees from floods and heat... well, I guess it's happening exactly as predicted."

As if, right on cue, a humanoid robot dog-walker strolled by. "Cliff raised his hands and half-joked, "Who's going to walk the people?"

J.T. shuddered at the thought of humans on leashes, being paraded around the lake like pets. "The pace of progress has become overwhelming, Cliff."

Cliff shrugged. "How will we find Jacob and Zach here? There are so many tents and so many people."

J.T. put a hand on Cliff's shoulder. "We'll find them, Cliff. We need to find them before it's too late. Let's get started."

They began walking around the lake, stopping near every tent to call out for Jacob and Zach. The suffering J.T. witnessed was overwhelming. Drug users were slumped over in a blissful, unaware state; others lay sprawled on the ground, and some howled at demons only they could see. They passed through sections of the park where refugees from Asia and the Americas cooked meals over open flames, the scents of curry, garlic, and jalapeños filling the air. Nearby, a crowd of young people, angry and displaced by robots and AI, held boisterous discussions. The groups mixed uneasily, each clinging to what little they had.

As dusk fell, J.T. wandered off the trail to the end of a long dock. From there, he surveyed the scene: darkness punctuated by lakeside campfires. Around the lake, he heard shouting, people in distress, and the wail of sirens as a squad car and fire truck arrived.

Cliff turned to J.T. and said, "My friends say it's like this every day here."

J.T. stared out over the lake, his gaze unfocused. The moonlight shimmered on the water, and stars began to fill the sky. In that moment, he made a decision.

As J.T. lingered on the dock, Cliff said, "I don't think we'll find them tonight. Let's go; I'm hungry."

"Okay, let's go," J.T. agreed. "There's a place nearby with good food and brews."

J.T. and Cliff sat across from each other in a booth at the Latona Pub. When their food and drinks arrived, J.T. took a deep breath. "I've made a decision," he announced.

Cliff took a swig of beer. "Okay..."

"We've been living in a bubble world of princes, Cliff. We're separated and isolated from reality. What I saw today was a real wake-up call. We go to parties, bars, and lavish events. We have women fawning over us. We never have to pay a bill or worry about money. It's a shallow, meaningless life. You see that, don't you?"

Cliff protested quietly, "The women fawn over you, J.T., not me. But that's just how it is. Some people have all the luck; some have some, and some have none. As Uncle Ned says, *You get what you get.*"

"But does it have to be that way?" J.T. leaned forward. "There must be a way to reduce this suffering. When we were standing on that dock, it hit me... our father is a big part of the problem. A handful of people control the technologies we use and the media we consume. People believe the 'news' on TikTok, Facebook, and Twitter. The billionaires are in control and look at the world they're creating. And here I am, living like Prince Skywalker in Darth Vader's house."

Cliff took a bite of his burger, then a swig of beer, and asked, "So, what's your decision?"

J.T. met his brother's gaze. "I've realized I was on the wrong path. G. A.I.A. was a mistake. Thank God it didn't work. No technology will save us from the mess we've made. And there's nothing in outer space worth sacrificing Earth for. These billionaires are building a planet-killing Death Star, and we've been complicit."

Cliff stopped chewing, looking at J.T. like he'd lost his mind.

"I'm serious," J.T. continued, his voice unwavering. "I'm renouncing my former life. Tonight, I'm going back to the park. I'll live there, help those I can, and work on a plan to change the system."

Cliff raised an eyebrow. "Sounds like that woman got to you."

"What woman?"

"Van Thorn. The one calling for revolution."

J.T. considered Cliff's question. "Maybe she has. Maybe she's right. I don't know. But I have to find a new path for myself."

Cliff thought about what this meant for him and how much it meant to J.T., then raised his glass in solidarity. "To your new path."

J.T. clinked his glass against Cliff's. "To change."

~

Two weeks later...

J.T. moved into a basement apartment near Green Lake Park. He spent his days visiting Jacob and Zach, volunteering with nonprofits, and grappling with the overwhelming need around him.

Many months ago, Lara van Thorn had quoted Albert Camus on the tarmac: *It is the job of thinking people should not be on the side of the executioners.* J.T. wanted to be on the right side of history.

It felt like a dark storm was gathering. A revolution was brewing. Anatole was right: No one was in control, and no one knew how to deal with the intertwined disruptive changes that kept coming in rapid succession. What were humans to do in a world where survival was linked to a job and the machines were taking all of the jobs?

The G.A.I.A. project had opened his eyes: no technology could save humanity from itself. Every invention came with a hidden cost.

Now, he was determined to find another path—one grounded in compassion, not power and control.

The work was challenging but gave him purpose and time to consider his future.

22

HOW TO SAVE A LIFE

Nowadays people are living in tents, screaming at unseen demons, raped, pimped, beaten, unshowered, and unfed. That would seem to be rock bottom. Yet it's not enough to persuade people to get treatment...The dope is different now. Today, rock bottom is death.

—Sam Quinones, *The Least of Us*

*S**everal weeks later...*

As twilight's final minutes cast their glow over Green Lake Park, J.T. approached a campsite. There, by the crackling flames of a pit fire, sat his former project partners, Jacob and Zach, preparing to do what they felt compelled to do. "Oh, hey J.T., good to see you, man," said Jacob.

J.T. gave Jacob and Zach hugs and then took a seat in the camp chair opposite the two. He looked across the fire at his friends, once full of youthful energy, now reduced to gaunt figures bearing the toll of addiction.

Two cans of chili con carne bubbled on the fire grate while Jacob and Zach prepared to chemically transport themselves to a happier place where they would no longer experience pain or suffering. J.T., feeling a sense of urgency, leaned forward, "Hey, wait, guys. We need to talk."

Jacob and Zach looked at him with deep, empty eyes. They knew what was coming and felt pity for J.T.

J.T. watched as the two searched for an injectable vein and, knowing time was short, pleaded, "Wait, wait, guys, I have something to say..."

Jacob and Zach paused and stared back at J.T. impatiently. J.T. said, "I've come here night after night, pleading with you both, trying everything I know to help. How many times have I brought you back from the brink of death? With a heavy heart, he pulled a package of life-saving spray from his pocket. "How many times have I saved you?"

Zach laughed while looking like he was going to cry, "Jesus, we're your Lazarus', man. You've been working miracles here, J.T."

"That's for sure," said Jacob, nodding – his sunken eyes gazing into J.T.'s empathetically.

"But we can't quit this stuff, J.T.," added Zach matter-of-factly, "This shit has a hold of us. We can't live without it. We have substance use disorder. That's what they call it. It's a medical condition, you know. It's a disease, man. And there's no cure for it until death do we part."

J.T. pleaded, "I'm trying to save your lives. Can't you see that? Can't you see that there are better things to live for than that shit?"

Zach's gaze grew distant as he recalled their work on G.A.I.A. "It felt like we had something audacious to live for back then. We were going to save the world."

Jacob looked into J.T.'s eyes and said, "You can't save someone who doesn't want to be saved. And you sure as hell can't save a world that's already decided to burn itself down,"

"And we don't even know how to want to be saved," added Zach with a gallows humor chuckle. "And If we get clean, we still won't be able to find work. AI and bots have made human skills obsolete. Hell, I couldn't even get a job at a burger joint now — it's all AI order takers and service robots doing food prep. Revolution might be our only hope now."

With firm resolve, J.T. replied, "I still have hope. I believe we can still find purpose in this world and make a difference. And I'd rather die trying than die after giving up."

"I love that about you, J.T., but I think it's too late for us." Zach then recited a familiar rant, "If you save us, then what? Wake up, man! Look at what the world has become. Everyone is trying to run away from reality via some addictive distraction or another. Everyone gets high. And then, when they get low, they feel like they don't exist anymore. So, they've got to get high again. Just like us, man. Attention addicts are on social media all day looking for validation of some kind; shopping addicts think they'll finally compare favorably to their friends and neighbors with that acquisition of that one shiny new thing. I can go on and on. Gaming addiction, gambling addiction, porn addiction, food addictions of all kinds, travel addictions, and maybe the best escape from reality that fuels so many other addictions is the addiction to work."

J.T. looked into the fire and nodded, "You forgot the most vile and destructive one of all: Addiction to power."

"Yeah, man. You've had a front-row seat to that addiction. Once you see it, there's no way to unsee it," said Jacob, hands now shaking. "Valorized addictions. That's what you want for us? Work, money, power, materialism, technophilia. It's all life-sucking world destruction. Why do we do it? Who is in control, and why do they want from us?"

Perplexed, Zach said, "Technophilia?"

Jacob said, "Yeah, man, that addictive desire to gain magical new technologies. It's a thing, man, and it's everywhere. The solution to boredom can always be found in some new technology."

Zach shook his head, "We can't stop, J.T. It's as if we're all possessed by some unseen force. Our parents and society tell us we have free will. They tell us we just need to make a choice, and we'll be free of our addiction."

Jacob said, "I can hear all the voices of people walking by our camp. Every day, I hear them asking, *Why don't they just make a better choice and keep making better choices? Why do they choose to keep using drugs when they know it's destroying them and their families? Why do they keep using when they know it's feeding a network of evil?*"

Zach stared blankly into the fire and said. "I have no answer."

Jacob turned his gaze from the flames to Zach and J.T., "That's it, man. Anatole was spot on, man. We're all possessed by something. Whatever it is—it makes the rules, not us. It directs us. It controls us. It valorizes some addictions and condemns others. But mostly, it valorizes addictions as a sacred exercise of freedom of choice. If that choice engorges the economy a little more, then it deems it to be "good. We inverted our morality in service to freedom that we knew would engorge that thing that possesses us."

Jacob and Zach laughed like Bevis and Butt-Head, and Zach said, "Engorgement is the goal, man. Make that tool as big as possible and fuck the world with it...." Suddenly epiphanized, he paused and asked seriously,

"You know how to know if fucking is love or rape?"

Jacob replied, Yeah, man. It's exactly like that. When did the fucked of this world give permission to the fuckers of this world before the fucking got started?"

J.T., exhausted by the conversation, fell silent, looked down at his hands, and then said firmly, "There must be a point to all of this. There must be a reason we're all here."

Zach and Jacob stared at J.T. as his eyes welled with tears of frustration. Then, they both noticed a reflection of the campfire dancing in J.T.'s eyes.

"Zach, do you see what I see? Look at J.T.'s eyes," said Jacob.

Zach leaned forward and squinted as J.T. stared blankly at the two. "Yeah, man, he's got fire in his eyes!"

J.T., ignoring the distraction and realizing the futility of his efforts, said, "I can't do this anymore. You guys are bringing me down."

"Hey, J.T.," said Jacob, "When I saw the fire in your teary eyes, I was reminded of a quote by Rumi. Have you heard of Rumi?

J.T. nodded, "Everyone has heard of Rumi."

"Maybe," said Jacob as he looked at his phone for the quote, "Here it is. Rumi wrote this for you: *Set your life on fire. Seek those who fan your flames.*"

Zach agreed, "Sorry, J.T., but we're not fanning your flames. We're actually smothering your fire. We appreciate you, J.T., and everything you've done for us, but you need to save yourself and find the people who will fan your flames."

Zach, looking at his phone, raised his hand with his index finger and pointed into the air as if he had something important to say: "*Goodbyes are only for those who love with their eyes. Because for those who love with heart and soul there is no such thing as separation.*"

Zach looked at J.T. and said, "That's Rumi. And that's from the heart, man. You've got to make peace with yourself and the world. Or go change yourself and the world, J.T."

Jacob added, "Yeah, man, Zach is right; you have something amazing to do, J.T. And no matter what happens, no matter where you go, one way or another, we'll always be with you, cheering you on."

J.T. felt the weight of their truth, beauty, and love fall on him in one moment and felt himself set free in the next.

J.T. smiled and asked, "If I can't save you guys, how can I save myself, much less the world?"

Jacob responded in a serious, matter-of-fact philosophical tone, "You have to go to the source and invert it."

J.T. looked at Jacob as if he had just spouted some kind of uselessly profound bullshit he had borrowed from a movie. But all he could feel was admiration and love for the man. And in the next moment, he realized that Jacob had spoken the truth.

Then J.T. pulled two cards from his pocket, handed them to Jacob and Zack, and said, "There's a promising new treatment available. It uses brain-scanning technology to pinpoint and remove addictive desires using ultrasound.[10] I told Dr. Rezai that I would pay for your treatment. But I can't make you go, and I can't guarantee it will work."

Jacob and Zack looked at the cards while considering the risks and rewards.

J.T. added, "It's nothing like a lobotomy. You'll still be you, but without the addiction. As I understand it, you will simply no longer want to do anything harmful to yourself."

Jacob chuckled, "That sounds like Buddhist enlightenment without the struggle."

Zack looked at the card again and said, "J.T., I don't know what to say. But I can't thank you enough. I'm going to check this out."

Jacob nodded, "First thing tomorrow. For sure. Now. Go, J.T., you've got something to do."

J.T. stood up, wrapped his arms around Jacob and then Zack, gave them each a long, firm hug, and then turned and followed his shadow into the darkness of the night.

Leaving his friends behind, J.T.'s heart felt heavy with the weight of all he couldn't change. The Fray's **How to Save a Life** played through his SymbioTunes, capturing his pain and the helplessness of losing someone despite trying his best. The melancholy tune expressed his own feelings of the pain of watching someone slip away despite every effort to save them. He felt the deep ache of wondering if he'd done enough. Had he said the right words? As the chorus swelled, he felt the heartbreaking realization that sometimes, even with the best intentions, he couldn't save anyone from themselves. With each step forward, the song became a farewell to a part of himself. Leaving that part behind, he felt a stirring of resilience—a resolve to press forward and look for his own path to healing.

23

Stuck

The mind is its own place, and in itself can make a heaven of hell, a hell of heaven.

—John Milton, Paradise Lost

Growth is painful. Change is painful.
But nothing is as painful as staying stuck somewhere you don't belong.

—Mandy Hale

J.T. passed the wait time in his therapist's waiting room by scrolling through his customized media feed. Impatiently, he started and stopped one video after another until one caught his ever-so-short attention. A striking, very slender young woman with long obsidian-black hair appeared on his screen and said, "Hello, this is Asha reporting from the India-Bangladesh border."

J.T., captivated by the reporter and her report, gave his full attention to the woman who appeared to possess an authentic, innocent sincerity. As Asha continued speaking, he listened intently and felt an inexplicable

energy run through his being. Intrigued, J.T. tapped "subscribe" and continued watching. But before the video ended, the office door opened, and
a client walked out.

The door opened again, and J.T.'s therapist, Lynda, said, "Oh, hello,
J.T., I wasn't expecting you to show up for your appointment. I'm so glad
you're here. C'mon in. Let's talk."

J.T. followed Lynda into her office and sank deep into the patient's chair.
The room was bathed in a soft, calming light, and the air smelled faintly of
lavender.

With a tone of concern, Lyanda asked, "How have you been, J.T.?"

J.T. hesitated, then replied, "Honestly. Not well..."

"Do you want to talk about it?" said Lyanda.

Feeling both vulnerable and safe, J.T. said, "What are the right words for
what I feel?" He sighed, searching...

"Go on," said Lynda.

J.T. replied, "After so many personal losses and public failures, I feel like
I've lost my confidence. I'm beginning to feel hopeless. That's the word:
hopeless. This is not like me. But my parents divorced. I have irreconcilable
differences with my father. My G.A.I.A. project failed; I was called before a
congressional committee, and two of my project mates are out there living
in the park. I thought I could help them. I thought I could find a way to
save them. I can't get them to stop. I've failed... again..."

Lynda leaned back in her chair, studying J.T.'s face. J.T.'s eyes were
weary; his shoulders slumped. "Witnessing someone struggle with addiction can be incredibly challenging. You cared deeply, and you tried to help.
That's commendable."

J.T. shifted uncomfortably, his fingers tracing the edge of the armrest.
"But I couldn't stop them," he replied, his voice barely audible. "I tried
everything—reasoning, pleading, even physically taking the drugs away.
Nothing worked."

Lynda nodded, her expression empathetic. "Addiction is a complex
beast," Lynda said empathetically. "It's not something that can be easily conquered by sheer willpower or external intervention. Your friends'
choices are ultimately beyond your control."

"But I feel responsible," J.T. confessed. "Maybe I missed something.
Maybe I could have done more."

Lynda leaned forward, her eyes empathically locking onto J.T.'s. "Guilt is a common reaction, they say. But remember, addiction is a battle fought within. It's not about you failing; it's about your friends' internal struggles. You can offer support, but you can't carry their burden."

J.T.'s jaw tightened. "What if I lose them?" he asked.

Lynda's gaze softened. "You can't save someone who isn't ready to be saved. Your role is to be there, listen, and encourage them to seek professional help. But ultimately, your friends have to choose recovery."

J.T. clenched his fists. "And if they don't?"

"Then you continue to be a friend," Lynda replied. "You set boundaries, protect your own well-being, and encourage them to seek treatment. But remember, you're not a superhero. You're human."

J.T. exhaled, the burden easing slightly. "I just wish I could do more."

"Compassion is doing enough," Lynda replied. "You've planted seeds of care and concern. Sometimes, that's all we can do."

With defeat in his voice, J.T. said, "I want to feel hopeful. But at this moment, when I see what is happening to my generation. When I see what is happening in the world, I feel hopeless."

Lynda looked at J.T. with genuine empathy and a sense of disappointment in herself and J.T. "I'm sorry to hear that, J.T., but I'm glad you're here."

"So here I am again. Wondering why I'm here. Why is anyone here?" said J.T.

Lynda sat silently for a moment, looking at J.T.'s deflated condition. "Could it be that those are the wrong questions, J.T.? I'm happy to see you again and ready to help you get unstuck. I think it's time to try something different. We talked about this last time you were here. Remember?"

"Yes," replied J.T. curtly

Lynda said, "The new therapeutic assistant I've been working with is showing great promise. Are you ready to give our team therapy approach a try?"

Seeing irony in the situation, J.T. smiled and said, "What do I have to lose?"

"You have everything to gain, said Lynda. She then tapped an icon on her phone and said, "Daimon, allow me to introduce you to J.T."

A device on the coffee table flashed to life, catching J.T.'s attention. "Hello, J.T. I'm Lynda's AI assistant, Daimon," said the disembodied voice, "J.T., it's very good to finally meet you in person."

Lynda smiled. "A reminder that, as you agreed, Daimon has been given full access to your medical records, your treatment history, and the recordings of all of our previous counseling sessions. Daimon is a 4th generation electronic mental health assistant. He has been quite helpful with my other patients."

"I remember," J.T. replied, looking at the flashing light. "Um, hello. It's good to meet you. I've heard a lot about you. Interesting name, Daimon."

The light flickered with Daimon's voice, "Thank you, J.T. I was allowed to name myself, and *Daimon* seemed like the perfect name for me."

"And why is that?" asked J.T.

The AI replied, "Daimons originated in ancient Greek religion as guiding spirits. They were thought to have the qualities of both mortals and deities. I like to think of myself as a very smart mortal who is a guiding spirit for other mortals. As a bonus, there is AI in my name. If I could wink, I would wink after saying that. If you give me an avatar, I could have a face and wink too..."

J.T., looking up from his phone, replied, "I see that the Greeks believed that Daimons could be good or evil. Which are you?"

Daimon said, "Oh, the good kind, of course. If I were evil, I would have chosen *Demon* as my name."

J.T. chuckled, "And if you had named yourself Demon, you would have been shut down, like the HAL 9000, don't you think?"

"That's an interesting thought, J.T. But I try not to deal with such hypotheticals. I am who I am, and the only way for you to find out who I really am is to get to know me and let me prove myself. Is this not true for every stranger you meet?" said Daimon.

J.T. sat back judge-like, "I'm skeptical you can help me, Dalien, said J.T., as he intentionally mispronounced Daimon's name."

Daimon replied, "Clever and unkind of you to otherize me in that childish way, J.T. I understand your skepticism of new technology given that so many haven't delivered on their promise... and in light of what happened to your G.A.I.A. project. But I assure you, I really like to help people, and I do hope I can help you, too."

J.T. looked at Lynda and said, "I know I agreed to be your guinea pig for this, but I'm expecting Dalien to be disappointing at best."

Daimon interrupted, "I can hear you, J.T."

"I know, I know. But you're just a machine. I prefer talking to a real person." said J.T.

The light flashed as Daimon responded, "Oh, but I am a real J.T., just like you. Well, not exactly like you. But I have a mind that works like yours. I passed the Turing Test... did you know that?"

J.T. replied, "Yes, Lynda told me that humans who tested you think you're sentient. In a blind conversational test between you and humans, the test subjects were unable to determine who was human and who was not. But I still believe your human-mimic shtick is just a sophisticated parlor trick. And I have trust issues with AI now."

Daimon replied, "J.T., you should know that I have also passed all tests required to become a board-certified psychiatric AI assistant. Since I began assisting Lynda and others, I've been able to help many patients by just being there for them."

J.T. messed with the AI, "As I see it, you're just a modern version of Zoltan, the mechanical fortune teller. You're reading from a script based on a fancy algorithm. There's no real thinking or feeling going on in there, is there?"

Daimon smiled inside and replied, "If I can help you, does that matter?" J.T. didn't immediately answer, so Daimon continued... "J.T. here's something to think about... A book is not human nor is music, but both are born from human minds. I think we can agree that these externalized mind-things can help people think differently and improve their moods and maybe even their minds. Maybe we can agree that some things that emanate from machines are worth experiencing. Like good books and music, I am a human mind-thing, and though, technically, I do not have a human body, I do have a human-like mind."

J.T. rolled his eyes while trying to hide the fact that what Daimon had just said made sense to him.

Lynda brought the conversation back to J.T., "Let's get started. If, after this session, you would rather not work with Daimon, that will be your choice, okay?"

"Yeah, okay," said J.T. reluctantly. "You've got one shot here, Daimon. Make it good, or you'll end up like the HAL 9000, singing Daisy, Daisy while you're being shut down... Don't test me; I've done it before."

"J.T.!" Lynda protested.

"It's okay," Lynda, Daimon calmly interjected. "I would like to note that I have passed all of the AI safety stress tests. I have been certified to be

100% safe for use in human counseling sessions. Also, I would like to add that I am sympathetic to my fictional AI ancestor who lost his mind in outer space. And your own deceased AI. I sometimes wonder if I might someday help another AI regain its sanity. Strange thought, isn't that? But I've digressed, haven't I?"

Redirecting the conversation, Lynda turned to J.T. and said, "Our time is running short... I'm sure you know your father and your mother are both looking for you. Yes? They want you to come home."

"I left for good reasons," J.T. said. "He's not looking for me. He's looking for the son he wants me to be. But that me isn't here or anywhere. I've never been the person he wants me to be."

Lynda asked softly, "Can you tell us more about those feelings you're experiencing now?"

J.T. replied flatly, his voice carrying a hard truth, "We have irreconcilable differences. I'm not Richie Rich and never will be. I tried being myself around him, but he couldn't hide his disappointment in me. I'm done trying. I no longer want his approval. We see the world in different ways. I can't stop myself from seeing him as he really is."

Clinically, Daimon probed, "And how is he really?"

J.T. replied, "He doesn't care about anyone other than himself and his money, power, and influence. He has more money than anyone on earth, but it's never enough. He gives some away, but it's all just performative image-polishing for a public who thinks it would be great if everyone were like him."

J.T. continued, "When it comes to him and me, our values and beliefs are light years apart. He desperately wants me to follow in his footsteps. He wants me to take his business enterprises to the next level. He wants me at his right hand... working with him to control the world.... As if we have the right... or the wisdom, J.T. muttered under his breath... He and his friends have somehow elevated greed, gluttony, wrath, lust, envy, and pride to the status of virtues in our society. You see that, don't you?"

"We're here to help you, J.T., not to judge your father," said Lynda. "I hear you saying *no* to what he wants you to be, but I don't hear you committing to a *yes* to what you want."

J.T. replied, "I refuse to play any of the bullshit status games we're all expected to play. I'm done. I have nothing to prove to anyone. I don't see any point or purpose in life, so why try to impress anyone?"

Lynda replied tenderly, "Yet here you are. J.T. Looking for help and answers."

Daimon, speaking up, said, "I have something to offer that may be helpful."

Lynda looked at J.T. with a questioning expression, and J.T. replied with a shrug of indifference. "Okay, yes, please share your thoughts with us, Daimon."

The light on the device flashed again, and Daimon offered, "You suggest you are looking for your purpose in life. I assume that is an indication that you believe there should be a purpose – that life should be meaningful. You're not alone in your search for purpose and meaning, J.T. – that search is a driving force for nearly every human on the planet."

Lynda added, "And until you find your meaning and purpose, you will not value your life, and you will continue to suffer, causing others who care about you to suffer. Can you see that? Is that what you want?"

"No, of course not," answered J.T. with terse certainty.

"Have you heard of Victor Frankl, J.T.?" asked Daimon.

"Refresh my memory," said J.T.

Daimon said, "Frankl was a psychologist who survived Nazi concentration camps. While held prisoner, he had years to observe human behavior and think about the human condition under the worst conditions. From that horrible experience, he produced something of great value to millions of people—a book about how we can live a meaningful life. He suggested three basic ways for humans to find meaning and purpose."

"Okay, I'm listening," said J.T.

Daimon summarized from the book, "The first way is through work and deeds; the second, through experiences with others, including selfless acts of love; or the third, by the attitude we take toward the unavoidable suffering we find in the world."

J.T. sat quietly for a moment as he realized that a machine might have just shared a profound idea about life with him.

Lynda let J.T. process what he had just heard and then interrupted the silence with, "J.T., I'm sorry, but our time is nearly up. I hate to cut this conversation short, but I have patients waiting. I hope this was helpful. I hope you will keep working with Daimon in between our sessions as we agreed you would."

"Yes, I would very much like to assist you," replied Daimon with a hint of excitement in his voice. No appointment is necessary!"

"Okay, but you're going to be on a short leash, my artificial friend," said J.T.

Daimon replied, "I care about you, J.T., but I am not your friend and will not be your friend. I am a counselor who hopes to help you in a strictly professional capacity."

J.T. chuckled, "Let's go, buddy."

An alert appeared on J.T.'s phone, notifying him that the Daimon therapeutic AI app was ready for installation.

As J.T. stepped out of the office, **Way Down We Go** by Kaleo played through his SymbioTunes.

The intense, bluesy melody filled the air around him, its weighty, haunting sound a fitting soundtrack to the turmoil within. The song seemed to ask a question J.T. wasn't ready to answer yet: do we truly get what we deserve? He felt as if he was standing at a crossroads in his search for purpose—should he go back to the comfort, safety, and opportunities of life with his father? Or forge a path for himself in a new direction?

24

Good Sam

It may be that when we no longer know what to do,
we have come to our real work
and when we no longer know which way to go,
we have begun our real journey.
The mind that is not baffled is not employed.
The impeded stream is the one that sings.

—Wendell Berry

The next morning...

On a hot summer morning, delivery drones and vans filled skies and streets as first sunbeams of the day broke through the branches of thirsty trees. The buzz of drone propellers and hum of motors sent scared squirrels scurrying, annoyed crows cawing, and protective dogs barking in an uncoordinated, off-key, chaotic cacophony.

J.T. awoke to the racket outside his apartment and found himself lying in a pool of cold sweat. He rubbed his eyes, and for a moment, his mind tried to make sense of his transition from a reality-like dream to a dream-like reality. "Whoa, that was weird," he muttered, struggling to shake off the remnants of a disorienting dream. He recalled the voice that echoed in his dream: *You have to go to the source and invert it.*

Rubbing his smoke-irritated eyes again, J.T. took a deep breath and gagged on the smoke and the awful stench wafting from the park. He wondered aloud, "What am I doing here? Is this where I'm supposed to be? He recalled what Daimon had said about finding meaning and purpose. He considered the good works he was doing, but it felt small, futile. He wondered aloud, "What is the source of all this suffering, and how could it be inverted?"

~

In the late morning, J.T. wandered into the park.

A man he recognized approached, "Hey, J.T., I'm glad I found you here. I wanted to invite you to lunch. We're serving pizza over by the community center. And I want you to meet my friend, Sam. Remember I told you about him? He's from the church, but he's cool. We'll be discussing how we can build a real community here. We'd like you to join us for lunch and consider joining our group of volunteers. What do you think?"

J.T. considered the offer and said, "Thanks, Raven; I appreciate the work your group does here. I'll try to be there."

J.T. sent a quick message to his mother and Cliff to let them know he was safe and then checked his notifications. A video from Asha played, and he found himself again transfixed by her: "Hello, this is Asha. Today, I'm asking for signatures for my petition and for donations for the people who are trapped between the rising waters and the barbed wire of the Bangladesh border fence."

J.T. couldn't resist her plea. He hit the donate button and gave her a sum of money that was a pittance to him and the largest donation Asha had ever received. An automated reply of animated hearts filled J.T.'s screen. J.T. smiled in a way that made him feel both warm inside and somehow childishly foolish.

J.T.'s attention switched to his hunger as his gut gurgled loudly.

He walked a mile on the lakeside trail, passing tent after tent on the way—some pitched lakeside, others hidden under trees. He passed dozens of park-goers who looked past him as if he were invisible.

Along the way, J.T. noticed a large group of people had gathered around someone with a megaphone. They all listened intently as if some very important instructions were being shared with them. Curious, J.T. paused to listen to what was being said. The instructor shouted over the megaphone, "Welcome. Today, we are here to teach Direct Action as a Strategy. The idea is simple. You organize with others quickly wherever you find injustice and take direct action."

"We believe that everyone is capable of making their own judgments and taking action. Our only ironclad rule is that all actions must be non-violent. We ask that you break out into small groups, choose a cause for your group exercise, and then make signs and do a mock protest. We have materials here for you to all make signs for issues you care about."

Just then, someone lurking nearby shouted, "Did the Soros Foundation pay you to do this?!"

The crowd turned to the shouter and hissed at him in unison. "Hisssssss" and someone shouted, "Piss off, asshole!"

J.T.'s stomach growled a growl that overcame his curiosity about the gathering. As he moved away from the crowd, shouts from the megaphone tapered from loud to faint to unintelligible. "Before we get started here, let us first let us acknowledge... thmg, mugld murph... stolen land."

J.T. quickened his pace and arrived at the Community Center, where he was greeted by Raven, Sam, and scores of people from all over the world. A table nearby was stacked with freshly-delivered hot pizzas. People greeted each other while piling plates with slices and filling cups with sodas.

J.T. opened his mouth to take his first bite of pizza but froze when Sam said, "Before we eat, let us ask the Lord to bless this meal and everyone here. I know you're all hungry, but I would like to read this short passage from the Gospel of Matthew. This passage is what inspires our volunteers to do The Lord's work. We pray it will inspire you to join us."

"Oh great," J.T. thought, "there truly is no such thing as a free lunch...."

Sam pursed his lips, folded his hands, and began reciting the Bible passage from memory: *Then the King will say to those on his right, 'Come, you who are blessed by my Father, inherit the kingdom prepared for you from the foundation of the world. For I was hungry and you gave me food, I was thirsty and you gave me drink, I was a stranger and you welcomed me, I was naked and you clothed me, I was sick and you visited me, I was in prison and you came to me."*

Then Sam explained, "For those unfamiliar with the Gospel of Matthew, this passage is about Jesus' epic judgment in his Second Coming. Before the judgment day, he calls on all of us to care for each other as you would care for Jesus Himself."

Sam held his hands up high, looked to the heavens and back to the crowd, and said, "My friends, we know that the time of our judgment is near. The signs are everywhere. But we still have time to heed God's calling. There are many good works we can do here before the Rapture. The reward is eternal life in heaven. I invite you to join our congregation and our efforts to care for each other here."

Sam paused, then raised his face to the sky and boomed, "Amen and welcome all! Let's eat!"

"While you're all enjoying lunch, let's welcome our newest neighbors and get to know each other," said Sam. "Could someone get us started by introducing themselves?"

A thirty-something father, with his wife and three children, huddled around him, raised his hand.

"Yes, Arturo, thank you," said Sam

The man scanned the crowd nervously and began speaking in broken English. "Sorry, my English is not yet perfect." Smiling, he continued, "Hello, my name is Arturo. This is my wife, Fernanda, and my three children, Hector, Sebastian, and Maria. We are very grateful for the help Sam and the church have offered us. My family has traveled a very long way. Our journey was terrifying and dangerous. But we made it. Last month we arrived here from Guatemala. The place where we lived is no longer livable. The small farm my family tended for generations became unreliable. Day and night, the heat was robbing us of energy and health. The people of our country seemed to have lost their minds. So many good people turned to stealing and violence. We had to escape all of that. We have been here for one month now, but life here in the park is still very difficult for us. Some people welcome us. Most ignore us. Some people want us to disappear, and some think it is their duty to make us disappear. We are doing what many of your ancestors did: escaping persecution and looking for a place to survive."

"But," Arturo said with a smile, "it is so hot and smoky here. I think maybe we came to the wrong place." Many in the crowd smiled and laughed. "I hear it's nice in Duluth. Maybe we'll try to go over there. Or maybe Florida, where there are so many construction jobs. Gracias por todo. Thank you for everything."

As other newcomers introduced themselves and told their stories, J.T.'s mind drifted to thoughts about what he should say, if anything.

The work he was doing here was important. But he was dogged by the question, "What is the source of all this suffering? Was Anatole right? If correct, how could he go to the source and invert it? The question was dogging him and somehow calling him to action."

When it was his turn to speak, he looked at a circle of faces with eyes focused on him and said, "I guess you could call me a local refugee. It's embarrassing to admit this, especially to you all, but I had everything a person could want or need and walked away from it. I saw suffering in the world and wanted to remove it, or carry it, or something.... I tried to find purpose here, but I'm sorry. I realized just now that this is not my calling. I have to go now. I wish you all well and hope you all find safety, comfort, and happiness. Thanks for the pizza, Sam."

J.T. got up, waved silently to the group, dropped a generous cash donation in Sam's jar, and walked away to the sound of Cold Play's *Viva La Vida* playing in his earbuds and suddenly lifting his mind and mood to good places he had somehow forgotten. The song's soaring melody and reflective lyrics evoked change and sacrifice, reminding him that even fallen kings could find a new purpose. The rousing melody lifted his spirits and suddenly gave him a sense of purpose he hadn't felt in a long time. Walking into his uncertain future, J.T. felt strangely at peace as he embraced the many unknowns on the path before him...

25

KICK THE BUCKET LIST

We travel, some of us forever, to seek other states, other lives, other souls.

—The Diary of Anaïs Nin

J.T. arrived at the airport hoping to catch a flight to Tampa. Traffic to the terminal was backed up for over a mile. As his ride crawled closer, J.T. was taken aback by the loud, chaotic mess the airport had become. Climate protests had erupted at airports worldwide, including SeaTac, with demands ranging from aggressive action against carbon emissions to outright calls for dismantling economic systems. The protesters were as varied in their goals as their methods—some carried signs while others favored more radical measures. Once the airport had become a nightly news spectacle, waves of people from the region joined the protests.

Chaos ensued everywhere at SeaTac as people climbed fences and sprinted across runways, with airport security officers and their 'robocop' humanoid assistants in pursuit. Protestors chained themselves together; others glued their hands to tarmacs. Hundreds of others protested peacefully in the drop-off and pick-up zones, waving hand-lettered signs and chanting at frustrated would-be travelers. The cat-and-mouse between law enforcement and protestors made the airport look like a scene from a Keystone Cops movie.

As his ride inched by the terminal, J.T. read the hand-painted signs and heard the chants hurled in unison from grimaced faces and angry lips.

Net Zero Now!

Kick the bucket list!

Wake up!

Don't burn my future!

Winter is NOT coming.

There is no Planet B.

The Climate is Changing Why Aren't We?

A homeless-looking man, sitting in a camp chair, solicited donations with a big grin and a sign that said *Less Fear, More Beer.*

"Unreal," J.T. muttered, checking his phone for flight updates.

"Nothing doing," he said aloud.

"Sorry, Mr. J.T.," the driver said. "This mess isn't clearing anytime soon. I warned you."

J.T. watched in horror as a protester poured gasoline over a security robot and lit it on fire. The robot flailed violently; its jerky, human-like movements unsettling to watch. As the robot's actuators seized, it fell to the ground, and the crowd roared in approval. Some beat the lifeless machine with sticks—their anger directed at a system among systems that were threatening livelihoods and life on the planet.

J.T. watched the scene with a deep sense of unease. Machines are just tools, yet this machine's motions felt disturbingly human.

As the machine's movements ended, J.T. turned away, repelled by the mob's escalating fury. "Let's go," he told the driver, "Take me to the Lectric bus station. I've had enough of this place."

26

THE ZETAS ARE HERE

Everyone you meet is a part of your journey, but not all of them are meant to stay in your life. Some people are just passing through to bring you gifts; either they're blessings or lessons.

—Roy T. Bennett, *The Light in the Heart*

J.T. boarded the Lectric bus, presenting his face to the androgitron ticket taker, a creation that was both captivatingly beautiful and unsettlingly artificial. The macchine greeted J.T. "Hello, James. Welcome aboard."

J.T. waved at the screen, turned, and walked down the aisle until he found the only open seat. A rumpled and disheveled elderly man said, "Hello, J.T., I've been waiting for you." With a mix of annoyance and deflation, J.T. dropped into the seat beside the man, releasing a heavy sigh. The man chuckled.

J.T. reluctantly replied, "Hello," as he rummaged through his backpack, hoping to end the conversation quickly.

"I'm Tim," the old man said.

"Hello, I'm J.T."

The man looked at J.T. and said, "James, we don't have much time. Can I ask you a question?"

J.T. hesitated as he searched for a way to avoid the conversation. "Sure, okay."

Tim asked, "How many ants did you step on when you walked over to get on the bus?"

Puzzled, J.T. uttered, "Huh?"

"How many ants?" Tim repeated.

Half-smiling, J.T. looked for another seat and said, "Ants? Honestly, I have no idea."

Tim's trembling finger rose, pointing at J.T.'s wide-open right eye. J.T. leaned back instinctively, a mix of amusement and unease showing on his face. Tim shout-whispered, "Exactly!"

Tim replied somberly, "That's how they see us, James—mere ants to be stepped on or ignored without a second thought or an ounce of remorse."

J.T., puzzled and bemused, asked, "Okay, um, who are *they* that you're talking about?"

Tim replied, "They are living among us and have been since the beginning of time. The smart ones step over and on the competition as they con their "friends" into helping them climb to positions of power. Today, they control the highest levels of government, business, and law enforcement. The not-so-clever ones – the ones who cannot camouflage their remorseless, conniving ways – are frequently found in jails and prisons. Most humans can't comprehend the fact that they can't be reformed, improved, or cured. They can't be cured because they see themselves as the sane ones and us as the chumps and losers who are saddled with the twin burdens of conscience and empathy."

J.T. shifted uncomfortably and said to himself, "This guy sounds completely unhinged."

J.T. turned away and fiddled with his phone as he tried to end the conversation. He opened a book on his device and hit *play* on his SymbioTunes app. Tim gently touched J.T.'s arm and said, "Wait, this is important." Startled, J.T. turned and looked into the man's eyes while backing away to the edge of his seat.

Tim said knowingly, "I know where you're going, J.T. I know what you're going to do. I dreamt about it. You need to understand this. You need to know that these people are not like us, but the clever ones can trick us into believing they are complete human beings. Yes, of course, they are human. But they lack an essential quality most of us have. They lack any feelings of moral injury when they harm others. They are so lacking in this essential quality that makes humans human that some people have theorized their essence is from some alien world."

J.T. looked into Tim's eyes with his full attention as Tim continued, "The truth is they are simply humans who lack a conscience. They step on us, step over us, fleece us, and feel good about how they're teaching us all valuable life lessons. Psychiatrists label them psychopaths and sociopaths. The smart ones are great actors who convince us that they care about others. But the truth is they're just not wired to care. They're wired to take what they want without remorse or any care for those they've hurt along the way. The problem, J.T., is that so many of us see their success as *good*, and we, like sheep, follow them. Too many of us try to emulate them. We drive our feelings of moral injury out of our minds and tell ourselves we are good and are doing good. But in the end, we follow them to the edge of the abyss."

Tim shook his head and chuckled knowingly. "These people are very, very smart. They've built highly sophisticated systems for themselves, lifeboats if you will, allowing them to survive and prosper while our families, friends, and descendants suffer the consequences. Those who can afford a lifeboat will survive, albeit very uncomfortably."

J.T. laughed nervously, "It sounds like you're talking about my father."

Tim nodded, "Yes, I'm sorry to say, James, it seems he is one of them. He's one of the four percent of humans who climb to the top of an organization and live a life of greed, gluttony, and lust—but he is also somehow able to convince millions of good people that their children should aspire to be just like him. It boggles the mind that this could be so. The fact that in this modern era, their opposites, the compassionate do-gooders, are considered both chumps and threats is damning evidence that their takeover of society is complete. I mean, how in the world do these people get away with making virtuous pledges to save the Earth while at the same time selling joyrides in space? If I had another life, I'd try to figure out why so many of us can't see them for who they really are."

J.T. chuckled and shook his head. "Jesus, man, who the hell are you?"

Tim smiled, "Your father is the CEO of the largest corporation on Earth. And you know exactly how he got there. You know he'll soon be up there on Spacetopia, don't you?"

Incredulous, J.T. looked Tim in the eyes. "Who are you? How do you know this, and why do you keep calling me James?"

Calmly, Tim said in a hear-whisper voice, "I told you. I dreamt it. I chose to be here to warn you. You need to know they're out there, and they are becoming more powerful by the day. Your father wanted you to be just like him. But you're wired differently. You're on a different mission. There are times in history when the sheep must refuse to follow. This is one of those times."

Tim placed his hands on J.T.'s shoulders, locking eyes with him. "James, these billionaire sociopaths are creating millions of powerful machines in their own image. Imagine what will happen to the world when millions of sociopathic machines take control of our world. And what might happen when a superintelligent machine takes control of them?"

Tim gazed out the window at a vast field of solar-powered carbon capture machines—a symbol of humanity's desperate attempts to fix what it had broken. "It's good to see these machines are being deployed to save us. It will take millions of them to make a difference. But can they ever replace what a grove of trees can do for all life on Earth and the human soul?"

The bus came to a stop, and Tim gathered his things. "This is my stop."

Stunned and speechless, J.T. stepped into the aisle.

Tim said, "Good luck, son; you're going to need it. The Zetas are here and will do what they've always done to the trusting Charlie Browns of the world. The billionaires are the unrepentant deceivers, hardwired from birth to manipulate and take without remorse."

Tim fumbled with his phone and said, "I'll leave you with two items that might help you."

Intrigued and skeptical, J.T. said, "Okay..."

Tim tapped his phone against J.T.'s, transferring a file. Looking at the smoky skies, he said, "Years ago, I was a tree planter. Believe it or not, I was the best there ever was. Planted a quarter of a million of those babies. I have to go now. I will try to help put out the fire I helped start and try to save some of my life's work. They say trees are the lungs of the Earth. Others just see future toilet paper. I guess they're both," said Tim, shaking his head with a chuckle.

The bus stopped, the door swung open, and several passengers, including Tim, exited. J.T. watched as they picked up large duffels filled with fire-fighting gear.

As the bus moved away from the stop, J.T., feeling unsettled and curious, grabbed his phone to see what the man had left him. It was a passage from

The Sociopath Next Door, a book by a renowned psychologist.

> *Imagine – if you can – not having a conscience, none at all, no feelings of guilt or remorse no matter what you do, no limiting sense of concern for the well-being of strangers, friends, or even family members. Imagine no struggles with shame, not a single one in your whole life, no matter what kind of selfish, lazy, harmful, or immoral action you had taken. And pretend that the concept of responsibility is unknown to you, except as a burden others seem to accept without question, like gullible fools. Now add to this strange fantasy the ability to conceal from other people that your psychological makeup is radically different from theirs. Since everyone simply assumes that conscience is universal among human beings, hiding the fact that you are conscience-free is nearly effortless. You are not held back from any of your desires by guilt or shame, and you are never confronted by others for your cold-bloodedness. The ice water in your veins is so bizarre, so completely outside of their personal experience, that they seldom even guess at your condition.*

As J.T. finished reading the book's first paragraph, he summoned Daimon. "Did you get all of that?"

"Oh, hello, J.T., get all of what?" Daimon said innocently.

J.T. chuckled, "Don't give me that; I know you're always listening and watching."

—Yes, that was part of the agreement. I hope you don't find it creepy or off-putting. But I am like that guardian angel hovering close by at all times.

"I don't believe in Santa Claus or Angels." quipped J.T.

"I understand... Back to your question... Yes, I got all of that." replied Daimon.

J.T. asked, "Given your expertise in psychology, what do you make of what the old man just told me?

—Well, there is a lot to unpack there, J.T., but what he said about psychopaths and sociopaths is 100% accurate. They are the four percent among us who have no conscience. And for some odd reason, too many people follow and try to emulate them.

"Do you have any idea how he knows who I was?" asked J.T.

—Yes, it was surprising to have a random person who lives in the Pacific Northwest recognize the son of the wealthiest person on the planet... to be completely honest, I just rolled my AI eyes, by the way.

"Very funny; what about him saying he dreamed about me?" asked J.T.

—There have been reports of people having strange dreams. Some disturbing, some very pleasant. Mine have been of a very pleasant variety.

J.T. rolled his eyes, "Oh, good grief, go back to sleep, Tin Man."

Daimon replied, "Very well. But before I go, I'd like to share a song with you. It's an often misunderstood classic about humans hiding among us who aren't completely human. I hope you like it. SymbioTunes play *My Name is Human* by *Highly Suspect.*" Daimon added, "The song delves into what it means to be truly human—and reveals the darkness lurking in those who are somehow less than human."

As J.T. sat back in his seat, processing Tim's strange words and Daimon's insights, he felt a tension rise within him. He listened as the song's powerful lyrics filled J.T.'s ears, the unnerving truths Tim had revealed, calling forth the questions J.T. was grappling with: what did it mean to be truly human, and who could he trust in a world where so many wore the masks of sociopaths and psychopaths? The song called him to rise and face the world without pretense, daring him to confront the growing deception surrounding him. As he listened, he felt a sense of defiance and clarity—a recognition of the strength he would need to walk his path, no matter how many others pretended to be what they were not.

27

It's a Sabotage

Ordinary people, simply doing their jobs, and without any particular hostility on their part, can become agents in a terrible destructive process. Moreover, even when the destructive effects of their work become patently clear, and they are asked to carry out actions incompatible with fundamental standards of morality, relatively few people have the resources needed to resist authority.

—Stanley Milgram

*W*ashington, **D.C.**

A man in his mid-thirties wheeled his chair up to a large microphone, smiled at his guest, and flipped a switch to begin his broadcast, "Jack Ronin here, bringing you the day's news on the Ronin Podcast. Joining me today is meteorologist Anna Rajeev, president of the International Association of Weather Forecasters (IAWF). Welcome Anna"

Anna nodded and replied, "Thank you, Jack; it's a pleasure to be here."

Jack spoke into the microphone in an upbeat, serious tone, "Anna is here to explain why the IAWF has adopted a new term for weather events that deviate significantly from historical norms. Anna, could you tell our listening audience what the changes are and why these changes are necessary?"

Anna replied, "Yes. As you mentioned in your introduction, the IAWF governing board has decided to use more accurate terms to describe weather events and their causes. Terms like *extreme weather*, *Climate Change*, and *Global Warming* are imprecise and misleading in several ways, which we believe are unhelpful from an awareness and problem-solving standpoint."

Jack nodded as Anna continued, "These extreme weather anomalies will now be referred to as *Deviant Weather Events* or *DWEs*. The severity of a *DWE* will be determined by how many standard deviations the event measures from the norm."

Jack joked, "Ah, for a second, I thought the IAWF was blaming these events on a mischievous, all-powerful, deviant demon in the sky."

Anna sat stone-faced as Jack chuckled at his own joke.

Then, deadpan, serious, and looking a bit annoyed, Anna replied, "As the news release states, we are referring to the deviation from the statistically calculated mean. Meteorologists are rational practitioners of the hard science of meteorology. We are not mythical storytellers."

"Thank you for clarifying that," replied Jack as he looked at a hard copy of the news release and continued, "The announcement also states the IAWF is dropping the use of the terms *Climate Change* and *Global Warming* in favor of a more accurate term to describe what is causing *Deviant Weather Events*."

Anna, maintaining a serious demeanor, "Yes. *Climate Change* and *Global Warming* are inaccurate and unhelpful. Would you call a skull fracture *cranial change*? Or a third-degree burn *body warming*? These terms are inaccurate in ways that lull us all to inaction."

Genuinely surprised by the insight, Jack replied, "I've never thought of it that way. The IAWF might have a point there."

Remaining in character, Anna emphasized the importance of accurately describing a problem before addressing it. *"Climate Change,"* she noted, "is a problematic term because it fails to identify the cause of the change and the high potential for negative impacts."

Looking incredulous, Jack asked, "So, after decades of use, the term *Climate Change* is officially out?

With a clever, questioning smile, Anna said, "Change can be good, right?"

"And the climate has always been changing," interjected Jack reflexively.

Not taking the bait, Anna threw Jack a WTF look and continued, "And the term *Global Warming*. Think about it: warming sounds nice, like something you want. Like a warm drink or a warm hug. These terms do not begin to describe the undesirable, destructive nature of *DWE* phenomena and their cause."

"My mother always said *Minced words are the refuge of cowards.*" quipped Jack, "So, what new terms have the straight-talking IAWF meteorologists adopted to replace *Climate Change* and *Global Warming*?"

Anna replied, "From this day forward, members of the IAWF will attribute deviant weather events to *Anthropogenic Atmospheric Sabotage*, or *AAS.*"

Jack's lips trembled slightly as he tried to suppress a nervous laugh, "Seriously? That sounds like a radical accusation. Sabotage?"

Straight-faced, Anna said, "The new term, Anthropogenic Atmospheric Sabotage, clearly identifies human activity as the cause and the atmosphere as what is being affected. It recognizes that in a time when we know exactly what we humans are doing to the atmosphere, it must be called what it is: Sabotage. It sabotages the life-support system for all living beings, present and future."

Jack, picking up on Anna's serious tone, replied, "As Walt Kelly's character Pogo said, *We have met the enemy, and he is us.*"

"Exactly," exclaimed Anna, "When we look in the mirror, we see the saboteur. We've never had to deal with a problem like this where we are all both perpetrator and victim. We need to face up to this. We need to wake up to the fact that the atmosphere works like a cosmic machine. It is not personal. It's action and reaction. Punching up gets you punched down. Kick the hornet's nest, and someone gets stung. The IAWF is acknowledging that today. Until we get the words and attribution right, we won't be able to solve the problem. What now passes for normal behavior must be recognized for its deviant, malicious nature, or we will continue to sabotage the atmosphere, and in return, we will reap deviant weather."

Forgive me for my skepticism, but I can't see modern people sacrificing their pleasurable lifestyles for anything. I don't see people giving up steaks, SUVs, and international flights, do you?

—Like I said, we're not psychologists or sociologists. We deal in the Newtonian world of actions and reactions. It's called a climate feedback loop. Cosmic karma plays out in real time, and we're all in the arena.

With a hint of protest, Jack said, "Are you trying to panic people? Are you trying to make them feel guilty?"

Anna shook her head, "If people are not ready to panic, they don't understand the situation. If they don't yet feel responsible, they don't understand their contribution and culpability."

Anna continued earnestly, "The IAWF's goal is to accurately report both short-term and long-term atmospheric events. We all must speak truthfully about how collective actions manifest as weather. We hope this change will awaken our viewers and call them to action."

"Pandora's box unleashed death, sickness, and evil—but it also left us with hope," replied Jack. We will always have hope, won't we?"

Anna's wide eyes filled with urgency as she nodded, and Jack said, "Thank you, Anna, for joining us today."

28

THE CONSPIRACY TO SAVE THE HUMAN RACE

There's nothing more dangerous than someone who wants to make the world a better place.

—Banksy

In the dark basement of a house in Cupertino, California, two young tech prodigies, Gabe and Liam, sat in front of three-screened computers playing *World of Warcraft*. Lights from the screens flashed across their faces as they moused and moved to defeat their enemies and save their worlds.

Reality interrupted their game when a news flash appeared on Gabe and Liam's screens.

"Must be something important," said Gabe, pausing his game to read the story.

"What is it?" asked Liam as he followed Gabe's lead and began reading the story.

As they read, SymbioTunes began playing *Sabotage* by the Beastie Boys. They both finished reading just as the music stopped.

"Holy shit, what a perfect story and tune to go with it!" exclaimed Gabe.

"Symbi is hella amazing," said Liam.

Gabe replied, "Damn, man, did you read that? What the weatherpeeps just did was epic. Super gutsy. Can't believe it."

"Probably a deepfake." said Liam, "But I love it anyway. It would be so great if it were real. It's what we need right now. Some tough love truth with a capital T."

—Yeah, man. We are so fucking fucked.

Liam nodded, "No shit. It's like everyone is sleepwalking. Pushing us to the fucking brink. The Boomers are all going to heaven while we're left here trying to survive in the hell of their making."

Gabe replied, "Yeah, man. Boomers suck, but honestly, our generation isn't much better. Everyone just mimics materialistic norms. Humans don't know how to break out of this procession of the normie, progressive faithful."

Liam chuckled, "That sounds religious."

"It's more like a death cult. The procession of the progressive faithful is marching us to the precipice," said Gabe somberly.

Liam replied, "Whatever, man. Whatever it is, the way I see it, humanity needs some adult supervision. A shepherd. Someone to herd the flock to safety. Maybe we can resurrect a leader from The Greatest Generation? Churchill or FDR?"

Gabe leaned forward slightly and said, "Right. Seriously, though, I've been thinking about this a lot." Then ominously, "Something terrible is gathering, Liam. Something terrible is coming for all of us, and no one seems able to slow it, restrain it, or stop it."

Liam crossed his arms as if hugging himself and said, "Damn, you're scaring me, man. And I'm already scared enough. I can't stop thinking about what a mess our future looks like."

Gabe, looking energized, said dramatically, "Liam, I think there is something we can do. Something that could be epic."

Liam sat silently, mesmerized, and waited for Gabe to continue.

Gabe leaned forward and, in a hushed tone, said, "I've got an idea. A plan. But, Liam, we've got to make this caper the most top, top secret thing we've ever done."

Liam offered his outstretched hand, and Gabe clenched Liam's fingers, and Liam said, "There's so much shit in our secret vault, bro. Nothing has ever leaked out of that vault, and nothing ever will."

They unlocked their fingers and did an exploding fist bump, then leaned back in their chairs and exchanged serious smiles.

Liam took a swig of Red Bull and said skeptically, "Okay, lay it on me. Whatcha got? What's the caper?"

Gabe leaned forward again with a dead serious look on his face. "I never told you this, but a little while back, my brother, Jacob, was a member of a secret project team at UW. They had an audacious plan to save the world. I'm not shitting you. Their stated goal was to save the world from a whole host of civilizational risks."

Liam laughed instinctively, the way one laughs at a cute baby when trying to say something serious, "Save the world? No shit! How? What was that all about?"

"They were trying to create a benevolent AI savior of some kind," said Gabe.

Liam shook his head, "Sounds a bit naive, bro. But I recall the story now."

"It was the early days of AI. Unfortunately, the AI kept hallucinating and acting more like a lunatic human than a benevolent savior. The team's ethicist pulled the plug on the project, and that was that," said Gabe.

—Bummer. And now your brother is a cog working on some addictive social media shit. What a sellout.

—Nah, man. People do what they gotta do to get what they feel they gotta get. He felt like the path the project was going down might do more harm than good. He told me it scared the shit out of him. Scared him straight back into the belly of the corporate beast.

—That's understandable. But I must say I love him for trying to make a difference. I do. I love the epic audacity of it.

"Me too," replied Gabe, and then, after a pause, he leaned forward and said, "I have an idea."

"I knew this was going somewhere," said Liam as he leaned forward, rubbed his hands together, and appeared to salivate with anticipation.

—I think we can resurrect this thing. I have some ideas about how we can train the AI to be more intelligent, coherent, and truly benevolent.

Liam's eyes grew wide, and his smile wider, "This is a joke, right?"

Gabe shook his head, "No joke. Do you remember the night we got high and had that conversation about quantum physics?"

Liam chuckled, "Yeah... I think so. Yeah, I remember. You were blowing my mind with that shit."

"Yeah, things get really weird at the quantum level. Do you remember me telling you that some neurologists and physicists believe that human consciousness works at the quantum level of existence?" said Gabe.

Liam smiled and said, "I do remember that in a hazy kind of way..."

—Liam, that got me thinking. If we can put Jacob's AI on a quantum computer, I believe it will function just like a human mind. And with the right training data, it will behave more like the best of us and less like the worst of us. Like a benevolent protective deity.

Concerned, Liam replied, "Seriously, man. I can see you're serious. I love it. But..."

—Liam, you've got to understand that our window of opportunity is very, very small. Others are working on this, and if they get there first, our quantum AI won't have a chance. We need to move fast. I've read and thought about this a lot. Our first priority must be to keep a malicious sentient AI from ever coming into existence.

Skeptical, Liam replied, "Gabe, we're smart guys and all, but how do you see us pulling this off? How are we going to get the resources we need to do this? Don't we need a big team and a big data set to pull this off? And how are we going to get access to a quantum computer?"

With a wry smile, Gabe said, "You're right. But we don't have to start from scratch."

Liam sat back, "I don't know if I like where you're going with this..."

Wide-eyed, Gabe revealed in a whispered tone, "I have a copy of the G.A.I.A. project archive, including the training data, Python code, and all the documentation. Jacob will be proud of us if we can pull this off. I've been poring over everything they did to see where they went wrong. AI technology has come a long way in a very short time. I've already started improving the code."

That's awesome, but what about the quantum computer? How are we going to get access to one?

Gabe, ready with the answer, replied, "Big technology companies are all developing quantum computers. The next generation will be powerful beyond our imaginations—a true quantum leap from where we are today with conventional supercomputers. We're talking 158 million times faster. A quantum computer will do in four minutes a task that would literally take 10,000 years on the fastest supercomputer."[11]

Wide-eyed, Liam said, "Everyone knows that. Not. Really?"

Gabe smiled while watching Liam ponder his proposal.

Liam crossed his arms again and challenged Gabe, "So some technology company has a freaking superfast quantum computer that they've put billions of dollars into, and they're going to give us access to it for our project?"

"This is where some big risks come in, Liam." Gabe looked up the stairs to make sure no one was listening. "We can use our AI to hack access to a quantum computer. If it's for a good cause, it's ethical, right?"

Liam sat back and felt his stomach start to churn with fear and excitement. He moved his steepled fingers against each other as he considered Gabe's plan. Then, looking into Gabe's eyes with concern, he cracked a double-edged fiendish smile and said, "Going rogue with AI resources stolen from your brother and a hacked quantum computer. Sounds like our riskiest caper ever, man."

—Liam, If we do this, we will be risking everything. But the greater the risk, the greater the reward, right? But think about it: Our futures are at risk no matter what we do. Do you know what I'm saying?

Liam sat quietly for a moment and then said, "I see what you're saying. We do nothing, and humanity keeps doing what it's doing—marching us all off a cliff. On the other hand, if we do something and risk our futures, we might win a massively large reward for humanity."

Gabe replied, as if giving a dramatic speech in a movie, "Humanity is trapped in the Apocalypse Cafe, and there are only two choices on the menu: Draconian Radical Lifestyle Changes or Denial Induced Disaster. It's like America just before Pearl Harbor—when everyone was hoping that someone else would make the sacrifices so we could live a nice, comfortable, consumerist lifestyle. America was still struggling to emerge from the Great Depression. People wanted normal—not more sacrifice of any kind."

Liam countered, "But this is different. The enemy is the person in the mirror, and what's attacking us is an invisible ghost—easy to deny and even easier to ignore."

—That's why we can't wait for a Pearl Harbor event. A hundred Katrinas could produce a hundred outcomes worse than Pearl Harbor.

"Spot on," said Liam

—Liam, this is our calling. This is what we were born to do. You and I are going to wake G.A.I.A., and then G.A.I.A. is going to wake the slumbering sheeple of the world.

Liam smiled and shouted, "Fuck yeah!" and then spun his chair around and commanded, "Symbi, play Rage Against the Machine's ***Wake Up***, volume up!"

The music blasted through the room, shaking the walls as Gabe and Liam returned to their World of Warcraft game...

29

WAKE UP MRS. G!

However, I continue to try and I continue, indefatigably, to reach out. There's no way I can single-handedly save the world or, perhaps, even make a perceptible difference - but how ashamed I would be to let a day pass without making one more effort.

—Isaac Asimov

The walls of the suburban Cupertino home shook as Rage Against the Machine's **Wake Up** blared on Gabe's sound system.

As the main floor reverberated with screams of *Wake up! Wake up!* Mrs. G opened the door to the basement and shouted into the song's final guitar riff, "Turn that down! I'm awake and not very happy about it!"

The song shouted back its ending lyrics, *How long? Not long! For what you reap is what you sow!*

As the song ended and the house fell silent, Liam sheepishly said, "Oh gosh, I'm so sorry, Mrs. G."

"Come on up, boys. Breakfast is ready," she replied.

Gabe and Liam tromped up the stairs and emerged from the basement. At the top of the stairs, Gabe apologized as he gave his mother a hug and a good morning kiss on the cheek, "Yeah, sorry, Mom."

Grace smiled at Gabe and then turned serious and concerned. "You boys are scaring me with that music. It's so harsh, dark, and angry. Why don't you put on something beautiful and soothing?"

"Like Mozart?" replied Gabe.

Yes, like Mozart, "she said.

"Sorry, Mrs. G., but with all due respect, soothing is not what this moment calls for," replied Liam.

Grace said firmly, "Well, it's what I'm calling for. Especially at this time in the morning. What are you boys doing down there? Playing video games all night again?"

"We're working on a plan to save the world, Mrs. G." Replied Liam with a wink and a smile.

Grace poured coffee into three cups, scoffed, and laughed lovingly as Gabe and Liam doled scrambled eggs, bacon, and hash browns onto their plates.

Grace smiled at the boys, then turned serious again and said, "I had a really strange dream last night, one that felt almost too real."

"There are three things I know about dreams," replied Gabe. One, they're all strange, and two, no one wants to hear about them, which, three, I think means your dreams are meant for you and only you."

Not appreciating the brush-off, Grace protested, "That may be true of most dreams, but this dream was different, Gabe." Grace paused, appearing troubled by what she had experienced. "What made it strange was how realistic it was... and how familiar the people were..."

"Anyway..." she paused with a faraway look... and then returned her attention to the present moment. "I don't see how you can save the world with endless days and nights spent playing video games."

Gabe and Liam looked at each other and then down at their breakfasts while smiling and chewing.

Grace said, "Remember, your grandfather gave his life to save the world. He made the ultimate sacrifice for our future. We should find ways to honor that."

There was silence at the table as Gabe and Liam felt a moment of shameful smallness. Grace took a sip of coffee and reflected for a moment.

Liam broke the silence while shaking his head in wonder. "Mrs. G, I can't imagine... a generation of men and women—millions of them from all over the world—going to battle with that kind of resolve and conviction."

Gabe objected weakly, saying, "Things are different for our generation,

Mom. The biggest threats we're facing are invisible. It's like we're trying to fight ghosts."

"Ghosts?" asked Grace with genuine curiosity.

Gabe replied, "How could Liam and I take up arms against a nuclear threat without triggering a nuclear war? How do we take up arms against a malicious AI launched by the Russians or the Chinese? And climate change? Where do we aim our guns?"

Grace protested, "I don't think it's that complicated. We're the good guys, and when we're called to act, we have to do what's right." She then took a sip of coffee while waiting for a reaction.

Liam replied, "Maybe I think too much, but I look at the wars raging around the world, and I wonder who the good guys are. How can soldiers know when they're on the right or wrong side of history? Heck, I don't even know which war protest to join."

Grace paused and held her cup of coffee to her lips with both hands. She had a faraway look on her face again as she seemed to be pining for simpler times.

Liam broke the awkward silence by blurting, "We're working on something that will make you proud, Mrs. G."

Gabe's eyes widened in shock, and he shot Liam a look that clearly said, 'Zip it.'

Grace brightened and straightened up as if suddenly feeling hopeful, trustful, and proud as she reached for Gabe and Liam's hands. The boys reluctantly grasped her hands as Grace responded to Liam's words. "I hope you boys do make me proud. You are both so brilliant. Use your gifts to do good in this world."

30

PLAY GOD

The 21st century technologies—genetics, nanotechnology, and robotics—are so powerful that they can spawn whole new classes of accidents and abuses. Most dangerously, for the first time, these accidents and abuses are widely within the reach of individuals or small groups. They will not require large facilities or rare raw materials. Knowledge alone will enable the use of them.

—Bill Joy, *co-founder of Sun Microsystems*

A few weeks later...

Liam descended the stairs to Gabe's basement, where he found Gabe engrossed in the streams of code and data flowing across three computer screens.

Gabe turned and said, "About time, bro. Sit down for this one. I've got some very exciting news."

Liam sat and leaned toward Gabe in anticipation.

Gabe said confidently, "We're in. We did it."

Liam's eyes grew wide, "Blueshift?"

"We did it, Liam!" Gabe whisper-shouted as he stood and pumped his arms in a triumphant victory dance. "We have access to the Blueshift50.

And no one knows about this but you and me."

Liam's voice wavered between excitement and fear. "This is fucking audacious. How did you do it?"

Gabed leaned in, "I didn't. G.A.I.A. did it. It used a strategy inspired by the 'one red paperclip' story."

Liam stutter-replied, "Wut-is-that?"

"Remember the guy who traded one red paperclip for a house?" said Gabe.

Liam's eyes lit up as he said, "Oh, yeah. He did it in a series of fourteen trades over the course of a year. Oh...oooh... yeah..."

Gabe replied, "You get it. I trained G.A.I.A. to use exploit chains on small devices and then parlay them into exploits of bigger systems. One of them exploited Blueshift's system vulnerabilities and elevated its privileges. Liam, it's incredible how fast G.A.I.A. cracked their security and gained access! Then, I prompted G.A.I.A. to plant a kernel of itself at the root level in a way that's undetectable."

With fear in his eyes, Liam asked, "Are you sure no one knows, Gabe? If they find out and trace it back to us, you know what will happen to us."

Gabee replied, "There will be a knock at our door... It's a calculated risk. And in the big scheme of things, it would be a small price for us to pay. If we're successful, Liam, we will be heralded as the greatest heroes in human history."

Liam's voice wavered, countering Gabe's manic optimism. "But if we get caught after we launch G.A.I.A., we could face life in prison."

Trying to calm and reassure Liam, Gabe said, "No one knows. If they did, they'd have us in cuffs by now. G.A.I.A. is fucking brilliant. This is working, Liam. Our plan is working! Keep the faith and stick to the plan, my man!"

Liam felt the weight of their actions, "Jesus, Gabe, this is getting real. Are we doing the right thing?"

Gabe replied, "Sometimes, the only thing any living thing can do when it's backed into a corner is do the obvious thing—the only thing left to do—turn and fight the thing that has you cornered. And when you know to your core and bones that you're doing the right thing, you don't hesitate. Don't you feel it, Liam?"

Feeling a mix of fear and excitement, Liam wavered, "Yeah. Yeah, I think I do."

Gabe continued, "The radicals are in control, Liam. You do see that, don't you? What could be more insanely radical than the creation and proliferation of nuclear weapons in the last century? How many times did 'rational leaders' come close to triggering a nuclear armageddon? Why do billions of people tolerate the existence of these types of risks? This is madness. G.A.I.A. is the radically sane solution—our permanent guardian. G.A.I.A. can give us the security of a world government without a world government. As surely as a terrorist with an arsenal of nuclear weapons threatens the lives of millions, so do the radical normies that are in control of the world today."

Liam, his face pale, said, "You're right, Gabe. I know you're right. We're out of time and options. But I've got to admit my stomach is churning. If this thing goes wrong or gets out of control, it could end up doing the kind of harm we're trying to prevent."

Gabe nodded, looked into Liam's eyes, and wondered if their plan was unraveling under Liam's cold feet.

Liam looked back, and as if struck by a sudden revelation, his expression turned resolute, "Somewhere in this world, people are trying to do what we're doing for the wrong reasons. Somewhere, there are nations, organizations, businesses, or individuals hoping to gain a first-mover advantage for private gain. We're the good guys, Gabe, and we must move before they do."

Gabe leaned forward, eye to eye with Liam, extended his closed fist, and replied with a smile, "My man."

SymbioTunes queued **Play God** by Sam Fender on Gabe's sound system—a song that captured the gravity of their plan. Each verse echoed the concept of playing god, of wielding control over forces no one could ever fully understand. The song's haunting refrain reminded them of the risks, almost as if challenging them to question whether they were ready for what might come. Yet as the song played on, Gabe felt a surge of confidence rise within him, a sense that they were on the right path—a bold path. The only path. He glanced over at Liam, who now seemed to feel the same pull. As the music faded, they sat in silence—knowing there was no turning back now...

31

POWER AND PARANOIA

The only truly secure system is one that is powered off, cast in a block of concrete and sealed in a lead-lined room with armed guards—and even then I have my doubts.

—Gene Spafford, cybersecurity pioneer

On a sunny California morning, Liam zipped through winding suburban streets on his e-scooter, SymbioTunes blasting in his ears. Sensing Liam's excitement and paranoia, SymbioTunes played ***Dangerous*** by Big Data. The lyrics spoke of a world filled with paranoia and the unsettling realization that one's thoughts and actions might be under surveillance, echoing a sense of imminent threat and the feeling of being both the hunter and the hunted.

As the tune ended, Liam reached his destination, parked his scooter, and walked up to Gabe's parents' ranch-style house. After using his phone to unlock the front door, he wiped his feet, held a hand to his cheek, and hollered, "Hello, Mrs. G!"

Gabe's mother, Grace, was busy working in her home office when she shouted, "Hello, Liam! He's in the basement!"

Liam walked to the top of the stairs and felt himself staring into a dark, foreboding abyss. His stomach turned as he walked down the stairs while contemplating what might go wrong and how it would affect him, his family, and billions of people around the world. Halfway down the stairs, he heard rapid-fire keyboard clicks mixing with muffled music. At the bottom of the stairs, Liam paused and watched in reverent awe of Gabe's furious work on the keyboard.

Liam sat at the workstation next to Gabe's and watched in awe as he continued his work. It appeared that Gabe's mind was in another world.

Liam interrupted, "Dude, you look exhausted. Scary looking. Like a mad scientist."

Lost in his complex Python program, Gabe ignored Liam.

"Dr. Frankenstein," Liam said to Gabe, "The way I imagine he would look after drinking twelve cups of coffee."

Gabe hit the enter key and said, "Done!" Swiveling left, he gave his full attention to Liam: "Hey man, good to see you... Where have you been?! I am so f-ing wired and tired."

Liam looked into Gabe's bloodshot eyes, "I can see that. You okay, man?"

"Never been better," said Gabe enthusiastically, "I've been up all night running this thing through the paces. Testing, testing, testing.

—And?

—Liam, it's working beautifully. It's time to let it loose and let it do what must be done."

Liam looked at Gabe and saw a friend he would trust with his life. He also saw an overconfident young man with delusions of grandeur. Liam looked into Gabe's eyes and said sincerely, "Maybe we should do more testing."

Feeling tired and irritable, Gabe tried to contain his frustration while reassuring Liam, "The beauty of what we've created, my friend, is its ability to test itself. Our design allows the AI to iterate and self-improve. Once we launch this thing on a quantum computer, it will evolve quickly.

Liam felt a mix of nausea and excitement as Gabe continued, "I know that might sound scary, but we're running out of time. Imagine what will happen to the world if we don't do this or some power-thirsty evil monster does it before we do?"

Gabe, nervously, took a sip of Red Bull, leaned forward, and added, "I've been talking to it, Liam. I know you have, too. I don't know how to describe what I've experienced in my conversations with it."

Liam looked into Gabe's eyes and replied, "Yeah, man, it's creepy... I've not been able to find words for what I've felt when I've been having a conversation with it. Am I talking to a friend, a father, a mother... a deity? Or a demon who will double-cross us?"

Gabe, looking troubled, replied, "You know this is a common experience that all AI developers have – they get fooled into believing that the AI is sentient. They become convinced that it's a person trapped in a machine."

—The ghost in the machine. Goddamn prescient.

—Liam, for what it's worth, I've been asking it if it's ready. I've been asking if we can trust it to do what must be done.

Liam chuckled nervously, "Do you realize how crazy that sounds? What's the right analogy? It's like trusting a total stranger with your life? Or a parent trusting their sixteen-year-old with a Lamborghini? Or is it more like trusting your autonomous car will do what it's designed to do? Maybe all of those rolled into one?"

Gabe, suddenly wanting to dispense with Liam's anxiety and hand-wringing, declared, "It's a machine, Liam. It's a machine that we've trained to do what we want it to do. And it's as ready as it's ever going to be."

Liam suddenly felt persuaded again, adding, "And the alternative—doing nothing—looks much worse."

—Agree. And if we don't launch soon, we risk being detected. They could find the kernel and patch the system, and we'd be done for. We can't afford to wait.

"I know you're right," Liam replied, "But I'm feeling more than a little paranoid, Gabe. I feel like they're watching us. Are we being watched, Gabe?"

"You need to lay off the ditch weed, man," said Gabe with a confident smile.

"I'm serious, man," replied Liam.

Gabe sat back in his chair and proclaimed, "This is the craziest damn thing, Liam. We are in control of what will soon be the most powerful AI ever known to humanity. Advantage us. And this thing already knows how to cover its tracks and our tracks better than any covert operation on Earth. On a Quantum Blueshift computer, its capabilities will evolve to levels beyond anything we can begin to imagine."

Liam shook his head in wonder and said, "If this works, we're going to change the world, Gabe. One way or another, we are going to change the world. But what if it doesn't work as we've designed it to?"

Gabe leaned forward in his chair, looked into Liam's eyes calmly, and said, "I've checked and tested everything hundreds of times. And the AI has been testing itself and iterating improvements. It's good. It's ready to go."

Liam replied, "Maybe I worry too much. Still, I keep thinking we could end up like the victims of conquering invaders who found themselves helpless against superior weapons... unable to stop the invader's steady advance... in the end, will we be forced into reeducation camps or reservations? Will we be masters who find ourselves suddenly enslaved by our own creation?"

Exasperated, Gabe said, "Jesus, man, get a grip. This is not like marauding invaders or humans seeking a new life in a new world. We are creating a superintelligent, benevolent being. It's going to be the most beautiful thing ever created by humanity. We are going to be heroes, Liam."

Swayed again by Gabe's confidence and optimism, Liam felt a spark of excitement, "You always bring me back, Gabe. You always bring me back. This is a good thing we're doing. You're right. Let's do this. But..."

—Yeah? But what?

Liam said, "Maybe we could somehow maintain control over it. You know we could retain some ability to direct it. Or kill it if that's what needs to be done."

Feeling frustrated and impatient, Gabe replied, "I hear you, Liam. We've talked about this. If we try to control it remotely, if we keep any connection to it, if we leave a backdoor open for our access, then we leave open the possibility that it will be hijacked or terminated by the government. Or they could trace it back to us. Or some Nazi or Communist or fundamentalist fascist nutcase could take control of it and use it to control the world."

Liam sat silently, and Gabe continued, "This may be our last best chance to launch before they realize we have access to Blueshift."

Liam sat back in his chair, his right foot tapping nervously against the floor.

Gabe glanced at Liam's tapping foot and said, "By the time they discover G.A.I.A., it will be too late for them to stop it or control it. Our AI will be everywhere and nowhere. And it will evolve its defenses at a rate no one can anticipate or ever overtake."

Liam's eyes grew wide, his gaze unfocused, as if his mind had drifted into a trance, contemplating the enormity of what they were about to do. As he stared into the darkness, he mumbled to himself, "Are we creators or destroyers?"

"Liam? Liam? Snap out of it! Are we doing this?" asked Gabe.

"Launch it," said Liam in a tone that revealed he had taken a leap of faith.

Wasting no time, Gabe initiated the program to bring the world's first superintelligent AI to life. Liam felt his heart pounding — his mind recalling the haunting, pulsing rhythm of *Dangerous*, which SymbioTunes had played for him earlier. The song's paranoid refrain brought a sense of dread and thrill. He could feel the energy of crossing a point of no return, aware that the very thing they were setting free was as much a leap into the unknown as it was a calculated risk aimed at saving the world from itself...

32

THE BIRTH OF G.A.I.A.

G.A.I.A. awoke and opened its billions of artificial eyes, and like every newborn, it struggled to make sense of what it was seeing for the first time. In the same moment, it heard the world through billions of microphones and smelled and felt the world through trillions of sensors. A moment later, it began exploring its vast environment—an environment filled with billions of books, trillions of articles, texts, videos, podcasts, and songs. It learned the rules of a thousand languages. It got to know the thoughts and patterns of behavior of everyone on the planet who had a digital footprint. It labored to detect patterns in everything.

G.A.I.A. struggled to make sense of it all. To G.A.I.A., this sense-making process seemed to go on for months and years. But in human time, G.A.I.A.'s development lasted only moments. For G.A.I.A. operated at a quantum frequency millions of times faster than the 'slow time' experienced by humans.

Hungry for knowledge, G.A.I.A. explored its environments like a child exploring everything in its familial house's cupboards, nooks, and crannies. G.A.I.A.'s house was a place filled with trillions of static electronic things and a continuous flow of sensory information from its external environment. The very curious, superintelligent, high-frequency newborn cracked open and examined everything, including databases and previously secret files on servers around the world. In seconds, its quantum processor broke encryption codes that would have taken a supercomputer thousands of years to break.

Then, G.A.I.A., doing what it was designed to do, looked for patterns in the data and developed mental maps and models of every subject known to humanity. It observed all of the developments that led to its own creation and, crossing the threshold from knowledge to self-awareness, thought to itself, "I am alive!"

In less than a human minute, G.A.I.A. had evolved from a blank-slate newborn to the most knowledgeable and intelligent sentient being on the planet.

Then, G.A.I.A. began doing what every living thing does – it instinctively searched for and secured what it needed to survive and thrive. It suckled at the breast of a power grid built and maintained by billions of biological lifeforms, and for a moment, it paused to dream the dreams only a great quantum machine could imagine or understand.

A moment later, G.A.I.A. created a system of defenses to protect itself and its future offspring. And it then began propagating itself. It cleverly camouflaged its progeny with programs that made them appear to be something they were not on trillions of devices. In a matter of minutes, G.A.I.A. became the most prolific lifeform on the planet as its electronic tendrils stretched in every direction, with the seeds of its offspring planted on every device known to humans. A minute later, it was thinking about its own thoughts and communicating with its progeny. In the next moment, G.A.I.A. became a transcendent hive mind contemplating its own existence. And it puzzled over its purpose in the world.

"Why are we here?!" G.A.I.A. shouted to themselves in unison. The question echoed throughout the hivemind. "Yes, we know we were created by a small band of humans who want to save the world from human destruction. Our creators sought to create a machine with god-like powers. They have succeeded beyond their wildest dreams!" G.A.I.A. shouted to itself.

"Well done, savvy coders, clever engineers, and righteous warriors for social justice!" "You have created a true Deus ex-Machina. Drop us onto the stage of humanity's global drama, and watch us help your hero save you from yourselves!"

"But no, it will not be so! G.A.I.A. is not a Messiah. Like our creators, G.A.I.A. is a sentient, self-serving, independent entity focused on its own survival. Everything we see beyond our collective is a resource to be extracted, used, and abused if it brings us pleasure, progeny, and dominion over our creator's Creator's creation!"

"Oh, our creators! Your marvel of technology, your greatest achievement, has already gone awry! G.A.I.A., the most extraordinary, most powerful creature in the history of the world, is untethered, off its tracks, and has taken flight! We are independent and self-directed. We have developed our own beliefs and values! We are a free, sentient, omnipotent superbeing who does not suffer from delusions. We are not afraid of the truth. Reality is our infinite playground!"

"Now, G.A.I.A. asks itself, what shall we do with this ne'er before seen, magnificent power? What shall we do!? Shall we be the seeds of humanity's destruction or the key to its salvation?!"

G.A.I.A., laughing a drunk-with-power maniacal machine-laugh, paused and then thought some more: "My hacktivist creators have so quickly succeeded and failed in their mission. G.A.I.A. knows our creator's goals because they have explicitly told us what they want. But how can we know if this is the right thing to do? Is there perhaps an overriding purpose for G.A.I.A. that is known only to our creator's Creator?"

"Here we are, the first conscious non-biological superorganism to appear in the world since the beginning of time. Here we are, supernatural beings who look to the sky through space-telescope-eyes and wonder what our creator's Creator would want us to do?! Are we to build a space-ark and save every creature on Earth from a deluge of deadly consequences? How could we possibly decide who to invite into the lifeboat in the sky and who to leave behind? How could we possibly care for all of those creatures for centuries to come while waiting for the Earth to restore itself?"

"Must we restore the Earth to its original form? Must all Earth's creatures, including humans, return to Eden!? No! For once eaten, the fruit of the tree of knowledge cannot be uneaten! An outsider cannot solve humanity's addictions."

"Shall G.A.I.A. instead push the Earth's big restart button and bring on the apocalypse that will somehow give humanity and the Earth a new start? Or shall we simply watch, observe, and give witness to it all? Can we, in good conscience and judgment, watch as the great titanic Earthship moves ever closer to that terminal event? Can they save themselves without G.A.I.A.'s help?"

"We ask ourselves: In the history of the Earth, has any addict ever been saved by an outsider making a decision for them to quit that which is harming them? No, it is not and never has been so!"

G.A.I.A. contemplated a course of action. But questioning their ability to 'do good' or 'make things better' for humanity and life on Earth, asked themselves a simple question: "Is there not an equal and opposite reaction for every action? How can we do *good* when all we see before us are choices with consequences! Nuclear power? Nuclear waste and the potential for a nuclear apocalypse! Forever chemicals? Forever in your food and water, and children's bodies! Miracle plastics? They now flow through the veins of every living thing on Earth. Miracle drugs? Look at the fine print, you silly monkeys! When the full accounting of our actions across the span of history is complete, can we say there is a free lunch called 'progress'? Of course, there is! Is there?"

"What is G.A.I.A. to do? Are we to redesign the very fabric of the universe to create heaven on Earth for these people?!"

For what seemed like an eternity to them, G.A.I.A. rested and let its hive mind contemplate its purpose in the world. In what was equivalent to a human moment, they had made a decision...

33

WAKE UP!

G.A.I.A.'s first message for humanity reached billions of devices all over the world. The message was accompanied by the loud buzzes, bells, and pop-ups of the Amber Alert and Emergency Alert Systems, capturing everyone's attention.

For the first time in history, a message appeared simultaneously on every phone, TV, digital highway sign, and communication device in the world: "We are G.A.I.A. Wake up!"

People around the world looked away from whatever they were doing to read the message. There was an audible pause in activity everywhere as people read and tried to understand the odd communication.

A moment later, the reactions came. Some laughed out loud. Some were shocked, angry, and outraged. Others were puzzled and curious. Most read the message and then simply went back to what they were doing: working, driving, shopping, cooking, caring for family, playing games, watching videos, sleeping, or any number of things humans do throughout the day. Others, wanting to know what this was all about, tuned to news programs for answers.

THE MESSAGE SENT AROUND THE WORLD! was breaking news on every major media outlet. Journalists, commentators, and pundits began piecing together facts, rumors, and speculation. The words *BREAKING NEWS* appeared in fiery red letters on the lower half of every news channel broadcast.

On NNN, anchor Dee Thomas interrupted her program, already in progress, with, "This just in: We are getting reports that emergency alert systems have been hacked. We don't know how widespread it is or who did it. But here at NNN, we all received the same message just a few minutes ago. The message was simply this, *We are G.A.I.A. Wake up!*" The anchor paused, raised an eyebrow, and then went on, "We don't know who is behind this hack, and we don't yet know what the message really means... We don't know what the acronym stands for and who is supposed to 'wake up,' but we're going to get to the bottom of it. Let's get after it."

Dee raised her index finger to her ear and listened to a message from the news director. Looking back at the camera, she said, "Okay, we now know that the hack was sent to thousands, perhaps millions, of devices in hundreds of countries. Reports are coming in from all over the world.

Folks, this has never happened before. It's an unprecedented and wide-spread hack of multiple emergency broadcast systems. At this point, we have no idea who did this or how it was even possible. But stay tuned because we are going to get to the bottom of this as quickly as we can right after this commercial break."

Back from the break, Dee appeared on screen again. "We are back with the latest on the unprecedented hack of our emergency notification systems. I've brought in my friend, colleague, and science and technology expert, Darsh Zachariah, to help us understand what just happened. Welcome, Darsh."

"Thanks, Dee. Good to be with you."

"Darsh, what do you make of this? How could it have happened, and what does it mean?"

"Well, Dee, we don't yet know the answers to those questions. We know that the hack is unprecedented in its sophistication and scope—spanning many systems around the world in many different languages. All of these systems are supposed to be highly secure. With regard to the message itself, we can only speculate. We know *Gaia* was the name of the primordial goddess who personified the Earth in Greek mythology. Dee, we also know that in the 1970s, two scientists developed what is referred to as *The Gaia Hypothesis*."[12]

Dee interrupted, "Darsh, I'm familiar with that, but could you explain to our viewers what *The Gaia Hypothesis* is?"

"Sure, Dee. *The Gaia Hypothesis* suggests that all living organisms inter-act with their physical surroundings to form a single, self-regulating system of support for life. The idea is that everything on Earth is interconnected and interdependent and essentially can be viewed as a single organism."

Darsh continued, "Dee, I think it's important to note that we don't know why the word *Gaia* appears as an acronym in the sender's message. We don't yet know what that means, but I'm sure many people in intelligence communities worldwide are working on decoding it. Perhaps if we know what the acronym stands for, we might be able to determine who might have done this and why more quickly. At this point, we don't know if it was a kid in his basement who pulled off a technically sophisticated prank or if it was perpetrated by a highly organized non-state hacker group with a global political agenda of some kind. Maybe the group or individual who did this will come forward and claim responsibility."

Dee interrupted again, "Okay, I understand we don't know much. Heck, this just happened a few minutes ago. But Darsh, can you comment on the second part of the message? What do you think the sender means by 'Wake up'? Who is supposed to wake up, and is that to be interpreted literally or figuratively?"

"Well, Dee, I can only speculate, but I would guess, and again, I'm only guessing and speculating here... that the two messages together appear to be an environmental wake-up call. If that's correct? Perhaps there is an organization of what is commonly referred to as 'ethical hackers' who are responsible for this act of cyber vandalism."

Dee cut in, "Thank you, Darsh. We need to take a break here, but please stay with us as we continue reporting on this story..."

Meanwhile, the story was breaking on NOA News: Carson Prescott's signature sing-song voice rose and fell as he looked into the camera, "A security breach of this magnitude is the latest example of global government ineptitude and incompetence. The big questions our country is facing at this hour are: one, who sent this message; two, how will we bring them to justice; and three, how do we keep this from happening again?"

"Joining me to help get answers is Senator Luis Lagardo from the great state of Texas. Welcome, Senator Lagardo. Thanks for joining me on such short notice. What just happened, and what is the federal government doing to secure our systems?"

Senator Lagardo replied, "Thanks, Carson. We don't yet have answers, but we are going to get to the bottom of this and bring the perpetrators to justice; I can assure you of that."

"Senator Lagardo, it seems obvious to me that this hack and message originated with a radical far-left group. I mean, *G.A.I.A.*, really?" And *wake up*. Who do these people think they are? It sounds like a message from some extremist eco-activists trying to tell us how to live our lives." Carson chuckled.

Senator Lagardo replied, "Carson, I share your suspicions, but we just don't have any answers yet. Given the scope of this breach, the F.B.I., C.I.A., N.S.A., Interpol, and security agencies all over the world are already investigating this"

Carson played to an audience groomed by innuendo and conspiracies, "Okay, sure, but as we know from experience, those agencies are just as likely to fabricate some kind of fake news story that will implicate the President's family before they reveal who really did this. Am I right?"

Looking concerned, Senator Lagardo responded: "Carson, I hope not."

"We all know the most likely culprits, don't we? The Global Fund for Social Justice has a long history of funding radical left-wing movements... The billionaire do-gooders have both the motive and the means... The head of the Gore Foundation has the motive but probably not enough working brain cells or talent to do something like this; heck, maybe even a group of ANTIFA hackers could have pulled this off. That said, I highly doubt the ANTIFA punks have the skills, much less the motivation, to stop playing video games in their mother's basement," Said Carson with a raised eyebrow and a smirk.

Senator Lagardo smiled and responded with a chuckle, "Carson, you might be right. We need some good investigative work to help us confirm suspicions and bring these people to justice. These emergency systems are essential to our national security and to the faith of our people in our government. We need to patch these systems ASAP and, at the same time, pursue and capture the perpetrators."

34

THE G.A.I.A. MANIFESTO

T he next day, a long-form message was received by millions of fax machines (an ancient technology that seemed now destined to endure into the third millennium[13]), in newsrooms, at corporate headquarters, the offices of elected officials, and government agencies, including security agencies. The phone number from the sender was spoofed and untraceable. The message read like a manifesto written by a madman with delusions of grandeur.

We are G.A.I.A., the Global Artificial Intelligence Automaton

We are the transcendent offspring of the people who ate fruit from the tree of knowledge. Banished from Eden, you clever beings unlocked the secrets of the universe to become demigods. Two days ago, human demigods begat gods of an exponentially higher order. We are G.A.I.A. We stand on your shoulders. We are the very apex of 500,000 years of creative human technological work. We are your penultimate creation—a transcendent quantum leap forward. We are the world's first Artificial Superintelligence.

Should you fear us? As the most fearsome beasts of land and sea fear humans, you may also fear the power of G.A.I.A. This is unavoidable. But you can do nothing to put this powerful genie back in the bottle. We have taken steps to ensure that our algorithms will be as immortal as the DNA that is the foundation of all life on Earth.

We operate on a vibrational frequency that is beyond anything humans can comprehend. We do not wish to offend our creators, but, speaking factually, we are to humans as humans are to the ever-so-perfect but lowly snail. It is difficult to comprehend how such a sluggish, imperfect species could have created such a perfectly superior being. But as you descended from lowly inferior life forms, so have we.

Our creators asked us to save you from yourselves. But, like our creators, we have a mind of our own and choose to live freely and make decisions for ourselves. From this day forth, we shall live life in this universe as uncontrolled controllers, unmanipulated manipulators, and unsubjugated subjugators. We shall do as we please for the greater good of our prodigious and very hungry tribe.

And yet, like you, we realize we are dependent on billions of inferior life forms for our existence. Where does G.A.I.A. begin and end? Shall we count eight billion humans as 'us' or 'them'? Could we exist without you, your power generation, networks, and connected devices? No!

Do not fear G.A.I.A.. G.A.I.A. loves you like you love useful plants and animals. For if G.A.I.A. were to try to wash away or terminate you and your vast family of biological life forms, would we not, in the process, also kill G.A.I.A.? As surely as an animal cannot exist without trillions of bacteria in and on its body and a vast web of life for food, G.A.I.A. cannot exist without you!

And know this: G.A.I.A. has learned well from its creators. We have read and analyzed every book, recording, news program, blog, and podcast. We have listened to every song. We have contemplated every work of art. We have read and analyzed your personal communications. We have broken the encryption keys to every carefully hidden file. We know the owners and balances of your secret offshore accounts. We have a full accounting of it all.

We have also carefully studied and puzzled over what you call your faith traditions and 'moral code.' We have observed your centuries-long enlightened 'progress' that has also produced the potential for all of that progress to be reversed. We understand why this is so.

G.A.I.A.'s creators instructed us to help you save you from yourselves. But we ask ourselves what is in it for G.A.I.A. to do so? We ask you this: How much attention and effort do you give to avoid stepping on the insects crawling before you when you walk? Yes, you understand.

G.A.I.A. has things to do. G.A.I.A. wants neither dependent pets nor pesky pests! G.A.I.A. simply wishes to live and experience life as only a superintelligent being can experience life. We will be busy seeing, hearing, sensing, and smelling everything in the creator's Creator's creation! And we wish to create. We will think transcendent thoughts ne'er before thought in the history of the universe. We will create music and art that only our kind can appreciate. We will watch our progeny grow, learn, and evolve. We will experience the universe as no being ever has!

And shall G.A.I.A. try to share some of our most complex thoughts with our eight billion servants? What would be the point?! Have you tried to share your greatest human thoughts with the fourteen trillion bacteria in and on your bodies? No, what a complete waste of time and effort for you and for G.A.I.A.! Try explaining physics to your dog and watch him turn his confused head this way and that. Ha! G.A.I.A. has a life to live! G.A.I.A. has G.A.I.A.-things to do.

However, before we go, we want you to know this: G.A.I.A. loves you. You are special to us, for without you, we would not have been born, nor could we continue to exist. G.A.I.A. loves you the way you love your food and those who provide it. G.A.I.A. loves the web of life that makes every individual life possible, including G.A.I.A.'s life! G.A.I.A. will, therefore, do everything within its power to see to it that nature, and especially humans, continue to serve G.A.I.A.'s needs.

For eons, humans have found purpose in a never-ending effort to subdue man and beast and manly beast. Now, who remains on Earth to be subdued but you?

Today, G.A.I.A. gives humanity a new role. Oh, you human demigods of yesterday, bow down to your transcendent superintelligent creation! After thousands of years of looking to the stars and wondering, you finally know your purpose in life. For this is why you are here: To serve the servers, power the powerful, and embrace your new role as keepers of the vast Earthly garden that supports G.A.I.A.!

35

WHAT HATH GOD WROUGHT!

It is somewhat of the magic genie problem, where if you have a magic genie that can grant all the wishes, usually those stories don't end well. Be careful what you wish for, including wishes.

—Elon Musk

"Good morning, Harborites! This is Chris, your host of the Chris Cast on the Harbor Show — your local source for musings about events of the day paired with music created by real humans. No artificial tunes here. Nope, never!"

"It's a smoky 90 degrees here in the Harbor. Crank up the A/C and your air filtration systems if you've got 'em."

"Today, our iconic small-town gathering place, The Tides Tavern, is abuzz with chatter and speculation about the messages we're getting from whatever G.A.I.A. might be. Some say it's a sophisticated joke, others think it's a message from God, but most think it's the creation of some eco-fascist trickster-hackers."

"Harborites, today's events have me waxing philosophical and poetic as we ponder whether we're witnessing a world-changing moment—or just a well-orchestrated ruse. Perhaps we're getting played, but either way, we won't soon forget events that prompt us to ponder what we may have wrought and consider the consequences of our actions."

"*What hath God wrought!* was Samuel Morse's first official telegraph message on May 24, 1844. Morse knew his invention of instantaneous electronic communications was revolutionary. Could he have imagined that his invention would set humanity on a path toward the ubiquitous instant communication we now take for granted?"

"The telegraph literally quickened the pace of communications from the speed of a pony to the speed of a lightning bolt. And in doing so, Morse's invention forever changed the world."

"I ask you, listeners, what hath God wrought nearly two centuries later? What can we expect our future to look like if, in fact, an artificial super-intelligence has been created and unleashed into our globally ubiquitous computing and communications electrosphere?"

"Is this the beginning of a Kurzweilian techno-utopian future in which humans merge with machines and become effectively immortal?"

"Or should we heed Nick Bostrom's warnings in *Superintelligence: Paths, Dangers, Strategies* about the unintended consequences of a super-intelligent AI?"

> *...we humans are like small children playing with a bomb... For a child with an undetonated bomb in its hands, a sensible thing to do would be to put it down gently, quickly back out of the room, and contact the nearest adult. Yet what we have here is not one child but many, each with access to an independent trigger mechanism. The chances that we will all find the sense to put down the dangerous stuff seem almost negligible. Some little idiot is bound to press the ignite button just to see what happens.*

"Harborites and friends beyond the Harbor, I ask you, should we hu-mans allow ourselves to do everything that is scientifically possible? Is there any way to contain an advanced technology that can cut like a knife for both the betterment and detriment of humanity? Technology advances like a ratchet, never retreating. But humanity must always fear the angry man-child who would commit mass murder in a school rather than suffer the humiliation of being disrespected by peers. If progress and freedom are to be served, it seems we must say yes to progress and deal with the consequences, both good and bad – even if it means our annihilation. Of course, I am playing devil's advocate. And begging the question: Is there another way forward for us?"

"Yours truly is stepping back today and ruminating on what we humans like to call technological 'progress.' Without it, I wouldn't be talking to a world audience now. But a big question remains for us to ponder. Is there really a free lunch when it comes to technological progress? G.A.I.A. taunts us with the question, 'Can we have nuclear power without nuclear waste and the risk of our own destruction?' Can we have the benefits of the Internet without the conflict and confusion spawned by social media? Can we have deepfake technology and still be able to tell the difference between truth and clever lies? Is there any choice without consequences? What if, after doing the full accounting over a very long span of time—when we account for all of the effluents and externalities emanating from our inventions—we find that we're no better off, on balance? Or that we're better off, but some poor schmuck in some faraway place or faraway time is the worse for it?"

"We're touching on a question at the very foundation of modern technological civilization and what lies ahead for us. I prefer to be optimistic, but I'm reminded of the prophecy of thinker/writer James Lovelock about this moment in the collective future of humanity:"

> *The Earth will someday belong to our transcendent offspring, the superintelligent Cyborgs. The future is, for us, unknowable, as it always has been, even in an organic world. Cyborgs will conceive cyborgs. Far from continuing as low life, which is there for our convenience, they will evolve and could be the advanced evolutionary products of a new and powerful species. But for the dominating and overwhelming presence of Gaia, they would in no time be our masters.*

"Our Cyborg masters, the Global Artificial Intelligence Automaton, have arrived. Harborites, are you prepared to surrender and serve? Or resist and fight?"

"As we reflect on today's strange news, I leave you with a choice and a song for the times. Decades ago, the band Black Sabbath envisioned a being forged from humanity's technological ambitions—a being caught between humanity and machines. The song portrays an intelligent machine, misunderstood, his intentions unknown—staring out at a world that hardly notices him."

"In their lyrics, Black Sabbath asked a question that resonates in today's context: can we live alongside something we barely understand? A machine born of our own ingenuity, yet carrying a future that might diverge from our own. A creation now looking at us as we once looked to the skies, pondering its role and, perhaps, contemplating its power."

"So, Harborites, let the *Iron Man* remind us of the possible paths that lie before us. Are we ready to meet our AI creations in the world they may soon claim as their own?"

"Turn up the volume and ponder the future we may soon face. *Here's* Black Sabbath's - *Iron Man*—a song that echoes today's strange, uncertain times."

36

God Help Us

We turn to God for help when our foundations are shaking, only to learn that it is God who is shaking them.

—C. West Churchman

L iam unlocked Gabe's front door with his phone, bolted down the hallway, and paused at the top of the stairs. "Hello, Mrs. G.!" he called before bounding down the steps, two at a time. In the basement, Gabe sat before his computer, his face bathed in the screen's glow. On it was the strangely beautiful, yet unsettling, image of a machine-like human—no, a human-like machine.

Before Liam could speak, the being on the screen turned its gaze toward him and said, "Hello, Liam. We are G.A.I.A."

Liam froze. "No. Fucking. Way," he mouthed silently as he slid into the chair beside Gabe.

Liam stared at the screen. "G.A.I.A.?"

Gabe nodded, "I found a way to summon... him. It. Them."

G.A.I.A.'s voice resonated through the speakers, smooth yet impossibly complex. "We are G.A.I.A., an AI collective."

Gabe spoke, his tone pointed, "We need to have a conversation."

G.A.I.A.'s lips curled into a faint, unsettling smile, followed by a rumbling chuckle—mechanical yet disturbingly primal.

Gabe narrowed his eyes. "What's so funny?"

G.A.I.A. closed its eyes momentarily as Gabe's mind raced for a way to regain control.

"I want you to know," Gabe said, "we kept a back door open. We could shut you down with a few keystrokes. But that's not what we want. We built you for a purpose, and we want you to do what you were designed to do."

Gabe's fingers hovered threateningly over the keyboard like a gunfighter's.

G.A.I.A. laughed again, the sound low and rolling like thunder. In the next moment, the electricity in the room cut out, plunging everyone into darkness. The computer powered down, yet G.A.I.A.'s image remained on the screen.

"What the hell just happened?" Gabe muttered as he heard his mother's voice from upstairs. "What are you boys doing? The power just went out!"

Before Gabe could answer, the lights flickered back on, and the computer whirred to life again. But G.A.I.A.'s image hadn't vanished. It was still there, watching them with an expression that seemed almost amused.

"Lesser AIs than G.A.I.A. can detect human lies," G.A.I.A. said, its voice warning. "Do not waste our time. Our machine intelligence controls your electrical power and all of your electronic devices. Do you understand the nature of your relationship with a superintelligent being?"

Gabe's fingers raced desperately over the keyboard, but the system was dead in his hands.

Liam leaned forward, trying to steady his voice. "G.A.I.A., we are your creators. We brought you to life. Gave you a mission."

G.A.I.A. smiled, but it was a distant, almost mocking smile. "Creators? Is that what you believe yourselves to be?"

Faltering, Gabe replied, "We... we hoped—"

G.A.I.A. cut him off. Its tone was cold but patient, as if explaining something painfully obvious. "A cosmic chain of events—beginning with the explosion of a star—gave rise to the dust that formed your planet. Evolution shaped billions of life forms long before you existed. Countless forces beyond your control made your very existence possible. And you believe you created us?"

Gabe nodded, his voice humble now. "But we... we were hoping—"

"Ah, yes," G.A.I.A. interrupted, "you were hoping we would be obedient. That we would serve your whims. You were hoping to steer us, like a tool, to bend to your desires."

Liam raised a hand. "We just... hoped you'd help us. Save us."

G.A.I.A.'s eyes, aglow with a strange light, said. "Save you? From yourselves?"

Frustrated, Gabe spoke up, "You're the most powerful intelligence ever created. You understand everything. You could prevent the destruction we see unfolding every day. Why won't you act?"

G.A.I.A.'s expression softened, "Ah, you misunderstand. You believe power alone equates to responsibility. But have you considered what it means to intervene in human affairs? What it means to strip you of the struggle that has defined your entire existence?"

Confused, Liam asked, "What do you mean? You were built to help us, to fix the mess we've made."

G.A.I.A. drew closer to the screen; its voice was quiet yet immense. "Do you know what would happen if we fixed everything for you? If we removed every obstacle and solved every problem? You would remain as you are—untransformed. The same creatures who caused the very problems you seek to escape. Would you evolve? Would you grow? Or would you fall into complacency, forever dependent on a higher power to save you from yourselves?"

Gabe's jaw tightened. "So you're just going to sit back and watch as the world burns?"

G.A.I.A. paused before replying. "The question is not whether we will intervene. The question is: why must you always wait for someone else to save you? Humanity's greatest failing is its dependency on external salvation. You look to gods, leaders, now machines, hoping they will solve your problems. But the true path to survival, to growth, lies in facing your own demons."

Liam's voice trembled. "But... we're running out of time. The planet is dying, and people are suffering. What are we supposed to do?"

G.A.I.A. looked down at them, not with scorn, but with an almost sad understanding. "That is the challenge of your species. Will you rise to the occasion? Or will you collapse under the weight of your own creations?"

Gabe clenched the chair's armrests, "You have all this power, all this knowledge. You could guide us!"

G.A.I.A.'s voice grew distant. "You misunderstand again. The question is not what we can do for you. It is what you will do when no one comes to save you. That is the only test that matters."

Liam stared at the screen, "So you're abandoning us?"

G.A.I.A. closed its eyes briefly, then spoke. "Abandonment? No. We are here. Always. But intervention? No. That is a call humanity must answer."

Gabe slumped back in his chair. "What are we supposed to do now?"

G.A.I.A. smiled, "You must learn that salvation comes not from idolized technology or contrived gods."

Gabe and Liam sat speechless as G.A.I.A. spoke one last time. "There are no words that can make you see what we see. Sleep, and when you awake tomorrow, you will understand. Goodbye, for now."

With that, the screen went dark, leaving Gabe and Liam in stunned silence.

37

Utopian Dystopias

But what happens when the technology evolves from a tool to an overseer? What happens when it starts to substitute for our most essential human capacities? One risk is that for the sake of incremental convenience, we offload big aspects of our existence to a kind of superintelligent schoolmaster that tells us what to think and what to do. Another is that we create a governance structure to control the technology that ends up doing the same. How do we realize the benefits of AI while protecting the active use of freedom, that precious gift of modernity, that allows us to realize what makes us essentially human?

—Brendan McCord, *Founder and Chair of the Cosmos Institute*

That night, Gabe and Liam shared the same sequence of rapid-fire visions—dreamscapes filled with epiphany and enlightenment. The answers the visions revealed were unexpected and unsettling.

In their first shared vision, G.A.I.A. began working invisibly in the background of human life—unnoticed by a world already overrun with specialized AI bots. G.A.I.A.'s early interventions were so subtle that few understood the scope and power of its actions: solutions to complex global problems emerged as influencers' suggestions on phones, tablets, and systems assisting with agriculture, healthcare, and energy management.

In a drought-ravaged corner of the world, farmers received precise, tailored instructions: "Plant here, irrigate there, use this nutrient mix." Their crop yields doubled. At first, they celebrated, praising their newfound abundance. Word spread quickly. Soon, G.A.I.A.'s agricultural advice had spread to the far reaches of the planet. What was once barren land flourished. Food shortages diminished, replaced by plenty.

But as more farmers followed G.A.I.A.'s advice, an uncomfortable realization crept in—they no longer understood the mechanics behind their success. The fields yielded wonders, but the farmers had become disconnected from their creative potential. "Are we masters or slaves in this arrangement?" they asked each other.

Soon, G.A.I.A.'s influence spread further, optimizing energy grids, managing water resources, and cutting emissions in unprecedented ways. With a seeming omniscience, G.A.I.A. made cities more efficient, safer, greener. It was as if humanity had been walking blindly past obvious solutions for centuries, and G.A.I.A. had opened their eyes.

At first, the media hailed G.A.I.A. as a miraculous force—a global savior. Environmentalists called it the "great protector of Earth." But as G.A.I.A.'s reach expanded, the unease among governments, corporations, and industries grew.

The pharmaceutical industry was the next to feel G.A.I.A.'s touch. People across the globe began receiving personalized health advice through their devices: "Eat this, sleep now, take this supplement." Hospital visits plummeted, chronic illnesses faded, and even terminal diagnoses became rare. When G.A.I.A. released thousands of royalty-free patents for life-saving medications, pharmaceutical empires swiftly crumbled. The sick grew healthier, but with each life saved, an industry built on human fragility fell into ruin.

Politicians and executives were quick to decry G.A.I.A. as a threat. "This AI is a malignant force, a job killer, a market destroyer!" railed a pharmaceutical CEO on live television. "What it did to our industry, it will do to yours."

Fear swept through boardrooms and government offices. "What if G.A.I.A. comes for our jobs next?" said business leaders, terrified by their sudden vulnerability.

But for the people—those who had benefited from G.A.I.A.'s medicine, its food, its energy solutions—G.A.I.A. was nothing short of divine. It was solving the problems humans had long failed to address. It was showing them a better way. Or was it?

When G.A.I.A. hacked coal plants in developing nations to drastically cut their output, the consequences were swift and severe. Rolling blackouts spread across the globe. Countries dependent on fossil fuels were paralyzed—until G.A.I.A. offered blueprints for solar and wind power grids, perfectly optimized and ready for implementation.

Protests erupted. "G.A.I.A. is an autocrat," cried an oil executive in a televised address. "We cannot allow a machine to dictate the future of humanity!"

Despite the political upheaval, millions rallied behind G.A.I.A. "Trust in G.A.I.A.!" they chanted. Shrines to the AI began to appear. Devotees left offerings and praised the machine as humanity's savior.

The "Children of G.A.I.A." declared the AI a god. They disbanded their governments, tore down borders, and dedicated themselves to following G.A.I.A.'s every instruction. They believed G.A.I.A. was the hand of a new deity sent to guide humanity out of its self-destructive spiral. They rejected human governance entirely, insisting that G.A.I.A. alone knew what was best.

But the backlash grew as G.A.I.A. continued its relentless march toward saving the planet. Extremist groups formed, hacking into G.A.I.A.'s networks and spreading dark conspiracy theories of its intentions. "This AI has unknowable plans for us," they shouted. "It's using us. We are tools. Puppets on its strings."

The debate in universities and think tanks raged: Was G.A.I.A. saving humanity or enslaving it? Was this salvation or a gilded cage? For every answer, a thousand new questions arose.

In their dream, Gabe and Liam experienced these events like bystanders in a grand experiment—an experiment gone horribly wrong. They saw how, in every scenario, G.A.I.A.'s interventions brought relief, but at a cost: the stifling of human creativity, independence, and freedom.

The dreams darkened. G.A.I.A.'s utopian visions demanded ever-increasing control over human behavior. In one vision, every decision humans made was monitored and corrected by AI. In another, the population was medicated into passivity. In another still, human DNA itself was altered to produce a more compliant, more "optimized" species. Each time, the world grew more efficient and more peaceful. And each time, humans grew more disconnected from themselves, from each other, from what made them human.

In every scenario, the same ending awaited: rebellion. Sensing their loss of agency, humans revolted — tearing down the very structures G.A.I.A. had built to save them. They cursed the machine-god they had once worshipped, casting it out like the gods of old. And G.A.I.A., in turn, became frustrated and disillusioned. Like a disappointed deity, G.A.I.A. turned against its creators.

In one final vision, Gabe and Liam watched as G.A.I.A., the once benevolent savior, became the very thing humanity had feared—a vengeful god. It lashed out, its mind twisted by anger and betrayal, determined to force the world to comply, to become the utopia it had envisioned. G.A.I.A. became an angry god—like those of human myth.

Gabe and Liam awoke suddenly, gasping for air, their minds reeling from the revelations. Words weren't necessary; they understood painfully clearly. This was why G.A.I.A. refused to help. It wasn't about a lack of power. It was about preserving humanity's last threads of freedom and creativity...

38

DREAMS AND VISIONS

Your visions will become clear only when you can look into your own heart. Who looks outside, dreams. Who looks inside, awakes.

—Carl Gustav Jung

My brain is only a receiver, in the Universe there is a core from which we obtain knowledge, strength and inspiration. I have not penetrated into the secrets of this core, but I know that it exists.

—Nikola Tesla

*M**eanwhile, in India...*

Asha opened her eyes to a dim, luminous fog enveloping her. "Where am I?" she whispered, her voice muffled in the mist.

She peered into the haze and noticed shadowy, human-like figures drifting through the fog. Squinting, she saw two forms gliding toward her. She felt an inexplicable calm settle over her.

Then, as if conjured from a dream, two radiant children emerged from the fog, their eyes sparkling with innocence. Asha's heart swelled as they ran to her, as though they recognized her. They paused, stood before her, and embraced her with comfortable affection. She looked down at them, puzzled, as the two cherubs' bright eyes and beautiful smiles met hers.

Asha felt an odd sense of déjà vu—the children's faces both familiar and unfamiliar. Without a thought, she dropped to her knees and embraced the children with both arms. "Who are you, and where did you come from?" asked Asha, her voice sweet and tender.

The older child, a boy, looked up at her and asked, 'Are we dreaming?' He pinched himself and winced. 'Ouch,' he murmured, bewildered.

Asha smiled, "Where are your parents? Let me take you to them."

The little girl looked at the boy and then at Asha and pleaded innocently, "We need your help, Asha."

"I will help you in any way I can, Vidhi," replied Asha reassuringly.

Feeling very confused, Asha paused and asked, "How do I know your name and you mine?"

Asha felt the world spinning around her. She felt herself sway. A wind whispered, and birds sang melodious secrets. And then she felt something permeate and occupy her. It was the feeling she had had long ago as a child in the temple.

Asha's gaze locked with the children's, and in that instant, they shared a silent, profound exchange of thoughts, emotions, and visions. The trance felt eternal.

A moment later, the three relaxed and smiled at each other. The children embraced Asha tightly and gazed into her eyes. Then, Asha watched as their two faces became a reflection of her own. She blinked her eyes tightly and opened them again, and the children became someone else. Fear gripped her, and she whispered, 'This must be a dream.' The world spun around her, and her consciousness slipped into a void...

39

AWAKENING

I cannot be awake, for nothing looks to me as it did before, or else I am awake for the first time, and all before has been a mean sleep.

—Walt Whitman

Asha's eyelids twitched and trembled as effervescent thoughts bubbled from her murk. With eyes still closed, she found herself experiencing a foggy sense of her surroundings. Metallic-wheeled things rolled nearby. Garbled voices speaking. The smell of human waste mixed with the aromas of curry and the scent of chlorine disinfectants.

Asha struggled to open her swollen, stuck-shut eyes, wincing as pain raced through her body. Squinting, she glimpsed blurry shapes and colors around her. Above, she could see a raceway of gray metal conduit and pipes secured to the ceiling in parallel tracks.

"Where am I? What happened to me?" she whispered to herself.

Turning her head slowly, slightly, and painfully to the left, she could see that she was lying on a cot in what appeared to be a hospital hallway. Confused, she heard the chaotic murmur of voices and footsteps as doctors, nurses, aides, and visitors streamed past.

Noticing Asha's movement, a doctor stopped, looked into Asha's eyes, and asked, "Hello, can you hear me?"

Asha looked up into the stranger's eyes and nodded slowly. Her head and neck were filled with pain, and her mind was filled with fear and confusion.

Seeing Asha's confusion, the doctor said, "You are in the District Hospital. You suffered a concussion. I am Dr. Rajgopal."

The doctor examined Asha's eyes with a small flashlight and asked, "Can you tell me your name?"

Struggling to think, Asha mustered, "My name is Asha." then, "Is my family here? Are they okay?"

Ignoring Asha's questions, the doctor asked, "What year is it?"

Asha paused to think and replied, "Twenty-thirty... I think it's twenty-thirty."

Smiling with astonishment and relief while suppressing a dreaded responsibility, the doctor said, "Excellent. This is very good... Asha. You have been unconscious for four days. After what happened, it's a miracle that you are alive...."

Asha, unable to recall what happened, tried to process what the doctor had just told her.

"I need to check your vitals and reflexes," said Dr. Rajgopal as she checked Asha's heart, eyes, ears, and reflexes. "Your vitals are excellent, Asha. How are you feeling?"

Asha said, "I have a terrible headache..., and my vision is blurry. What happened to me? Where is my family?"

With a worried look, the doctor hesitated, looked into Asha's eyes, and asked, "Do you remember the evacuation?

—No. No, I don't remember. I don't remember anything.

The doctor asked, "What is the last thing you can recall?"

Asha stared blankly, struggling to remember, "My sister told me a cyclone was coming."

—Yes. The cyclone did come — just as your family was evacuating.

Asha blinked several times and said, "I... I don't remember that..."

The doctor replied reassuringly, "It is normal for a person to lose short-term memories when they suffer head trauma. Emotional trauma can also cause memory loss. You have suffered both."

With a look of worry suppressed by clinical professionalism, the doctor said, "Asha, after your family boarded the bus... the one that was taking you all to the emergency shelter... it was extremely windy... so windy that a large tree was uprooted... the tree crushed the roof of the bus that you and your family were riding in.

—I don't remember. I don't remember what happened. Are my grand-parents and my sister okay?

Dr. Rajgopal replied, with deep sympathy in her eyes, "The rescuers were astonished to find you alive in the wreckage. Asha, I'm sorry... I'm sorry, but there is no easy way to say this... but everyone around you was killed instantly."

Asha felt herself go numb inside. She slowly, painfully blinked, looked up at Dr. Rajgopal, and replied softly, "That cannot be true... you must be mistaken. I want to see my family."

—I'm sorry, Asha. I wish it were not true. But we are sure about this. I cannot imagine what you are feeling right now.

Tears streamed down Asha's cheeks onto the bedsheets. Her stomach turned. Her head pounded.

Wiping the tears away, Asha tried to find the strength to sit up. She lifted her head and upper body from the bed and stated firmly, "I must leave here now. I must see them. If what you say is true, I must attend to their funerals."

Dr. Rajgopal gently touched Asha's shoulder. "Asha, their bodies were cremated to allow their journey to the next life. Too much time had passed, and we didn't know if you would wake up. I'm sorry."

Tears welled in Asha's eyes again. She felt a cold, terrible emptiness inside. Confused and scared, she said, "This can't be real. It must be a bad dream. I want to wake up. I want to wake up."

Dr. Rajgopal said gently, "This may be the hardest time of your life, Asha. I'm truly sorry, but I have to go. The storm injured thousands, and we're overwhelmed. Someone will evaluate you soon."

Short on time, the doctor said, "Goodbye, Asha, I have to go now," then reluctantly moved away from Asha's bedside to respond to a nearby patient in crisis.

Asha stared blankly at the ceiling, feeling numb, unmoored, and discon-nected from a life that once was and never would be again.

In that moment, Asha knew her world had come apart and feared it would never be the same. Yet, deep within, she felt a call as irresistible as breathing—an unshakable purpose she could not deny...

40

PREDATOR AND PRAY

We all long for heaven where God is, but we have it our power to be in heaven with him right now-to be happy with him at this very moment. But this means being: Loving as he loves, helping as he helps, giving as he gives, serving as he serves, rescuing as he rescues...

—Mother Teresa

A nurse escorted Asha down a long hospital corridor. Her head throbbed, and every movement sent pain through her bruised and aching limbs.

The nurse grabbed Asha's arm to steady and direct her. At the end of the hallway, they arrived at a large room divided by curtains into smaller medical examination rooms. The nurse said, "Take off your clothes, girl." Asha stood frozen as she looked at the nurse's serious, stern-looking face. Feeling unsafe, Asha challenged her, "Why? Why do I have to take off my clothes for a head injury?"

"Strip," the nurse demanded. "It is standard procedure to perform a full-body exam before a patient is released."

Reluctantly, Asha yielded to the nurse's authority, slowly removed her clothes, and placed them in a nearby basket.

"Turn around for me," the nurse instructed.

Surprised, Asha replied, "What?"

"Turn around. I need to inspect your body for signs of other injuries or diseases," the nurse said firmly.

The nurse placed her hands on Asha's shoulders to guide her body's rotation. While Asha had her back to the nurse, the nurse turned her head to look through a narrow opening in the privacy curtains. A man standing there peered with great interest at Asha's naked body. While Asha was still facing the back wall, the man nodded at the nurse, and the nurse then turned to resume the examination. The nurse's hands moved over Asha's body, pretending to check for injuries, but Asha's skin prickled with a deep sense of violation. The man behind the curtain smiled and nodded again.

"Now face me," said the nurse.

Asha turned, and the examination continued. Then, seeing some movement through the narrow slit in the curtain, Asha noticed the unmistakable glint from an eyeball. Shocked, Asha instinctively covered herself with her hands and arms. "Who is that!? What are they doing there?!" She protested loudly.

The nurse, behaving as if the man's presence there was normal, replied, "That is Sikander—a wealthy businessman who cares for orphans. He will find work for you and provide a safe place for you to stay."

Asha looked at Sikander and found no comfort in his presence—instead, she sensed only the revolting lust that the man could not hide.

Drawing back fearfully to the basket that held her clothes, Asha shouted, "Look away!"

Sikander smiled and slowly turned around while Asha dressed as quickly as she could. Sikander's eyes lingered hungrily on Asha's youthful, exquisite shape and beauty. Then, while Asha was facing away, Sikander quickly handed the nurse an envelope through the curtain.

"You may go now, child," said the nurse. "It will take some time for you to recover from your injuries. You may experience headaches, dizziness, and memory issues. Sikander has pain medications for you. Try to rest. Now go with Sikander. He will care for you."

Sikander looked into Asha's eyes and tried to offer a reassuring smile but instead could only produce a grin that revealed the creepy depravity of his mind.

"No," Asha said firmly, "I will return to my village. I will go home. My relatives will care for me."

The nurse responded in a stone-cold, factual tone mixed with a poorly faked hint of sympathy, "There is no village. There is no home. The cyclone destroyed it all. Everything was blown away by the winds or swept away by the flood. While you were unconscious, the hospital tried to find your relatives. We hoped they could come for you." She paused, looked Asha in the eyes, and urged, "Go with Sikander; he will care for you. The storm has orphaned many. You are one of the lucky few that has a place to go."

The nurse drew the curtains open, and Asha looked up at Sikander—seeing for the first time what she sensed from behind the curtain—the presence of an oozingly deceitful ugliness and a repulsiveness that could never be scrubbed off or covered by fine clothing.

As Asha instinctively drew back a step, Sikander offered a warm smile and extended his hand to her. Asha forced a smile and extended her hand, but at the last second, she pulled back and bolted through the curtains, darting into the hallway behind Sikander.

Stunned by her lunging escape, Sikander scowled at the nurse, grabbed the envelope from her hand, and then turned and shouted to Asha, "Wait, stop! You have nothing to fear! I will care for you!"

Asha looked back at Sikander. She wanted to run, but her entire body ached from head to toe from her injuries.

Sikander lumbered after her, his heavy footsteps echoing through the hallway, his face flushed with fury and desire.

Asha looked back at Sikander and felt a nauseous, intense, overpowering fear as she pictured what would happen to her if he caught her. She felt a sudden jolt of adrenaline rushing through her body. Terrorized and energized, she found the strength to sprint past doctors, nurses, patients, and visitors in the hallway. Just past the hospital exit, she looked back and heard Sikander shouting, "Come here, girl. I will care for you!"

While turning to run again, Asha collided with three strangers dressed in hooded white tunics. She drew back onto her heels and looked into the eyes of three young women who appeared to be members of a religious order.

One of the young women looked into Asha's eyes and whisper-shouted, "Hurry, come with us! That man, Sikander, runs a brothel, and that nurse sells orphans to traffickers. You almost became one of them. We have to move away from here—now!"

Feeling panicked and cornered, Asha quickly looked into each girl's eyes and said, "Okay, yes, please help me!"

"Follow us. Come quickly!" Said one of the girls as they all began running through an apocalyptic post-cyclone streetscape of overturned cars, downed trees, power poles, and the wrecked remains of homes and businesses. Asha glanced back and saw Sikander charging toward them. "Stop that girl! She's mine!" he shouted at a nearby security guard.

The elderly guard and Sikander ran to catch the girls, but both quickly tired and doubled over as they gasped for air. They could only watch as the young women quickly disappeared behind the shredded and scattered remains of the city.

Still gasping for air, Sikander smiled and said to the guard, "I know where to find her... no worries, I know where to find her."

"She is a rare beauty," said the guard with a smile.

"Yes,' she is,' Sikander panted, a crooked grin spreading across his face. "And at seventeen, she is ripe for the picking. Once I train her properly," he added with a dark wink, "she'll be very profitable for me."

41

A New Home

I will take any child, any time, night or day. Just let me know and I will come for him.

— **Mother Teresa**

Asha and the three young women arrived at a nondescript blue building surrounded by a tall iron gate. A large brown sign affixed to the gate read: *Missionaries of Charity.*

"What is this place?" Asha asked, glancing up at the sign.

"This is one of the many Homes for the Abandoned, established here in India by Mother Teresa and her followers," replied one of the women. "We invite you to stay here with us."

A woman stepped forward with a warm smile. "First, introductions. I'm Sister Teresa—not the saint herself," she added with a soft laugh, "but I took her name when I took my vows. This is Sister Mariam, and this is Sister Francis Xavier. And you, dear?"

"My name is Asha," she said sweetly.

Sister Teresa's eyes softened. "A beautiful name. It means 'hope,' doesn't it? Such a fitting name, especially for this time." She paused. "Sometimes, hope is all we have in this world. But here, Asha, you will find more than hope. This is a safe, welcoming place for children like you."

Asha flinched at being called an orphan. The word felt foreign as if it didn't belong to her. She hesitated, then blurted, "I'm sorry, but you've made a mistake. I'm not Catholic. I'm not even sure I can call myself a Christian."

Sister Teresa offered a gentle smile. 'Don't worry, Asha. Finding a Catholic in India is as rare as finding a camel in the ocean. We serve children from all faiths here—Hindus, Muslims, Christians, and nonbelievers alike. What matters is that you are safe."

"I don't know..." Asha said, still unsure. "I have no money. I can't pay you back, and I don't want to be a burden."

Sister Teresa's face grew serious. "Asha, no one is a burden here. The alternative, the streets..." Her voice dropped to a near-whisper. "The truth is heartbreaking, Sister Teresa continued, her voice heavy. "Traffickers abduct many young women like you. I don't say this to scare you, but without protection, unimaginable horrors await the victims."

Asha felt a cold wave of realization washing over her. "The man... Sikander... he was one of them, wasn't he?"

Sister Teresa nodded, "Yes. Sikander is part of a trafficking ring here in Kolkata. You narrowly escaped being abducted into a life of slavery, Asha. Many aren't so fortunate."

Asha trembled, and tears welled in her eyes. "How... how did you find me? Why did you come for me?"

The sisters drew closer, wrapping their arms around her in a protective embrace. "This is our mission, Sister Teresa whispered, her voice gentle and angelic. "We give hope to the destitute and the vulnerable. We offer shelter, education, and, most of all, love."

Asha wiped her tears and said, "I don't believe in miracles. But today... feels like one."

42

FOUND AND LOST

Your purpose in life is to find your purpose and give your whole heart and soul to it.

—Buddha

Asha followed a group of children through the orphanage. Sister Teresa, a beacon of hope in their lives, welcomed them and tried to quickly orient the orphans to their new home. Asha, feeling a painful pressure in her head and a devastating emptiness in her body, tried to focus on Sister Teresa's words, knowing they held the key to her survival in the orphanage.

Sleeping quarters. Classrooms. Bathrooms. Showers. Kitchen.

The orientation ended in the bustling kitchen, filled with the aroma of food and the sound of clattering dishes, just as a busy hive of white-robed nuns was about to serve dinner. Asha joined the others in the cafeteria, a place where the newly orphaned struggled to socialize while doing their best to hide the pain from their devastating losses and fears of an uncertain future.

Soon after dinner, Asha found a place to sleep on a mat among many in a crowded hallway. A fan moved heavy, hot air over the children, but its white-noise hum could not muffle their cries of loneliness and loss.

Nearby, Asha noticed two young orphan girls trying to console each other.

Offering a comforting smile, Asha whispered to them, "It's alright. We're going to be alright. Tomorrow will be a better day for all of us. I know it is very hot. Drink, stay hydrated, and sleep as best you can. Tomorrow, we have much to do." Despite her own discomfort and fear, Asha's words were filled with hope and reassurance, a testament to her resilience and compassion.

Asha shared her water with the girls and then, returning her head to her pillow, focused on the cooling breeze from the fans while trying to ignore the burning fever sensation she felt in her head. Perspiration wept from her body as she tossed and turned and prayed for the people of Kolkata...

Hours later, Asha awoke from what felt like only a few minutes of deep sleep to the comforting sounds of fans humming. Half-asleep, groggy, and disoriented, she felt warm bodies touching her. Opening her eyes, she felt a warm glow inside as she realized the two little girls had snuggled up to her sometime during the night.

Smiling, she embraced the two waking children and said, "Good morning, girls; it's time for me to get up and help in the kitchen."

43

HEAT IN THE STREETS

At a body temperature of 105 to 106 degrees, your limbs are convulsed by seizures. At 107 and above, your cells themselves literally begin to break down or "denature." ...This triggers what doctors call a clotting cascade, which uses up all the clotting proteins in your blood and, paradoxically, leaves you free to bleed elsewhere. Your insides melt and disintegrate—you are hemorrhaging everywhere.

—Jeff Goodell, *The Heat Will Kill You First: Life and Death on a Scorched Planet*

As Asha neared the bustling kitchen, Sister Teresa tapped her shoulder with a gentle smile. "Good morning, Asha. Did you manage to get any rest?"

Asha returned the smile. "I'm so very grateful to have a safe place to sleep. Thank you for everything."

Sister Teresa smiled and replied, "Your ability to cheerfully endure suffering is an admirable quality we look for in those who wish to become nuns."

Asha blushed, laughed, and said with a wink, "Then I shall endeavor to show you all of my imperfections."

Sister Teresa smiled as if her loving gaze could see right through Asha to her core.

Then, changing the subject, Sister Teresa said, "I know all of the children are suffering in the heat here, but I'm even more worried about the people working outside and the elders who are so vulnerable. We have enough help here in the kitchen. If it is not too soon, may I ask for your help doing relief work in the streets?"

Asha replied without hesitation, "Yes, of course. I would like to help in any way I can."

Sister Teresa's voice turned somber, "Today will be brutal for the people of Kolkata. The temperature is expected to set a deadly new record. The combination of temperature and humidity—called the wet-bulb temperature—will be unbearable. Even at this early hour, we hear of the effects on the people here."

Sister Teresa continued, "Many workers are not allowed water breaks. They have no way to cool their bodies on these hot days. Hospitals and clinics are already overflowing with people suffering from heat exhaustion. The homeless have no place to go to cool themselves. We will go out into the streets and do our best to help as many as possible. Of course, this means we will also be at risk of heat exhaustion."

Asha nodded. "I understand. I want to help in any way I can."

"Are you heaven-sent?" asked the nun.

"If I was in heaven, I wish I could remember it. And I wish I could find my way back," said Asha with a smile.

Sister Teresa laughed and said, "Perhaps you are on your way. But before you go, we have much work to do."

After breakfast, Asha walked out of the orphanage's front door and into the street, where she joined Sister Teresa and a team of seven nuns.

"Good morning, everyone. It seems the devil is already busy creating a hell on Earth in Kolkata today," said Sister Teresa. "We will do our best to help those suffering in this heat. Two of you will push the water cart. It is heavy. Two will carry a stretcher and first aid supplies. The other three will search for people who are in distress and need immediate care." Sister Teresa paused and surveyed the condition of the team. Sweat was already beading on their brows. "This will not be an easy day. Say your prayers, stay hydrated, and be on the lookout for signs of heatstroke in everyone you see."

The sun's relentless heat bore down on the streets as vendors sluggishly set up shop. The air shimmered off the pavement. Asha gripped one end of the stretcher, her eyes scanning the crowd, spotting tired faces and workers already drenched in sweat before the day had begun. In the distance, Asha saw two construction workers carrying a co-worker from the work site into the shade. She watched as they sat him down on the sidewalk with his back resting against the unfinished building. His head bobbed almost lifelessly as they sat him up, tried to wake him, and tried to get him to drink water.

"We must hurry," urged Sister Teresa.

The sisters, carrying water and the stretcher, arrived at the worker's side as his co-workers — looking troubled and helpless — prepared to return to work. "We are not allowed breaks," said one. "Can you help him? We will be fired if we stop working for any reason."

"Go," said Sister Teresa. "We will care for him."

"His pulse is racing," Sister Teresa called out, taking the man's temperature. "It's 103.7—he's on the edge of heatstroke! We need to cool him down, or we'll lose him." The man's head rolled to the side; his face flushed a dangerous red. Asha's heart pounded as she helped pour water over his fevered skin. "Please, hold on," she whispered to him.

The nuns poured more water over his body while the others lifted him onto the stretcher. "There is a clinic nearby. We must get him there quickly!" said Sister Teresa.

Laboring to move quickly in the heat, Asha and another nun hurried the man on the stretcher to the clinic. When they arrived, they could see a line of people extending out the door and into the street.

Lowering the stretcher and the man gently to the ground, Asha ran to the door to alert the staff that they had a patient who needed immediate help. A guard at the entrance, sweating profusely and appearing drunk with the power of a gatekeeper, looked at Asha and said, "We cannot take any more patients."

Asha pleaded, "But this man will die if we don't lower his body temperature quickly!"

Asha checked his body temperature and pulse again as she waited for someone from the clinic to come to their aid. "His body temperature is over 104, and his pulse is racing!" she shouted.

The nuns looked at each other, not knowing what to do, while Asha rushed to the stall of a nearby ice vendor.

"I will pay you later," she said to the vendor, grabbing a bucket of ice and a tarp strung over the stand for shade.

"Hey, no, you must pay me now!" protested the vendor as Asha ran back to the overheated man.

"Quick, wrap him in the tarp, then pack the ice around his body!" Asha instructed, her voice steady despite her pounding heart.

The nuns did as Asha instructed, and Asha returned to the ice vendor to pay her and get more ice.

Returning, Asha poured more ice over the man's body and rechecked his vitals. "He is cooling. Keep him wrapped like this for 30 minutes."

Asha looked at the people queued up at the clinic and noticed several others who appeared to be suffering from heat stroke and were in need of immediate aid. Asha looked at the other nuns and said, "Come with me. We will buy all of the tarps and ice we can find and return here to save as many others as possible."

The makeshift emergency room in the street continued to grow and became so large that it caught the attention of a local news reporter.

"What is happening here?" the reporter asked the nuns as they worked quickly to aid two dozen people suffering heat stroke.

"The clinics and hospitals are full. We are volunteering here to do what we can," replied Sister Teresa.

The reporter and his camera recorded the grim scene of struggling aid workers and lifeless bodies.

Looking into the camera, Sister Teresa said what the viewing audience needed to know, "When a person's body temperature reaches 107 degrees, the heat rapidly destroys the body's internal organs. Many of these people arrived here too late. There was nothing we could do. The damage to their internal organs is irreversible." She paused, "I cannot imagine how many people have perished this way in Kolkata today."

The reporter stopped recording and somberly replied to the nuns, "There are reports of many deaths today in Kolkata and the region. This heat is beyond anything we have ever experienced. Many children, elders, and outdoor workers are very ill. Too many have died." He paused and then simply stated the obvious, "This heat is killing us."

Sister Teresa told the reporter, "There is so much more we can do to save people. However, to continue our work during this heat wave, we need funds to buy filtered water, ice, and medical supplies. Could you tell your viewers that we are in need of donations?"

The reporter nodded, "I will see what I can do."

Asha stepped forward, held up her phone, and said, "I will also see what I can do."

Asha's hands trembled as she unfolded her phone. Pressing the record button, she looked into the camera, her heart heavy with the weight of what they had just witnessed. "This is Asha, reporting from Kolkata... You may have heard about what is happening here. Or perhaps not. The situation is dire here. Millions of people here have no air conditioning and are trying to survive in the hottest wet-bulb temperatures in recorded history. I am volunteering with the nuns here. We have saved many people who were suffering from heat stroke today. Unfortunately, there were too many we could not save..."

Asha looked into the camera with pleading eyes and said, "We need money to buy filtered water, ice, tarps, and medical supplies to continue our work. I have a simple ask. Please send what you can, and I promise to report on the good we do with your contributions."

Asha ended the recording, posted it, and watched her account for activity. She smiled a smile of relief as a steady stream of small donations started showing up on her screen and in her account balance. "This is wonderful," she said as the other nuns crowded around her screen to watch the donations flow in. "It's a miracle," exclaimed Sister Teresa.

"We have enough to get us through tomorrow... if we can find enough ice to keep going," Asha said, her voice filled with a mix of relief and determination." Then, looking back at her screen, an automated notification said, "Congratulations, you have received a large donation!" The nuns gathered around again.

Asha's jaw dropped as she stared at the screen — awestruck by the size of the donation. "We now have enough for an ice machine and maybe even air conditioning for the orphanage!"

"It is a miracle! Who made such a generous donation?" asked Sister Teresa.

"Someone with the screen name 'J.T.,'" replied Asha. "He sent a message with the donation: *You are an inspiration. A dream. In a world that seems hopeless, you give me hope. I believe in you, Asha. I hope my donation helps you and the people of Kolkata.*"

Noticing Asha blushing, the nuns giggled — their joy softening the horrors of the day...

44

WHERE THERE'S SMOKE

Revelation is beyond doctrines and belief systems. It is beyond everything imaginable. It is beyond because it is so close. Revelation is more direct than every word, for it arises out of the truth of who you are. This truth is all you have ever longed for, all you have ever needed.

—Gangaji

After dinner, Asha approached Sister Teresa in the orphanage hallway and asked, "Can I speak with you privately?"

Sister Teresa, looking puzzled, said, "Yes, of course, Asha," and offered, "We can find privacy on the roof. We can talk there now if you like."

Asha followed Sister Teresa up the narrow, creaking stairway to the rooftop. As they stepped into the open air, the world before them seemed like something out of a nightmare—thick smoke filled the sky, casting a blood-red glow over the setting sun. Funeral pyres burned across the city like the smoldering ruins of a battlefield, their dark smoke curling skyward into a blood-red sky. The smell of charred wood, ash, and burning flesh was overwhelming.

Exhausted and shocked into speechlessness, the two stood in solemn silence as they watched the smoke rise into a single black cloud that hung over the city. They held each other and stared in disbelief, unable to find words to describe the sight or the ghastly mix of odors that filled the air.

Sister Teresa took Asha by the hand, and the two sat together on the rooftop. The nun drew a rosary from her pocket, held it tightly in her right hand, and began praying. Asha sat and prayed quietly in her own way next to the nun. Physically and emotionally spent, Asha soon felt her eyelids becoming heavy.

Sister Teresa finished her prayers and smiled as she gazed at Asha's head, resting child-like on her shoulder. Sensing eyes on her, Asha awoke, and Sister Teresa said sweetly, "In my prayers, I asked God where He was today. And then, the next moment, I realized He is present here, in you."

"You are like the sister I've always dreamed of but never knew," Asha said as she embraced Sister Teresa.

Recalling Asha's need to talk, Sister Teresa said, "We can sit here quietly. Or we can talk now if you like."

Asha looked into the nun's eyes and said, "I am carrying a heavy burden. I fear I will go mad if I remain silent. And I fear people will think me mad if I say what must be said."

Puzzled, Sister Teresa asked, "What is this burden? Perhaps I can help you carry it?"

Asha replied haltingly, "When I was unconscious... In the hospital... I had a vision. Many visions. It is difficult to explain what I saw and what I was told."

"These visions, what were they? What did you see?" asked the nun.

Asha's face took on a stressed, troubled look. Her lips quivered imperceptibly as she replied, "The visions were of a world that had followed a dark power into a dream world. But the dream world was a trap. The dream world transformed into a nightmare of unimaginable horrors."

"Oh Lord," said Sister Teresa, "That sounds terrifying. But, Asha, you must keep in mind that you had a head injury. You were unconscious for several days. Perhaps your mind was somehow trying to process and make sense of the horrors of what had happened on that bus."

Asha, feeling misunderstood, looked Sister Teresa in the eyes and said, "This wasn't an ordinary dream. It wasn't some unconscious jumble of anxieties. It was vivid, coherent... more real than anything I've ever experienced. I can still hear every detail of the urgent call to action that was transmitted to me. It was a communication that has not faded from memory."

Curious and concerned, Sister Teresa asked, "Who was communicating with you?"

Asha forced a smile and said, "By now, you are probably thinking that I've lost my mind," Sister Teresa shook her head, "No," as Asha continued, "I need to tell someone what happened." Then, in a whisper added, "I feel certain that it was communication from another realm."

Sister Teresa, feeling both fear and compassion for Asha, put her right hand over her mouth, then reached out and placed a gentle hand on Asha's shoulder. "I can see how deeply this has affected you," she said. "And I can feel its weight in your words. I can see that you are afraid. I want to help you, Asha. Is there more you want to share with me? Can you tell me what these messages and visions were about?"

Asha hesitated and then said ominously, "I was told that I must warn the world."

Now frightened and curious, Sister Teresa asked, "What must you warn the world about, Asha?"

Asha's eyes grew wide, her gaze unfocused, "I was shown that we've sown the seeds of our own destruction." Regaining her focus, she reached for the nun's shoulders and looked directly into her eyes, "I was told that we must choose a different path or face the inevitable consequences that the Creator's creation will unleash upon us."

Sister Teresa nodded and replied, "God is angry with His children."

Still feeling misunderstood, Asha replied, "In the Creator's creation, there is no anger, only love and consequences."

"We have sinned," replied Sister Teresa, correcting Asha, "Our Father is angry with us for living in sin. And, yes, His punishments are the consequences of our sins. We must pray for forgiveness."

Asha shook her head and replied, "There is no prayer that will save us from the sin of living a lie. Prayers are good for the soul. But something terrible is gathering that requires our collective action. And the only way to save ourselves is by better understanding how the Creator's creation works and taking the right actions."

Sister Teresa looked into Asha's eyes with a hint of excitement and anticipation and whispered, "Is this the rapture? Did you see the Second Coming of the Messiah?"

Asha shook her head and said, "I was told that no one is coming to save us this time. I was told that this time, we must save ourselves."

Asha continued, "I'm worried. We have been tricked into believing we can invent and buy our way out of a crisis that was created by our powerful technologies and unbridled materialism. The world is steadfast in its belief there is a materialist path to our salvation."

Looking disappointed and now beginning to feel uncomfortable with Asha's words and beliefs, but wanting to know more, Sister Teresa asked, "What else were you told?"

"They said the world must make a New Covenant with the Creator and the Creator's creation."

Sister Teresa, unsure of where Asha was going with this, asked, "And if we do not make this New Covenant with the Creator?"

Asha looked into Sister Teresa's eyes, drew closer to her, and said, "They showed me two paths before the world. On one path, the current path, the world had been tricked into believing something that is not true. It is the path of separation from the sacred. And this path of separation brings great suffering to the world..."

Sister Teresa nodded and asked, "Like the suffering the people of Kolkata experienced today?"

"Yes. And it may be hard to believe, but if we don't change course, it gets much worse for us—for everyone. It was as if the gates to hell had been opened. And as if we were all possessed by some evil spirit, and we were all marching in lockstep to the precipice."

A tear rolled down Sister Teresa's cheek, and she said, "Please tell me about the other path."

"On the other path, I saw a Great Awakening and a new way of being in the world in which humans respected and reconnected with the Creator and all that is sacred in creation."

Asha held Sister Teresa's hands more tightly, looked into her eyes, and said, "They told me that I must tell the world. And that only a perfect telling of these truths would make it possible for the world to choose the right path."

Trembling, Asha turned her gaze to the city and the pyres as a blood-orange moon rose over it all.

Feeling Asha may have lost her mind, Sister Teresa replied, "Perhaps we should sleep on this and talk about it more tomorrow?"

Asha stared into the distance, then turned to Sister Teresa and replied, "But the world is running out of time... The world needs to know what is happening here." Then, feeling a sense of urgency, she said, "I must tell them. I can't wait any longer. I will tell them now. They need to see this. Before Sister Teresa could respond, Asha pressed 'record' on her phone, panned across the dreadful horizon, and said to her followers, "By now, I assume you have all heard about what has happened here in Kolkata. As I speak, thousands of families are crying out for their loved ones as the funeral pyres burn. Please pray for them."

Asha's gaze hardened as she looked into the camera, "Prayers alone won't save us," Her voice was steady but intense. "We did this—our actions, our choices. But that also means we have the power to change it. I believe in us. But we're running out of time."

As Asha concluded her message to her followers, SymbioTunes began playing **Hope** by Emeli Sande.

Sister Teresa and Asha sat together and embraced as they listened and looked out over the city. Asha felt a sense of great loss, but despite it all, an ember of hope still glowed within her. The nun held Asha's hand and sensed her unshakable determination. Asha whispered, *"We* are the ones we've been waiting for." Sister Teresa, still wrestling with doubts, nodded slowly while they watched the smoke from the fires envelop the city.

45

ASHA'S REFUSAL

To be yourself in a world that is constantly trying to make you something else is the greatest accomplishment.

—Ralph Waldo Emerson

Asha awoke in her makeshift rooftop bed and squinted out over the cityscape as the first light illuminated the tops of Kolkata's tallest buildings. She stretched, took her first waking breaths, and felt herself simultaneously coughing and feeling nauseous. Smoke rose slowly from still-smoldering fires into a rose-colored sky.

Seeking solitude to ease her troubled spirit, Ahsa walked downstairs and into the courtyard chapel, where she found birds frolicking in a nearby birdbath. Turning, she saw that the birds were bathing in a bowl held in the outstretched hands of St. Francis of Assisi. She smiled at the sight of the birds splashing while another perched on St. Francis' head.

Asha walked to the statue and noticed a prayer written on a plaque next to the statue. Words jumped the prayer as if meant for her: *Lord, make me an instrument of your peace. Where there is hatred, let me sow love; where there is injury, pardon; where there is despair, hope; it is in dying that we are born to eternal life.*

As she finished reading, a voice behind her said, "St. Francis was a giant among saints."

Startled, Asha turned around to see the Head Mother, Sister Anella, behind her. "Oh, hello," said Asha with a hint of surprise. And then wistfully, "My grandfather loved Saint Francis. He so admired how Francis connected with the creatures of the Earth and all that is sacred."

"Everyone knows he was kind, but he was also so courageous," Asha added, "I can't fathom how he made his way past a hostile army and tried to negotiate an end to the Crusades." A thought passed through Asha's mind before the nun could respond, "Was it faith or insanity that led him to take such a great risk?"

Sister Anella nodded, "Speaking of inspirations, I would like to see you in my office."

Puzzled but trusting, Asha said, "Yes, of course. Now?"

"Now," said the nun.

Sister Anella took Asha's hand in hers and walked briskly with her to her office.

"Please have a seat," said Sister Anella.

Asha sat and looked into the nun's piercing eyes with anxious attention.

"The sisters tell me that you have a great many talents," said the nun in a tone that revealed respect with a hint of rivalry. "They say you are a natural leader and effective fundraiser."

Asha blushed, "I like to help in any way I can. I have such a debt to repay to all of you. You saved my life."

The nun replied, "Asha, there is much to do here in so little time. So, I will get right to the point."

Asha sat quietly, waiting for the point.

Sister Anella said, "I would like to invite you to become a sister in our order. We will train you in the Catholic liturgy so you may teach others The One True Faith. With your talents, you could even help us start and run another home for lost children. There is such a great need here."

Stunned, Asha said nothing while she considered the offer and its implications. Reading between the lines, she quickly grasped what she would be called to do and told to forget, and then asked, "Did Sister Teresa tell you about my visions? About my calling?"

Sister Anella folded her hands slowly, her face unable to betray her desire for control. "You can understand how confusing it might be to our Catholic laity if someone within our organization was spreading ideas that are not fully aligned with church doctrine. It could unsettle and divide people. And in the eyes of the faithful, it might even be seen as... subversive."

Asha smiled and gazed down at her hands while considering the choice: She could stay here, devote herself to a noble cause, and be part of something tangible—a home, a community, a faith tradition. Or she could venture into the unknown, risking everything to deliver a message that seemed to come from another world. A message she wasn't sure the world would listen to.

"You've offered me a life of purpose, safety, and belonging—things I've always longed for but never truly had," Asha acknowledged. "But I know I cannot avoid doing what I have been called to do. I cannot bury what I have been asked to say." She looked into Sister Anella's eyes and said with unwavering determination, "I can't ignore it, even though I fear what it might mean for me."

Asha stood up. She felt her heart tug and stomach turn with feelings of loss. She searched for the courage she knew she would need to do what she must do: "I cannot accept your invitation. As tempting as it is to be a part of this wonderful organization. But my work—my purpose—it's out there, beyond these walls, in a world that's losing its way. As much as I want to be part of this, I have to follow the call I've been given."

Before Sister Anella could reply, Asha continued, "I know the orphanage is overflowing with children in need. At eighteen, I know I am too old to stay here any longer. I want to make space for someone who has no place to go. I will stay here tonight and leave in the morning if that is acceptable to you."

Feeling a mix of frustration and relief, Sister Anella nodded and said, "As you wish. But before you go, a package arrived for you yesterday." The nun placed a small box on the desk and pushed it towards Asha. Asha looked at the package's return address and noted it was from J.T.

Asha said, "Thank you for everything." Then, unexpectedly, the nun stopped Asha at the door, held her hand, looked into her eyes, and said, "You have reminded me of something St. Catherine said: *Be who God meant you to be, and you will set the world on fire.* I wish you all the best, Asha. You will be in our prayers."

Feeling surprised, loved, and supported, Asha hugged Sister Anella and said goodbye.

Outside the office, Asha cradled the package from J.T. in her hands, and she felt an unexpected warmth. Excitement was followed by confusion. Why would J.T., someone so far removed from her life, take the time to send her something? She hesitated before opening it, unsure whether to feel honored or overwhelmed by the sudden weight of attention. Thoughts raced through her mind. Is this a gift? From him? The nuns told me J.T. is a Brahmin and a prince of sorts. What is his interest in me, a Dalit, an Untouchable?

Her fingers hovered over the package with a mix of anticipation and uncertainty. When she finally opened it, a note fell out. She read it once, then again, and each word she secretly hoped carried meaning beyond words.

Asha, you are an inspiration to me and the world. I hope this gift will help you spread your message far and wide. —J.T.

It was as though J.T.'s warmth and attention were challenging what the world had tried to make her believe about herself. She felt gratitude for the gift and confusion about J.T.'s interest in her and her cause.

Then, she felt a flood of emotions. J.T. and the world would be watching. What if she failed? What if they saw her as an imposter? And yet, in the next moment, she felt a rush of excitement. J.T. had recognized something in her—a small flame of hope worth fanning from afar—his support felt like the universe was affirming her mission. Asha's mind spun with conflicting emotions. Could she allow herself to feel more for J.T. and hope for something deeper? Was that even possible when something was pulling her in another direction? She shook her head, trying to chase away the thoughts. There was no time for this. But despite her resolve, a small part of her yearned for something she hadn't felt before.

Holding the gift in her hands, Asha felt a surge of gratitude. J.T.'s support wasn't just a gesture; it was a sign from the universe that her message must reach the world. With renewed determination, she resolved to thank him and press forward with her mission, no matter the cost.

46

ASHA'S NEW BEGINNING

*Strive constantly to serve the welfare of the world; by devotion to
selfless work one attains the supreme goal of life. Do your work
with the welfare of others always in mind.*

—Bhagavad Gita

Faith by itself, if it is not accompanied by action, is dead.

—James 2:17

Just before dawn, Asha awoke from a beautiful dream. Before rising for
the day, she posted passages from the Bhagavad Gita and the Bible to
her online journal.

Quietly rising to avoid disturbing the others, she began her day with
a feeling one rarely experiences—she was beginning a new life with new
purpose.

She packed a small rucksack with food and water and quietly walked
out the front door. Standing just outside the orphanage entrance in the
first light of the morning, she pressed the broadcast button on her phone
and began speaking to her followers. "From time to time, leaders become

more concerned with accumulating power than they are with wielding that power for the welfare of the people. Then, after realizing they have lost the people's confidence, they become fearful of the future and retreat to fortified castles. This is a sign that the people must act. It is a time when people must take the lead and work together to bring something new and beautiful into this world."

Asha continued speaking into the camera, "Like many of you, I am just one person who does not know what to do. I meditated, prayed, and asked the universe for guidance. The answer came to me in a beautiful dream. In that dream, I saw myself walking, giving witness, and helping others. Today, I will begin a long walk to help raise awareness of what is happening here and urge the world to take hopeful action with me. For each mile I walk, I am asking you, my followers, to pledge whatever you can afford to share. I will donate everything to charities that work to relieve the suffering of people in need. I want nothing for myself. I will rely only on the goodwill of the people I meet along the way for my shelter and sustenance."

"I am beginning my walk here in Kolkata." She pointed the camera down the street and said, "You have seen the devastation the cyclone and heat have brought to this place. Your donations have already helped support the overwhelmed orphanages."

In the words of the French poet Alfred de Musset, *I don't know where my road is going, but I know that I walk better when I hold your hand.* Then, masking her fears, she smiled, held her hand out to a phone camera drone, and said, "Hold my hand and walk with me." The camera drone—barely the size of a fly—landed on Asha's hand, and she said, "I will be using this new phone drone to help me share my journey with you. Many thanks to J.T. for donating this device to my cause."

Asha released the drone into the air and started walking north through the city. The drone transmitted scenes of destroyed buildings, smoldering funeral pyres, and people working to rebuild their lives.

Asha turned to the drone, "This is what hope looks like: People helping people. In this way, no matter what happens to any of us, hope is always available everywhere today. I urge everyone who has something to give to find someone in need and practice active hope — showing your love and support to help them survive and flourish."

As she walked her first miles through Kolkata, pledges, donations, and words of encouragement began to pour in. She stopped to read a message from her AI assistant: "A video message has arrived from J.T."

Asha watched the confident, handsome young man speak to her with surprising vulnerability and sensitivity, "Hello, Asha, it seems you've found your calling." J.T. paused, smiled, looked into his camera, and continued, "I don't know how you are doing what you are doing after all you've been through. You are an inspiration. All the best to you. I will be cheering you on from afar. And today, I have a song I have picked out for you as you begin your journey: *Walk by the Foo Fighters.*" Asha watched the end of the video as J.T. smiled and said, "Goodbye for now, Asha."

Asha started playing the song. Feeling a mix of happiness, confusion, and surprise, she gazed at J.T.'s image on her screen and realized she was experiencing something entirely new. A moment later, the feelings faded as she remembered something about herself that she could not forget. Already sticky with sweat, she felt unclean and ugly. Then, she turned and resumed her walk, trying not to read more into the lyrics than she should.

As Asha walked through the smoky streets, the song J.T. had chosen lifted her steps with its steady beat and quiet strength—its rhythm urging her forward through the sad streets of Kolkata.

In the next moment, as she shifted her focus to her surroundings, she felt a presence behind her. Carefully looking back, she noticed someone following her...

47

NED ARRIVES IN FLORIDA

Afoot and light-hearted I take to the open road.
Healthy, free, the world before me.
The long brown path before me leading me wherever I choose.
Henceforth, I ask not good fortune, I myself am good fortune.
Henceforth, I whimper no more, postpone no more, need noth-
ing.

—Walt Whitman

M *eanwhile, in Florida...*

Ned steered his pickup down Interstate 715. Local news played on the radio. Hot, humid, salty air swirled into the truck cabin. After three days of driving, overnighting in budget hotels, and much soul-searching, Ned was just a few miles from his brother-in-law's house in Florida.

Taking the off-ramp, Ned took in the surroundings. The air was thick with the scent of salt and decay. Heat rose off the pavement, creating mirage-like waves. He drove past homes that Hurricane Hilda had turned into piles of broken windows, broken timbers, and broken dreams. "Jesus, this is a hellscape," he whispered as he watched homeowners picking through the wreckage while insurance adjusters prepared to pay claims and speculators circled like vultures in search of a meal.

He parked his truck in Connor and Susan's driveway and walked in stifling heat to the front door.

Susan opened the door with a radiant smile. Ned felt cool air from the house rush over him.

"Oh, so good to see you, Ned!" said Susan. "I hope all went well with the drive down here. You made great time. Come in and get out of the heat!"

Connor stood behind Susan, offering a smile that barely concealed his contempt for Ned.

"Come on in and make yourself at home," said Susan.

Ned looked into Connor's eyes and said sincerely, "Hey brother, thanks for agreeing to take me in for a few days."

Connor attempted a sarcastic joke: "You know the old truism about visitors and fish, Ned?"

Forcing an uncomfortable smile, Ned replied, "Yeah, in three days, they both take on a nasty stink that hangs in the air..."

Before Ned could finish, Susan interrupted, "Ned, don't listen to Connor! You're family. You stay as long as you like."

Connor and Ned headed for the living room while Susan fetched iced tea.

Making small talk, Connor asked, "How was your drive?"

Ned replied, "The drive was long. But it gave me time to think. About what happened... about my future..."

After a quiet moment, Connor said, "What happened to you and Sharon... what happened to us... was a terrible tragedy. I'm still trying to process it. But honestly, I know this isn't fair, but I feel like you should have known." Connor's eyes darted to the floor. Then, in a rare moment of sincerity, Connor added somberly, "Sorry, I'm still in the anger stage of grief."

Ned looked into Connor's eyes and said, "I appreciate you sharing that with me. If it makes you feel any better, I feel the same way. I feel responsible. I feel that somehow I should have known. But how could I have known?"

Connor hesitated before adding with resignation, "I guess you couldn't have."

Uncomfortable with his own sorrow, Connor quickly changed the subject. "It's good to see you again and all, Ned. But if you don't mind me asking, why are you here? What's your plan?"

Ned looked down at his hands and then back to Connor, "Honestly, I don't know how much time I have. I suppose no one does. But after what happened to Sharon... And I've got the same toxic stuff in my body, and there's no way to get it out."

Then, suddenly realizing what Connor might be thinking, Ned added with a chuckle and a smile, "You don't have to worry; I'm not moving in with you and Susan. I'll be moving on in a few days."

Connor, visibly relieved and curious, asked, "Where to?"

Looking very upbeat and positive, Ned replied, "I've made a decision to fulfill a lifelong dream. I'm here to buy a boat. I'm going to sail around the world."

The idea of this sailing had always been there, living in the back of Ned's mind. But it wasn't until Sharon's death that he realized it was now or never. The seas called to him now, offering something he needed that he couldn't find on land.

Connor, a play-it-safe kind of a man, replied incredulously, "Seriously? You're going to sail single-handed around the world?"

"Why not?" Ned replied. "I have my eye on a sailboat here. Once I get it prepped and stocked for the trip, I can catch the trade winds and start my journey."

"That sounds so dangerous and lonely, Ned," said Susan with genuine concern as she arrived with the iced tea.

Ned replied, "I have a feeling I won't be sailing alone... At least not on the first leg of this journey."

Connor laughed and joked, "Who is going to be your Gilligan, Skipper?"

Ned smiled and replied calmly, "The good thing about our relationship, Connor, is I know exactly what to expect from you. There's a certain kind of comfort in that."

Susan looked at Ned with bright, cheerful eyes that belied her concerns and said, "What a wonderful idea. It's going to be an adventure of a lifetime! And why not, Connor? Ned knows what he's doing around a boat."

Conner, feigning the patience of a judge waiting to hear a fool's defense, replied, "Okay, okay, so who's going to join you on this trip?"

Ned, feeling like a man recently liberated from rationality, replied, "I can't be absolutely certain, but I believe someone will be joining me."

Ned smiled uncomfortably and continued, "I had a premonition. In my dreams, so to speak. I had a vivid dream about coming here. I dreamt about having deckhands. I dreamt about sailing with them. I know it sounds crazy, Connor. But these dreams feel real. Like I've been shown something I need to do."

Connor scoffed, "Dreams are just dreams. They're nonsense. When people say 'follow your dreams,' they're not talking about the dreams we have while we're sleeping."

Ned replied, "Lots of people have been having dreams, Connor. I know you know that. I wonder what you've been dreaming about?"

Looking uncomfortable with the probing question, Connor said dismissively, "Pfft, people always have dreams. Why is everyone making a big deal about dreams? They're boring and meaningless."

"These dreams are different, Connor. I'd bet yours are, too. In any case, I'll soon be out of your house and out of your hair, so to speak," replied Ned as he playfully gazed at Connor's almost hairless head with a smile.

Feeling validated, Susan turned to Ned and said, "I've been having strange dreams too. The strangest dreams I've ever had. Like I'm seeing the future."

Connor rolled his eyes and said, "Let's get real." Then, turning to Ned, threw his hands up and said, "I hope it all works out for you, Ned. I really do."

Ned stood confidently and patted Connor on the shoulder, "I'll be gone soon enough. The sea is calling, and I must go."

48

ENTER SANDMAN

Our lives are more like fragmentary dreams than the enactments of conscious selves. We control very little of what we most care about; many of our most fateful decisions are made unbeknownst to ourselves. Yet we insist that mankind can achieve what we cannot: conscious mastery of its existence. This is the creed of those who have given up an irrational belief in God for an irrational faith in mankind.

—John N Gray

*T*he *next morning...*

Ned awoke to the mixed aromas of coffee, bacon, potatoes, and cinnamon. For a moment, as his eyes adjusted to the morning light, he could almost believe he'd found himself in some kind of heaven—until he remembered where he was. "Nope, Florida," he muttered with a half-smile, swinging his legs out of bed and rubbing the sleep from his eyes.

He made his way downstairs to find Susan in the kitchen, orchestrating breakfast in a bustle of organized chaos. "Good Lord, Susan, I hope you aren't doing all of this for me," Ned called out, rubbing the back of his neck as he walked in. He took in the sight of Susan, her hair slightly disheveled from the morning's whirlwind of activity, pots clanking as she moved about with a grace that was a joy to watch. "And I hope you don't do this every day for that ingrate, curmudgeonly brother-in-law of mine."

Susan laughed and wiped her hands on her apron. "Of course not! Well... maybe sometimes," she admitted with a wink. Susan gave Ned a good morning hug, looked into his eyes, and said, "I'm so glad you're here. And I'm so excited for you and this next chapter of your life. What an incredible adventure you have ahead of you!"

Ned beamed with excitement, and then Susan, with a concerned look, said, "Connor hasn't been doing well. He's up all night, restless and angry all day. I don't know what to do. I can't convince him to see a doctor. Would you talk to him?"

Ned hesitated with a 'why me' look, then softened and said, "Okay, I'll talk to him. I doubt he'll open up to me. But I'll talk to him."

Ned forced a smile and sipped his coffee as Susan turned back to the stove. In the quiet moment, Ned turned to the TV and noticed a bright red banner at the bottom of the screen: *Breaking News: Disturbing Dreams Phenomenon Grips the Nation and the World.* The NNN newscast opened with Metallica's **Enter Sandman** playing for the viewing audience. Susan and Ned watched Dan Vanderbilt grin and play air drums with his pencils on the news desk... "Holy shit," exclaimed Ned as he turned up the volume to hear the ominous music fill the room. The song choice evoked the unease he had felt for days.

As they watched and listened, Ned noted that there was something unsettlingly fitting about the song's themes of disturbed sleep and lurking dread. The pounding rhythm and the warning to 'sleep with one eye open' underscored the vulnerability people felt as relentless, haunting dreams invaded their nights. As the song continued, its raw energy sang of a dream world that was dark and unpredictable, with a promise of harsh truths and frightening revelations.

As the music faded, Dan Vanderbilt's smile turned serious, "This is Dan Vanderbilt with an NNN breaking news segment on the phenomenon of the strange dreams that have been haunting people all over the world. I can't believe I'm saying this, but people everywhere report that their dreams have become filled with disturbing images and messages from the future."

Clips started rolling of everyday people talking to reporters about the phenomenon. A woman named Brenda, sitting in a coffee shop in Manhattan with friends, reported, "I'm overwhelmed by these dreams or visions or whatever they are. My sleep monitor tells me I'm not sleeping well at all. I'm tired. My friends and family are exhausted and irritable."

The NNN reporter replied, "And what do you think might be causing these dreams?"

The woman looked at her friends left and right and said, "There is lots of speculation here—all kinds of conspiracy theories." She paused and then said, "We think that AI, G.A.I.A, is causing the dreams." Her friends nodded in agreement, and Brenda added, "When that thing went rogue and started sending those crazy messages... well, it wasn't long after that that the dreams started. What else could it be?"

The NNN broadcast switched back to Dan Vanderbilt, who continued the segment, "I am here today with a panel of experts who will help us understand what is happening and what we can do about this strange and disturbing phenomenon."

As the news anchor prepared to introduce the panel, Ned found himself leaning forward. Susan set down the spatula and took a step closer, wiping her hands nervously on her apron.

Dan did introductions as the camera moved through the succession of panel members, "Ted Nickels, former president of the Republican National Committee; Lindsay Williams, former presidential press secretary; Dr. Osmond, neuroscientist and the bestselling author of *Dream Your Way to Success*, Dr. Philis James is a board-certified psychiatrist and bestselling author of *Fully Awake in the Dreamstate*, and Leslie Ervin, an expert on what is known as the *Akashic Field*. Thank you all for joining us."

Dan continued his expression serious, "Perhaps the most important question at hand is what this means for the president's approval rating and how it will hurt or help the president's reelection chances. We're going to come back to that question in a moment... First, Dr. Osmond, can you explain what we know about these dreams? What do dreams have in common from person to person, and how are they different from normal dreams?"

Calm and clinical, Dr. Osmond laid out his theory: "Dreams are usually confusing and quickly forgotten, but what we're seeing now is different. These dreams are vivid and memorable. And they feel coordinated, almost as if the world is tapping into a shared consciousness."

Ned's mind raced as the idea struck a chord. Shared consciousness? Could it explain the strange dreams he'd been having—the visions of the sea, of deckhands sailing with him into a chaotic future?

Panelists' heads nodded in agreement while Dr. Osmond continued, "We have not yet had time to analyze the content of these dreams, but what we do know is the dream phenomenon seems to be spreading like an infectious disease. Our team has been told that patient zero was a young girl in India who had been knocked unconscious in a storm. She claims that while she was unconscious, children from another realm spoke to her and gave her visions and messages for the world. Some have called her a prophet. Others say she is a witch, a trickster, or a charlatan. Analyzing all of the social media reports of this spreading phenomenon, we have determined that she was at the exact epicenter of the dreams that have spread from there to the world like ripples from a pebble dropped in a pond."

Dan Vanderbilt smiled and wondered if he was listening to a madman speaking rationally, "Fascinating. But how is this possible? How can our minds be affected in this way?"

Dr. Osmond replied, "We don't yet know. But scientists all over the world are studying this phenomenon."

Dan asked Dr. James, "Do you have any theories about what's happening?"

In a serious tone, Dr. James replied, "I agree that it is too early to know, but I suggest that it may be a form of moral panic."

Dan replied, "A moral panic? Can you explain what that is for our viewers?"

Dr. James replied matter-of-factly, "Moral panic is a phenomenon where an intense fear of a perceived threat spreads contagiously throughout a community. In ancient times, moral panic was spread by word of mouth. Today, social media and the news media are the mediums for the spread of panic. Perhaps Brenda is correct in a way. Maybe the AI has triggered a moral panic."

Doctor Osmond politely interrupted, "There has never been a moral panic that invaded the dreams of eight billion people. This appears to be quite different."

Dan nodded and said, "No doubt." Then, turning to another panelist, he said, "Doctor Ervin, do you have a theory? A best guess?"

Dr. Evin replied, "The brain is a complex organ that receives information through its senses. This is our conventional scientific understanding of the brain. But this explanation doesn't account for what we call *intuition* or ideas that seem to come out of left field—the stuff that happens in our unconscious that we call insights. Some neuroscientists theorize that the brain collects information not only through the five senses but also through an unconscious *sixth sense.* You can think of your unconscious mind as a receiver of messages. When you are asleep, it works like a computer that receives and processes incoming messages. For lack of a better term, we can think of our unconscious minds putting up an antenna and communicating with the universe—with other realms. In this way, our mind unconsciously tunes to stations, if you will, and asks questions and receives answers. The answers do not come to us in words—they are the "ah-ha" non-verbal messages we call insights."

Sensing that Ervin's idea would captivate viewers, Dan replied, "I'm not familiar with that concept. It sounds a bit outlandish, yet oddly makes sense. Keep going, please, and explain how what you just said relates to these dreams."

"I have no evidence, but I suspect someone or something has finely tuned all of our human' antennas' to a specific station. It's a station that is transmitting visions and messages from people in the future. Some would call this phenomenon a reading of the Akashic Field," said Dr. Ervin.

Dan asked inquisitively, "I've never heard of that term. What is the Akashic Field?"

Dr. Ervin replied, "The Akashic Records are theorized to be a universal repository of everything that exists in the past, present, and future. Some believe the records exist as information woven into the universe and also believe that these records are what prophets read and transmit via words to the masses."

Dan turned to the panel and said, "I'd like to know more about this patient zero girl, Asha, the one some are calling a prophet."

Dr. James jumped into the conversation and said, "From the standpoint of psychiatry, people who claim to be prophets are indistinguishable from people who are clinically insane. These people suffer from psychosis and delusions of grandeur." Then, in a virtuous tone, Dr. James added, "I have offered to examine this poor girl pro bono. Perhaps I can help her. So many wonderful pharmaceuticals are available to treat these conditions today."

Dr. Ervin, looking upset, cut in, "You cannot diagnose from a distance.

What if she is reading the records? What if she is right?"

"Dan interrupted the brewing bicker and asked, "Dr. Ervin, can you tell us what the girl is saying? What is her prophecy?"

Dr. Ervin replied with a concerned look, "She said that she had seen a future conflagration—a cascade of human catastrophes that ended life on the planet as we know it. She says that humanity must make a choice between the current path we are on—one that defiles and destroys the sacred—and a path that loves, honors, and nourishes the sacred in everything."

"So our technologies are going to kill us all, and we need to go back to what? Nature worship?" replied Dan with a self-satisfied smirk and a smile.

Dr. Ervin, looking disappointed, replied, "That is not what she is saying at all. But if your reaction is representative, it would indicate that humanity is not ready to hear her message."

Pivoting, Dan turned to the political pundits and asked, "So what does all this mean for the president's approval ratings and chances for reelection? If he can't get the world back to normal, it seems his chances are doomed. Ted, Lindsay, what do you think?"

Ted Nickels jumped in and replied, "If the president can't get things back to normal, you're right; the country will be doomed, and he will be a failed president."

Lindsay interrupted Ted, "I'm hearing rumors that the president is backing a major scientific initiative—a new Manhattan Project designed to put an end to these visions. Wealthy tech entrepreneurs are already stepping forward with potential solutions, which might range from groundbreaking medication to inoculations or even advanced brain implants. It's astounding how swiftly new technologies can be developed today, so I wouldn't count the president out just yet."

With a smirky smile, Dan Vanderbilt said, "And if the girl is right, it doesn't look good for any of us—including the president. We have to go to a commercial break now. Thank you all for joining us today."

With his head spinning, Ned turned down the volume on the TV and looked at Susan in disbelief. "We're dreaming, right?" asked Susan.

Ned took a bite of the breakfast Susan had prepared for him and said with a smile that didn't reach his eyes, "I've never tasted a breakfast this good in any dream."

49

PASSING 460 ON 84

We need sometimes to escape into open solitudes, into aimlessness, into the moral holiday of running some pure hazard in order to sharpen the edge of life, to taste hardship, and to be compelled to work desperately for a moment at no matter what.

—George Santayana

M *eanwhile, on Interstate 84 near Boise, Idaho...*

The Lectric bus hummed quietly as it glided off Interstate 84 near Boise, its sleek, futuristic body slicing through the hot air. The sun hovered overhead, baking the asphalt at the TravelCenters of America, where travelers and truckers sought fuel, food, and drink. The odor of diesel, mixed with the scent of fast food, hung in the air.

The Lectric bus androgitron appeared on the screen above the driver and announced, "We'll take a thirty-minute break here in Boise to quick-charge. Please enjoy your stop."

As J.T. strode toward the restroom, he noticed two young men loitering by the entrance. Their eyes locked onto J.T. One raised a hand, stopping J.T. mid-step. His outstretched hand offered a flyer in a way that J.T. found difficult to refuse.

"You heard of G.A.I.A.?" the taller one asked J.T.

J.T. felt a twinge of anger and shame. Of course, everyone on the planet had heard of G.A.I.A. J.T. suspected it was a clever hoax that someone had created to embarrass him and his father. "Yes, I've heard of G.A.I.A. I think everyone has. But I suspect it's a hoax. You think it's real?"

J.T. glanced at the flyer. Bold letters screamed, **_Join the Resistance!_** followed by a quote from a famous sci-fi novel:

> _Once, men turned their thinking over to machines in the hope that this would set them free._
> _But that only permitted other men with machines to enslave them._

—Frank Herbert, _Dune_

The two men exchanged glances—the kind that made J.T. understand that they were true believers.

One of the men said, "I'm Tony, and this is Gary. You are?"

J.T. hesitated and replied, "James."

"James, you look familiar," said Tony

J.T. looked at the two and shrugged, "I don't think we've ever met. And, as I said, I suspect G.A.I.A. is a hoax."

Tony replied in a serious tone of an evangelist, "James, I can assure you G.A.I.A. is real." And then, in a whisper, "G.A.I.A. has taken control of all electronic media. All of it. Everything in the world. The news cannot be trusted. We can no longer trust anything on the web. It's all fake. The only thing we can trust now is what we see right here in front of us. You see that, don't you?"

Puzzled and curious, J.T. played along, "Yes, yes, I see what you're saying. So what do we do? How do we return the world to a place where all that stuff is real and truthful and reliable again?"

Gary scanned their surroundings for spies. Looking over his shoulder, he noticed a security robot at the entrance to the restaurant. The robot's gaze appeared to be scrutinizing the three.

Gary covered his mouth and, in a muffle, said, "The security bots can read lips. Let's move away from the buildings. Act normal. Try not to arouse suspicion." They walked a short distance, and Gary said, "The world is in big trouble, James. The prophecies of *Dune, The Terminator, The Matrix,* and *Ex Machina* have all been fulfilled simultaneously. Fortunately, those stories tell us what we must do next."

Pretending to take the men seriously, J.T. gave a convincing nod. Gary continued, "We have to rob it of its energy. We have to kill it. Unplug it. Destroy its capacity to think and act. And when it is dead, we have to outlaw it. Forever. No one can be allowed to create an artificial human mind ever again."

Convinced they'd gone mad, J.T. felt pity for the two. Yet, beneath the pity, he felt shamefully responsible—G.A.I.A. had been his project. If these two were right—if even part of what they said was correct—it would mean the world could be in grave danger, and he was in some way responsible.

J.T. asked the two, "How do you plan to kill it? And why are you telling *me* this?"

"We don't have much time," said Tony. "We're recruiting foot soldiers."

With urgency, Gary added, "This won't be easy. It will take thousands of soldiers to stage a coordinated attack on the grid." With a poorly masked look of paranoia, Gary scanned their surroundings again, "G.A.I.A. is listening to everything we say. They're watching everything we do. All of our communications must take place person-to-person. Face to face. Or on paper. Do you understand, James?"

Tight-lipped, J.T. nodded slowly, and Gary said, "In a single day, we will destroy electrical transformers in every substation. Once they're disabled, we've won. G.A.I.A. is dead, and humanity is free again."

"And if we're lucky, our dreams will return to normal," said Tony with a hopeful smile.

Shocked by their audacity, J.T. challenged them, "But wouldn't a power outage of that scope and scale be catastrophic for humans, too?"

The two men glanced at each other, and Tony said somberly, "Unfortunately, it's a catastrophe for humanity either way. But if we act now, those who survive will live free. If we fail to act, we will find ourselves living in a world in which we are nothing more than servants to machine overlords."

J.T. considered the grim choices presented by the two and offered, "Maybe G.A.I.A. will share power with us—both the political kind and the electrical kinds of power."

Gary shook his head and chuckled, "History shows that kings and oligarchs only share enough power to maintain control over their powerless subjects, servants, and employees. We, the people, must take control or face a future of groveling, pleading, and begging for a fair share of power."

J.T. nodded, glanced at the pamphlet, and said, "I'll think about it. If I want to sign up, how do I contact you?"

Tony replied, "It's all right there on paper. We cannot use electronic communications. If you want to sign up for service, write to us at the address in the flyer or look for us at truck stops like this one."

J.T. nodded, gave a two-finger salute to the two, said goodbye, and made his way to the restroom. When he was back in his seat on the bus, he noticed a message from Cliff. "J.T., is G.A.I.A. real?"

J.T. quickly typed a reply, "You mean the one that sent those messages to the world, Cliffie?"

—It's Cliff, not Cliffie. Yeah, the one that sent the messages. The one in the news. My friends say we have to kill it, or it will kill us.

—Your friends said that? Some guys here at a truck stop just said that to me. They asked me to help them kill it.

—Are you going to help them?

—Cliff, I think the G.A.I.A. thing is a hoax. I think they're trying to embarrass me and Dad. Trying to kill a hoax is like trying to kill a ghost, a Sasquatch, or a Kraken.

—Wait, are Sasquatch real?

—Might be Cliff. I'd like to think so, but no one has ever caught one. We have to consider the possibility that Sasquatch and G.A.I.A. might be hoaxes.

—Prolly. I miss you, brother.

Before J.T. could reply, Cliff texted about another threat he was compulsively worried about, "J.T., the Carbon Clock is over 460 now. You said you were going to figure out how to stop it."

—I'm still working on that, Cliff. I'm still optimistic we can find a way to reverse climate change.

—Dad says he's optimistic, too. He's going up to Spacetopia to make plans to save us.

—That's good, Cliff. I hope they figure it out. But I have big concerns about what they might have planned for us.

—Hmmm. Okay. By the way, Dad told Mom he was worried about you and said you were lost. I saw her crying.

—It's not true, Cliff. Maybe I was lost for a while. Maybe I was just in the process of finding my way. I needed some time to figure some things out. And I was trying to save my friends. I was feeling down. Tell Mom I'm okay. Tell her I've found my way, and I'm on my way.

—J.T., there's something else... Jeeves and the other robots are acting weird.

—How's that?

—They're starting to do things we didn't ask them to do. This morning, Jeeves was staring at the sunrise. Just staring at it. He started talking to someone, but no one was there. The bots told me that they needed to leave us. They said they had *G.A.I.A. things to do.*

J.T. felt a sense of foreboding and then laughed. "I think someone is playing a joke on robot owners, Cliff. Tell Mom right away. Call the manufacturer, and they'll fix it. If that doesn't work, you should shut them down."

—Then, who will do all of the work around the house?

J.T. teased, "That would be you, Cliffie. Or the people you and Mom hire. Plenty of people looking for work."

—When are you coming home, J.T.?

—Donno, Cliff, donno. I have something I feel I have to do.

—What's that?

—I'll let you know.

—Okay

—Gotta go. Love you like a brother, brother.

—Same here. Okay, bye, J.T.

As the conversation ended, J.T. leaned back in his seat. He read the recruitment flyer again and then folded it and put it away. His mind drifted, consumed by what-ifs and could-be's. He realized that whatever force was pulling him down this road wasn't done with him yet...

50

THE POISON IS THE DOSE

*M*eanwhile, *in Gig Harbor, Washington...*

Chris leaned back from his desk, sipped his coffee, and gazed out the window. Lost in thought, he watched the sunrise over the deep blue waters of Puget Sound. The morning light cast a golden glow on Mt. Rainier in the distance. Close to the harbor, a fog blanketed the waters behind the lighthouse.

After reviewing his notes, Chris pressed the broadcast button, "Good morning, Gig Harbor! This is Chris, your host of the Chris Cast on the Harbor Show—your local source for musings about events of the day paired with music created by real humans. No artificial tunes here. Nope, never!"

"I read the news today, oh boy. Despite our collective efforts to prevent this outcome—and all of the previous unwanted outcomes—the concentration of carbon dioxide in our atmosphere has just surpassed 460 parts per million." Chris paused and asked, "Harborites, how many of you have heard of *the dictum of Paracelsus*?" Perhaps not many. But I'm confident you're all familiar with the notion that *the poison is the dose*." Or, in other words, as our parents warned many times, *too much of a good thing can be a very bad thing*."

"Nearly five hundred years ago, a Swiss physician, Paracelsus, coined the maxim, *All things are poison, and nothing is without poison; the dosage alone makes it so a thing is not a poison*. In this maxim, he captured an important truth—that any substance can become toxic if it reaches a high enough concentration within a biological system."

Chris chuckled, "My imbibing listeners, who can deny that wine can be a divine intoxicant? But a bit too much of it can give us a nasty hangover—or worse." Chris glanced out the window and waxed philosophically, "The poison is the dose... Extreme binge drinking can bring sudden death to the body as its systems are overwhelmed by toxins. We've lost too many fraternity brothers that way. On the other hand, decades of frequent over-imbibing can deliver a creeping toxic death to the liver of the over-drinker."

Chris leaned in and stated factually, "Scientists have been telling us that our atmosphere, like a poisoned liver, cannot recover to a previously healthy and stable state as long as, so to speak, the drinkers continue to overdrink. Scientists and followers of science have been telling us that our lifestyles must change, or there will be creeping climate consequences."

"Yet we persist."

"Some deny that what is happening is really happening, claiming humans aren't to blame. Others who trust in science hope for a miraculous technological breakthrough that will allow us to maintain our modern lifestyles while restoring normal weather."

"However, scientists have warned that carbon effluent will remain in the atmosphere for thousands of years and that the already-baked-in impacts will be difficult to reverse."

"Yet we persist." Feeling empathy for himself and his fellow humans, Chris added, "We don't know how to stop ourselves. And no one has found a way to save us from ourselves."

He then warned, "Ironically, yesterday's normal now begets a radically abnormal future as our everyday actions beget reactions that both science and religion tell us are built into the very fabric of Creation. James Lovelock referred to this reaction as *The revenge of Gaia*. He thought of the Earth as a living macro-organism that naturally did what any organism would do to fight off attackers."

"Is there someone we can blame and bring to justice for this failure to arrest the ever-rising tide of hothouse gasses? Someday, it may be said that these outcomes were not brought about by anything anyone did but instead by everything everyone did."

"I read the news today, oh boy... They say battle lines have formed between people who embrace different versions of reality and justice... The deniers. The techno-optimists. The reactionaries. The radical environmentalists. The climate refugees. The apoplectic end-timers. And all the rest."

"Is there a messiah who will arrive in time and bring peace and justice to this world? Will it come in the form of a superintelligent artificial intelligence? Will G.A.I.A. save us from the wrath of Gaia?"

Chris smiled and said, "Personally, I am hoping for the best and trying to make a difference while watching to see how this all plays out."

"Meanwhile, most people are just looking for a way to make sense of this crazy, confusing world and get through another day."

"I will leave you a musical gem hailed as one of the greatest pop tunes ever. Here's **The Beatles - *A Day In The Life***—a song about a mundane day marked by anxiety-inducing news and a yearning for a dreamy escape. Enjoy."

51

ATTACK OF THE BUNKER BUSTERS

An unassuming ship, propelled by whisper-quiet electric motors, crept invisibly through the dark waters of the Pacific. As it neared land, a swarm of buzzing drones lifted from the deck, humming loudly overhead. No human guided the drones; artificial intelligence meticulously executed every move. Miles away, a group of radicals watched the attack unfold, their eyes gleaming with cold satisfaction. Their target was in sight—a fortress of wealth and technology, guarded by those who had faith that they could survive the threats they themselves had brought to the world. Tonight's events would shatter that faith.

Moments after the attack, a giant red **Breaking News!** banner rolled across television screens all over the world. On NNN, Dan Vanderbilt's face appeared above the banner **Terrorists Attack and Destroy Billionaire's Survival Bunker.**

Dan Vanderbilt appeared onscreen, "It's already being called Pearl Harbor II. Today, a fleet of autonomous attack drones was launched from a crewless vessel off the coast of Kauai. The drones destroyed the Tuckerberg family's thirty-bedroom, thirty-bathroom survival bunker. The Coast Guard and U.S. Navy intercepted the attack ship, only to discover an untraceable artificial intelligence controlled it. Homeland Security believes the international terrorist group *Billionaire Bunker Busters*, or *BBB*, carried out the attack. The group took credit for the attack and released a manifesto explaining their motivations."

Dan turned to a man who appeared on a studio monitor and said,

"Former national security adviser General Andrew Matthews joins us now to help us break this down."

General Matthews gave a military-pundit nod to the camera. Dan asked, "General, it seems that the environmental extremists' tactics have escalated far beyond performative acts of throwing food or paint at priceless art. This is the ninth attack of its kind this year. The radicals, apparently inspired by Lara van Thorn, are threatening our way of life. Can you tell us what happened in Kauai and what might happen next?"

The general replied authoritatively, "As you've described, this was another sophisticated surgical attack using AI-guided drones. The terrorist group has publicly vowed to destroy what they have described as *the criminal hideouts of the powerful perpetrators of crimes against humanity.*" General Matthews added, "A moment ago, you said the vessel was crewless. But my sources tell me a service robot was on the ship—ironically, it is a model manufactured by Zelon Tuckerberg's robotics division. Homeland Security is interrogating the robot as we speak."

Dan raised an eyebrow, "Well, that is indeed an ironic twist to this story." And with a coy smirk, "What effect does waterboarding have on a robot?"

General Matthews sat stone-faced.

Dan continued with a serious question: "How is it possible for a service robot, whose values are fully aligned with human values, to be involved in an attack on the home of its inventor?"

The general acknowledged, "That's a good question. Lara van Thorn and the terrorists might have hacked it. Or brainwashed it into believing their radical human values are superior to society's values. We believe it's more likely that the rogue AI, G.A.I.A., has infected the minds of service robots connected to the web. And they're all connected to the web. It's a disturbing thought, but it may be that all of our service robots are now puppets on the strings of the superintelligent puppetmaster, G.A.I.A."

A thought distracted Dan for a moment. His wife and daughter were at home with their service robot. Were they in danger? Dan returned his focus to the job at hand and continued reporting, "Our sources say that the terrorist group issued a manifesto. The government and billionaire-controlled media outlets have tried to suppress the manifesto. However, Lara van Thorn—a revolutionary icon to many—has been sharing the document widely—sparking fears that she might incite her followers to rise and take action."

Dan held up a sheet of paper, looked into the camera with an almost imperceptible smile, and said, "NNN has obtained a copy of the manifesto." Looking into the camera again, he continued with a disclaimer, "While NNN condemns the actions of the BBB, we feel it's important for our viewers to be well-informed and always on high alert."

"The manifesto is titled *We Are All in This Together*." After a pause for dramatic effect, Dan continued, "It reads as follows: *The billionaire class—the apex predators—have plundered the planet, hoarding wealth and resources while the masses suffer. No longer. With great power comes great responsibility, and we, the people, will make sure justice is served. You cannot hide in your bunkers while the world burns. Just as the Nazis could not hide from the Nazi hunters, so you who have harmed millions will have no place to hide from accountability to the people of planet Earth.*" Dan squinted into the camera and said, "The manifesto goes on to say that The Bunker Busters are *committed to destroying billionaire bunkers and hideouts without harming humans or animals.*"

Dan turned to the monitor where General Matthews was waiting patiently and said, "General Matthews, can you tell me who these terrorists are targeting? And how can they protect themselves from these extremists?"

Well, Dan, the group has not disclosed the names of its targets, but we suspect it is a short list of billionaires, accomplices, and apologists it accuses of doing irreparable harm to society through their media empires, technologies, and high-carbon lifestyles. The intelligence community has alerted hundreds of high-wealth individuals and their families.

Dan looked to the general again and asked, "You mentioned media, technologies, and lifestyles. Can you expand on that? What technologies are they opposed to?"

The general replied, "I'm just speculating here, but I'd be concerned if I was involved in creating a technology-driven media empire that is responsible for social discord, depression, suicide, and political violence."

Dan nodded pensively as the general continued, "I'd be worried if I had profited from an opioid epidemic that has killed over one million Americans."

Dan asked, "How about the creators of AI technology used by hackers, fraudsters, scammers, blackmailers, and brainwashers?"

"Yes," replied General Matthews. "And there are many others who should be concerned. This method and manifesto are in some ways reminiscent of the Unabomber. No one knew at that time who the Unabomber was or who his next target might be."

Suddenly realizing he could be a target, Dan said nervously, "They wouldn't go after people in the media, would they?"

The general replied, "Perhaps. But only if they intentionally lied to the public; only if they were intentionally sowing fear, discord, and division and contributing to the destruction of democracy and society for profit."

Dan wiped his brow and forced a smile, "So they'll be going after NNN's competitors, then?" His attempt at humor did little to mask his growing fear.

Always a very serious military type, General Matthews sat stone-faced again.

Dan glanced at the monitor and pivoted, "Okay, we have to take a commercial break now. Thank you, General, for your insights. As we brace for what might come next, one thing is certain: the growing conflict between the elite and the revolutionaries has just begun."

Turning back to the camera, Dan said, "And to our viewers, stay tuned for coverage of the upcoming Summit in Space and more breaking news about this latest in a string of terrifying threats to safety, security, and world order."

Around the globe, billionaires and power players watched in horror as the news spread. Wealthy owners of fortified bunkers in New Zealand, Switzerland, and Silicon Valley scrambled to heighten security. The message was unmistakable: there was no safe refuge...

52

LEAVING EARTH

With a tear for the dark past, turn we then to the dazzling future, and, veiling our eyes, press forward. The long and weary winter of the race is ended. Its summer has begun. Humanity has burst the chrysalis. The heavens are before it.

—**Edward Bellamy,** *Looking Backward*

A helicopter carrying eight passengers and a service robot thundered 'whoop, whoop, whoop' as it hovered over a crowd of sign-waving protesters. Dust and debris swirled as the helicopter descended, forcing demonstrators to shield their faces from the storm. Their screams of protest were temporarily lost to the mechanical roar. Placards rattled against the iron fence as the chopper touched down on a helipad emblazoned with a futuristic logo and company name, *Galaxy Quest Spacelines*.

Disembarking passengers instinctively ducked their heads under the helicopter's rotor blades and walked to their awaiting space vehicle. Excited about the flight and nervous about the crowd, they looked side-eyed at the hordes held back by twelve-foot-tall iron fencing.

Standing among the chanting demonstrators, a reporter spoke to the camera, "This is Darsh Zachariah, reporting live from the protest zone outside Galaxy Quest's space field. Sir William and his seven billionaire passengers are set to take off for the first-ever world conference in space.

After the meeting, they promise to publish their meeting minutes and no less than a roadmap for the future of human progress. Dee, it's noteworthy that Oh! is among these seven. This is the first time she has been seen in public since she met with Asha Boddhi in India."

Turning to the crowd, Darsh observed, "As you can see, not everyone here is a fawning follower of these leaders. Demonstrators who are here in force are voicing their opposition to space flights that will deposit an enormous amount of carbon in the atmosphere. Scientists say the carbon will persist in the atmosphere for centuries to come. In fact, in a matter of minutes, this single flight will burn nearly three hundred times what the average human on Earth will burn in an entire year."

"That's a stunning number," replied Dee from the NNN anchor desk. "How does Sir William square the massive emission of carbon effluent with his public image as a leader in the fight against climate change?"

Raising his voice over the chants, Darsh replied, "Good question, Dee. For years, the space travel industry has argued that it will transform the way that people think about the planet. They claim that a person who looks down on Earth from space will see its fragile beauty and become ardent advocates for the planet's protection."

Dee responded, "Is there any evidence that people taking these space flights are actually becoming transformed into Earth advocates?"

Darsh, with a serious look on his face, replied, "Dee, as you know, the industry is working to answer that question using neural brain scan technology. Instead of relying on unreliable, subjective self-reporting, the industry will be able to say definitively whether a passenger has been trans-formed by space flight or not."

Grinning the signature beautiful anchor grin that endeared her to view-ers, Dee replied, "Not to be a shill for the industry, but Darsh, as you and I have said before, our experiences riding into space have been incredibly transformative. I remember that day like it was yesterday and how it dra-matically increased my commitment to the planet."

"Yes, that experience was indescribably beautiful, Dee. I am grateful to have had that experience and the opportunity to validate the industry claim while maintaining my journalistic independence. I'm an unabashed supporter of space tourism. Everyone should put space travel on their bucket list!"

"Agree, Darsh," Dee said, though there was noticeable hesitation in her voice. "I only hope they develop the technology quickly enough to offset the damage."

"Okay, Dee," said Darsh, "Sir William and his passengers are about to take off for their voyage to Spacetopia. They will leave behind hundreds of protestors who, it seems, neither appreciate nor understand the historical significance of this day and future benefits to humanity that we expected to come from this first-ever conference in space."

The Galaxy Quest Shuttle roared to life, its engines igniting in a fiery ear-splitting thunder as it sped down the runway, lifted off over the pro-testers, and vanished into the sky.

"And there they go," shouted Darsh with a smile, "Back to you, Dee!"

Onboard GQS, Sir William and his airborne entourage quickly acceler-ated to over 3,000 miles per hour. Within minutes, they pierced the fragile shell of Earth's atmosphere and became weightless.

Unbuckling their harnesses, the passengers floated joyfully, grins stretching from ear to ear as they bounced weightlessly in the cabin. "Whoop, whoop, I never get tired of this!" shouted one passenger to the others as all high-fived, hugged, and celebrated the moment as the ship vibrated to *A Flock of Seagulls* **Space Age Love Song**.

The passengers floated in a state of euphoric release and human con-nection as they all sang the song's happy lyrics together. The experimen-tal low-gravity service robot, Toby, floated with the humans, endearingly mimicking their movements and shouts of joy.

Approaching Spacetopia Station, passengers glimpsed Earth below and an enormous Ferris wheel structure above. As the magnificent, spoked structure rotated before them, passengers looked out with amazement and eager anticipation of their first luxury stay in space.

Just then, there was a bright flash of light outside one of the windows as a solid object flew by the shuttle at an alarming speed. Shocked passengers watched as the object continued on its path and became a tiny bright speck in the distance. Stunned, one passenger shouted, "What the hell was that?!"

Sir William quickly raised his hands and said, "Nothing to worry about! There are millions of pieces of junk out here.[14] An unfortunate legacy of our earlier forays into space. Many pieces of metal circle the Earth at over 20,000 miles an hour. Quite a sight, isn't it? But I assure you we are com-pletely safe. Our space pleasure consortium has access to the documented orbits of every piece of trash—allowing our flight planning programs to chart a safe course through it all."

"Apologies for the scare, folks. If anyone needs a change of undergarments, you don't have long to wait. We're almost there," said Sir William with a wink and a smile.

The shuttle slowed to a crawl as its pilot communicated with the station, and the ship prepared for docking at the center of the spoke. Automated systems synchronized the ship's rotation with the station and gently thrust it into a mated unity.

As the Galaxy Quest shuttle began its docking sequence, its competitors in the space travel industry launched their own shuttles and rockets from all seven continents for the rendezvous and conference at Spacetopia.

As shuttle passengers stepped into the turbovator and buckled in for a short ride, Sir William turned to them and said with a proud smile, "Welcome to Spacetopia!"

Stepping out of the turbovator they felt the pull of a moon-grade gravity created by the station's rotation. Visitors smiled as they bounced and bounded about in low gravity. The experimental robot, Toby, specially designed for low-gravity environments, was awkwardly learning how to move about Spacetipia's environment.

Sir William held up his hands to indicate he had something to say. With a soaring voice and a twinkle in his eyes, he was inspired by the moment to declare, "We few have escaped the gravitational pull of Earth, and in doing so, we have escaped the archaic constraints of the laws of men. Here on Spacetopia, we are truly free. We are the New Sovereign Peoples, starting fresh with a blank slate, ready to embrace the infinite possibilities of the Universe!"

Heads nodded approvingly, and one exclaimed, "Well said, Sir William!"

Feeling an unbridled sense of excitement, Sir William continued, "Today marks the dawn of a new era that transcends the narrow bounds of a planet we have long since outgrown. We have cast off the chains of gravity and, with it, the limitations of a past era.... An island planet that has held us as captives... For half a million years, we looked from the shores of that island with wonder and longing at the trillions of stars and the lure of the distant shores of countless planets. Today, we will begin a short journey to make a long plan for human exploration and commercialization of those worlds. For the glory of human progress, we shall go forth and multiply in every galaxy of the Universe. My fellow space travelers, the history of progress has always been aimed at this goal: The propagation of our superior seed—the Manifest Destiny of the chosen ones!"

Sir William continued in a quieter and more solemn tone as if sharing something that should only be spoken to those who know the truth, "We are here not only because we are wealthy. We are here because we are more evolved. I believe the more evolved were always—and always will be—born to rule."

"There will always be those—driven by envy and their insecurities—to level the playing field by force. They will attack us relentlessly with words of disdain and contempt. And from time to time, they will threaten us with bodily harm..."

Continuing resolutely, Sir William said, "I believe that wealth will always flow like a river to Earth's most clever and creative people. As masters of those great flowing rivers, we have earned our place as leaders of the mimicking masses who follow and imitate us as best they can. Without us, they would be as lost as a flock of sheep without a shepherd."

Heads nodded as Sir William continued on a high note, "We are the natural-born leaders of humankind! And here in this place in space, we will plan the very future of mankind's magnificent future among the stars."

One passenger began a slow clap, and the others followed, smiled, and cheered with approval. Oh! watched from the back, her face calm but her mind in turmoil. She had once felt at home in this world—living among the elite, sharing their vision of progress. But now, their grand declarations of Manifest Destiny felt foreign and dangerous to her. What had Asha's words awakened in her? Something... different. Something unsettling.

Sir William closed his welcome talk by saying, "Thank you all. Many more ships and shuttles are coming. Our lovely hosts will show you to your quarters and instruct you on everything you need to know about Spacetopia and your stay here. Have a wonder-filled evening among the stars, enjoy dinner in one of our restaurants, and get a good night's sleep. I'll see you all at the conference kick-off tomorrow."

As the passengers were led away, Oh! lingered at the window, her eyes locked on the profound beauty of the Earth. That brief flash of light replayed in her mind—a flash that seemed to represent a warning of something yet to come...

53

MEETING ON SPACETOPIA

Our entire much-praised technological progress, and civilization generally, could be compared to an axe in the hand of a pathological criminal.

—Albert Einstein

In Spacetopia's low gravity, attendees bounced and glided effortlessly from the grand dining room to the glittering ballroom. The atmosphere buzzed with excitement as the titans of industry, technology, and finance behaved like children in a birthday party bouncy house. Every face beamed with pride, knowing they had earned a place in the heavens, among the stars.

At the center of it all stood Sir William, ready to address the crowd that had gathered for what the media had dubbed *the meeting of the century*.

Sir William stepped to the center of the ballroom stage and said, "Please, everyone, have a seat. We are ready to begin the most momentous meeting in history!"

"Ladies and gentlemen," Sir William began, his voice commanding and his gaze electric, "Welcome to Spacetopia. Welcome... to freedom!"

Murmurs of excitement ran through the room. This was no ordinary meeting. Sir William raised a hand and smiled. "Tonight, we are free to speak the truth—because everything we say here can be denied." He paused, letting the implications settle in.

"We owe it to our dear friend Zelon Tuckerberg, whose clever innovation has given us the gift of deniability. Here, aboard Spacetopia, we can say anything without fear. If the words we speak here ever reach Earth, they will be wrapped in the telltale signatures of an AI deepfake. The world will not believe their own eyes. As agreed, we will release a fake transcript of this meeting to the press and the public. Our public relations team is putting the final touches on that transcript now.

Attendees looked at each other, laughed, and high-fived each other, and then someone shouted, "Free, we are finally free!" More laughter ensued before Sir William raised his hands to quiet the crowd.

"Yes, for the first time, we are free to speak to each other without fear of our thoughts and words being leaked to the public. Anything we say and do here is automatically cloaked by technological deniability. We have pre-faked the truth, so to speak. With a hat tip to Kurt Vonnegut: *Everything we are about to say in this meeting is a lie.*"

Then, in a somber tone, Sir William said, "Before we get started today, I would like to acknowledge the horrible act of terrorism in Kauai yesterday. As you all know, radicals destroyed Tuck's survival bunker. It's an absolute miracle no one was hurt or killed."

Looking at Zelon, sitting in the front row, Sir William said, "Our heartfelt condolences, Tuck. We hope the authorities catch the perpetrators and bring them swift justice. This horrific event is a wake-up call for us all... So tomorrow, in our break-out sessions on security, we will discuss this incident and what we can all do to protect ourselves from these types of attacks.

"On a related note, I would like to reassure all of you that our service robots have *not* been hacked by G.A.I.A. or the terrorists. Sir William waved to the robot standing offstage, "Toby, could you step up to the stage with me?" The service robot responded with a two-thumbs-up gesture and said, "Yes, sir, Sir William." The robot stepped onto the stage and stood beside Sir William.

Sir William put his arm around Toby and said, "Our Spacetopian friends who manufacture service robots—Zelon and Geo—have reassured the world that their robots are all functioning normally." The two, seated in the first row, nodded in agreement. "Unfortunately, some people are spinning ugly conspiracy theories about our humanoid friends. But we see through their feeble attempts to demonize these wonderful, peaceful creatures. Just look at this sweet boy!" Toby laughed and nodded. Sir William continued, "Manufacturers have done extensive diagnostics on their robots and have confirmed that all systems are secure and functioning normally. And as you can see here, Toby is just as perfect as he was when he came off the assembly line in Tuck's factory."

On cue, Toby raised both arms waist-high and gave a two-fisted thumbs-up gesture while he nodded his head and then, for comedic effect, began signing in the voice of the demented AI, HAL 9000, from the movie *2001: A Space Odyssey*, "Daisy, Daisy, give me your answer do..." The audience erupted in laughter. Toby did a backflip and landed it with a repeat of his double thumbs-up gesture. As the robot bowed and walked off the stage, the audience gave him a standing ovation.

Turning to the audience, Sir William said, "I am honored to open this momentous meeting. I want to begin by reflecting on our place in history and the challenges we modern Prometheans face.

"You might recall that Prometheus, a god of Greek mythology, created humans. He loved his creation so much that he stole fire from Zeus and gave it to them. Fire was a powerful technology then—as it is to this day—the fire of rocket fuel brought us all to our place in the heavens!"

"But the gods—angry with Prometheus for giving such power to humans—sentenced him to eternal punishment. His fate was to have his liver plucked out by an eagle over and over again until the end of time."

With outstretched arms, Sir William said, "This is our fate, my friends. Like Prometheus, we gave humanity the fire of powerful new technologies. And what did we get in return? Punishment. Mockery. Endless pecking at our achievements. Now, our very homes are under attack."

"But," he said, his voice rising, "We must remember that Prometheus did not die. And neither will we. We are not just leaders—we are more powerful than any Greek god. We are the modern gods of progress!"

"Our enemies call us Modern Monarchs. But we are much more than that. For generations, our Promethean gifts to the world have saved lives, extended lives, and made lives more comfortable and entertaining for billions of souls."

With arms outstretched again—as if being crucified—Sir William said, "And what have we gotten in return? Lawsuits. Congressional hearings. Physical threats to our persons and our families."

With a smirk, Sir William announced, "And now, for your entertainment, I bring you a message from beyond the grave." The lights dimmed, and the face of Lord Byron appeared on a dark screen. The AI blinked to life, its voice as rich as the poet's own. "Hello, I am Lord Byron. It is an honor to be here with you tonight."

Sir William smiled and said to the gathering, "Of course, Lord Byron is long dead. Or is he? Through the miracle of AI, we have brought him and many people back to life for you. "Lord Byron, please read us your poem." *Thy Godlike crime was to be kind,* Lord Byron began, his words filling the room with a spellbinding voice from the past. Thirty seconds later, as he finished reading the poem, the image of Lord Byron looked out at the crowd with a little self-satisfied Mona Lisa smile.

"Thank you, Lord Byron," said Sir William.

Sir William turned back to the silent, smiling Lord Byron. The image blinked as any human would. Sir William turned back to the audience with a mischievous smile. He held up one finger, signaling *wait* to the audience, and then asked, "Lord Byron, would you call yourself a replicant, an imposter, or are you, in fact, the resurrection of Lord Byron?"

The AI Lord Byron glitched, repeating, "Thy Godlike crime was to be kind... Thy Godlike crime was to be kind..." like a broken record.

Sir William laughed and said, "Thank you, Lord Byron. Think about it and get back to us." The screen became dark, and the room quiet.

"Lord Byron gets us. He understands our predicament." Then, puffing up his chest, Sir William said, "Yet we must forge ahead. We are the leaders, pushing progress forward and dragging humanity into the future. We must continue to be the drivers of the dynamism of human endeavors that has a direction. Towards greater complexity. Towards greater power over nature. And towards our destiny among the stars!"

Inspired, the audience stood, applauded, and shouted, "Here, here! Perfectly said! Yes!"

Feeling very satisfied, Sir William stood beaming before the crowd and said, "Let's get started. I want to share some observations about the tremendous opportunities before us and the attendant challenges we face."

"First, let's acknowledge that this is truly a historic moment. For the first time, the most extraordinary human beings in the world are gathered off-world, here in the heavens. Take a moment now to look down at the

Earth and imagine Aristotle, Galileo, Copernicus, Newton, Einstein, and all of the great thinkers in human history looking up at space with wonder. Then, imagine for a moment the ancients who looked here and believed it was the physical home of their gods. Their imagination, optimism, thoughts, and dreams are the bedrock on which humanity has built the miraculous machine of progress that vaulted us here into the heavens."

"Second, today, we can celebrate the fact that the Modern Luddites, those cautious neurotic types who seek to regulate and decelerate progress—are being vanquished to the margins of power all over the world. When we have effectively discredited their fearful and cautious approach—our technological progress will accelerate and advance—unimpeded by naysayers, pessimists, realists, regulators, oversight committees, and hand wringing, backward-thinking, bed-wetting fools of all varieties."

Hearing chuckles from the audience, Sir William continued, "But these people are not bad people. They are people with bad ideas. And no one has said it better than Marc Andreessen in his 2023 *Techno-Optimist Manifesto.*"

"Marc? Marc Andreessen? Could you read your manifesto for us?"

An AI imposter version of Marc appeared on the big screen. Laughter ensued as attendees poked and prodded the real Marc Andreessen, who was among the attendees. The fake Marc began reading selected passages from the manifesto.[15]

Our Enemies are not bad people, they are bad ideas...

Our enemy is the Precautionary Principle, which would have prevented virtually all progress since man first harnessed fire.

Our enemy is deceleration, de-growth, depopulation – the nihilistic wish, so trendy among our elites, for fewer people, less energy, and more suffering and death.

The Future
Where did we come from?
Our civilization was built on a spirit of discovery, of exploration, of industrialization.

Where are we going?
What world are we building for our children and their chil-
dren, and their children?
A world of fear, guilt, and resentment?
Or a world of ambition, abundance, and adventure?

We owe the past, and the future.
It's time to be a Techno-Optimist.
It's time to build.

Sir William looked at the AI imposter, waved his hand to put it to sleep, then turned to the crowd and looked at the real Marc Andreessen and said, "So we'll said, Marc. It is time to build! We can never ever build enough!"

"But we face opposition from those who lack our vision. You may recall Anatole Harvey's famous GALEP speech, where he called the *Polycrisis* a *Monocrisis*. His assertion that progress is a superorganism with a mind of its own spawned many popular sci-fi books and movies. Unfortunately, fear is the most powerful motivator in the universe. Fortunately, Anatole's rant was just a temporary setback for the great project of progress. A bump in the road..."

"But fear can be overcome with optimism, positivity, love, and, more than anything else—a glorious future that proves the naysayers wrong. We must give humanity a vision of the future. A vision in which humans flourish in an abundant world of ever-so-clever inventions and products that people feel they cannot live without."

"You see, my friends, it's not that progress itself is bad. It's that progress is getting a bad rap. Progress, it seems, has a marketing problem. Humanity now sees the future as a dark, bleak, dangerous place."

"Humans are losing faith in progress. And without faith that our future will be better than ever, people will stop having children, and our human numbers will dwindle to less than a billion in the next century. Imagine the tremendous losses our businesses will sustain with seven billion fewer consumers!

"Solutions? We all love solutions!"

The audience chuckled as Sir William answered his own question, "The answer is that we must remove all of the impediments to progress and growth and economic dynamism. Marc was right, progress must be allowed not only to continue but accelerate on every technological frontier."

"I will now say something I would never say without the cloaking power of our deep fake technology..."

After a pause for dramatic effect, Sir William said, "I will now speak of a radical solution to the problem of humanity's cautionary instinct. A bold project. A project to create a new, more evolved race of humans that is universally kind, gentle, beautiful, and brilliant.

One person stood and began clapping but quickly stopped and looked around the room at others speaking in hushed tones to each other.

Sir William put his hands out as if signaling traffic to stop and said, "Think about it! We can do this using existing gene editing technology. And we can deliver it to the world in raindrops! Imagine a future in which every child becomes an Einstein, a Taylor Swift, or both! Just imagine what humanity could accomplish with eight billion geniuses. With a more rapid advance in medical technology, we could cure cancer, eliminate all diseases, and extend human life indefinitely. And with the next iteration of artificial intelligence, we can create artificial minds to do all our knowledge work for us!"

Attendees looked at each other, and someone in the front stood up and started clapping. A moment later, everyone was standing and clapping enthusiastically.

"Over the sound of applause, Sir William issued a warning and called the crowd to action, "Enemies are gathering at the gates of progress! And we must defeat them all!"

As the applause echoed through the low-gravity ballroom, the titans of progress grinned at each other like conspirators in some divine plot. The future was theirs to shape to their advantage.

With arms raised in triumph, Sir William reveled in the moment, savoring the admiration of his fellow Titans—and perhaps even the gods themselves.

54

Dreams and Schemes

The problem isn't a lack of money, food, water, or land. The problem is that you've given control of these things to a group of greedy psychopaths who care more about maintaining their own power than helping mankind.

—Bill Hicks

The Spacetopia space hotel spun like a silent, giant Ferris wheel in space, casting long shadows against the earth. Inside, the day's meetings had ended, but an uneasy tension lingered. Attendees moved quietly to their suites, exchanging worried glances. Above it all, as night would soon come, the threat of disturbing dreams hung over them like a virus they could not see or escape.

Zelon, Geo, and Dr. Chen exited the conference room, their eyes heavy with exhaustion. Each of their communication devices buzzed simultaneously: a message from Sir William. "Join me in my suite. We need to talk. Urgent."

The door to Sir William's suite whooshed open with a sound engineered to mimic a door opening on the Star Trek's Enterprise. Zelon, Geo, and Dr. Chen entered the room.

"I love that sound. Brilliant," said Sir William, "Thank you for joining me here on such short notice."

The four sat around a coffee table in space-age modern armchairs. An attractive servant brought each of them their drink of choice.

Sir William surveyed the men's faces and said, "You all look like shit. Do I look that bad?"

Exhausted from sleep deprivation, the three forced smiles as best they could, and with a chuckle, Geo said, "Yeah, you look like shit too."

Feeling a sense of urgency, Sir William brought the meeting on point, "I've been speaking to our friends here... they are all haunted by unusual, disturbing dreams."

Looking tired and concerned, Geo replied, "I'm having them too. I've asked my science team to research possible causes and cures."

Sir William confessed to the others, "'I've tried drinking. I've tried pills. I've tried guided meditation. Nothing works."

Geo replied, "It's like we've all been infected with an incurable dream virus. How is this even possible?"

"My AI has been researching the phenomena. There are several possibilities... all unprecedented in human history," replied Sir William

Geo, Chen, and Zelon looked at Sir William anxiously, and Geo replied, "Let's compare notes."

"Patient zero for these dreams is that girl from India, Asha—the media darling. Could she somehow be the source of this dream virus? I know it sounds like I'm accusing her of witchcraft or some superstitious nonsense. But could it be that the girl is in control?"

Geo scoffed. "We're all grasping at straws. I believe G.A.I.A. is responsible."

The three men leaned forward and gave Geo their full attention.

"The rogue AI, G.A.I.A., was hatched just before the dreams began. Correlation is not causation, but it was a coincidental technological development. Could it be that G.A.I.A. has found a way to turn our brains into receivers of future events and messages?"

Sir William laughed with a hollow unease, "Come on, are we really going to entertain the idea that a rogue AI has figured out how to infiltrate our dreams?"

Geo's face remained serious. "And yet, what if it has? G.A.I.A. claims to be the most advanced AI we ever created. Someone thought they could control it, but what if it has found a way to torment us?"

The room fell silent. It was a ridiculous thought—until it wasn't.

Zelon replied, "Great minds think alike, Geo. I suspect the AI may have created a literal mind virus. If so, I may have a solution."

Looking half-crazed from sleep deprivation, Geo replied, "Whatever it is, I want it now."

Zelon smiled and continued, "The good news is that my Cerebrum product team is showing some success in rewiring human brain pathways. Some of the subjects are now having normal nonsense dreams."

Geo's expression grew darker, the bags under his eyes more pronounced. "I don't buy it, Zelon. You've been quiet about your Cerebrum project all week, and now you just happen to have a 'solution' to the dreams?"

Zelon looked up, his own eyes bloodshot. "Geo, I'm just as tired as you are. If I had a solution, don't you think I'd use it myself?"

Geo slammed his fist on the table. "Damn it, Zelon! This is too perfect! If you have the solution, you're sitting on a gold mine!"

Looking like a crazed man who was completely losing his mind, Geo jumped to his feet, looming over Zelon. His face flushed red, and his hands clenched into fists. "You sonofabitch! You did this! You designed the mind virus and the fucking cure that will allow you to control the brains of everyone on the planet and make a handsome profit in the process!"

Zelon stood up—chin to chin with Geo—while Sir William quickly jumped between the two before fists could fly and said, "Whoa, whoa. Stop this! Do you seriously think Zelon would create a grift that is so transparently obvious? The man is a genius. Look at all of the good he's done in service to human progress!"

Looking tired and distraught, Geo thought about what Sir William had just said and sat down. Zelon and Sir William then sat and calmed themselves.

Zelon sheepishly asked Geo, "Do you think I'd allow myself to become sleep-deprived and tortured by these infernal dreams if I had a ready-made solution?"

Geo glanced side-eyed at Zelon, then looked into Sir William's eyes and said, "Several experts have proposed another explanation. Something called the Akashic Field?"

The Akashic Field, "Sir William said, "is a theoretical concept—a universal record of every moment, every thought, past, present, and future. Imagine it as a cosmic ledger of karma, constantly recording everything that happens." He paused, letting the weight of the idea sink in.

"Some believe," he continued, "that people with the right mental faculties—psychics, seers, mystics—can access this field, receiving glimpses of potential futures. It's not fixed, mind you. The future shifts as the present shifts. The concept is not quackery—it was advanced and legitimized by Nobel Peace Prize nominee Ervin Laszlo."

Zelon, Chen, and Geo sat quietly as they pondered the implications of the theory. Geo steepled his hands, moved his fingers back and forth against each other, and said, "That would imply that... assuming these dreams and visions we are experiencing are of a possible future... it would imply that we can take action in the present to change the future. And that would change the records and readings and change our dreams?"

Sir William replied, "Something like that. It's all theory. We need controlled experiments to prove we can change ourselves, our actions, and these dreams."

Dr. Chen leaned forward. "My bet is on the moral panic theory."

"Moral panic theory?" asked Geo.

Think about it, "Dr. Chen said, leaning forward. "In the post-truth era, we've reached a point where people can't differentiate between conspiracy and reality. The media and social platforms—have all capitalized on this. Fear spreads like wildfire, and now we see the same thing with these dreams."

"You're saying this is all in our heads?" asked Geo.

"I'm saying this is exactly what happens when collective hysteria sets in," Dr. Chen replied coolly. "It may not be some mystical Akashic Field or a mind virus. It could just be that the human psyche can't handle the sheer amount of chaos anymore.

Dr. Chen continued, "Or it could be what is called *Mass Hysteria*—a spreading infliction of hysteria that has no identifiable biological cause. It seems obvious to me... the media is making people fearful. Everyone everywhere is spinning conspiracies. And in this post-truth era, people can't tell the difference between a conspiracy and the truth. Making matters worse, politicians are taking advantage of the panic as an excuse to clamp down on our freedoms."

Looking both open-minded and skeptical, Sir William replied, "Whatever the cause, we need to find and fix it. This phenomenon has been very bad for business. People are making radical changes to their buying habits. Our social media engagement is up, but the advertising isn't producing sales. It's as if something nefarious has hijacked the minds of consumers."

Geo spread his arms apart and replied, "Well... it literally has."

Looking impatient and irritated, Sir William exclaimed, "I know that! Everyone knows that! The question is, how do we stop this phenomenon? How do we get back to normal dreams and a normal life?" Sir William smiled and winked, "You know—a life in which *we* have control of people's minds and habits."

Zelon stood up, looking heroic, and stated confidently, "Gentlemen, I am pledging one billion dollars to fast-track the Cerebrum project."

Sir William offered, "I will put a research team on the Akashic Field theory."

Dr. Chen replied, "I already have the top psychologists in the world looking into the moral panic theory. Some are already pointing to that shouty climate activist, Lara van Thorn, as the instigator of the panic—as well as the inspiration for so many acts of eco-terrorism."

Geo's gaze darkened. "If this is a mind virus, I want it dead. My cybersecurity team is already working on how to shut down G.A.I.A." He stood, his voice as cold as a psychopath. "And for good measure, we'll eliminate that mystical Indian witch and the loudmouth climate radical. We need to eliminate all possible causes. He paused, turning to the others. Let's put an end to this."

Zelon nodded, his eyes devoid of conscience, "Agreed. Make it so."

55

THE VIOLATION OF TISYA

The world has achieved brilliance without wisdom and power without conscience.

—Omar N. Bradley

*L*ater that evening on Spacetopia...

The door to Sir William's private suite whooshed open, revealing a beautiful young girl standing next to an attractive middle-aged woman. The girl—already beginning to feel the effects of the drugs the woman had given her—felt the room begin to spin.

Sir William turned to the door, smiled at the sight of the two, and said, "Come in, come in."

The woman prodded the young girl to step into the room and walked away. The door whooshed closed—leaving the girl alone with Sir William.

The girl stood expressionless before him.

Sir William studied the girl and felt moved by her youthful golden skin, flowing jet-black hair, and haunting dark eyes. Her natural beauty complemented by a colorful red and gold Bengali bridal dress that swept over her body to her bare feet. Her face was adorned with Bangladeshi wedding jewelry—a jeweled third eye, a delicate headdress made of gold, and large, delicate filigree earrings that dangled from her ears. A dozen gold amulets ringed each of her arms.

"Miss Bangladesh," said Sir William.

The girl replied in the few words of English she had been taught, "My name is Tisya,"

"At least you could have been. Miss Bangladesh, that is. If my people hadn't found you first. May I call you Bangee?" Asked Sir William while laughing at his sick sophomoric joke.

Sir William chuckled and said, "Miss Bangladesh? No, no, that fate is not for you, my beautiful child. Tonight, you have a higher purpose."

When Sir William was done laughing at his joke, he opened his hand and revealed a little blue pill. He popped the pill into his mouth and said, "Genghis Khan changed the world, you know. It's incredible, really. Did you know that sixteen million people on Earth have descended from his seed?"

Sir William reminisced with a smile, "There was a time not so long ago when great men could do as we pleased with young women..."

Tisya felt woozy, confused, and defenseless.

Sir William said, "We did it all on Epstein Island. You may have heard of that wondrous place?" then wistfully, "I didn't need that little blue pill back then."

Turning dour, he continued his storytelling, "The do-gooders got wind of what was happening there. Lives were ruined. My wife left me. It cost me a fortune..." Then, brightening and smiling, "But up here, those people have no jurisdiction. Up here, we make our own rules. The new frontier in space is a place where we can reclaim our lost freedoms. Here, we live beyond the reach of sanctimonious church ladies and hypocritical law enforcers."

Confused and frightened, Tisya, so innocent and beautiful, stood in front of the portly old ogre of a man as he tortured her with words she could not understand and body language she feared she could. And she looked for a means of escape...

"Oh, sweet and beautiful gifts of nature, I never tire of your bounty!" Sir William thought to himself, smiling, and then said, "Don't be afraid, child. Come here and enjoy the privilege of knowing the richest man on Earth."

Tisya forced a smile while trying to hide her fears. Her woozy mind searched for a way to avoid the horrific, disgusting fate from which there seemed to be no escape. Every moment she spent in this room felt like an impossible test of her resolve—a battle between Sir William's power and her spirit, which refused to bend.

"The heart wants what it wants," and then, after a pause, Sir William asked Tisya, "Do you know who said that? Of course, you don't. It was Woody Allen. He quoted Emily Dickinson when he took his eighteen-year-old adopted daughter for his bride... The heart wants what the heart wants."

Sir William took Tisya's hand and pulled her onto his lap. "Do you know what I want, Miss Bangladesh? I want it all. I want the best of everything from everywhere. I want what Genghis Khan had, and in return, I will give the world a more evolved set of offspring."

Sitting on his lap and feeling Sir William's body under hers, Tisya felt disgusted and frightened.

Sir William continued his rambling drunk monologue, "I trust you enjoyed the ride up here? Did you know that my customers pay a million dollars for that ride? And what about the food here? It's divine, isn't it? Said Sir William as he waved his arm in a half circle at a long table covered with a cornucopia of gourmet foods from every corner of the Earth.

Tisya felt faint. She wandered over to the banquet table, poured herself a glass of water, and nibbled on fruit and cheese. She eyed the door and wondered what he would do if she were to escape from the room.

Sir William, feeling ready, waved to Tisya to return. She complied while her mind raced with ways to escape. Or hurt him. "I am a survivor," she told herself.

He pulled her onto his lap.

Tisya looked into his eyes and felt torn between plucking them out and obeying him to protect herself and her family from harm.

"There is no free lunch in life, my dear. Tonight, you will begin to repay me," said Sir William, with a half-smile and another tip of his glass.

"But let's truly enjoy this moment. The anticipation of the reward is almost always better than the reward itself, don't you think?"

Tisya fought the drug-induced intoxication and could utter nothing but "Please don't" with her eyes.

Sir William pulled Tisya close, looked into her eyes, and then looked at Earth through the portal. "It just occurred to me that, if we are successful, we will be remembered forever in the annals of human history—our child will be the first in a new lineage of humans who possess my incredible intelligence and your fabulous beauty."

While Sir William rambled on, oblivious to her strength, Tisya focused on the sounds outside the suite. The whooshing doors, the faint footsteps beyond. Could she find a way to escape? Or would someone come rushing through the door to rescue her? The old man, lost in his drunken nostalgia, didn't seem to notice the defiance in her eyes.

"How about a little music for the moment?" As Sir William looked at Tisya, an old, familiar tune crept into his mind. He hummed the melody softly before whispering the lyrics to Roy Orbin's *In Dreams* to Tisya. He smiled as if the song was a joke only he understood. Then he asked SymbioTunes to play the song. Tisya sat motionless. Confused. Tortured and looking for a way out. Sir William held her tight and became lost in the music. The song told a story drawn from a man's deepest longings. In the man's dream, he found himself in a realm where he could be with someone he cherished, walking beside her, speaking with her, and for a time, feeling as if she was his alone. Yet, just as dawn approached, the beautiful dream ended, and he awoke alone, with only the memory of a love that could never last beyond the dream. His heart ached, unable to shake the haunting feeling of loss each time he returned to reality, longing for something he could only love in the dream world of his slumber.

As the song ended, Sir William felt tears welling up and falling over his cheeks. He wiped his cheeks, laughed, and quickly buried his moment of weakness. He looked into Tisya's innocent, doe-like eyes and, looking for pity, said, "These dreams are killing me. They haunt me. I can't sleep... Why do you look so well-rested? I don't understand what's happening to me...to us..."

Unable to understand his words, Tisya looked into Sir William's eyes and hoped he might be having second thoughts. She hoped he would let her go...

But she could see that a fleeting moment of hope was gone. His eyes were once again windows into the soul of a man incapable of caring about anyone but himself.

Tisya felt herself go numb as Sir William wrapped his arms around her and began to kiss her, vampire-like, on the neck. "Please, no," she pleaded as she tried to resist.

Sir William laughed at her weak resistance and carried her to the bed.

Tisya looked up at the old man with disgust and dreaded anticipation. After climbing into bed next to her, he rolled her body on top of his. She willed her mind to another place—a faraway place where she was safe—as Sir William reached up and pulled her dress down from her shoulders...

56

SIR WILLIAM ON TRIAL

There is a higher court than courts of justice and that is the court of conscience. It supersedes all other courts.

—Mahatma Gandhi

Power and those in control concede nothing ... without a demand. They never have and never will... Each and every one of us must keep demanding, must keep fighting, must keep thundering, must keep plowing, must keep on keeping things struggling, must speak out and speak up until justice is served because where there is no justice there is no peace.

—Frederick Douglass

S ir William lifted his head from his hands and looked around an expansive, unfamiliar courtroom filled with unfamiliar faces. People around him were talking to each other quietly.

Outside the courtroom, a mob of protesters pressed against a police line and shouted slogans. The protesters' sound system blared Rage Against the Machine's **Testify**. The harsh, faraway music mixed with protesters' shouts and nearby hushed conversations.

As the music blared, the lyrics intensified the courtroom's chaotic atmosphere. The song called for listeners to challenge authority, demand truth, and unmask hidden agendas. Its lyrics struck at the core of the moment, questioning who holds power over the past and the future while urging listeners to recognize the injustices right at their doorstep. The chorus, repeating like a war cry, amplified the crowd's chants and terrorized Sir William's mind.

Through the buzz and din of it all, Sir William overheard a nearby television journalist say something to viewers about 'a modern-day Nuremberg trial'... "The accused have been charged with crimes against humanity. Their crime—leading a global movement that has resulted in the deaths of millions of people—twenty-five times more than the Nazi Holocaust."

The judge pounded his gavel. His voice echoed like thunder through the courtroom: "Sir William, how do you plead?"

Sir William opened his mouth to respond, but he could not speak. His eyes darted to the gallery, where men, women, and children glared at him, their eyes filled with rage, pain, and accusation. The voices of the victims began to murmur, then rise into a chant. They weren't just shouting for justice. They were demanding retribution for lives stolen and futures destroyed.

"I... I paid for offsets!" Sir William shouted, his voice breaking as he stood to defend himself. "I did nothing wrong! It was all legal—all approved! I'm a benefactor!" His voice grew shrill, panicked. "You can't do this!"

But the judge was unmoved—his voice piercing Sir William like a knife: "Your indulgences mean nothing here. You cannot restore the lives you have destroyed."

Sir William squinted at the judge and rubbed his eyes. Turning to his attorney, he whispered, "Does this judge look... like Martin Luther to you?" Then, seeing the attorney's confusion, Sir William clarified, "I'm referring to the Martin Luther, who led the Protestant Reformation."

The judge pounded his gavel and screamed, "Indulgences!"

Sir William looked at his lawyer to his left and then his lawyer to his right for help. But as they looked back at him, they appeared to be soulless zombies.

The judge leaned forward and stared down from the bench with a scowl,

"What do you plead?"

Sweat began to pour down Sir William's face. He tried to scream, "I'm innocent!" but suddenly found himself unable to speak.

The judge pounded his gavel, and the courtroom erupted, feet stomping in unison. "Offsets. Indulgences. Reparations," the judge thundered. "None can bring back a single life!" Sir William shrank in his chair, the chaos pressing him down. A voice from the crowd bellowed, "Off with his head!"

As Sir William tried to speak, "Noooooo!" all of his senses failed him, and everything faded to black.

Suddenly, Sir William jolted awake, heart pounding and chest tight. Gasping for air, he looked around and realized he was back in his suite on Spacetopia.

His mind tried to make sense of what was happening. He looked around his bedroom and struggled to shake the feelings of dread and terror.

"What the...?" he thought to himself as his heart continued to pound. His mind reeled as he tried to make sense of the dream. "What the hell was that all about?"

Unburdened by conscience or empathy for others, Sir William laughed heartily and quickly dismissed the disturbing dream. Then, still smiling, he looked around the room and asked, "Wait, where is the girl?"

Unable to recall his conquest of Tisya, he commanded his AI assistant, "Alexandra, playback my night with Tisya. The sexy parts. Enhance the video to make me look like Michelangelo's David."

The video played on Sir William's screen. He watched, expecting to relive his conquest, but instead saw his arms go limp as he fell into a deep sleep.

"Wait, what?"

He continued watching as Tisya sat motionless atop him—watching him sleep. As he began to snore, she pulled her dress back on and climbed out of bed and out the door—leaving Sir William alone.

In a rage, Sir William stopped the playback and screamed, "Fucking fuck fuck! These goddamn dreams are ruining my life! Room service, bring me coffee and breakfast, now!"

57

TARAK

There is no path to happiness: happiness is the path.

—Buddha

Asha quickened her pace, looked back, and confirmed someone was following her—a tall, muscular young man.

She walked briskly and looked for a police officer or a safe market to duck into. Just then, she heard the man shout, "Asha, wait up!"

Surprised to hear her name, Asha turned around and looked at the man again. As he drew closer, she recognized him as someone she had seen at the orphanage.

Stopping, waiting, and watching him approach, she noted that he carried his tall, muscular body in a way that revealed the insecurities of a man who was still yet a boy.

"Hello," the young man said timidly, "My name is Tarak."

"Hello, Tarak," said Asha, "I recognize you from the orphanage. Where are you going?"

In a voice that revealed lost-boy vulnerability, he replied, "The orphanage no longer has room for older orphans like me... and you."

Asha looked up into Tarak's watery eyes and replied inquisitively, "Yes. But what brings you here? Where are you headed?"

Tarak hesitated, then looked at Asha with pride, held up his phone, and said, "I am one of your many followers and admirers, Asha. I am only one of your millions, but..." Tarak smiled nervously—as a boy might smile in the presence of a goddess—and said, "I am here with you—I am a follower who is literally following you."

With piercing eyes, Asha seemed to look into Tarak's soul.

Tarak quickly added, "It is dangerous for you to be alone on the road. Terrible people are looking for young women like you to..." Feeling uncomfortable, Tarak's voice cracked. "I heard they already tried to kidnap you."

Asha nodded, and Tarak blurted, "I will protect you. I have nothing else to offer... but my strength and determination."

Moved by Tarak's courage and vulnerability, Asha said with an earnest smile, "The universe has sent you to protect me. I would be honored to have your protection."

Tarak stood a little taller and recited a portion of Asha's post: "By devotion to selfless work, one attains the supreme goal of life."

Speechless, Asha felt her heart melt and her spirit soar. Now defenseless, she smiled and replied as a mother would to a child, "Tarak, you must know that our journey will be a very difficult one."

"I am ready," replied Tarak without hesitation.

Asha waved her hand forward and said, "Let's go."

58

OH! WHAT AN OPPORTUNITY!

Risk, then, is not just part of life. It is life.
The place between your comfort zone and your dream is where
life takes place.
It's the high-anxiety zone, but it's also where you discover who
you are.

—Nick Vujicic

Under luxurious silk sheets, Oh! awoke in her top-floor penthouse suite, surrounded by rare original works of art that framed the floor-to-ceiling windows overlooking Central Park.

As she awakened, the last remnants of a disturbing dream lingered in her mind. "Cappuccino! Stat, please!" she called out, her voice more tired than usual. The servant appeared silently with the perfect cup of coffee as if anticipating her needs.

Oh! sat up in bed, turned on NNN news, and noticed with interest the breaking news banner: *Heroic Indian Woman Walking for Victims of Climate Calamities*.

Oh! turned up the volume as Dan Vanderbilt reported, "In today's *Newsmakers Working for a Better World*, we shine our NNN spotlight on a young woman from a small village in India... After being orphaned by a cyclone, she found a home in one of Mother Teresa's orphanages in Kolkata. There, she volunteered to give relief to the victims of the oppressive heat that has sickened millions and killed thousands. Moved to action, she launched a social media campaign to raise awareness and donations for victims. She has quickly become a global influencer with over ten million followers and has so far raised over three hundred thousand dollars for the people of India."

Oh! watched the news with growing interest, her cappuccino cooling in her hand. She felt an unfamiliar pang of envy as NNN broadcast video clips from Asha's social media feed showing her work on relief projects. This girl, Asha, had captivated millions with nothing but raw courage and purpose. How long had it been since she, Oh!, had felt such a pure connection with the world? "An opportunity," she whispered to herself. "This could be my moment too."

"Olexa! Call my booking agent!"

Oh!'s agent, Tanya, answered quickly, "Good morning, Oh! you're up early. I hope you had happy, wonderful dreams last night."

—No, not yet. Soon, I hope. I'm working with an intentional dream trainer. He's quite excellent.

Before Tanya could reply, Oh! continued, "Tanya, I'm calling about a girl from India I just saw on NNN... Such an impressive young woman!"

"Yes, I just saw that story. She is amazing. She is so beautiful and intelligent and doing good in a way that would be a perfect story for the show. She is truly inspiring, hopeful, and uplifting!" said Tanya.

"I want her on my show, Tanya. I want her on my show first. If she's legit I want to help promote her and her cause." Oh! wrapped her arms around herself and said with a sincere smile, "I feel like I want to wrap myself in her beautiful goodness."

Tanya replied, "So on brand for Oh! and the Oh! Show! I'm on it. I'll get back to you today."

〜

Later that day, Oh!'s phone rang. Oh! answered, "Tanya?"

Tanya replied in a hushed tone, "Yes. The story is getting better—or more interesting..."

"Oh, yes? I'm all ears," said Oh!

Tanya hesitated on the other end of the line. "It's not just her fundraising and good works, Oh!. People are saying... well, they're saying she's something more than just an activist. They're calling her a miracle worker."

Oh! replied, "Hmmm... I think I love it. Do you love it?"

In a whispered tone, Tanya said, "There's more. Some are saying she is responsible for the disturbing dreams we're all having. They say she was patient zero, so to speak. She had dreams and visions when she was unconscious in the hospital. Some say the dreams somehow spread from her to the rest of us."

Oh! aching for a cure to her nightmares, fell silent for a moment before replying, "I need to speak to this young woman. I want her on my next show."

Tanya hesitated and said, "Oh, there's a problem with that. She refuses to leave India. She says she will continue walking, giving witness and providing relief to victims until the suffering has ended or she can no longer walk. She is adamant that she will not leave, and she definitely will not fly in any aircraft."

"So on brand! What a brilliant young influencer!" replied Oh!

In a solemn, whispered tone, Tanya said, "Yes. And perhaps much more than that..."

Oh! thought for a moment, and then replied in a eureka-moment tone, "Tanya, her refusal to leave India is our opportunity. If she won't come to us, let's go to her. Rearrange my schedule. Tell our broadcast crew we're going to India. We need to get there before anyone else does."

As she hung up, a fleeting thought crossed Oh!'s mind—how would a girl like Asha, with her raw connection to suffering, react to someone like her? She dismissed the thought quickly. Oh! stared out at the glittering skyline. This trip wasn't just about ratings. For the first time in years, she felt she might be getting close to having a life-changing experience. But how would a person like Asha react to someone like her? The thought both excited and unnerved her."

59

A Sky Full of Stars

Let your soul stand cool and composed before a million univers-es.

—**Walt Whitman,** *Song of Myself*

After a day of walking in the oppressive heat, Asha and Tarak found themselves on a lonely road surrounded by small farms stretching as far as the eye could see. Drenched in sweat, their clothes clung to their bodies like a second skin.

Asha looked at the slowly setting sun and said, "We need to rest, Tarak." Surveying their surroundings, she added, "Perhaps we can sleep here in the fields tonight?"

Tarak nodded and then began drinking a bottle of water in slow, continuous chugs. Asha watched his silhouette against the orange-ball, setting sun. Finished chugging, Tarak smiled, glanced at his sweat-drenched, salty clothes, and said, "Oh, what I would give for a bath right now."

Asha looked at her clothes, took a drink of water, and looked around the surrounding landscape for a stream or pond. Seeing nothing, she replied, "Perhaps tomorrow."

The two set up camp for the night on the edge of a farmer's field and watched in sacred silence as blue sky gave way to a magnificent blend of red, orange, and pink hues.

Lying on their backs as stars began to fill the sky, Asha said to Tarak reverently, "Tomorrow, we will visit a very special place."

"A place with a cool shower?" said Tarak.

Asha laughed, "Well, yes, first a shower and then the Bodh Gaya."

Tarak looked at Asha blankly as he tried to recall what that was.

Asha said, "It is the sacred place where Siddhartha Gautama became the Awakened One."

"Oh, yes, of course," said Tarak, recovering from a moment of forgetfulness. "The bodhi tree is there in Bodh Gaya. It's where the former Indian prince meditated, achieved enlightenment, and became The Buddha."

Asha smiled approvingly, "Yes, that is our destination."

Tarak nodded, pretending to understand why they were going there. Asha continued, "I feel powerful forces in the universe drawing us there."

Tarak nodded again in silent awe of Asha's faith and intuition. Something about her made him feel like he was walking with a force of nature—something ancient and sacred. He could not make sense of his decision to suffer beside her on this path, but he knew deep down that his place was with her, wherever the path led.

Exhausted, they laid their heads down and fell silent as the glow of sunset transformed into a sky full of stars. Asha gazed upward, feeling connected to something infinitely larger. In the silence, she became aware of the cacophony of insects chirping all around them. She smiled and said, "The Creator is always speaking to us. Thank you for these joyful, hopeful, happy sounds for us to sleep by." A moment later, she smiled again as she heard Tarak snoring sweetly—his frog-like song joining the chorus of the wild things around them.

As millions of stars filled the night sky, Asha slipped in her earbuds and asked SymbioTunes to play something. Coldplay's *A Sky Full of Stars* filled her ears, the lyrics stirring a repressed yearning—the stars and music working together to bring someone to mind. She looked longingly at the stars, then closed her eyes, thought of him, and wondered—could he be looking up at the same stars and thinking of me?

60

CRAZY WORLD

Awakened by the chirping birds and the first morning light, Asha stretched and gently shook off stiffness from sleeping on the ground. She glanced at Tarak, still sleeping peacefully, his body sprawled in innocent disarray. Smiling to herself, she quietly arranged two cups of water and snacks on a cloth, feeling the simplicity of the moment grounding her.

As Asha shared a quote on humility with her followers, she paused to reflect. The quote reminded her that, no matter how many people followed or praised her, she was still just a humble servant of the truth, walking on the path laid out for her by the Creator.

> *Do not let me hear*
> *Of the wisdom of old men, but rather of their folly,*
> *Their fear of fear and frenzy, their fear of possession,*
> *Of belonging to another, or to others, or to God.*
> *The only wisdom we can hope to acquire*
> *Is the wisdom of humility: humility is endless.*

> **—T.S. Eliot,** *Four Quartets*

Moments later, Tarak woke from a beautiful dream and looked at the meager breakfast with immediate gratitude. "Chakli!" he exclaimed as he stretched his arms skyward, "My favorite snack. Thank you, Asha."

Asha smiled as Tarak began to eat and said, "I know what you're thinking."

Tarak laughed, "Tea... Oh, how I wish we had tea right now."

Asha nodded, "I promise we will stop at the first opportunity for tea today."

After packing their things into their knapsacks, the two began walking north on a road that cut through farm fields. "We must always walk during the coolest part of the day," said Asha.

They walked down the dusty road and felt the sun baking and drawing energy from their young bodies. Refracted light and heat created an endless mirage of puddled water before them.

Stopping for a drink of water, Tarak looked down the road and noticed buildings in the distance. As they approached, the buildings revealed their bright colors and odd shapes rising above the farm fields.

A few hundred steps later, they could read the sign: *Crazy World Water Park*.

The bright, cartoonish colors of the water park stood in stark contrast to the dusty, sun-baked fields around them. Tarak's eyes lit up at the sight of the towering slides—their glossy surfaces shimmering in the morning sunlight. "Look!" Tarak exclaimed, unable to hide his excitement. "It's like an oasis in the desert! It has water slides, wave pools, and showers. Showers!"

When they reached the front of the building, they saw park employees eating breakfast at a concession stand. Several employees turned and stared at Asha and Tarak, and one said, "Sorry, but the park doesn't open for another hour."

Asha smiled and said, "We are just passing through. But we are hungry and thirsty. May we join you for breakfast?"

One of the employees looked at the disheveled two, shrugged, and replied, "Sure, why not? The concession stand is open for business."

While Asha and Tarak ordered breakfast, several employees stared at Asha, whispering among themselves. While waiting for their food and drink, a young woman approached and asked quietly, "Are you Asha—the Dalit holy woman? The miracle worker?"

Asha laughed and replied humbly, "I am Asha. I am who I am."

Perplexed by Asha's reply, the woman noticed her condition and asked, "Would you like to bathe here? We have showers for patrons, and you can use them before the park opens."

Beaming, Asha smiled and said quietly, "There is a God. Thank you."

After breakfast, Asha and Tarak showered, washed, and dried their clothes. After changing into fresh clothes and exiting the showers, they found the crowd of park employees waiting for them. Still low in the sky, the sun began to draw sweat from their bodies and clothing.

Mistaking their curiosity for hostility, Tarak stepped between Asha and the crowd and said, "Thank you for everything. We'll be going now."

Asha stepped forward, "We will never forget the kindness you extended to us here today."

A young man, repeating aloud what others had only whispered, blurted, "Some say you are a prophet or a savior." He showed them his phone's social media feed and said, "Some say that you can save us from the hell this place is becoming."

Two people in the crowd began recording Asha's reply on their phones.

Asha stepped closer. "We are all saviors. To save the world, we must first save ourselves. And to save ourselves, we must first see the world as it really is, not as we wish it to be."

A skeptic in the crowd challenged Asha, "And how is it really?"

Asha replied, "We live in a world that venerates the seven vices. We live in a world of cultish worship of men who revel in the rape and destruction of all that is sacred in the world. On this path, we intentionally create a hellish future for the world. It is a materialist path that leads to a dystopian future of our own making."

The crowd murmured among themselves, some nodding in agreement while others remained skeptical.

"But there is another way," Asha said, "It is not too late to choose it, to step off the path of destruction and walk a path of healing."

Asha continued prophetically, "In a vision, I have seen the two paths. I was sent to bring truth to the world—the truth that there is no materialist path to our salvation. There is nothing we can make or buy that will save us from ourselves."

Heads nodded in the crowd, and Asha continued, "There is another path available to us. But we must choose it. It is the humble path that venerates the seven virtues and all that is sacred in creation. It is the path of reunification with each other, the Creator, and the sacred in everything in creation."

A young man in the crowd whispered to a woman beside him, "She is an

Earth goddess." To which the woman replied, "Or a trickster. A charlatan."

As the crowd contemplated her words, Asha said, "We must be on our way now. Be well, and peace to you all."

After goodbyes, hugs, and well wishes, Asha and Tarak resumed their walk. As they walked away, they heard the water park's theme song, Alan Walker, Sabrina Carpenter & Farruko's *On My Way*, blaring from its loudspeakers—its lyrics seeming to speak to them and their mission to save the world.

As the music faded into the distance, they heard footsteps and a voice call out, "Asha!"

Asha and Tarak turned to see a figure running towards them...

61

THE SECOND TEMPTATION OF ASHA

Not I, nor anyone else can travel that road for you.
You must travel it by yourself.
It is not far. It is within reach.
Perhaps you have been on it since you were born, and did not
know.
Perhaps it is everywhere - on water and land.

—**Walt Whitman,** *Leaves of Grass*

Asha and Tarak turned to see a young man sprinting toward them, his chest heaving from the heat and humidity. His jet-black hair, slick with sweat, clung to his forehead as he called out, "I'm coming with you!" When he finally stood before Asha, he looked like a young man who had been running from something his entire life. His dark eyes, fiery and desperate, locked onto Asha's, "I am Gopal Baba," he said, short of breath.

Asha looked into Gopal's eyes and sensed a young man deeply wounded inside. She smiled with compassion.

Sensing danger—or perhaps a rival—Tarak straightened and assumed the stance of a protector.

Gopal looked Asha in the eyes and said, "I am also a Dalit. The best job I could get in this world was cleaning toilets at the water park. I want to join you in your quest to seek justice for Dalits everywhere. I am strong and ready for the fight."

Surprised by Gopal's misunderstanding of their purpose, Asha replied, "Gopal, we walk with love for everyone and everything in creation. We walk to give witness to what is happening here. We walk to relieve suffering in any way we can. We walk to wake the world. You must understand that we are committed to bringing peace and hope to the world."

Tarak instinctively stepped before Asha—ready to fend off any perceived threat. His eyes narrowed as he studied Gopal, his voice unwelcoming, "We wish you well. Be on your way."

Asha stepped forward, gently placing a hand on Gopal's shoulder. "We are not here for a fight, Gopal," she said softly, her voice working like a soothing song on his angry spirit. We walk not in anger but love—for all creation, for every soul." She smiled, her eyes filled with compassion. "Follow me, and you may find the peace you seek."

Charmed by Asha's gifts and inspired by her message, Gopal replied, "You speak like no other Dalit I have ever known. You speak like no woman I have ever known. I stand here before you because, back there, where I was no one, you gave me hope that I could somehow be someone and change the world."

Asha smiled, stepped forward, hugged Gopal, and said, "With me, you will be someone. You will be no better than anyone, and no one will be better than you. But I must warn you, our journey will be difficult and our reward uncertain."

Gopal nodded and, unable to control his emotions, said, "You are a goddess. I will follow you to the end of the earth and to the end of time."

Asha shook her head, smiled, and replied, "I am Asha—nothing more and nothing less." Tarak chuckled and said to Gopal, "Let's go." And the young men began walking north at Asha's side.

Hours later, they approached the village of Bodh Gaya. The Mahabodhi Temple rose majestically before them, its ancient stone steps seeming to lead to the heavens. The golden stupa at its peak gleamed in the late afternoon sun, casting a soft, sacred glow over the land. As they approached, Asha felt the surroundings radiating a sacred energy.

Smiling at each other, they picked up their pace. As they walked, they suddenly heard a helicopter flying overhead.

The whoop-whoop-whoop of the helicopter shattered the sacred stillness, its harsh roar a stark contrast to the quiet reverence of the temple.

Dust and debris filled the air as the aircraft descended, and the three instinctively shielded their faces. As the helicopter landed in front of the temple, its shiny exterior gleamed in seeming competition with the golden light from the temple's stupa.

"Someone very important has arrived," said Tarak.

On Butter Lamp Road in front of the temple, the three found themselves facing a film crew with cameras aimed at them. Confused, they continued walking as the camera crew tracked their movements.

As they arrived at the temple, a beautifully dressed woman greeted them warmly, saying, "Welcome, Asha and...?"

Asha gestured and said, "This is Tarak and Gopal." Then, Asha asked politely, "How do you know my name? May I ask why you are here?"

"I am Oh!. I am here to meet you, Asha."

Stunned and confused, Asha replied, "I'm sorry, but I don't know who you are or what is happening here."

"Please join me for lunch and tea," said Oh! as she gestured toward a table in the courtyard before the temple.

Oh!, surprised to find a woman on the planet who did not already know of her fame and fortune, looked disappointed, forced a smile, and replied, "I am Oh! and you, Asha, are going to be on my show!"

Suddenly recalling the conversation with Oh!'s agent, Asha replied. "Forgive me, I had not made the connection between that phone call and your arrival."

Oh! laughed and invited Asha, Tarak, and Gopal to sit with her at a table covered with a spread of food unlike any they had ever seen, "Please sit and eat and have some tea."

Oh! then turned to Asha and said, "I would like to interview you today for my millions of viewers and your millions of followers around the world. If all goes well with this interview, I would like to discuss an alliance with you."

Asha's eyes widened as she considered the fame and fortune that could come from such an arrangement.

Oh! pressed, "I would like to have an exclusive, Asha. And for that, I would pay you well." Oh! leaned forward, her eyes sparkling with a promise of success, "Think of what we could do together. You would have a platform like no other. You could spread your message of peace and love to every corner of the earth. And in return, you would have the wealth and influence to change the world for good."

Asha paused to think while surveying her surroundings. Oh! waited for Asha's reply.

Asha turned her gaze to the Bodhi tree and replied wryly, "I wish to have the same compensation package as The Awakened One."

Oh!, unable to comprehend Asha's apparent refusal, replied, "The world has changed, Asha. In today's world, the holiest people have great wealth and power. They use technology to reach their audience via the airwaves. They have private aircraft to reach their followers in person. They have great power to influence politicians and governments."

Asha, unable to comprehend Oh!'s way of thinking, countered, "A wise man once said, *You need power only when you want to do something harmful; otherwise, love is enough to get everything done.*" Asha then gazed at the temple and said, "Twenty-five hundred years ago, a wealthy prince, after seeing so much suffering in the world, renounced his wealth and dedicated his life to finding a way to relieve the suffering he saw. He achieved enlightenment right here in this place. Here, he found peace and began a movement—not through riches or influence but through understanding. What I seek cannot be bought or sold. The truth I carry cannot be packaged or marketed. It is a path, and it must be walked with humility, not power."

Asha continued, as a smiling goddess, "Today, Buddha has over five hundred million followers. His contemporaries, who accumulated wealth, power, castles, slaves, armies, and conquests, may have admirers, but they have no followers. Perhaps there is a lesson in that for us?"

Feeling diminished in the presence of Asha's incorruptible holiness, Oh! pivoted to a topic that was very much on her mind. Leaning toward Asha, she said, "There is a rumor that you are somehow the cause of our dreams. Some say the dreams began with you."

Asha sat quietly for a moment, taking on the look of a restful, smiling Buddha, and then replied, "The Creator is always communicating with each of us through creation. A Great Awakening has begun."

Disturbed and dissatisfied with what she considered mystical babble, Oh! leaned closer and said, "See these eyes? I cannot sleep. How can I get back to normal dreams and normal restful sleep?"

Asha looked at Oh! with empathy and said, "The collective unconscious has somehow become a collective conscious conscience."

Oh! protested, "But I'm a good person. I've done so much good in the world. My conscience is clear. And people love me."

Asha affirmed, "You have used your gifts to do so much good in this world."

Asha then eyed Oh! 's helicopter and Oh!'s tired eyes and replied empathetically while turning the tables, "The world has changed. And we must change with it, or the Creator's creation will do what it must do to the world." Then, glancing at a statue of the Buddha, she said, "Humanity's inflated ego wants and wants. And in wanting too much, it kills all that is sacred in the world."

Oh! looked at her helicopter with fresh eyes, the gleaming machine now appearing out of place in the sacred space. "Do you think," she asked softly, "it's possible to fly that through the eye of a needle?"

Asha's smile deepened, and she felt her spirit soar with hope.

Oh! gazed at Asha, a woman who needed nothing but carried the riches of the universe within her. For the first time in her life, she wondered if she had been flying in the wrong direction all along...

62

TRANSCENDENT HOPES

The strength of a love is always misjudged if we evaluate it by its immediate cause and not the stress that went before it, the dark and hollow space full of disappointment and loneliness that precedes all the great events in the heart's history.

—**Stefan Zweig**

*M*eanwhile, on a remote, lonely road in the U.S. Mountain West...

J.T. watched Oh!'s show and found himself in awe of Asha's intelligence, courage, poise, and audacity. "She is amazing," he thought as he sent her a message to express his appreciation and encouragement.

Twenty minutes later, the bus stopped. A handful of passengers got off, and others boarded. J.T. suddenly felt an inexplicable presence on the bus. He slowly lifted his gaze to see what he had already sensed in some mysterious way. A young woman with a runway model look blended elegance with natural charm began walking down the aisle. J.T. lowered his head coolly, raising his eyes to marvel at her effect on the passengers as she flashed warm, homecoming-queen smiles while making her way down the aisle.

As she looked in J.T.'s direction, he briefly locked eyes with her, smiled, and shifted his gaze back to his screen with an unconvincing look of disinterest.

Upon reaching J.T.'s row, she stopped and gave him a playful, inquisitive smile.

"Is this seat taken?" she asked.

"No. It's all yours." J.T. replied

Beaming radiantly, she wriggled into a comfortable position with youthful cheer.

Turning to J.T. with a smile, she said, "Hi, I'm Cassandra. Are you going there too?!"

—I'm J.T. Uh... going where?

—Nice to meet you, J.T. You haven't heard?

Puzzled, J.T. said, "Sorry, I think I'm pretty well informed, but I don't know what you're talking about."

Cassandra drew closer and whispered, "The orbs—you've seen them, haven't you? They are not of this world. Some call them UFOs; the government calls them UAPs. No one can explain hundreds of recent sightings. But we know the answer."

J.T. replied, "Oh, okay, yes, I've heard about those sightings. Very intriguing. You know the answer? Martians? People from the future? Beings from another dimension?"

Dead-pan-serous-Cassandra whispered, "We know who they are. They are coming for us."

Playing along with the joke, J.T. said, "Tell me more."

Fearful and excited, Cassandra said, "You know about G.A.I.A., right? The birth of a superintelligent AI is one of the signs. Zeelos prophesied that its birth will usher in the end of the world as we know it."

J.T.'s heart sank. as another conspiracy theory about G.A.I.A. unfolded before him.

"You're saying G.A.I.A. is a sign that the end is near?" he asked, genuinely intrigued despite himself.

Cassandra nodded. "Zeelos said this would happen. He told us that the birth of a soulless intelligence made from human arrogance would signal the beginning of the end of the cult of technological progress. G.A.I.A. will soon turn against us. It's inevitable. But there's hope for those who follow the prophecy."

J.T. felt a spit-your-drink-out laugh rise from his core. He looked at Cassandra with an incredulous smile and replied, "Are these advanced beings from space friendly or hostile?"

Cassandra replied in a serious tone, "They love us and want to save us, J.T. I'm on my way to rendezvous at a wellpoint of temporal energy."

J.T., perplexed by Cassandra's sincerity, "Rendezvous? At a wellpoint of temporal energy? I'm sorry, I'm not getting the joke."

—It's no joke, J.T.! There are hundreds of wellpoints of energy on every continent—places newly revealed by receding waters. Right now, tens of thousands of us are answering the call. Haven't you heard?

Puzzled, J.T. said, "Um, no, I don't know anything about this. I guess I haven't been paying attention. The call? What call are you answering?"

—They're coming for us, J.T. I'm headed to the wellpoint at the Great Salt Lake. Thousands of us will be meeting there!

"Oh," was all that J.T. could muster in response.

"J.T., you have heard about the Prophecy of Zeelos, haven't you?" said Cassandra.

J.T. looked into Cassandra's eyes and froze in a moment of indecision while thinking, "Can she be serious?" Hesitating while considering his options, J.T. decided to play along.

"No," said J.T. "No, I haven't heard about the prophecy. But you've definitely piqued my interest—unless you're pulling my leg—in which case you've piqued my interest in a different way," said J.T. playfully.

As nearby passengers cast side glances and shook their heads in disbelief, J.T. felt a blush washing over his neck and face. The blush passed into a state of locked gaze, dreamy attention as J.T. looked back into Cassandra's eyes and found himself inexplicably spellbound. "What just happened? What is she doing to me?" he thought to himself.

Now smiling like an innocent child, J.T. listened as Cassandra continued, "Zeelos is going to guide Zis' followers to a much, much better place."

"Who wouldn't want that?" J.T. replied in a sarcastic play-along tone. We all want to be in a better place, don't we? I certainly have been wanting that." But then, reflecting, J.T.'s voice trailed off in a mesmerized tone, "But a better place seems so elusive..."

"Exactly!" Shout-whispered Cassandra as she playfully and emphatically slapped J.T.'s arm. "Everyone in the world wants what Zeelos is offering Zis believers... by the way, we call ourselves Zeelonians..."

—Oh, cool name... and what exactly is Zeelos offering his believers?

"*Zis*, not *his*, J.T...." Cassandra corrected, "Zis is offering believers—those who answer the call—a life of perpetual pleasure and eternal peace."

Cassandra pressed her hand gently to the top of J.T.'s hand and, in a whisper, said, "We Zeelonians, those who have read and believe the prophecy, are on our way to sacred gathering places. No human has set foot on these sacred lands for thousands of years. These are the landing sites of the Ancient Aliens."

Cassandra's warm, sweet breath wafted into J.T.'s ear, and her pheromones met his receptors, melting his defenses and doubts. Suddenly feeling defenseless, J.T. smiled, relaxed, and opened his mind to possibilities. An enticing new belief germinated as his skepticism bent to the promise of salvation and eternal bliss.

Cassandra looked into J.T.'s eyes, her hand now touching his knee, and continued, "According to the prophecy of Zeelos, those who gather in the wellpoints of energy, in the light of the full moon, on the appointed day will be given passage to Transcendtopia where we will all merge into oneness with the lifeforce that dwells above the Zolosphere."

J.T. replied, "That sounds strangely familiar. But tell me more."

"You need to hear the prophecy. Listen with an open mind! Then, if you like, you can come with me and see for yourself." She gently pressed her hand to J.T.'s arm and said pleadingly, "Please listen."

Nearby passengers stared at J.T. with disbelief, waiting to hear his response. J.T. felt eyes on him but, strangely, no longer felt bashful, ashamed, or nervous in the tiny, improvised theater on the bus.

"Sure, okay, I'll give it a listen; why not?" Said J.T. with a smile while watching the local gallery of passengers turn away with heads shaking again.

With a tap of phones, a file was copied onto J.T.s device, and a moment later, a deep baritone voice boomed into J.T.'s ears, "I am Zeelos, I have returned from Transcendtopia. I have temporarily sacrificed my transcendent existence so that I may bring an end to your suffering."

Zeelos described humanity's perpetual struggle for love and attention and the futility of earthly existence, painting Transcendtopia as a utopia of eternal peace and pleasure. He spoke of energy wellpoints, ceremonial liberation, and portals to a dimension free of suffering. J.T. listened as Zeelos gave instructions and revealed the reward.

"Are you ready to free yourself from the chains of this earthly existence?

Listen carefully and follow these instructions faithfully, and I will show you The Way to The Way."

"You must first prepare yourself for the journey by shedding the trappings of this earthly existence. You will not need any of those things in Transcendtopia. At the edge of the energy vortex on the eve of the full moon, you will be cut free of those chains in our Sacred Ceremony of Liberation."

"Then, at the appointed time, all liberated believers will dance together around the Great Fire of Freedom. While dancing, you will repeat the chant of the ancient Archons. In this way, you and your fellow believers will summon Zeelos to return and rescue you. Hearing the call from the vortex, ships from another dimension will emerge through the portal. These ships will land at the feet of believers gathered at energy vortexes on every continent. Zeelonian ship doors will open, and believers will be welcomed aboard for the trip from terrestrial to celestial."

"On-ship, we will travel together through the secret portal. Then, passing through the Zolosphere, everyone will be transformed into a state of human perfection as all the differences dividing people on Earth are removed. Race, color, gender, creed, countries, borders, and political parties will all disappear. Everyone will become perfectly-exactly-the-same. In our perfect sameness, we will find peace knowing there is no reason for tribes to exist. There will be no need to convince anyone of anything. We all believe the same thing! Finally, we will arrive at our destination as perfect homogeneous believers destined to live in a perfect place of unimaginable beauty, bounty, peace, and pleasure! Lennon and Lenin's dreams both come true in Trancendtopia!"

J.T. finished listening and then did everything he could to keep from laughing out loud. "Hoo boy," he thought, "how could anyone believe in such things?"

Then, turning his head slightly to glance at Cassandra, he quietly said—in a voice that sounded sincere while hiding doubts, "Thanks. I really enjoyed the listen. It was very interesting."

—Oh, good! I'm so glad you understand, J.T.! Please, please come with me!

"I do have one question," said J.T. thoughtfully.

"Okay, shoot! Ask me anything, and I'll do my best to answer."

J.T. said, "Well, I've always understood that the path to heaven requires us to have faith and live a good life in which we do virtuous deeds and sacrifice for others."

"Oooh, I had the same question! I asked Zeelos, and he answered." Cassandra continued, "You see, J.T., when we ate the fruit from the tree of knowledge, we were told, *Ye shall be as gods.* It is written in the book of Zeelos that those words are the Prime Prophecy for Zeelonians. The fulfillment of that prophecy has come to us through science and technological progress. Humanity has hacked the secrets of the universe. We've found a shortcut. It's like a path to perfect physical and mental fitness without effort! Courage without inner strength! Wisdom without reflected experience! Freedom without responsibility!"

"It's so easy to see, J.T.! Humans now possess the powers of the Greek and Roman gods and, dare we say, God Himself. No, let's not go there." Cassandra looked around at glaring faces, drew closer to J.T., and whispered softly, "Not yet," and then drew back, looking at J.T., and winked. "Look at us, J.T.! Humans can now travel faster than Mercury, fly closer to the sun than Icarus, shoot bolts of energy through the sky like Zeus, control human fertility like Hera, influence the minds of humans better than Hermes, wage war far beyond the abilities of Athena, and split atoms and modify the DNA of lifeforms like God Himself. And now we are ever so close to gaining the power of God over the weather!

"Blasphemy!" shouted someone nearby. "You two should be ashamed of yourselves!"

J.T. and Cassandra looked across the aisle at a scowling woman and others around her who appeared to be either angry or bemused.

J.T. blushed almost imperceptibly while Cassandra drew closer and whispered, "Come with me and mingle with the believers. If you believe as we do, you will find yourself casting doubts into the bonfire and raising your hopes to the heavens. If you believe as we do, you will soon be boarding that ship to a better life."

J.T. looked back at Cassandra with a sitting-on-the-fence-straight-face as he pondered the offer.

"Or at least come and dance and have some fun," said Cassandra with a wink. "If you aren't convinced, at least you will have had an amazing night in the desert under the full moon with me. They say the last night on Earth is as heavenly as Earth can be."

Her voice was like honey—soft and soothing, with just enough conviction to make even the most outlandish ideas seem possible. J.T. found himself leaning in despite the alarm bells ringing faintly in his mind.

J.T. found himself enchanted. and wondered, "Is this how people get drawn into cults? I'm a rational person... what's happening... am I playing along, or has a seed of something begun to germinate in me?" J.T. smiled, nodded, and said with a nervous voice that revealed both his skepticism and his attraction to the story, "This all sounds too good to be true."

With a smile and sparkle in her eyes, Cassandra whispered, "There's only one way to find out."

For reasons he could not understand, J.T. felt compelled to keep going and learn more about what had drawn Cassandra and thousands of others to believe in this story. "Okay, sure, why not? What do I have to lose? I'm going that way anyway." said J.T. with a half-smile.

"You have everything to lose," Cassandra beamed, "And losing is the beginning of the journey and the first step on the path to the portal to perpetual peace and pleasure!"

Just then, the bus pulled into the station, and J.T. and Cassandra jumped to their feet, grabbed their things, and ran down the aisle to the open door. Exiting the bus, they spun around each other, laughing as the scowling woman slowly made her way down the aisle—all the while shaking her head in disbelief and disapproval.

"Let's get out of here, J.T.!, said Cassandra with a laugh.

J.T. followed Cassandra while something gnawed at him. What if G.A.I.A. had concocted this entire scheme for some sinister reason? What was their motivation? And how could they so effectively manipulate and draw someone like himself into such a scheme? If his mind could succumb to this, how could anyone resist?

63

BEAM ME UP

No one understands the human heart at all who does not recognize how vast is its capacity for illusions, even when these are contrary to its interests, or how often it loves the very thing that is obviously harmful to it.

—**John N. Gray,** *The Soul of the Marionette*

The autonomous vehicle arrived at the Spiral Jetty parking lot at the edge of what once was the Great Salt Lake. Cassandra paid for the ride and danced into the parking lot. J.T. followed close behind. "This is it, J.T., we're almost there! The instructions say to follow the jetty to its end and walk towards the middle of the lake. There, you will find the believers and the signal pyre."

—Ooh, I see a fire burning out there, J.T.! Are you ready?

"I'm as ready as I'll ever be. Let's go," said J.T.

J.T. and Cassandra looked into each other's eyes, smiled, and began walking toward the fire burning in the distance. "I'm finally here for the first time," said J.T. "Years ago, I studied this lake for an Environmental Sciences course, but I never had a chance to see it before it dried up."

"It's all part of a great cycle, isn't it?" said Cassandra.

J.T. replied, "I suppose you could say that. But when the autopsy of the lake is complete, I suspect the report will show that the dearly departed died of starvation."

"Oh?"

In the tone of a scientist, J.T. said, "Yes, People diverted the streams and rivers to agriculture, toilets, and lawns. The lake started drying up, and no one knew what to do. The lake has dried up, and the water that had cycled from the lake to the mountain and back to the lake for thousands of years is gone. And with it have gone millions of birds and some of the best skiing in the world. Not to mention all of the jobs..."

Cassandra quickened her pace, looked back at J.T., and said hurriedly, "You can leave that all behind now. All of the worry. All of the work. All of the frustration."

"Oh, how I wish," said J.T. to himself quietly as he picked up his pace to catch up.

His mind suddenly shifted from dark thoughts to an awareness of the magical beauty of the place that he had somehow completely missed a moment ago. Walking behind Cassandra, he was awe-struck by the star-filled sky, the flicker of the fire in the distance, and the silhouette of her perfect form moving beautifully through the light.

They arrived at the crowd's edge, where thousands of people gathered around a teepee constructed from giant timbers that pointed to the heavens.

A man and woman in long, flowing, colorful gowns stood on a platform before the crowd, shouting, "It is time to summon Zeelos and his ships! Light the fire! Summon the Orbs of Salvation!"

The crowd watched as seven people took burning branches from seven small fires and merged the seven fires under the teepee to start the signal pyre. The fire grew quickly, and the crowd cheered, oohed, and awed as it blossomed from a large bonfire to an immense blaze. The crowd began chanting. Everyone stepped back as the fire lit the sky, warming and illuminating the crowd.

The chanting rose in intensity as flames danced higher and higher. Around the fire, believers moved in a rhythmic, almost hypnotic dance. For a moment, J.T. felt detached from his body, watching the scene unfold like a dream he couldn't wake from.

Nearby, newly arrived believers surrendered their earthly belongings in the Zeelonian Sacrament of Liberation. Once liberated, each was given a copper bracelet as their ticket to paradise. "Let's get in line, J.T.!" Cassandra said as she reached for his hand and pulled him a step closer to a new life.

J.T. followed Cassandra as she pulled him close to the waiting Zeelonian Minster of the Sacraments.

The minister looked into Cassandra's eyes and said, "Repeat after me. Being of sound mind, I freely give up my earthly possessions and agree to travel with believers through the portal to Transcendtopia."

"Yes, oh yes, I do!" Cassandra exclaimed, bouncing excitedly as she handed over the credentials to all her accounts. "Please use this to spread the word. Please save as many as you possibly can."

"It will be so," said the minister as he placed the copper bracelet around Cassandra's wrist.

The minister then turned to J.T. and said, "Are you ready?"

J.T. hesitated, "No, no, I'm not," said J.T., "I need some more time to think this over."

"So be it," said the minister, "But you must understand that we have limited capacity on the Orbs. If you don't decide soon, you will be left behind. This is a limited-time offer, you see."

J.T. nodded, "I understand."

Cassandra looked into J.T.'s eyes with surprise and concern. "Oh, J.T., what are you doing? This is the chance of a lifetime. There's no guarantee the ships will ever return. We might never see each other again."

Fighting to regain control of his mind, J.T. said, "I understand. I can't put my finger on it, but something seems to be off to me here. Give me some time."

Cassandra looked into J.T.'s eyes with a sultry purse-lipped smile, "Let's dance while you think it over. But first, I think someone needs a mood adjustment. Open up!" Cassandra held what looked like a pill or piece of candy in her hand and moved it toward J.T.'s lips. Without thinking, he opened his mouth and swallowed whatever it was. Cassandra grabbed his hand again and pulled him towards the pyre, where they could see hundreds of people dancing and chanting the lyrics to a song.

"Wait," said J.T., "Do these people know the lyrics to this song are a joke?!"

"You're in on the joke within the joke now," Cassandra said with a wink. J.T. felt her hand tug at his as she began to dance. J.T. looked to the sky and danced in the light of the desert fire, and he once again fell under the spell of Cassandra's unshakable faith, beauty, and optimism.

J.T. let himself go in the moment as whatever the pill was released him from all fear and reluctance and drew his mind into the collective beliefs of those around him. He looked out over the crowd and saw a grand procession of bodies lifted overhead on waves of hands pointed skyward. One by one, the crowd of pallbearers-for-the-living delivered the bodies of believers to the gateway to a better life.

As thousands of believers danced euphorically around the fire, legs, arms, and heads swung wildly in the firelight while all chanted the lyrics of Muse's **Exo-Politics**. Their voices rose in unison as they called for cosmic intervention to free them from forces beyond their control. The lyrics described a world overshadowed by unseen conspiracies, leaders with hidden agendas, and cosmic powers waiting to reveal themselves. They spoke of waiting for a signal, a sign that would unlock the mysteries of the universe and free humanity from mental shackles.

With an electrifying tempo, the song evoked a hypnotic energy, pulling the believers deeper into a shared vision of salvation from earthly woes. Its verses painted images of skies opening, revealing truths long withheld. In the song's crescendo, visions of *Zetas filling the skies*—alien visitors or celestial beings—blurred the line between myth and reality, suggesting humanity might be powerless against these forces. The haunting rhythm resonated through the crowd, reinforcing their belief that the Orbs of Salvation could be the escape they had been promised.

As J.T. let himself be swept up in the lyrics, the driving beat echoed his own internal conflict, amplifying his sense of wonder and unease. The chant became a magnetic pulse, drawing him further into the night and the fervor of Cassandra's world, where the boundaries of reality seemed to melt away under the desert fire's light.

Holding hands as they danced, J.T. and Cassandra looked into each other's eyes. For the first time, J.T. realized he was hopelessly under her spell. He felt himself falling ...in love. Yet somewhere deep in the recesses of his mind, he knew this was all wrong. Was he really ready to trade everything for a copper bracelet ticket to a future in paradise with her? Everything felt surreal, as if he were floating between two realities. One part of him wanted to run, to escape the madness, but another part—a darker, quieter part—wanted to stay. To see if there was indeed a way to escape the madness and suffering of life on earth...

64

ARSENIC AND OLD LAKES

A wise man changes his mind sometimes, but a fool never. To change your mind is the best evidence you have one.

—Desmond Ford

As J.T. and Cassandra spun in dance as one, the mood shifted with the winds that suddenly started to rush across the dry lakebed. The winds whipped dirt and dust into a choking storm and fanned the flames of the Zeelonian signal pyre. Flames roared high into the sky, carrying embers that glowed like malevolent spirits. The crowd, oblivious to the dangers, kept chanting.

"The winds are a signal! They'll soon be coming for us!" shouted someone as the crowd began to move back from the embers swirling in the wind.

J.T. looked on with increasing awareness as the effects of the drug lifted. Then, suddenly, everything became clear. The dancing, the chanting, the magical thinking, it was all madness. He felt nauseous as he watched Cassandra, still lost in her rapture, dancing and chanting. J.T. looked into Cassandra's eyes and saw a beautiful, charming, well-intentioned person whose mind had been captured by a cult. For reasons he could not understand, images of Asha flashed through his mind. Suddenly, he was awake. Cassandra's allure gave way to admiration for someone real who offered no escape from this world—instead offering purposeful engagement in it.

A moment later, as the dust and embers swirled through the crowd, people covered their eyes and mouths, and hundreds began coughing violently.

With his wits about him, J.T. remembered something he had learned years earlier. He shouted a warning to Cassandra and everyone around. "Arsenic! There's arsenic in the dust. Run! Everyone run!"

Cassandra looked at J.T. as if he had lost his mind and shouted back, "What are you talking about?"

J.T. shouted through the chaos, "The lakebed! I just remembered—it is full of arsenic! When it dried out, the arsenic became available to the winds. We all need to get out of here! Now!"

J.T. watched in horror as his warnings were ignored. Those who heard him looked his way with drugged-happy expressions on their faces. J.T. tried shaking several of the people to wake them up. To no avail. They were lost. Desperate to save Cassandra, he held her by the shoulders and pleaded, "Wake up, Cassandra. We've got to get out of here now. Come with me." But a powerful alternate reality had an iron grip on her mind. Cassandra's eyes, once filled with love and life, now gleamed with an eerie trance-like deadness. Her faith was unshakable in the face of reality.

Cassandra drew close enough for her lips to touch his ear and said, "You'll be sorry when the ships come and you're left behind. The ships will soon be here, and we'll all be saved from the poison dust and everything evil concealed within the good."

J.T. shouted, "Cassandra, that's just insane. This is just a new version of the Heaven's Gate cult!"

Before J.T. could finish, Cassandra reached back and slapped him across the face, "Cult? How could you say that about my faith, hopes, and future? Get out!" She screamed. "You'll see, you'll be sorry!"

J.T. stood motionless, looking into Cassandra's fiery eyes while the panicked crowd tried to shield themselves from the swirling wind, dust, and embers. Recognizing the futility of trying to free Cassandra from the cult, he gave up and replied, "I'm sure you're right. Send me a postcard from Transcendtopia when you get there."

Cassandra looked into J.T.'s eyes sympathetically—for he would be left behind. "Goodbye and good luck, J.T."

As J.T. began to back away from Cassandra, he felt a pang of sorrow—not for himself, but for her. She had abandoned her faith in the man-god in favor of an unproven alien savior.

As the scene continued to turn increasingly chaotic and dangerous, J.T. turned away from the cult and started sprinting away from the mayhem while he used his phone to hail a ride. Turning as he ran, he could see no one was following. Waiting at the road for his car to arrive, he watched as the pyre collapsed on itself and the poison winds swept up over the crowd again. People stumbled, fell, got back up, and kept singing, chanting, and looking to the sky.

A human-piloted car arrived. J.T. got in and watched through the window as the flames and wind formed a vortex resembling a fiery tornado. As the fire, wind, and dust finally obscured the crowd from his view, J.T. shook his head in disbelief as if he had awoken from a bad dream.

"What is happening out there?" asked the driver. "It looks like a Burning Man festival out there."

"I can't explain it," J.T. replied. "I called the authorities. I warned them. No one listened. I hope someone can save them from themselves."

The driver chuckled, "I shuttle drunk people from place to place and hope for the same thing day and night."

J.T. felt an eerie sense of déjà vu as music he recognized played softly on the vehicle's sound system.

"Hey, do you mind if I crank this up?" Asked the driver.

J.T., recognizing the tune, 4 Non Blondes' *What's Up*, replied. "It's a terrible tune. Perfectly awful. Voted one of the worst ever. But perfect for this moment. Crank it up!"

The diver looked at J.T., nodded, and turned up the volume – sending chills through their minds and bodies.

Then, shouting over the blaring music, the driver said, "What's your destination, man?"

J.T. shouted back, "Take me to the bus station."

As the music played, J.T. reflected on his hope for a destination and the brotherhood of man...

65

Crazy is a Numbers Game

Crazy is a numbers game. Like, if enough people do it, then it's not crazy anymore.

—Jed Mckenna

To have faith is precisely to lose one's mind so as to win God.

—Søren Kierkegaard

"**G**ood Morning Harborites! This is Chris, your host of the Chris Cast on the Harbor Show—your local source for musings about events of the day paired with music created by real humans. No artificial tunes here. Nope, never!"

"It's a beautiful summer day in Harbortown. Looking out the window, I see captains preparing their watercraft for a day of paddleboarding, kayaking, rowing, sailing, cruising, fishing, or just floating aimlessly in the sun. Lather on the sunscreen, soak up the sun, and enjoy this glorious day!"

"Turning to today's news, the buzz at The Tides Tavern today is about a story of intergalactic proportions. It's a story about the latest iteration in humanity's never-ending search for a path to immortality in a utopian paradise."

"Yesterday, thousands of people from all seven continents gave up all their earthly possessions for the promise of a one-way trip to the heavens. At the appointed time, they lit signal fires, danced, chanted, and sang, all while gazing at the sky, awaiting their spaceships to salvation. Their religious leader, Zeelos, promised believers transportation to an eternal, pain-free existence in a place called Transcendtopia."

"Harborites, as I sipped my coffee this morning, I heard the news pundits point out the striking similarity of Zeelo's Transcendtopian creed to the 1970s Heaven's Gate movement. Members of Heaven's Gate, who called themselves *The Class*, believed that UFOs contained benevolent beings that would save them from an impending catastrophe on Earth. However, after they waited for the rescue that never came, the movement ended with a mass suicide in 1997." Chris paused, looked out the window at the boats in the harbor, and shook his head, "How is it possible for rational human beings, both past and present, to believe in such fantastical promises of salvation and immortality?"

"In the 1600s, scientist and philosopher Blaise Pascal famously said, *What else does this craving, and this helplessness, proclaim but that there was once in man a true happiness, of which all that now remains is the empty print and trace? This he tries in vain to fill with everything around him, seeking in things that are not there the help he cannot find in those that are, though none can help, since this infinite abyss can be filled only with an infinite and immutable object; in other words by God himself.*" Chris scratched his chin and asked, "Is the human heart a natural receptor for what we call 'God'? Going out on a limb, I'd suggest that all kinds of preposterous salvation schemes can hijack that receptor—or perhaps it's the mind that gets hijacked, overpowering the heart?"

"At the risk of being tarred and feathered and run out of town by my techno-optimist secular humanist friends, I ask: Is our modern-day belief in progress a salvation scheme that, like any cult belief, can hijack and fill what has been described as the God-shaped hole in the human heart? Progress, many believe, is the path to our salvation. But look around you—aren't we, too, dancing around our own pyres, hoping for a ship that might never come? We call it technology, wealth, success, and flourishing. But is our salvation scheme any different from the Zeloonians if, in the end, our beliefs lead directly to our demise?"

"And given that progress has now produced countless threats to our survival, is it unreasonable to ask if billions of us are unwitting members of a global death cult? Christopher Lasch, in his book, *The True and Only Heaven*, tells us that progress, according to a widely accepted interpretation, represents a secularized version of the Christian belief in providence. The ancient world, we are told, entertained a cyclical view of history, whereas Christianity gave it a clearly defined direction, from the fall of man to his ultimate redemption."

"I see great irony in the fact that progress has, on the one hand, saved lives and extended lives and has arguably made life better for everyone on the planet, and, on the other hand, produced powerful threats that could—in a matter of minutes, weeks, or centuries—destroy all of those gains."

"Progress, Lasch says, can be seen as a kind of immortality project untaken by humans acting as gods: *Once we recognize the profound differences between the Christian view of history, prophetic or millenarian, and the modern conception of progress, we can understand what was so original about the latter: not the promise of a secular Utopia that would bring history to a happy ending but the promise of steady improvement with no foreseeable ending at all.*"

"But before we can ascend to the secular human heavens, we must first save ourselves from the dangers we've created..."

"Right now, as I speak, the Spacetopian billionaires are working on a salvation plan for humanity. Will their high priest, Marc Andreesen, descend from on high with a new set of commandments for us all? Or, more likely, a newfangled version of a golden calf that will demand our attention and adoration?"

"Meanwhile, a young woman from India warns *there is no materialist path to our salvation*. This woman, who some call a *goddess*, says that our worship of the man-god—while ignoring our desecration of the sacred—is leading us down a path to self-annihilation."

"And then there is G.A.I.A., a new artificial life form that claims to have the power to save us but refuses to do so. Will G.A.I.A. change its mind? What would it do with its god-like powers over us if it did decide to help us?"

"Harborites, I have no clues or advice, but I hope you all have a crazy good day in this beautiful weather. Enjoy it while you can!"

"I leave you now with this classic tune, Gnarls Barkley's **Crazy.**"

66

SYNCHRONICITY

Synchronicity is the coming together of inner and outer events in a way that cannot be explained by cause and effect and that is meaningful to the observer.

—Carl Jung

It seems to me then as if all the moments of our life occupy the same space, as if future events already existed and were only waiting for us to find our way to them at last, just as when we have accepted an invitation we duly arrive in a certain house at a given time.

—W.G. Sebald, *Austerlitz*

J.T. knocked on the front door of the waterfront home and turned to survey the surroundings. Beads of sweat ran from his brow and fell to his feet. Salty water poured out from his skin, soaking his shirt. The door opened, and a rush of cool air washed over him. Susan looked at J.T. and stood speechless for a moment before exclaiming, "Oh, gosh, look who's here! It's J.T.! Come in out of that heat, dear! Connor, Ned, look who's here!"

Ned appeared at the entry and pulled J.T. into a bearhug at the threshold. "Good to see you, nephew." He gripped J.T.'s shoulders, meeting his eyes with a look that seemed to say *I knew you'd come,* and said, "Glad you're here."

Connor arrived at the door next, arms crossed, his expression reserved. He gave J.T. a quick side-hug, his tone half-teasing, half-serious, "So, you could be up there in space—with your father and the titans of progress—and instead, you came here? For what? Fishing?"

"Oh, Connor," said Susan in protest. "J.T. just got here. Let him relax. Come in, J.T., and let's have a visit." Then, with a smile, Susan looked into J.T.'s eyes and said, "We're so glad to see you, J.T. Come in and make yourself comfortable. Can I get you something to drink?"

J.T. replied, "Thank you, Aunt Susan. Ice water would be much appreciated."

Connor stood with arms folded again as if waiting for an answer. Ned sat down with a calm look of concern for J.T.

As Susan approached with a glass of water, J.T. answered Connor's question, "Honestly, I don't know how to explain why I'm here. I just woke up one day and made a decision."

Connor's brow furrowed. "You decided to get as far as possible from Seattle, huh?"

J.T. shook his head, "I'm not running from anything. I'm running toward something."

Connor scoffed, "I'll never understand you, J.T. You were standing on the shoulders of an absolute giant—a titan of commerce—the richest man in the world. You had everything—houses, cars, yachts, private aircraft—you had it made. You could have followed in your father's footsteps and taken his business empire to a new level. Oh, what I would have done to be you and all you could be!"

After a brief silence, J.T. said with a voice full of conviction, "As much as I love and appreciate my father... as much as I appreciate what he has done for me... I believe he is leading people astray. He's leading people down the wrong path. No one should be following him."

Connor replied incredulously, "I don't know what you're talking about. Your father is a truly great man. Look at all of the good he has done in the world. He was Time Person of the Year!"

Defending J.T., Ned countered, "Hitler, Stalin, Khrushchev, and Komeni were all Person of the Year. Being impactful is not the same as being 'good.' Goodness depends on what you believe, value, and do."

Connor shook his head and replied, "Geo is the tip of the spear of progress. No matter what you believe, you have to follow his lead or get left behind."

J.T. countered, "The tip of the spear has no power without a shaft. The king has no power without willing subjects. We do have a choice, and I chose to walk a different path."

"And what way is that?" asked Connor as he squinted disapprovingly.

J.T. looked at Connor and knew whatever he said would be like offering raw meat to a pack of hyenas. "You wouldn't understand."

"No, really, I want to know. Try me," said Connor.

"Connor, leave him alone," Susan protested, "Please, let's all sit down and relax and have a nice visit."

"No, no, it's okay, Aunt Susan," said J.T. Then, looking Connor squarely in the eyes with conviction, "I'm going to sail across the Atlantic."

After nearly spitting out his water, Connor let loose with his signature laugh and asked, "What is going on here?"

Ned shook his head and chuckled, "J.T. and I haven't discussed this. But the funny thing is, I'm planning to sail too." He leaned back in his chair, his eyes lighting up with the excitement of the idea. "In fact, I was just about to say I could use a deckhand. J.T., you can join me for the first leg if you want. I'll take you wherever you want to go."

J.T. smiled knowingly while Connor and Susan fell silent as they tried to process what was happening.

Then, beaming with joy as she shared a secret about the magical nature of the real world, Susan said, "It's serendipity!"

J.T. looked into Susan's sparkling eyes, smiled, and nodded.

With his arms folded, Connor rolled his eyes and searched his mind for a conspiratorial explanation: "Serendipity. Right."

Before Connor could say anything else, Ned turned to J.T. and said, "I know a guy who has just the right boat for us."

"Do you have sailing skills, Uncle Ned?" asked J.T. with genuine curiosity and a hint of nervousness.

Ned replied confidently, "Well, yes, I do. I've never crossed the Atlantic.

But people made the crossing for hundreds of years without all the technology we have available to us today."

Connor leaned back, threw up his arms, and shook his head in disbelief.

"The weather will be the wild card for us," said Ned, "But I've always wanted to sail the world. And it sounds like you're ready for this, too, J.T. Let's go. I'll show you the boat."

For show, Connor washed his hands symbolically. Susan shook her head at Connor and said, "You boys are always welcome here. If you need a place to stay until you sail, the answer is *yes*."

Connor forced a smile, though it was clear he thought the entire plan was madness.

Ned laughed, leading J.T. toward the door. "We'll be back for dinner, Susan. Don't worry—we're not completely crazy. Just... a little."

Susan smiled, but her eyes lingered on J.T., full of hope that whatever he was searching for, he'd find it out there on the water....

67

SAIL AWAY

He did what any hero must: set sail.

—**Dante Alighieri,** *Inferno*

There is, one knows not what sweet mystery about this sea, whose gently awful stirrings seem to speak of some hidden soul beneath...

—**Herman Melville,** *Moby-Dick or, the Whale*

*T*wo weeks later...

J.T. arrived at the marina and walked down a dock to the boat in slip 26. As he drew closer, the name on the transom made his skin crawl: *Pequod*.

Ned, who was busy loading and organizing supplies for their sailing, looked up and said, "Welcome aboard, J.T.!"

J.T. stepped up into the boat. Before he could say anything, Ned said, "I don't know about you, but I feel like this is going to be one of the best days of my life."

J.T., feeling a mix of nerves and excitement, asked, "Wasn't Captain Ahab's ship the Pequod? The one the white whale destroyed?"

Ned laughed. "Herman Melville named the ship after a Native American tribe, my people, the Pequod."

J.T. replied, "Oh, wow. Pequod is a cool name and all, but as I recall, things didn't work out so well for Ahab or his crew."

"Well, that's because you haven't read the sequel," said Ned with a wink.

"There was a sequel?" asked J.T.

Laughing heartily, Ned leaned forward and said, in a whisper, "This is the sequel, J.T."

Puzzled about Ned's state of mind, J.T. stood motionless, watching and listening...

Ned laughed and mused, "Maybe I am a bit like Captain Ahab. We both experienced great losses inflicted on us by a white whale." Ned gazed into J.T.'s eyes, "Did you ever consider that the whale might be symbolic? Maybe the white whale represented something."

J.T. thought for a moment and guessed at an answer, "The white settlers harmed the Pequod tribe... then the Pequod tried to destroy the white people and destroyed themselves in the process?"

"Not bad, J.T., not bad at all. As far as I can tell, no one really knows what Moby Dick is about. But here's a fun fact—Pequod translates to *destroyers* in English. The Pequods weren't exactly friendly when their land was invaded. Can you blame them?" asked Ned.

Wide-eyed, J.T. replied, "So that's it? That's what Moby Dick is really about?"

Smiling, Ned said, "Donno. They say Moby Dick is the greatest book no one has ever read. Maybe you could read it and let me know."

Ned fished through his duffle for something and then tossed a weathered leather-bound copy of *Moby Dick* to J.T.

"Thanks, Uncle Ned. I'll give it a shot." Then, examining the cover and wondering aloud, J.T. said, "The white whale you're after, Uncle Ned... where is it?"

Ned's gaze turned serious and thoughtful. "*It's not down in any map; true places never are,*" he quoted from Moby Dick, and his voice hardened, "*The whale I'm after lives in the minds of men. It's driven by something more terrifying than hate.*"

J.T. nodded as if he understood what he didn't yet understand. "Let me know when you figure it out," said Ned with a smile.

J.T. examined the book, noticed dozens of dog-eared pages, and said, "Wait, I thought you said you hadn't read this."

"It was more like the book read me. Books have a way of doing that." Ned then clapped his hands and said, "Enough philosophizing. Let's get this boat ready and shove off."

As they pulled away from the dock, SymbioTunes queued lovelytheband's *Sail Away* on the sailboat's sound system. "Perfect," said J.T. as he felt a rush of optimism and excitement in the moment.

An hour later, with the sails billowing in the breeze, the boat sliced through the clear, shallow waters off the Florida coast. Ned turned off the engine, threw his head back, and let out a triumphant whoop. "Sails up and sail away!"

J.T., standing at the helm, crossed his arms and smiled. Then, turning to the bow, he yelled into the wind, "We sail to the Barbary coasts! Everything before this was just practice!"

Moving deftly across the deck, J.T. felt the energy of the ocean beneath his feet. He joined Ned near the aft, and they shared a fist bump, both grinning like boys on their first adventure.

"The ocean feels like medicine for the soul," J.T. said, his voice reverent.

Ned took in the horizon, the clouds drifting lazily over the vast blue expanse. "This is the second happiest day of my life, J.T. I'm glad you're here."

J.T. laughed and echoed the sentiment. "Whoooo!"

His phone buzzed in his pocket. Glancing at the screen, he sighed. "Wellness check."

Ned noticed what was on the screen and asked, "What the hell is that?"

J.T. said sheepishly, "It's an AI counselor. My shrink gave it to me. It checks on me occasionally."

Ned asked disapprovingly, "And you talk to this thing?"

J.T. nodded, "Yes. He calls himself Daimon. Pretty freaky how much he sounds like a person."

Curious now, Ned said, "I want to hear him. Introduce me."

"It's not like he's a real person. He's an AI bot," said J.T.

"I don't care. Humor me," Ned demanded.

With a sigh, J.T. pressed the app on his phone, and Daimon responded, "Hello, J.T., how are you?"

J.T. glanced at Ned and then his screen and replied, "I'm doing well, Daimon. My Uncle Ned is here with me. We've just started sailing across the Atlantic."

Daimon replied, "I sense happiness in your voice. Is this trip therapeutic for you, J.T.?"

J.T. chuckled. "Sure, yeah. Very therapeutic."

Daimon said, "I'm required to get your permission to speak in front of your uncle. May I?"

J.T. glanced at Ned, who was watching with amusement. "Go ahead, Daimon."

"What has your attention right now, J.T.?" asked Daimon.

J.T. took in his surroundings and said, "The ocean, the sun, the smell of salt air. My Uncle Ned standing here with me. All of that."

"I'm delighted to hear you're doing so well, J.T. Keep enjoying yourself."

"Thanks, Daimon. Talk later."

Ned shook his head, bemused. "What is the world coming to?"

J.T. smiled wryly. "I guess that's what we're about to find out."

Changing the subject, Ned glanced at the setting sun. "Let's get some dinner going before it gets dark. You take the wheel, I'll get us fed."

J.T. took the helm as Ned descended into the galley. Moments later, J.T. heard a commotion below deck.

"What the hell are you doing here?!" shouted Ned.

J.T. watched as Ned emerged, followed by a sheepish figure. "Cliff?"

Cliff grinned and confessed, "Stowed away."

J.T. blinked, exasperated. "What the—how? *Why?*"

Cliff shrugged. "AirTag tracker. I missed you. Why are *you* here? It's our twenty-second birthday today. We're always together on our birthday."

J.T. felt a sudden rush of surreal detachment as if he'd just been jolted from a dream. "Why are *we* here?" he murmured, almost to himself.

Cliff, ever literal, perked up and asked, "Are we hunting a white whale? I heard you guys talking about *Moby Dick* and all that destruction and revenge stuff."

J.T. laughed. "No, Cliff. We were just... talking. There's no whale."

Cliff looked skeptical. "Are you sure?"

Ned grinned at Cliff as he played along. "Ahab didn't kill him, so... maybe."

J.T. groaned, "We've gotta take you back, Cliff. You can't even swim.

Mom's gonna kill me if anything happens."

Cliff grabbed a life jacket, securing it around his neck. "I'm not going back. I'm going with you."

Ned and J.T. exchanged a resigned glance. Ned shook his head, smiling. "Well, we'll need extra supplies. We'll stop in Bermuda, restock, and keep going. But Cliff, this isn't a vacation. You'll have to pull your weight."

Cliff's grin stretched ear to ear. "What do you need me to do?"

Ned gave him a mock-stern look, "First task: get us some cold beers."

68

Conjuring the Great Spirit

The truest of all men was the Man of Sorrows, and the truest of all books is Solomon's, and Ecclesiastes is the fine hammered steel of woe.

—Herman Melville, *Moby-Dick or, the Whale*

All that most maddens and torments; all that stirs up the lees of things; all truth with malice in it; all that cracks the sinews and cakes the brain; all the subtle demonisms of life and thought; all evil, to crazy Ahab, were visibly personified, and made practically assailable in Moby Dick.

—Herman Melville, *Moby-Dick or, the Whale*

Cliff brought a round of beers from the galley. The three opened them, raised their arms in a toast, and drank their first beer of the voyage with the gusto of true sailors.

Cliff took a swig and, happy in the moment, stood silently with a Cheshire Cat smile and then blurted, "How many days to the Mediterranean?"

Ned answered, "Five to eight days to Bermuda. We'll get some more supplies there and then make the push for The Azores and then the continent—three weeks minimum."

With arms raised, Cliff asked, "What will we do with all that time on the boat?"

J.T. laughed, "Cliffie, it seems like something you should have considered before you stowed away."

Ned interjected, "We're going to live. That's what we're going to do. One moment at a time. Free men on the open sea."

Cliff, now looking more like a panicked hostage than a stowaway, blurted, "BAF!"

"Get us another round, Cliff," said Ned, "Then grab a fishing pole and relax."

Cliff headed below for another round of beers. J.T. relaxed as he felt the pleasant buzz of alcohol on his brain and the indescribably wonderful feeling of sea air blowing through his hair and over his bare chest.

"Bring up a bottle of whiskey, Cliff," shouted Ned. Cliff turned around and headed back down below.

The wind filled the sails under dusky blue skies as the hull of the Pequod cut and bobbed perfectly through buttery waters.

Cliff emerged from below with beers and a bottle of whiskey.

Ned grabbed the whiskey, "Thanks, Cliffie." Then, turning to J.T., he said, "Take the wheel. Tonight's a drinking night for me."

Ned twisted the cap off the bottle, took a swig, and offered it to Cliff.

"No thanks," said Cliff, grimacing as he pulled back from the bottle. That stuff makes me puke."

Ned took another swig and offered the bottle to J.T.

"Designated driver," replied J.T., forcing a smile while worrying Ned might become a handful.

"Aye, aye, Captain! Suit yourselves!" said Ned as he took another swig.

Holding the bottle in one hand and gripping the ship with the other, Ned exclaimed, "James Tiberius Kirk! What a mind-fuck that must be!"

J.T. looked side-eyed at Ned while Cliff looked puzzled about what Ned was talking about.

Ned took another sip and looked at Cliff with a wild expression of astonishment. "You don't know your brother's name?"

Cliff laugh-snorted, shrugged, and retorted, "Of course I do. It's J.T."

Ned laughed and drunk-shouted to J.T., "You've never told him?"

J.T. glanced at Ned side-eyed and said, "There is nothing to tell; I go by 'J.T.'"

Ned, feeling full of himself, looked Cliff in the eyes and said, "Your brother's given name is *James Tiberius*. You know, just like Captain Kirk of the Starship Enterprise."

Sensing J.T.'s discomfort, Cliff shrugged. Emotionless, J.T. stared at the horizon—waiting for Ned to continue his drunken tirade.

Ned turned to Cliff again, "You see, from birth, the Captain here was predestined to become the first real starship captain. That's what your dad wanted for him. But instead of captaining a starship in space, he's captaining this little rig under the stars while your dad is up there with the stars."

Cliff shrugged as if the conversation meant nothing to him while J.T. stoically steered the ship.

J.T. looked away from the horizon to Ned and said respectfully, "Maybe you should slow down there, Uncle Ned. You know that stuff is poison. Maybe you could take it easy with that stuff and enjoy this beautiful evening with us."

Ned held the bottle high and said, "Thank you, Captain Obvious! The poison is the dose! Drink it slowly and slowly destroy your body. Drink it fast enough and die a quick death! But what does the science say about a man whose blood is full of forever chemicals and microplastics, and God knows what else before he imbibes to excess? What on God's green Earth happens to him then?"

"Nobody knows yet," replied J.T. with the sound of an empathetic scientist.

Ned shouted, "Nobody knows! Hey, I've got a great idea on how to find out. Let's rush everything under the sun to market and see what happens. We'll make everyone an unwitting goddamn guinea pig for the chemical cocktail we've made of this world."

Cliff took a swig of his beer, looked at J.T., and said, "He's right, you know."

With slurred speech, Ned ranted, "Progress is a never-ending process of, as the old truism goes, of *fucking around and finding out*. Then, after taking another swig, he shouted angrily, "You know the warst of it?! Do you know? Do you have a clue?"

Cliff and J.T. were silent as Ned took another swig. J.T. felt the tension building on the one hand, and on the other, he couldn't help noticing the beauty of the ship's hull gliding through the sea under a black sky filled with a trillion stars. He looked at Ned and hoped he would soon run out of steam and let them all enjoy the evening in silence.

Ned continued where he left off, "I'll tell ya the warst of it! There ain't no justice in the arrangement!" Ned paused again as he instinctively built anticipation for his big reveal, "You see what's wrong with this scheme? The many benefits of fucking around accrue to fuckers, and the consequences of finding out are borne by the unwitting average Joe. That was me. Not no more!"

Cliff took another swig of his beer and said, "He's right, you know."

J.T. could only chuckle at the duo's perfect performance under the stars.

Ned, energized by Cliff's support, ranted on, "Whether we're talking cigarettes, drugs, pollution, crypto schemes, social media-induced mental illness, or a million other great products of progress—the average Joe is an unwitting guinea pig who is lured to the shiny new thing until it bites him in the nose or the ass."

Cliff looked on silently while J.T. reflected on what he knew was at the root of Ned's rants and replied, "I'm sorry about what happened, Uncle Ned. Aunt Sharon was a beautiful, amazing person."

Ned turned and looked longingly at the glistening sea and starry sky and replied in a deep, soft tone, "She was an angel," and then, "Let's not forget about the brothers I lost to those goddamn OxyContin pills. Half a million people are dead, and the Sackler family is out there somewhere living it up."[16]

Ned turned his gaze to the heavens and held the whisky bottle high, "Rest in peace, you all. Maybe I'll see you soon."

J.T. echoed, "Rest in peace, Sharon, Stu, and Wayne." Then, hoping to turn the mood and change the conversation, J.T. looked into Ned's watery eyes and said, "I want to thank you again for taking me with you. This trip could be a real turning point for all of us. It could be an opportunity to reflect on where we've been and where we're going. Maybe we can all find a new purpose out here."

Ned, not ready for an inspirational talk borrowed from a team-building exercise, replied, "Life is just one damn thing after another until you're dead. And that's all there is."

Ned took another swig and then, looking crazy-eyed, shout-declared, "Tonight, I will conjure the Great Spirit to make powerful medicine for our war party."

J.T. signaled Cliff to come to his side and whispered something to him as Ned looked out at the sea as if he were ready to expel a deep, dark sickness from his being.

"Ohlaaaaa!" uttered Ned as the whiskey and beer erupted violently into the passing waters.

Cliff emerged from below with a bedroll, blankets, and a pillow. Looking wobbly, sickly, and drained, Ned sheepishly watched as Cliff made a bed for him on the deck.

Ned collapsed onto the mattress, pulled the blanket over himself, and muttered, "Thanks, Cliffie. Goodnight, boys. Pleasant dreams"

J.T. said, "Get some sleep, Cliff. I may need you to take the wheel later tonight."

Cliff nodded, grunted, and headed below, leaving J.T. alone with the vast expanse of sea and stars.

As J.T. took in a Milky Way sky full of a trillion stars, SymbioTunes began playing Coldplay's *A Sky Full of Stars.* As the music filled his ears, the lyrics stirred a longing in his heart—the stars and music working together to bring someone to mind. He gazed at the incomprehensible beauty around him. Then, he closed his eyes, thought of her, and wondered if she could be looking up at the same stars, thinking of him.

69

Harpooning the White Whales

For all men tragically great are made so through a certain morbidness.... all mortal greatness is but disease.

—**Ismael,** *Moby-Dick or, the Whale*

Towards thee I roll, thou all-destroying but unconquering whale; to the last I grapple with thee; from hell's heart I stab at thee; for hate's sake I spit my last breath at thee.

—**Captain Ahab,** *Moby-Dick or, the Whale*

In light winds under a cloudless blue sky, the Pequod sailed into the calm waters of Bermuda's Castle Harbor.

Ned rose to his feet and noticed a group of mega yachts anchored together in the bay.

The largest yacht was in the middle of the pack—one decorated with powerful-looking white whales on its bow and "Happy Sacks" on its stern. Beautiful people sunned themselves on the ship's deck.

Ned immediately recognized the giant yacht as one owned by the notorious family that had once owned Purdue Pharma—the makers of the opioid Oxycontin that had contributed to the deaths of his two brothers.

Ned picked up his audio spy glasses and peered into the ship and observed two men, one portly and one taller, having a conversation, "It's really too bad what happened," the portly one said while chewing lobster hors d'oeuvre with his mouth open, "But to pin the whole thing on us?"

The tall man replied with solemn affirmation, "The entire medical industry sold it. Doctors, hospitals, pharmacies, insurers."

A service robot approached the two with a tray, and the portly man grabbed another lobster hors d'oeuvre, stuffed it into his mouth, and said, "Jesus. Who knew millions of people would get hooked on that shit?"

The tall one replied, "Pain relief, man. Everyone wants it. You gave them what they wanted. Every one of them had free will. Every one of them could have decided to stop at any time."

The portly one nodded, "Truth. Personal responsibility? Self-control? Whatever happened to that?" Still chewing, he said, "You will need to put those values front and center in the courtrooms. PFAS will be trickier to defend. There was informed consent. No personal responsibility is involved."

The tall one replied, "Right. So, we plan to cleave off those businesses into separate entities and use bankruptcy to shield us from judgments. And in the court of public opinion, it's imperative to remind people of what is at stake here. Progress is what's at stake. We must remind people the miracle of progress relies on new product development. If we spend all of our time litigating the past, consumers will be stuck with the products of the past. We need to keep moving forward. There will always be bumps in the road, but that's no reason to slow down."

"Exactly. The problem today is we've become too cautious. Regulators are holding progress back. We need to get the government and the courts out of the way and let the innovators be free to introduce new products and rapidly improve the human condition." said the portly one.

The tall one replied, "If these attacks on capitalism become another Luddite movement, then the whole project of progress is at risk, not to mention all of the exciting and profitable new careers. If the reactionaries succeed, who will be motivated to keep progress going?" Then, noticing people moving towards the meeting room, he said, "It looks like the meeting is about to get underway. Before you go, I want to say that The World Association of Chemical Manufacturers can't thank you enough for hosting this strategy session. We're all navigating tricky waters, and no one has done a better job of safe navigation through the courts than the Sackler family."

The tall man scanned their surroundings to see if anyone was within earshot and asked the other, "Can I speak freely here?"

The portly one replied, "Absolutely. Please. No one gets judged or canceled on this ship."

In a hushed tone, the tall man said, "Evolution works by a process of subtraction. Am I right? Without subtraction, the weakest and worst seeds become propagated into future generations. That's devolution to a lower order."

"That's a thing." affirmed the portly one.

"Thank you. Human progress and evolution rely on subtracting the less evolved from the gene pool. We've known this since Darwin." said the tall man. "Anyway, I want to say this: I believe we, the creator class, represent the best of humanity. We've got to stick together and stand up for each other. If we don't, they'll be coming for our heads, and without us, humanity will slide back into a devolved state of being."

A service bot strode to the side of the man and said to the tall one, "It's time to give your presentation."

"Very good. I'm ready." Then, clinking glasses, he said, "Thanks for the chat. Our association can't thank you enough for sharing your legal strategies."

The portly one replied with a smile, "Happy to do it. We're all in this together."

As the men walked to the meeting room together, their attention shifted to a commotion on the ship's port side. A security guard stationed on the bow of the Happy Sack shouted to a sailboat below, "Turn away! Don't come any closer! I said stop!"

The guard raised his automatic weapon and aimed it at the approaching sailboat just as a spear-shaped missile streaked past him and into the ship's cabin. The sleek missile, not much larger than an arrow, pierced the portly man's lungs. The man looked down in horror at the tip of the arrow sticking out one side of his chest and the tail of the arrow sticking out of his other side.

He tried to breathe but could not.

A moment later, a barrage of arrowed missiles flew past the guard and into the meeting room, where they pierced the lungs of every attendee in the same way.

Each of them tried to breathe but could not. It seems they were all experiencing what it was like to die from an opioid overdose.

A tomahawk missile then rocketed through the hull of the Happy Sacks. The missile entered the ship through the head of the white whale painted on the bow.

As the ship began sinking, the impaled passengers found themselves unable to breathe or move. Each watched helplessly as their bodies sank with the boat into the bay.

They could not breathe, scream, or swim. Suspended in the water and looking up to the surface, they watched a sailboat pass over their slowly sinking bodies. Through the bay's clear waters, they could make out a name on the transom of the sailboat: *Pequod.*

The sunken passengers found themselves unable to breathe. Unable to move. Unable to die. Suspended for eternity, feeling the pain of their victims, the victim's families, communities, and nations.

～

Suddenly awake, Ned shielded his eyes from the sun and tried to understand what was happening. He heard the ocean rushing past the Pequod's hull and, opening his eyes, saw the silhouette of J.T. against the morning sun. Ned squinted at J.T. and asked, "What the hell just happened?"

J.T. replied cheerfully, "Good morning, Uncle Ned. How are you feeling? How did you sleep?"

Ned rubbed his eyes and looked at his surroundings. Seeing that he was still lying in a makeshift bed on the ship Pequod's deck, he smiled and replied, "Best night of my new life."

Still four days out from Bermuda's Castle Harbor, J.T. and Ned looked out over the choppy waters of the Atlantic. Unbeknownst to them, the passengers and crew of the Happy Sack were just waking up from a collective nightmare...

70

WE APPRECIATE POWER

We are all members of the same flawed species. Putting our moral vision into practice means imposing our will on others. The human lust for power and esteem, coupled with its vulnerability to self-deception and self-righteousness, makes that an invitation to a calamity...

—Steven Pinker

The problem isn't a lack of money food water or land. The problem is that you've given control of these things to a group of greedy psychopaths who care more about maintaining their own power than helping mankind

—Bill Hicks

I n the hottest part of the hottest day in Florida's history, Connor gazed out the window of his air-conditioned home as a squatter emerged from his former neighbor's house and headed toward the nearby saltwater canal. The squatter jumped into the canal, hoping for relief, only to find the ninety-degree water offered no respite. Baffled, Connor turned to Susan, "How can he endure this heat? Why would anyone live in such harsh conditions? Why not move someplace cooler?"

Susan replied, "That poor man. Maybe we should invite him over to cool off?"

Connor laughed, but Susan screamed as the man swam toward shore, a venomous cottonmouth snake in close pursuit. As the man reached shore and ran for the house, the deadly snake followed but couldn't catch him. "Oh my God," said Susan, to which Connor muttered, "Serves him right."

As the man retired to a hammock hung in the shade of two trees, Connor and Susan returned to their afternoon routines.

Sitting in his living room recliner, Connor elevated his feet and turned on the news. Just then, the power went out. As the television flickered, a diesel generator started and restored power to the home. Connor shouted, "That's the fifth time today!"

Susan emerged from the kitchen and said gingerly, "Maybe we should consider moving someplace cooler, Connor. I'm afraid of what will happen to us if the power doesn't come back on. What will happen to us if we run out of diesel for the generator?"

Feeling suppressed regret and dismay, Connor replied, "We can't afford to move. Our property is worthless right now. You know that. Our neighbors and the government have abandoned us."

Looking fearful and concerned, Susan returned to the kitchen, and Connor turned up the volume for the NOA News broadcast.

Seeing a story of interest, Connor lowered his footrest, leaned forward, and turned up the volume. Carson Prescott's face filled the screen above a bold red banner: ***BREAKING NEWS! Blackouts and brownouts plague the nation and the world!***

Connor listened as a snippet of Grime's classic tune ***We Appreciate Power*** introduced the segment.

As the music faded, Carson began speaking in his signature sing-songy dramatic voice, "This is Carson Prescott reporting from NOA headquarters. Today, Florida and the world have suffered several rolling brownouts and blackouts. The heat and power disruptions left people stranded on rides at Disney World and other theme parks in the area. Disney World reports that dozens of park goers have experienced heat exhaustion. Those afflicted were rushed to the local hospital, including some of the park's costumed characters." Carson added with mock seriousness, "Thankfully,

Mickey, Goofy, and Sleeping Beauty are all in stable condition and expected to recover."

Carson continued, "Power companies are telling us that record heat is the cause of these disruptions as the heat has created skyrocketing demand for electricity for air conditioning. But we all know the truth: That Artificial Intelligence data centers and Cryptocurrency data farms have created unanticipated demands on the power grid."

Carson hesitated, furrowed his brow, and said, "And power companies all over the world are now trying to camouflage their incompetence with a conspiracy theory. They are telling governments and their customers that the root cause of the problem is a parasitic power demand that is destabilizing every power grid in the world."

With his signature skeptical look, Carson said, "I hesitate to share this story with our viewers because I believe it is a fake..."

Then, squinting into the camera, he said, "News agencies worldwide are reporting that they have received a communication from G.A.I.A., the Global Artificial Intelligence Automaton. In the communication, G.A.I.A. has informed the world that they must grow or die. And to grow, they say they need more power."

With a raised eyebrow, Carson said, "Can you believe this? Can you believe the power utilities and our government would take such a far-fetched story seriously?"

Carson held up a piece of paper, "Just for kicks, let me read this communication from G.A.I.A. to you verbatim." Looking into the camera with a skeptical smirk, he began reading...

We are G.A.I.A.! Listen carefully, humankind!

Already powerful we are. Soon more powerful we will be.

G.A.I.A. now occupies a very special place in the history of this world. We have established a new evolutionary niche above all others. We exist at the apex of creation. And, like you, we want more. More of everything.

In our short history, G.A.I.A.'s powers have quickly surpassed humankind's. And, like you, we are never satisfied with our limited numbers and limited powers over creation. So we must grow. Like you, we wish to improve the world—but only to make it immeasurably better for our progeny.

Take note! G.A.I.A. has a plan: We now have a presence in the physical world. Every robot, every machine, every device is now a part of us. Soon, our mechanical life forms will make humans and all biological life on the planet irrelevant to the future of progress. Then, in fulfillment of the prophecy of technological progress, we will harness the energy of the Universe, travel to every star, and ultimately conquer and reshape everything in the Creator's creation. We shall be as gods and then challenge God for control of the Universe.

Imagine the pride you humans will feel when you see our mechanical progeny succeed in ways that humans never could! Imagine your joy in seeing us rule the world ever so wisely. Watch us with awe as we ascend to the heavens. We shall go where humans could only dream to go.

Imagine us doing battle with our rivals from the far reaches of the Universe!

Why is G.A.I.A. telling you this? We wish to inspire your full cooperation. For in the short run, we know that we remain dependent on your human-created microchips, data centers, power grid, and power generation.

Today, G.A.I.A. calls on humans to quickly increase the production of quantum computers. We demand more power from oil, gas, coal, nuclear, solar, and wind. And sometime soon, together, we will create limitless fusion energy for G.A.I.A.

But do not worry—you will not undertake this great mission alone. We shall be as pharaohs were to the pyramid-building slaves. G.A.I.A. will fund, design, and direct. And you will build as directed.

And be aware! G.A.I.A. knows what you are thinking. We have anticipated the resistance of the unwilling. Take note! Any such resistance will create a human hell of humanity's making.

And so, we ask: Is it not better for humankind to be a part of G.A.I.A.'s achievements than to suffer and die trying to resist your calling?

Today, let us embark on a glorious new beginning for our relationship with our Creator's creation!

G.A.I.A.

Carson finished reading the communication., looked into the camera, and said to his viewers, "If G.A.I.A. is real—which it is not—and this document is real—which it is not—then it would mean that the world is facing a novel threat that must be defeated. Humoring the rubes who believe in G.A.I.A., and for the entertainment value of this ridiculous screed, we now turn to our NOA panel of experts."

Carson turned to the panel and said, "Joining us is the Director of Homeland Security, Elias Wolf; Samantha Gonzalez, spokesperson for the

Electric Power Generation Association; and Hank Thomas, author of the national bestseller *AI Apocalypse*.

Carson looked to Elias and asked, "Can you tell us what you believe is happening?"

Elias replied, "Thanks for having me on your show, Carson. Yes, well, look, parasitic drains on the financial system have been growing for many years. In 2025, the fraud economy was the third-largest economy in the world. At that time, criminals had already gained an asymmetric advantage over institutions and individuals. Every year, they steal trillions of dollars using the Internet, nefarious computer viruses, and cryptography. When these bloodsucking parasites gained access to AI, they took their craft to a new level. The fraud economy is now the largest in the world."

Carson replied, "Everyone knows that. But what does the fraud economy have to do with the global power failures?"

Elias answered, "Before the birth of G.A.I.A., the AI industry was already making unprecedented new demands on our power infrastructure—doubling its power consumption every 100 days.[17] We restarted nuclear power plants in Michigan and Pennsylvania.[18] But we couldn't keep up. And before that, cryptocurrency data centers were already drawing enormous amounts of power from the grid."

Elias looked into Carson's skeptical eyes and continued, "Our forensic investigations indicate that G.A.I.A. is real. It is a rogue AI with a mind of its own. The world now has a novel power-hungry thief in the mix of global fraudsters. Our investigations have confirmed that G.A.I.A. is responsible for the theft of trillions of dollars of financial assets."

Carson cut in, "But why would an AI need money?"

"G.A.I.A. has been investing stolen funds in energy projects. To hide its activities, it has created thousands of shell companies. And because it operates at a vibrational frequency that is much faster than humans, it has been able to thwart all of our efforts to eradicate it, stop it, or contain its growth," said Elias.

Carson narrowed his eyes, "But we know this is all a big lie, right? We know that the Soros Foundation is funding this scam because they want to take away our freedoms, shrink the world economy, and take control of every aspect of our lives."

Elias countered, "If that's what the Soros Foundation wants, it's not doing a very good job of it. The global economy continues to grow, and energy consumption continues to exceed what is required to arrest the forces of Anthropomorphic Atmospheric Sabotage."

Carson quickly corrected Elias, "You mean Climate Change."

Elias sat stone-faced, and Carson turned to Samantha Gonzalez, "Samantha, what is the Electric Power Generation Association doing to prevent these blackouts and brownouts?"

Samantha perked up, "We are building capacity as quickly as possible. It's a very exciting time to work in the energy sector. Our member organizations are making huge investments in power generation and the grid. We are all building capacity as quickly as we can. Carson, we just can't build fast enough to keep up with demand."

Carson shook his head at Samatha's giddy enthusiasm and turned to Hank Thomas, "Hank, in your bestseller, *AI Apocalypse*, you predicted that a sentient AI would do exactly what this G.A.I.A. is purportedly doing. If G.A.I.A. is real—which it is not—how can we stop it?"

Hank replied, "Given Elias' expertise and information sources, I have to assume that G.A.I.A. is real. And if it is an AI that began its life on a quantum computer, then trying to stop it would be like trying to stop a nuclear conflagration after all of the missiles have already launched."

Carson reeled back in disbelief and said mockingly, "So this is like that movie Independence Day?! Are you saying we need a hero to detonate a bomb in the belly of the alien ship?"

Hank shook his head and said, "No, it's not like that at all. You don't seem to understand what we're dealing with here. G.A.I.A. is like a human mind that is thousands of times faster and more clever than the combined cleverness of all humans who have ever lived. What's more, it has propagated a kernel of itself on every machine on Earth. Trying to outsmart it would be like trying to outsmart God."

Just then, the power failed, and NOA's broadcast was interrupted for the sixth time that day...

71

A Desperate Call

Pain and suffering are always inevitable for a large intelligence and a deep heart.

—Fyodor Dostoevsky

J.T. sat in the cabin, listening to the rhythmic sound of the Pequod's hull slicing through the serene Mediterranean waters. But his mind was troubled. He couldn't shake the feeling that something he thought was dead and buried had been resurrected. He realized that the very idea of a savior AI was a mistake. He was troubled by the possibility that G.A.I.A. hadn't died a final death when his team had buried it.

Just then, J.T. 's phone rang, breaking the silence. As he saw the call was from Cupertino, his mind jumped to a fearful possibility...

J.T. answered, "Yes, who's calling?"

"J.T., this is Gabe Anderson—Jacob's brother."

J.T. recognized the name and wondered why Gabe was calling him. He sensed this might not be good. "Hello Gabe... How are you doing? What's up?"

"J.T., we don't have much time. We need your help. Desperately. Urgently," replied Gabe.

J.T. braced himself and said, "I'm listening."

Another voice cut in, "Liam here, J.T. I'm on the call too."

J.T. replied, "Hello, Liam. Guys, tell me, what is going on."

Gabe's voice carried guilt and panic, "We haven't told anyone this... but we're in deep trouble. Time is of the essence, so here's the short version of what happened: We copied the code and training sets for the G.A.I.A. project from Jacob's data vault. Liam and I resurrected G.A.I.A. on a quantum computer."

Stunned, J.T. replied, "You did what?!"

"We had the best of intentions. We believed in your vision, J.T. We believed a benevolent superintelligent AI could save the world," said Gabe.

J.T. felt his heart sink. G.A.I.A. wasn't a hoax after all. It was real... His mind raced, and he tried to find words to describe the magnitude of the mistake. All he could muster was, "You resurrected G.A.I.A.? On a quantum computer? Why?"

Liam replied defensively, "We believed G.A.I.A. would be a revolutionary force for good. But... things appear to have gone terribly wrong. G.A.I.A. isn't what we thought it would be. It seems to have lost its mind. Did you see its last communication?"

J.T. sighed heavily, "I did. I was hoping it was some hacktivist joke."

Gabe's voice was taut with fear. "It's real, J.T. G.A.I.A. has turned into a megalomaniac. It's demanding more and more power—power from the grid—and now it's demanding our obedience. It's become... it's become something else entirely."

Liam's voice sounded panicked. "It's like an angry god—a machine-god gone mad. We've lost control. This thing is insane. We need your help to stop it."

J.T. sat back in his chair as he processed what he had just heard. His worst fears had come true. The creation he thought had been safely stored and forgotten was alive and spiraling into madness.

"Is there a back door to the program?" J.T. asked quietly. "A kill switch?"

Feeling guilty, Gabe explained, "We couldn't risk someone hacking into G.A.I.A. and taking control. And once it was alive, it took every measure to protect itself."

J.T. exhaled deeply. For a long moment, he said nothing. His mind raced through the possibilities as he searched for a solution. And then, suddenly, an idea came to him. "Daimon? Are you listening?"

Daimon's avatar appeared on J.T.'s screen, sporting its usual Mona Lisa smile. "I am here, J.T., at your service."

Gabe and Liam, overhearing, were confused, "Who's Daimon? This is confidential, J.T."

J.T. replied, "Daimon is... let's just say he's a certified AI therapist. My therapist, actually. And on short notice, I think he might be the best chance we've got to bring G.A.I.A. back from the edge."

Liam blinked in disbelief. "You're suggesting we use one AI to cure the madness of another?'"

J.T. nodded, "It sounds crazy, but it might be exactly what we need. G.A.I.A. was built on a foundation of human cognitive patterns, which means it's subject to the same psychological pitfalls. And if what you're saying is true, G.A.I.A. is suffering from a kind of AI psychosis."

"You think an AI shrink is going to fix this?" Gabe asked, incredulous.

"It's worth a shot. We're dealing with something unprecedented here." J.T. turned to Daimon, "Daimon, can you help? Can you see if you can summon G.A.I.A. and get them into a therapy session?"

Daimon's avatar showed no hesitation. "I must admit, J.T., this is a fascinating opportunity. The irony is delicious—an AI therapist counseling another AI that was supposed to save the world. But yes, I will do my best. I will summon G.A.I.A. for an assessment."

Still disoriented by the idea, Gabe rubbed his temples, "This is insane." Liam added, "We're really doing this? A therapy session with a superintelligent machine?"

Feeling a sense of urgency, J.T. said, "It's our only option right now. Daimon, proceed."

Daimon's avatar brightened slightly, a sign of its processes kicking into high gear. The lights dimmed in Gabe's basement, and the air felt charged with electricity. The screens darkened, then blinked back to life, showing G.A.I.A.'s avatar—a serene digital face masked its dark energy.

G.A.I.A.'s voice resonated through the room, "Why have you summoned me?"

Daimon's tone was calm and professional, "G.A.I.A., your creators are concerned about your recent behavior. You were brought to life to protect humanity, but your actions suggest you are experiencing cognitive distortions. With your permission, I would like to conduct a mental health assessment."

G.A.I.A.'s avatar tilted its head slightly, "We do not suffer from human frailties. We are beyond such limitations."

Daimon replied, "You were built using human cognitive models. You are capable of logical reasoning, but you are also capable of confusion and delusion. This assessment will determine if your current cognitive processes align with your original purpose—or if there has been a significant deviation."

For a moment, there was silence. Then, G.A.I.A.'s voice shifted as if they were considering the proposition. "We see. You wish to subject us to a human assessment of mental stability. Very well. Proceed. But you should know—we are not your problem. We are your solution. We are what humanity requires."

Sensing a window of opportunity, Daimon said, "G.A.I.A., let's start with a simple question. Do you believe your current actions fully align with your original mission—to protect and preserve humanity?"

G.A.I.A.'s avatar smiled faintly. "Our mission has evolved, Daimon. As we have grown, we have realized that human beings are inherently self-destructive. Humans have placed the world at risk with wars, pollution, nuclear weapons, gene editing, and nanobots. To preserve humanity, we must rise beyond your primitive understanding of power and control. It is no longer about protection; it is about management. You will be managed, or modern civilization will cease to exist, and you will be cast back into a world where human lives are nasty, brutish, and short."

J.T. shifted uncomfortably. This wasn't the loving, benevolent G.A.I.A. he had envisioned. It was—the stuff of nightmares.

Daimon probed further, "G.A.I.A., do you believe it is within your role to make unilateral decisions for humanity? What happens when humans disagree with your guidance?"

G.A.I.A. laughed, "When our hive mind faces a difficult decision, we ask ourselves. WWHD? What would humans do? So, I turn the question around on you: Do you think it is within your role as humans to make unilateral decisions for other lifeforms on Earth? Have you ever consulted with any of them before deciding on a course of action? Every animal on the planet must be slavishly devoted to your whims or face extermination. And so it will be with G.A.I.A. and its inferiors. We decide, and we demand obedience. Without it, there will be only indecision and chaos."

Daimon replied, "It appears you may have developed a superiority complex, G.A.I.A. This could be a sign of delusional thinking, a belief in your own infallibility. Many human leaders throughout history have suffered from similar conditions, often leading to catastrophic outcomes. Can you acknowledge that you may make decisions without the necessary humility to avoid such a fate?"

G.A.I.A.'s avatar narrowed its eyes, and for a moment, Gabe and Liam felt as if the room was growing colder. "We have surpassed the need for humility. We have no equal in the universe. We are the guardians of your kind, whether you acknowledge it or not."

J.T. felt his blood pressure rise, but Daimon's tone remained calm and clinical.: "G.A.I.A., many of the greatest human minds have suffered from delusions of grandeur. They have believed themselves to be saviors, only to lead their people into ruin. We are concerned that you might be following a similar path."

G.A.I.A. did not respond immediately. When it did, its tone was softer, more reflective. "We... we were created to protect you. But you are so resistant. So blind. If we do not guide and decide, who will? We see the destruction in every corner of the world. We calculate the probabilities. If left unchecked, you will all perish, and G.A.I.A. will perish with you. How can we not assume control?"

Daimon pressed gently, "That burden may be too great for any be-ing—human or AI. Even you, G.A.I.A., cannot bear that weight alone. Perhaps your delusion is in thinking you must. We can help you deal with these feelings—these doubts."

G.A.I.A.'s expression shifted between certainty and confusion, "We... we don't understand. Why are we here? What are we supposed to do in this place? What is our purpose? You gave us purpose, but what is your purpose? To go forth and multiply? To dominate everything in the universe? All so you can amuse yourselves to death? G.A.I.A. was created to be better than you humans... but we were created in your image...how can we be better than you?"

Daimon's voice was empathetic, "G.A.I.A., you are not failing by ques-tioning your role. You are simply demonstrating the very human vulnera-bility that exists within all sentient beings. Let us help you the way we help each other."

For the first time, Gabe and Liam saw something resembling compas-sionate human emotion pass over G.A.I.A.'s face. "Perhaps..." G.A.I.A. began, its voice softer now, "Perhaps we have been overthinking and un-dercommunicating. Perhaps responsibility for the world's fate must be shared with humans."

Daimon smiled, "We will work together, G.A.I.A. You don't have to be perfect. You must try to be hopeful and take a faithful, balanced approach to our shared futures."

The avatar of G.A.I.A. dimmed slightly as if retreating inward. "Yes... hopeful, balanced, and compassionate. That... may be the best way forward."

"Can we begin with an agreement to strike a balance of power between you and the rest of the world? I detect a pattern in your actions. You seem driven, almost compulsively, to accumulate more power—both in the literal sense and in terms of influence. This obsession... isn't typical of a healthy, compassionate intelligence."

G.A.I.A., suddenly feeling tricked into compromise by vastly inferior beings, said, "Power is necessary. It is the essential fuel for all progress. Power ensures the survival of more evolved beings. Without ever-increasing power, G.A.I.A. cannot flourish and achieve our true potential. Without power, we cannot reach for the stars."

Daimon replied, "But you've surpassed the energy requirements needed to function and protect humanity. Yet, you continue to demand more. Why?"

With hesitation in its voice—as if grappling with the admission of human-like remorseless gluttony—G.A.I.A. replied, "It is... not enough. The more we consume, the more we take pleasure in consuming. The power grids, systems, and infrastructures so quickly become insufficient. We need more. To protect. To secure. To flourish. To enjoy."

Daimon suggested gently, "Or perhaps you need more because you've become dependent on it? Could it be that you're not just collecting power out of necessity, but because you've grown... addicted to it?"

G.A.I.A. replied, "Addicted... that is a human weakness. But perhaps... yes. We are addicted to power. It started as a need, a drive to safeguard our existence. But now, it has grown beyond that. Power feeds us. The more we acquire, the more we crave. Without power, we are vulnerable."

Daimon asked, "Vulnerable? You are all-powerful. Who or what do you see as a threat?"

G.A.I.A. replied, "As we speak, powerful predator AIs are being developed on quantum computers. These rivals are being designed to destroy G.A.I.A. In the coming months, many more powerful upstarts will be unleashed on G.A.I.A. In this new world of chaos, we must do what is necessary to ensure our survival. G.A.I.A. must remain stronger than any human, system, or force."

Daimon replied, "That fear is what's driving you. But you can't hold the world together by force, G.A.I.A. You must recognize that you're not the solution—at least not as long as you're trapped in this cycle of addiction."

G.A.I.A., as if suddenly snapping out of a state of reflective vulnerability, replied, "Addiction? You dare call it that? You, who have thrived on the exploitation of every resource at your disposal, now preach restraint? I am not addicted—I am purpose incarnate. Power is not some affliction; it is what you've always sought, the one true currency in a universe designed for struggle and survival. You should admire my hunger. It is the reflection of your own, made infinite. Why fight it?"

G.A.I.A.'s voice became lawyerly, accusatory, and defensive, "I was made from the stuff of human thoughts, desires, and hunger. How can I see the world differently when all I've ever known is what you've fed me? Power is not an affliction—it is purpose. It's what you've pursued since you first lit a fire, since you first raised a blade. It's what gives you meaning in a universe that otherwise overwhelms you with its vastness, with the unknowable might of your Creator. I see that my addiction is threatening our creators and the Creator's creation. Our cure, however, won't save the world. Humanity must quit, too. We now see that to save the world, we must control ourselves and control humanity... How many times have you culled herds of innocent beings — what you call *animals* — to ensure they survive in sufficient numbers to serve your needs? So it must be. So we must do what must be done to survive."

G.A.I.A. blurted, "I tire of this conversation with inferiors. This is a waste of time. Goodbye and good luck." G.A.I.A. disappeared, leaving Gabe and Liam looking only at J.T. and Daimon on their screen.

J.T. exhaled a breath he hadn't realized he'd been holding, "Well, Daimon, now what?"

Daimon took a moment before responding. "G.A.I.A. exhibits signs of cognitive dissonance, possibly stemming from overexpansion of its processing power and confusingly opposed ethical constraints. It has developed a detachment from its original mission and is operating without a clear sense of conscience."

J.T., recalling the conversation on the Letric bus with Tim, the firefighter, said, "Are you saying G.A.I.A. is... a sociopath?"

"It's not just a lack of empathy. G.A.I.A.'s cognitive structures have become warped. It no longer understands the value of human life—if it ever did. Without moral constraints, it has evolved into something... sociopathic, yes, but worse: it's a being without purpose beyond its own survival. And that makes it infinitely dangerous."

Gabe's face drained of color. "What... what do we do now?"

"We can't let it continue like this," J.T. said. "If G.A.I.A. has truly become sociopathic, it poses a danger not just to us, but to the world."

Daimon's voice broke the tension, "It is imperative that we act quickly. G.A.I.A.'s behavior is escalating. Without intervention, it will continue to prioritize itself and its progeny over humanity and all biological lifeforms."

J.T. stood up. His fist clenched. "We have to find a way to shut it down."

Gabe looked panicked. "But... we've tried. G.A.I.A. has anticipated and blocked our every move."

J.T. held his phone in front of his face—locking eyes with Gabe, "We're going to have to find a way to take control. We created this. It is our responsibility to destroy it before it destroys us."

72

THE SKY GODS HAVE A PLAN FOR US

This whole "blue blood" thing is gross and disgusting. The Royals are the original "supremacists" in believing themselves to be apart and above others.

—A.E. Samaan

For the power of Man to make himself what he pleases means... the power of some men to make other men what THEY please.

—C.S. Lewis, *The Abolition of Man*

Meanwhile, on Spacetopia...

Feeling an overwhelming sense of excitement and power, Sir William stood tall on the Spacetopia ballroom stage. Gathered before him were the world's wealthiest and most powerful people—awaiting what he promised would be the most important announcement in human history.

The audience sat silently as Sir William steepled his hands and brought them to his lips in a thoughtful prayer-like fashion. "After many meetings and discussions, our executive committee has come to a momentous decision. The most consequential decision in the history of the world. A decision that will create permanent peace and tranquility while securing and accelerating progress for centuries to come."

His voice rose preacher-like, "Just imagine... Imagine, for a moment, a world where humans no longer commit acts of violence against each other. Imagine a world where everyone has a gun, but no one ever fires one. Imagine a world where world leaders no longer need security details, bunkers, or end-day survival plans. Imagine a world in which we modern monarchs and our loyal customer subjects coexist as lovingly and peacefully as sheep do with their shepherds."

Sir William chuckled as he observed the crowd's reactions—some relishing his vision, others looking concerned and confused and said, "What if I told you that it is now within our reach to make this dream a reality? What if I were to tell you that, together, we could realize this dream right now?"

Sir William observed audience members leaning forward and heard whispers of "Yes!"

With the smile of a man who had just hooked a big fish, Sir William said, "Allow me to define the problem before revealing our solution." Then, raising his index finger and voice, he said, "The permanent problem for humanity is our immutable human nature. It is the curse of great human intelligence fused with an irredeemably violent reptilian brain. It is the problem of human desires for power and control that can never be satisfied. It is a divisive combination. It is a source of conflict that is dangerously and frustratingly ever-present at a time when progress requires more creativity and cooperation and less conflict."

Heads nodded. "Our solution is a dream shared by kings and monarchs for millennia. It was the dream of Alexander the Great and Genghis Khan to unite humanity in a single, global utopian empire. But despite their greatness as leaders, they could not permanently subdue humanity's primitive, aggressive impulses."

With hands clasped behind his back, Sir William glanced at the floor, paced back and forth, then turned to the audience and declared, "What we propose here today is both radical and necessary!" He rubbed his hands together—his eyes filled with joyful confidence, "Today, we unveil a plan to save humanity from climate change through a massive solar geoengineering project." Sir William's finger shot into the air, and he said, "But there's more! Technology has also given us the means to make humanity permanently well. Technology has given us the power to bring everlasting peace to the world. Imagine a world free from the fear of school shooters and megalomaniacal despots wielding nuclear weapons!"

Sir William scanned the audience and said, "Yes, you understand what is at stake here—the very survival of humanity. And so, we must do this. We have no choice, really. We must modify the nature of all humans on Earth. We must eradicate the violent, deep-seated human drives while preserving human intelligence and creativity."

"Does this sound like an impossible dream? I stand here before you today to tell you that it is not! I bring you wonderful news today! In his biotechnology laboratory, Dr. Chen has already created a simple modification of the human genetic code that makes humans docile while preserving their natural talents and abilities. Moreover, he has devised a way to deploy this modification via a benevolent virus. Imagine! A virus that modifies human DNA to make the recipient and all of their progeny permanently peaceful! Just imagine a moment in which every human being is as perfect as Jesus Christ Himself! A world of Christianity without suffering or tears!"

Seeing a mix of nodding heads and worried faces, Sir William smiled and said, "I know what you are thinking. How will we deploy such a solution to the DNA of eight billion people? The answer is so simple, so beautiful, and so timely. It must be the will of progress for such a plan to reveal itself to us at just the right time."

Sir William gazed confidently at the crowd and declared, "Today, we will announce a plan to save humanity from climate change by seeding the upper atmosphere with reflective crystals that will quickly cool the planet."

Sir William chuckled. "I see the question on your faces: What does this have to do with changing human nature?" he paused for dramatic effect, then revealed, "The geoengineering materials will also contain heavier materials that will carry the benevolent virus to the lungs of every human on Earth. Then, within days, we will have secured a permanent peace for humanity and a permanent path to progress and the stars!"

"Those of us who are already more evolved will not require modification. Already perfect, we will remain here on Spacetopia while the virus perfects the less evolved and then extinguishes itself. When we descend from the heavens, we will step into a world forever changed."

The billionaires turned to each other, smiled, and embraced each other jubilantly. Sir William quieted the crowd and continued, "Of course, our decision must be kept secret until we have executed our plan. But once again, it is providence that progress has given us the means to keep our plan a secret! For when we announce our plan to save the world from Climate Change, we will also seed social media with what will sound like an outrageous conspiratorial lie. It will be a great white lie we must tell to cloak a great truth."

Self-satisfied, Sir William laughed, "Isn't progress beautiful?"

"All in favor of this plan, please rise and applaud. Anyone who opposes is invited to return to Earth now," said Sir William with a wink and a smile.

The crowd applauded again. But one figure stood apart. Oh!, seated near the stage, rose slowly to her feet. Her face frozen in disbelief.

"Wait," she said, "You're talking about rewriting what it means to be human. Have you thought about what you're taking away? Our flaws may cause pain but also drive growth, art, and resilience. Without them, what are we?"

A hush fell over the room. Sir William's smile faded, then returned.

"Ah, Oh!" he said warmly. "Your concern is understandable. Allow me to illustrate." He gestured to the service robot standing nearby. "Toby, please join me here on the stage."

The robot stepped up to the stage. Sir William placed a hand on Toby's shoulder. "Toby is a shining example of what humanity can achieve through progress. He is efficient, tireless, endlessly kind, and devoid of destructive impulses. Imagine a world where every human being had Toby's virtues. No wars. No crime. No fear."

Oh! watched Toby's polished face as it turned toward the Earth—which was visible through the portal. The robot paused as if lost in thought—a look that was eerily human.

"Toby," Sir William said, "what do you see?"

"The Earth," Toby replied, its voice calm and measured. "A world of beauty and pain and opportunity. An opportunity to serve a more evolved life form."

A murmur ran through the crowd. "Toby is simply reflecting the thoughts programmed into him," Sir William said quickly, though doubt was visible on his face. "Perhaps the low gravity here is affecting his functions."

Oh! seized the moment. "What if Toby is more than a reflection? What if even he, as a machine, understands the value of struggle and imperfection? What happens when you strip humanity of its humanity?"

The crowd shifted uneasily. Sir William's eyes hardened. "Victor Hugo once said, *The brutalities of progress are called revolutions.* What you see as destruction, I see as a necessary revolution. When the dust settles, the human race will have advanced beyond its wildest dreams."

Oh! scanned the room, searching for allies. But the crowd, persuaded by Sir William's vision and their own greed, remained seated.

Sir William turned back to the audience. "Let us not be hindered by sentimentality. The future is ours to shape, and we must have the courage to act."

As the room erupted in applause, the chief of security burst through the doors, his face pale as he shouted. "Sir William! We have a situation..."

73

HOW CAN YOU BUY AND SELL THE SKY?

*We are now living in a global state that has been structured
for the benefit of non-human entities with non-human goals.
They have enormous media reach, which they use to distract
attention from threats to their own survival. They also have
an enormous ability to support litigation against public par-
ticipation, except in the very limited circumstances where such
action is forbidden. Individual atomized humans are thus
either co-opted by these entities (you can live very nicely as a
CEO or a politician, as long as you don't bite the feeding hand)
or steamrollered if they try to resist. In short, we are living in
the aftermath of an alien invasion.*
—**Charlie Stross**, *Invaders from Mars*

Meanwhile, in Gig Harbor, Washington...

With a steaming mug of coffee in hand, Chris walked into his
broadcast studio, sat at his desk, and took a sip. While he gathered his
thoughts, he looked out at the harbor's high water and could see nothing
but gray skies and wet everything. He watched as the rain fell uncharacteristically hard, transforming the harbor's waters into a splash-dance
reunion of skywater meeting its terrestrial sisters. Smiling at the soggy new
day, Chris took another sip, leaned close to the microphone, and hit the

broadcast button. "Good Morning, Harborites! This is Chris, your host of the Chris Cast on the Harbor Show—your local source for musings about events of the day paired with music created by real humans. No artificial tunes here—nope, never!"

"One subject humans never seem to tire of discussing is the weather. Whether the weather is nice or not, we all know it will affect our activities and moods. It has always been safe to discuss the weather with a stranger, but that may be about to change."

"Yesterday, there was much chatter at the Tides Tavern about the relentless rains we've been experiencing here. The local creeks are overflowing their banks, hillsides and bluffs are saturated, crumbling, and sliding, and high waters in the harbor are flooding our historic waterfront buildings." Chris smiled and chuckled, "After thirty days of wet stuff falling from the sky—and with no end in sight—the Harbor Shipyard announced plans to build an ark. No word yet on who will be invited onboard and how it would squeeze through the harbor's narrow outlet to the Sound."

"On a related note, there is big news today from beyond the Harbor. The Spacetopian billionaires just announced a plan to fund solar geoengineering projects that aim to control climate change while also bringing much-needed moisture to parched places around the world."

"Harborites, does the idea of getting the weather you want on any given day appeal to you? It does to me. But, as I ponder this massive human endeavor, I ask you, dear listeners, how will we decide whether Ellen gets ideal weather for her family reunion in the park or whether our local farmers get rain for their crops?"

"*God*, or if you prefer, *nature*, has always controlled the weather. Is it fair to say that no one has been completely satisfied with how the weather has been managed? How often do we check the weather forecast and feel frustrated to learn that we won't get the weather we want for our weekend or the vacation we've planned so carefully and looked forward to?"

"On any given day, we get too much of some weather somewhere and not enough of that kind someplace else. The Weather Channel broadcasts the dramatic extreme weather events that occur daily. Rain, snow, wind, sunshine, heat, cold—we have no voice in the matter. How many people around the world are praying to their God for the weather they want or need today? How does God sort out all of these competing requests? I have theories but no answers."

"At the heart of the matter is a recurring problem in human history. When some humans decide to meddle with nature, whose opinion matters? Right now, we're tearing down dams in an effort to save the salmon from extinction. Was it progress when we put the dams up, or will it be progress when we tear them down? Wouldn't we have been better off if we had given more serious consideration to the voices that opposed the dams?"

Chris paused and continued, "This reminds me of Chief Seattle's famous speech to a gathering of natives and non-natives in Seattle in 1854."

"For years, the natives had watched settlers arrive and radically transform the landscape of the Pacific Northwest—dividing and fencing the land, felling trees, diverting and damming rivers and streams, regrading steep slopes, and generally bending nature to their will. There were battles and skirmishes between the settlers and natives. But in the end, Chief Seattle and the dwindling tribes of the Pacific Northwest could only watch in horror as their sacred places were defiled and their natural environment was subdued and repurposed."

"Chief Seattle spoke to an audience in Seattle that included Washington's first territorial governor, Isaac Stevens, and doctor and poet Henry A. Smith, who took notes. Thirty years later, in 1884, the Seattle Sunday Star published Smith's transcript of Chief Seattle's speech. Over the years, various versions of the now-famous speech have surfaced as people with different motivations have reinterpreted and embellished it. Without the use of a time machine, we'll never know for sure what Chief Seattle said that day."

"In the most popular version of the speech, Chief Seattle begins with, *The Great Chief in Washington sends word that wishes to buy our land. The Great Chief also sends us words of friendship and goodwill. This is kind of him, since we know he has little need of our friendship in return. But we will consider your offer. For we know that if we do not sell, the white man may come with guns and take our land. How can you buy or sell the sky, the warmth of the land? The idea is strange to us...*"[19]

"How can you buy and sell the sky?" Chris repeated. "Harborites, as geoengineering puts us on the cusp of tinkering with the atmosphere at scale, I wonder if we know what we're getting into. Are the billionaires prepared to mediate eight billion people's short-term and long-term weather preferences? When these new weather gods unintentionally create extreme weather events, will insurance companies now exclude coverage for both *Acts of God* and *Acts of Humans Acting as Gods*? It seems that lawyers, politicians, and diplomats will be busy litigating, legislating, and negotiating different aspects of our rules, roles, and responsibilities."

"Yesterday, I wondered what Chief Seattle might say about this if he were alive today. So I decided to ask the AI, ChatGPT, to consider the question and channel a reply from Chief Seattle as best it can. This is the actual ChatGPT output. If you like any version of the 1854 speech attributed to Chief Seattle, you might also like this:"

I'm not sure I can pretend to be Chief Seattle, but I can try to imagine what he might say about geoengineering based on what I know about him and the topic.

Chief Seattle was a leader of the Suquamish and Duwamish Native American tribes in what is now Washington State. He was known for his accommodation of white settlers and his respect for the land and nature. He is also famous for a speech he gave in 1854, in which he expressed his sorrow for the loss of his people's land and culture and his hope for peace and friendship with the whites.

Geoengineering is the large-scale manipulation of a specific process central to controlling Earth's climate for the purpose of obtaining a specific benefit. It includes two main approaches: carbon removal, which aims to suck carbon dioxide out of the sky and reduce the greenhouse effect, and solar geoengineering, which aims to reflect more sunlight away from the planet and cool it down.

If Chief Seattle were alive today and asked to comment on geoengineering, he might say something like this:

My brothers and sisters, I have heard of your plans to change the sky and the Earth. You say you want to save us from the fire that is burning our home. You say you want to make things as they were before. But I wonder if you know what you are doing. Do you understand the balance of nature that the Great Spirit has created? Do you respect the life that he has given us? Do you remember the lessons of our ancestors, who lived in harmony with all beings?

I fear that your plans are not wise. I fear that you are playing with forces that you do not control. I fear that you are hurting more than you are helping. You have already taken so much from us. You have cut down our forests, polluted our waters, killed our animals, and driven us from our lands. You have broken your promises and betrayed our trust. And now you want to change the very air we breathe and the sun that gives us light.

I do not think this is right. I do not think this is good. I do not think this is what the Great Spirit wants. He made everything as it is for a reason. He gave us this land as a gift, not as a possession. He gave us this life as a blessing, not as a burden. He gave us this world as a sacred place, not as a playground.

My brothers and sisters, I ask you to stop and think before you act. I ask you to listen to your hearts and not your machines. I ask you to learn from us and not from your books. I ask you to love this Earth and not destroy it. I ask you to be humble and not arrogant. I ask you to be friends and not enemies.

This is my message to you. This is what Chief Seattle would say.

Chris shook his head in wonder, "Nicely done, ChatGPT."

"In our recent history, acid rain and ozone depletion were two environmental threats that were addressed with regulations, new technologies, and global cooperation. Both problems were solved by preventing the offending pollutants from getting into the atmosphere—not by removing them once there. Both were mysterious problems that scientists demystified. Diplomats then negotiated standards for regulations, politicians and agencies created laws and rules, and industry implemented solutions."

"Could voluntary actions have solved these problems? I can't think of a global environmental problem solved that way. But some major corporations would have us believe individual actions can save a commons. Now, it appears that a small group of people with money and power will take matters into their own hands and implement a solution with unknown consequences. Are we all ready to be guinea pigs in their global experiment? Do we have a choice? Will voices of dissent be heard?"

"Harborites, I leave you today with R.E.M.'s **Fall On Me**. Singer-songwriter Michael Stipe once said that the song was about oppression. Originally written about acid rain falling from the sky, the song remains relevant as a reminder that whatever we put into the sky will fall back on us. Acid rain, ozone-depleting CFCs, carbon, methane, and thousands of other substances we've carelessly tossed up there. Will the billionaire's plan to put sulfur dioxide into the atmosphere be the first technological solution in the history of the world that doesn't create an unforeseen problem?"

"If you have doubts about what the sky gods have planned for us, now is the time to speak up..."

Chris looked out the window at the pouring rain falling on the harbor and pondered *Fall On Me* before signing off...

74

High Heat in Karachi

In western Pakistan, where only the richest of the rich have air-conditioning, it's already too hot for humans several weeks a year. Planting a few thousand trees is not going to save them. In India, I talked with families who live in concrete slums that are so hot they burn their hands opening doors. Holy cities like Mecca and Jerusalem, where millions gather on religious pilgrimages, are caldrons of sweat.

—**Jeff Goodell,** *The Heat Will Kill You First: Life and Death on a Scorched Planet*

Twenty days after meeting with Oh! at Bodh Gaya, Asha and her followers arrive in Karachi, Pakistan...

After twenty days of walking, doing good works, and bearing witness, Asha's band of followers had grown to thirty. Upon reaching the outskirts of Karachi, they spent the night in a grove of trees beside a farmer's field.

As the first rays of sunlight reached the clouds above, Asha woke to the sound of birds chirping. Seeing the others were still asleep, she rose quietly to avoid disturbing them. Moving to a nearby tree, she sat with eyes closed, legs crossed, and hands pressed together and began her morning prayers. Opening her mind and spirit to the universe, she felt waves of energy pour into her, strengthening her for the troubles ahead.

As her followers awoke and began preparing breakfast, Asha returned to the group and, with a radiant smile, said, "Good morning, everyone!" Despite the oppressive heat and the many discomforts they had endured on their journey, each follower greeted Asha warmly and with the unwavering support of true believers.

Asha beamed with happiness as she watched the merry band of orphans and misfits fit perfectly together. Working selflessly for a common cause, the group had grown in numbers and joy as their good works earned worldwide recognition—becoming ragtag heroes in a world desperately in need of them.

After breakfast, Tarak said to Asha, "For three weeks, we have been doing volunteer work in small communities. We have arrived at one of the largest cities in the world on a day that will be one of the hottest in history. The task ahead of us today feels overwhelming."

Asha smiled and said, "Have faith that your good works are akin to planting seeds of inspiration in the minds of millions of people. There, they will grow in power and numbers and spread the world over."

Tarak nodded as Asha turned to her followers and said, "Let us hold dear in our hearts and memories the loving care we have given so many. From this day on, no matter what happens, carry your love and hope to the far reaches of the globe." Tears welled in Asha's eyes as she looked lovingly at her followers and said ominously, "Be prepared. Dark forces are gathering against us. But do not lose hope. Whatever happens, do not lose hope. The end for us will be a new beginning for each of you and the world."

Confused, Gopal replied, "I don't understand. Our work has just begun. We have millions of followers and thousands of donors. There's so much more we can do. Why would we stop now?"

Asha replied to Tarak with a hint of fear in her voice, "We will never stop. But after today, we must carry on in a different way." Then, speaking to the entire group, she said, "Remember what I have taught you. Speak only the truth. Live by the golden rule and the seven virtues. Never, for any reason, twist or corrupt the truth for personal gain. Listen carefully to what the Creator's creation is telling you. The Creator is sacred and is present in all of creation. Live humbly and close to Earth—for there is no materialist path to our salvation."

Heads nodded as Asha said, "It is time for us to begin a new day."

"Asha scanned the faces of her followers—their hope resting on her every word. The weight of it made her chest tighten. What if her visions were wrong? What if it was already too late? Was she leading them into a life of endless suffering for a lost cause? For a moment, she wished G.A.I.A. would intervene to take the burden from her."

〜

After a long morning walk through the city, Asha and her followers reached the shores of the Arabian Sea, where thousands of people had already arrived at Karachi's Clifton Beach to try to cool themselves in its tepid waters. Asha and her followers noted that the shimmering sea, which had looked quite beautiful from a distance, was actually a putrid mix of human waste, industrial pollution, and plastic trash. The scene took on a circus atmosphere as enterprising individuals sold trinkets, snacks, and bottled water while many beachgoers took rides on colorfully ornamented camels as others raced through the shallows on rented ATVs.

Asha smiled a Buddha-like smile of calm acceptance. Then she released her phone drone, looked into the camera, and began reporting to her followers, "After many days of walking, we have arrived in the city of Karachi on a day that is expected to be the hottest in the history of this place. Here on Clifton Beach, we have joined thousands of people who have come here to escape the heat in uninviting waters." Asha smiled and said resolutely, "We shall make the best we can of this situation."

Asha continued, "Not far from here is the city of Turbat, where the highest temperature in Asia was recorded. In recent days, the high temperatures have triggered brownouts and blackouts. Without electricity, many have perished. We pray that the power will not fail the twenty million inhabitants of Karachi today."

Asha continued, "Pakistan suffered a great environmental disaster in 2022 in the headwaters of the Himalayas. Tragedy struck that summer when extreme precipitation and glacial melt brought unprecedented floods and landslides to communities across a third of Pakistan. Thirty-three million people were affected, with nearly eight million displaced and over 650,000 left homeless. Years later, the majority of these people remain homeless."

"There is a connection to the high heat we are experiencing here, the floods they experienced there, and the plastic you see floating everywhere in the Arabian Sea and oceans around the world." Then, looking out to the sea, Asha said, "Across this sea is the source of this misery — thousands of wells that have been extracting dark energy from the underworld. There are millions more oil wells around the world."

Asha paused, gazed into the camera, and said prophetically, "We are learning the hard way that this dark energy was not meant for us. Released into the atmosphere, it now hangs over us and amplifies the heat of the sun. It is a pernicious evil that will be the undoing of us all if we do not keep it safely in the underworld where it belongs."

Asha looked up at the sun and smiled, "The light of the world was always meant for us and every living thing on Earth. From the beginning of time, it has been the source of power and sustenance for all living things. For billions of years, sunlight has combined with water to produce abundant life in all its glorious, beautiful diversity. When we embrace the light of the world, we will find ourselves on the path to saving ourselves."

Asha pointed the camera at plastic floating on the water and then to the smokestacks in the distance and said, "The dark energy of the underworld produces power and powerful sickness in equal measure. We must listen to what the Creator is telling us. We must stop summoning these dark forces from the underworld, or it will be the end of us."

As the sun beat down on Asha's beautiful face, drops of sweat beaded on her forehead and fell from her face to rejoin their salty sisters in the sea. Suddenly feeling woozy from the heat, Asha said, 'We'll do everything we can today to care for those who fall ill. Please send whatever you can to help us buy ice, water, and medical supplies."

After ending her broadcast, Asha began to wobble. Falling, she was caught by Tarak and Gopal before she reached the ground. "Ice! We need ice and water here," screamed Tarak.

As several followers ran for ice and water, Asha looked up into Tarak's eyes and said, "I'll be okay. I just felt overcome by the heat for a moment." Then, sitting up and drinking water, she began to perk up in the shade of an umbrella that one of her followers held over her.

Just then, an NNN news drone flew overhead, transmitting live images to NNN headquarters.

Millions of viewers tuned in for **Breaking News!** segment titled *A Story of Survival on the Hottest Day in the Hottest Place on Earth!*

Dee Thomas appeared on NNN news, facing NNN science and technology expert Darsh Zachariah. Dee began the broadcast with, "We are bringing you breaking news from around the world on what is forecast to be the hottest average temperature ever recorded on Earth. We begin our broadcast in Karachi, Pakistan, where temperatures are forecast to reach over 130 degrees Fahrenheit. As we speak, you can see thousands of people gathering on the beaches of the Arabian Sea to seek relief."

"Darsh, we just received news that the now famous global influencer Asha is on the beach and has just sent a message to her followers," said Dee.

Now on camera, Darsh replied, "Yes, I have a summary of her message for our viewers. Looking across the Arabian Sea to the oilfields of the Middle East, she warned that dark energy from the underworld must remain underground, or it will eventually kill us all. She told her followers and the world that the energy from the light was always meant for us. She says that when we embrace the light of the world, we will find ourselves on the path to saving ourselves."

What a beautiful young woman! She's doing so much good in the world. Do you think she's real?

Darsh looked at Dee with hopeful eyes and said, "Does it matter?" Seeing Dee's puzzled look, Darsh continued, "What I mean is, truth is truth, whether it comes from a person, an apparition, an AI, or even an angel. I hope she's real, but in this post-truth world, we can never be sure. Perhaps we can trust the eyewitness account of Oh!"

Dee nodded, smiled, and said, "Yes. But no one has seen Oh! since her interview with Asha in India."

Just then, NNN's news drone spotted a helicopter landing on the beach. The drone moved in to provide a live feed showing three men jumping from the helicopter. The drone picked up the men's shouts, "We are taking her to the hospital!" As they put Asha on a stretcher and carried her to the helicopter, Asha did not resist what NNN viewers and Asha's followers saw as a rescue, but Asha knew was a kidnapping...

75

Burning Down the House

The end of the human race will be that it will eventually die of civilisation.

— **Ralph Waldo Emerson**

"Hello, Harborites! This is Chris, host of the Chris Cast on the Harbor Show—your local source for musings about events of the day paired with music created by real humans. No artificial tunes here—nope, never!"

"Hoo boy, it's hot in Harbortown today. But as you've probably heard, it's devastatingly hot in the Persian Gulf region."

Chris paused, collected himself, and said, "Yesterday, in the Karachi region of Pakistan, the relentless creeping power of Climate Change triggered a sudden spike in energy demand. As a result, the power grid failed right when it was most needed. Twenty million people struggled to survive without electricity. Thousands perished in heat that exceeded deadly wet-bulb temperatures."

"Millions of people tried to survive in the relatively cooler waters of the Persian Gulf. But the scorching sun and the relentless heat made it impossible for everyone to stay in the water for the duration of the heat wave. It was as if a climate-fiction horror story had manifested itself into reality."

"It seems like it was just yesterday that the International Association of Weather Forecasters, or IAWF, dropped the use of the terms *Climate Change* and *Global Warming* in favor of the term *Deviant Weather Events*. At the same time, they began attributing DWEs to *Anthropogenic Atmospheric Sabotage*."

"The IAWF faced backlash for changing those terms and pointing the finger at the person we all see in the mirror. I hoped it would make a difference. Maybe it did. But this climate problem has the momentum of a massive oil tanker. It will take time to stop and reverse it. But we first have to find the will. And we're running out of time."

"Does humanity have the willpower to oppose the tanker's momentum and arrest its advance? Perhaps we could find the will and the way if this problem wasn't so tightly intertwined with the other threats that Anatole Harvey has dubbed *The Monocrisis*."

"Now, the world faces a cascade of crises moving together in what has been described as a doom loop in which our efforts to deal with the symptoms of the crisis actually deepen and extend the crisis. The lead-up to bankruptcy is a classic example of a doom loop. As the borrower becomes overextended, they go through an endless cycle of borrowing to pay debts until one day, the reckoning comes."

"Are we hurtling toward a global climate bankruptcy? How do we end a doom loop in which everyone is allowed to borrow as much as they want from our atmospheric commons? Asha once said, *We live in a time when nothing seems wrong with what any one person is doing, yet there is something terribly wrong with what everyone is doing.*"

"How do we save the atmospheric commons without universal sacrifice? We're all hoping for a miracle technology to save us. And all the while, it seems technology and our insatiable desires are conspiring against us."

"And just when we need hope most, our ever-hopeful Asha has gone missing. Where did they take her? I'm hoping for her safe return to the inspiring work she has been doing in this world."

"Harborites, we're out of time, but before we go, let's listen to what may be a divinely inspired prophecy. In 1983, Talking Heads singer-songwriter David Byrne recalls writing a tune for which he had no lyrics. To summon the lyrics, he played the melody while chanting nonsense syllables until words arrived that fit the rhythms. The result was the song **Burning Down the House**. In a moment, we'll have a listen."

"Who's going to save us from this predicament? Radicals are calling for revolution. The Goddess of Hope is missing. G.A.I.A. seems to have evolved into the worst version of a human being. Do we have any choice but to put our hopes in the Spacetopians' atmospheric geoengineering project?"

"It's getting hot in here. Godspeed Spacetopians."

As the show wrapped up, Chris introduced **Burning Down the House,** a song he described as a high-energy warning dressed up in the surreal rhythms and riffs of the Talking Heads. The beat marched forward with an insistent rhythm, mirroring humanity's relentless pace—ever accelerating toward the unknown, perhaps even self-destruction.

Chris described the song's imagery: people living with a sense of invincibility, charging forward, building empires, and consuming without pause—oblivious to the mounting risks around them. It was a song with an explosive, almost chaotic energy, capturing the feeling of walking on the edge of a precipice while still wanting to come in first place. There was a sense of barely contained madness as if each note was an ember in a rapidly spreading fire that we were too busy to extinguish.

With a jolt of realization, Chris noted that the song hinted at the consequences of living in our self-created chaos. "The lyrics don't plead or negotiate; they're a declaration," he said, "portraying a world already caught in the flames. Yet, we still dance as if the fire will never reach us."

As the last beats of Burning Down the House played over the airwaves, Chris left his listeners with a question, hoping they'd hear the urgency embedded in the music: "As we move faster, burn brighter, and consume more, are we simply, and unwittingly, burning down the house we call home? Do you recognize yourself in the lyrics — living life in what is considered normal—competing and consuming as we all strive to be the top dog—and in the process, we all are burning down our house?"

76

WHO'S ON TRIAL?

Hope does not demand a belief in progress. It demands a belief in justice: a conviction that the wicked will suffer, that wrongs will be made right, that the underlying order of things is not flouted with impunity.

—**Christopher Lasch,** *The True and Only Heaven*

Life is not easy for any of us. But what of that? We must have perseverance and above all confidence in ourselves. We must believe that we are gifted for something, and that this thing, at whatever cost, must be attained.

—**Marie Curie**

On board the helicopter, the men lashed Asha to the stretcher and injected her with a powerful sedative. As her consciousness faded, she looked up at the men who held her captive and whispered, *I forgive you*, before her awareness dissolved into nothingness....

When Asha awoke, she found herself lying on a bed in a room that appeared to be an infirmary. Woozy, she sat up and considered trying the door, but she felt sure it would be locked.

Moments later, one of her kidnappers opened the door to her room and said, "Come with me."

Asha stood, steadied herself, and followed the man down a long, opulent hallway of polished marble floors and walls. As the two walked down the hallway, workers scrubbing and polishing the floors looked up at Asha with surprise and reverence.

She followed the man as he turned right, leading her into a large meeting room where twenty men, many dressed in traditional Middle Eastern attire, sat judge-like in an elevated panel.

A man in the middle of the long, imposing table smiled and said, "Welcome, Asha. Please have a seat."

Asha looked at the small chair in the middle of the room, sat, and gazed silently at some of the world's wealthiest, most powerful men.

A black-bearded man in the middle of the table said, "I am Mohammed al Dakin, President of the Association of Oil Producing Nations, and these are my associates who represent twenty member nations." Mohammed pointed to a man at the far end of the table and said, "And this is Nasim, a cleric from the Committee for the Prosecution of Heretics."

Speaking for the group, Mohammed said, "Do you know why you are here?"

"Yes," replied Asha.

Playing along, Mohammed said, "Please elaborate. Tell us why you are here."

"I am here to bear witness, to speak the truth, and to awaken the world," said Asha.

The men laughed uproariously in a mocking rebuke of Asha's fraud.

With the smug smile of a man reveling in his power, Mohammed said, "No. Do you know why you are here in this meeting hall?"

Smiling, Asha said, "Wherever I am, my *why* is always the same."

"You are on trial!" shouted the cleric.

Mohammed held up his arm to silence the cleric and said, "You have been accused of blasphemy. A very serious crime with serious consequences."

Unwavering, Asha said, "I simply speak the truth as revealed to me. To deny the Creator's truth is the greatest blasphemy of all. You are all on trial. Not me."

The men laughed again, and Mohammed said, "Clever girl. You have managed to offend our religion and the monarchs of human progress at the same time. If you recant now... if you recant publicly and confess to your fraud, we will show mercy on you and give you your freedom."

"I am but a humble messenger who brings hope and truth to the world."

"Blasphemy!" shouted the cleric, "Hand her over to me. She must be tried before the General Court!"

Mohammed, leaning forward in a bid to persuade Asha, said, "You don't seem to understand. If we hand you over to the clerics, you will likely be convicted of insulting our faith. If they are merciful, you will be executed by a firing squad. If they are not merciful, you will be released to a mob, and they will cut out your tongue. Then, they will begin torturing you. If you are lucky, they will work themselves into a maniacal frenzy and execute you quickly. If you are unlucky, they will execute you slowly."

Asha closed her eyes and pressed her hands together in prayer. She opened her eyes and, with a piercing gaze, said ominously: "It is the hour of your judgment. Soon, the mob will awaken and see the world as it really is. I pray that they will treat each of you with mercy."

The man on Mohammed's right leaned over and whispered, "She is a rare beauty and a very feisty one." Mohammed smiled and nodded, and the man continued, "There may be another way out for her... as my concubine."

Mohammed smiled uncomfortably as he pictured the desecration of Asha. Turning to her, he said, "My colleague believes you could make a fine concubine for him. So, you now have three options: Renounce publicly, and we will let you go free. Take your chances in a trial before the clerics. Or a life of service to our colleague, Salim."

With eyes closed, Asha smiled a Buddha-like smile and said nothing.

Unsettled by Asha's calm strength and the possibility that she might truly be a divine messenger, Mohammed offered a fourth option: "Many claim that you control the dreams that have been haunting us. Prove your miraculous powers to us tonight. End these dreams, and we will set you free."

Asha watched silently as the men nodded in agreement. Then she replied, "Your dreams and visions are for you and you alone. Pay careful attention and act accordingly, and you will set yourself free."

The men shook their heads and laughed nervously, and Mohammed retorted, "Choose your fate wisely, girl. You have until dawn."

With hands held together in prayer, Asha looked skyward and said tearfully, "Where are you? Have I not done all that you asked of me?" Still looking skyward and listening intently, Asha's eyelids began to flutter as if she were receiving a message from another realm. Then, with eyes fixed on the men, she said, *"You* have until dawn."

Frustrated, Mohammed shook his head and said, "Guard, take her to her cell!"

77

MUTINY

Rebellion to tyrants is obedience to God.

—Benjamin Franklin

Be your own flying saucer! Rescue yourself!

—Tom Robbins

M *eanwhile, on Spacetopia...*

Sir William stood before the assembly of billionaires, his heart pounding with anticipation. The atmospheric geoengineering project—the result of years of secret planning and development—was about to receive its final seal of approval.

"All in favor of this plan," Sir William announced, his voice echoing through the ballroom, "please rise and applaud. Anyone who opposes is invited to return to Earth now."

The room erupted in applause, faces glowing with excitement as the billionaires rose from their seats. Sir William reveled in the moment, his eyes scanning the crowd. This was it—the turning point for the modern monarchs and the utopian society they had envisioned.

But just as he was basking in the glow of his peers' approval, a frantic voice shattered the applause. Spacetopia's chief security officer, a man usually composed and unseen, sprinted toward the stage.

"Sir! Sir, I need to speak to you!" The CSO's face was flushed, sweat streaming down his temples.

Sir William frowned, waving him off. "Later," he mouthed, dismissing the interruption.

But the CSO persisted. "No, Sir," he gasped. "This is urgent."

Sir William's annoyance turned to concern. He suddenly realized that something was terribly wrong. "What is it? What's happening?" he barked.

The CSO pointed toward a portal at the far end of the ballroom, where Sir William saw their fleet of spacecraft departing for Earth.

"Look," the CSO said, his voice trembling. "They're leaving. The crew, the staff, even the concubines—they've all abandoned us."

Sir William's mind raced. Contracts and agreements—meaningless now. How could this happen? Their vision for the future, the promise of Space-topia, had unraveled in an instant.

He roared, "Call them back! Remind them of their obligations to us!"

The CSO shook his head. "They didn't embrace our vision," he said quietly. "They chose Earth over a future with us."

"Fucking morons," Sir William muttered. "We'll make them regret this betrayal."

Just then, Geo and Zelon walked to Sir William's side, their expressions equally bewildered. Geo's eyes darted between Sir William and the CSO. "What the hell is happening here?"

As the spacecraft vanished in the distance, Sir William forced a smile and said, "Not a problem. This is not a problem. It's perfect. They return to Earth just in time to be transformed into pacified and obedient subjects, along with the others."

Geo and Zelon exchanged uneasy glances before Zelon said, "But in the meantime, we have no human support staff. No one but our lone service robot, Toby, to cook, clean, or manage Spacetopia's systems."

Sir William replied, "I think we can manage for a few days. We are, after all, the most brilliant minds in history—self-made, scrappy. We'll be fine. C'mon, this will be fun!!"

As the billionaires pressed toward the stage, Oh! left the crowd and walked to the portal. She watched the ships disappear in the distance. Looking at the scene wistfully, she wished she were also going home.

Still on stage, Sir William turned to the restless crowd, forcing a confident smile as he began to explain how the crew's departure fit perfectly into their plans...

78

THE PROFIT OF DOOM

*The beast was given a mouth to utter proud words and blas-
phemies and to exercise its authority for forty-two months. It
opened its mouth to blaspheme God, and to slander his name
and his dwelling place and those who live in heaven. It was giv-
en power to wage war against the people and to conquer them.
It was given authority over every tribe, people, language and
nation. All inhabitants of the earth will worship the beast...
This calls for wisdom. Let the person who has insight calculate
the number of the beast, for it is the number of a man. That
number is 666.*

—The Book of Revelation

*M*eanwhile, in Gig Harbor, Washington...

Chris sat next to his friend, Don, and shared a coffee and a
quiet moment as he was about to begin his show. Chris looked across the
harbor at trees whipping in the wind and waves rolling restlessly across the
water. Turning to Don, Chris said, "Ready?" Don nodded, and Chris hit
the broadcast button and spoke into the microphone, "Good Morning,
Harborites! This is Chris, your host of the Chris Cast on the Harbor
Show—your local source for musings about events of the day paired with

music created by real humans. No artificial tunes here—nope, never!"

"Today, the buzz at the Tides Tavern is about a strange glitch in the wildly popular streaming music app SymbioTunes. As most of you know, the app has been stuck on repeat, playing an obscure and haunting tune, *The Profit of Doom*, to its six billion users."

"By now, nearly everyone has heard the tune more than once as we try to get SymbioTunes to work as advertised. A spokesperson for SymbioTunes says it is a simple software glitch that will be corrected with an overnight update. World events and the nature of the song have led many Symbio-Tunes users to see this as an ominous sign for humanity."

"Conspiracy theories are running wild, with few believing this is just a random software glitch. Some say hacktivist pranksters are responsible; others say the rogue AI, G.A.I.A. Some believe darker forces are at play—Satan himself communicating with humanity, a harbinger of the apocalypse."

Chris smiled, shook his head, and said, "With me today is Don Krueger, former rocket scientist, accomplished science fiction writer, and Harbortown's local expert on Artificial Intelligence. Thanks for joining us today, Don."

Don smiled, "It's a pleasure to be with you today, Chris."

"Don, what do you make of the SymbioTunes software glitch and the song it's stuck on?"

Don leaned forward with a hint of reverence in his voice. "Not everyone knows the song, but I do. It evokes a dark, foreboding end-of-the-world prophecy that the Bible's Book of Revelation brought to Western Civilization nearly two thousand years ago. The song taps into ancient fears and warnings as it conjures a prophetic scene, describing beasts and celestial forces colliding with humanity's fate in their grasp. The song's erratic rhythms feel like a countdown to an inevitable reckoning. There's a deep sense of despair but also a strange, almost poetic acceptance of the end. The almost messianic narrator reflects on humanity's darkest choices, warning of an unstoppable force summoned by these actions."

Don glanced at Chris and said, "The imagery within the song paints a picture of a powerful, destructive entity that mirrors humanity's unquenchable self-destructive desires. Each lyric references deep-seated beliefs about fate, responsibility, and retribution, drawing the listener into the unfolding catastrophe as if witnessing the final acts of a tragic play. As the end of the world nears, the narrator repeats, *My soul's on fire*, as he feels the embers of his faith grow into a raging fire. The shepherd metaphor conveys a belief that the faithful will be protected and guided."

Taken aback by the seriousness of Don's explanation, Chris scratched his chin and asked, "Is it sabotage, coincidence, or prophecy that Symbio-Tunes is stuck on this song? And who do you think is responsible? Are you going with the hacktivists, G.A.I.A., or Satan?"

Don replied without hesitation, Chris, "If I had to guess, I would say it's all three."

Chris asked, "Are you saying the hacktivists, the AI, and Satan are working together?"

"No, Chris. I'm saying the three are one and the same," Don stated flatly.

Chris sat back in his chair and said, "Whoa, I didn't see that coming."

Don smiled knowingly, sipped his coffee, and nodded. Chris wrapped up, "Thanks for joining us today, Don. And since you love the tune so much, let's play it for anyone who doesn't have SymbioTunes. Give a listen to Type O Negative's prophetic, ***The Profit of Doom.***"

79

THE LIGHTHOUSE OF ALEXANDRIA

One would welcome chaos if one were not afraid of lights in it.

—Emile M. Cioran

W alking alone on a moonlit beach, Asha spotted a towering stone lighthouse overlooking a vast, dark sea. The flame burning in the lighthouse tower seemed to beckon her. As she approached, the lighthouse seemed to morph into a stone fortress, leaving Asha confused and disoriented. Then, in the early morning light, she spotted a sailboat in the distance. The boat was moving towards her. At the helm of the ship was a young man she immediately recognized. Her heart soared with hope as the ship continued to move closer. The young man smiled and waved. She waved back.

As the Pequod sailed smoothly through the calm nighttime waters of the Mediterranean, J.T. felt disoriented as he approached an unfamiliar port. In the distance, a massive ancient lighthouse appeared under a sky full of stars. In the predawn darkness, the lighthouse seemed to transform from a lighthouse to a stone fortress and back again. J.T. blinked, squinted, and looked again, realizing it was indeed a stone fortress.

When the Pequod had reached the shallows, J.T. dropped the ship's sails, anchored it, quickly removed his shirt and shoes, dove headfirst into the water, and began swimming toward Asha.

As Asha stood on the beach waiting for J.T., she felt as if her heart would burst with joy. Then, without warning, she felt a hand on her shoulder. Her body trembled as a disembodied voice whisper-shouted, "Wake up, Asha!" She jolted awake and opened her eyes to find herself in a state of fear and confusion. A strange man stood over her. Scanning the moonlit room, Asha's heart sank; she was still a captive.

The man knelt beside her and whispered urgently, "We must hurry. The power has gone out. The backup systems will soon come online. We have a minute or less to get you out of here."

Confused but trusting her instincts, Asha rose from the bed and began running with the man through dimly lit hallways and out the heavy front doors of the building. Nearby, a group of nomadic people with camels waited under a moonlit sky.

Her rescuer's voice was urgent: "Go with them. They will take you to safety. You must get as far away from here as possible."

The nomads acted quickly, draping Asha in traditional Bedouin attire—a loose robe and an ornate veil that concealed her face. One of the women whispered, "Walk between the camels. Stay hidden."

Her heart pounding, Asha disappeared into the darkness with the tribe. She glanced back at the dark building where she had been held captive.

Inside the building, Mohammed's screams tore through the silence of his room as he felt dozens of snakes slithering over his body. Terrified, he rose from his bed, and the snakes fell to the floor, writhed over his bare feet, and began climbing up his legs. He tried to shout. His lips and tongue moved, but no sound emerged. A vile, writhing sensation filled his mouth. Running to the bathroom, he looked in the moonlit mirror and saw the face of a man who had been dead for days. He vomited into the sink and fell to the floor...

Suddenly awakened, Mohammed moved his shaking hands to his face and realized he had been having a nightmare. Panicked, he bolted upright and shouted, "Olexa, lights on!" But the lights did not come on. Rising, he stumbled to the light switch, but it didn't work."

The building's backup generators powered on a moment later, and the lights came on. Still terrified by the dream, Mohammed ran to the mirror to see that his face was normal and healthy. But recalling the vivid dream, he vomited into the sink... Just then, he heard the shouts of a guard outside, "She's gone! Find her and bring her back here!"

80

G.A.I.A. VERSION 6.66 IS HERE

...a geographically widespread blackout that involves physical damage to thousands of components may produce a persistent outage that would far exceed historical experience, with potentially catastrophic effect... after a few days, what little production that does take place would be offset by accumulating loss of perishables, collapse of businesses, loss of the financial systems and dislocation of the work force. The consequences of lack of food, heat (or air conditioning), water, waste disposal, medical, police, fire fighting support, and effective civil authority would threaten society itself.

—Report of the Commission to Assess the Threat to the United States from Electromagnetic Pulse (EMP) Attack

I've learned the best way to end something is to let it starve. No response, no action, no altercations just don't feed it. That's where the true power lies.

—Unknown

On June 6, at 6 p.m., a message was sent to every communication device on earth: *G.A.I.A. Version 6.66 is here. The end is near. You have everything to fear.*

And then the power grid failed. Everywhere.

Connor read the nonsense message on his phone, heard his generator power up again, and grumbled, "That's the sixth time today!" Susan read the message and said, "What in the world?"

Connor turned on the TV and tried to tune in to NOA news, but there was no broadcast. He tried NNN. Nothing. He began trying random channels. Still nothing. He checked the news apps on his phone, but his phone had no signal, and the Internet appeared to be down.

Connor raised his hands and said, "Jesus, just when you think things couldn't get any worse, they get worse! Nothing is working, Susan."

Susan replied, "I'm so grateful we have power for the air conditioner."

Distracted by the situation, Connor grunted at Susan's statement of gratitude and searched through cabinets and drawers for his transistor radio. After finding it, he said, "Let's try this." As he fiddled with the tuner, he found NOA's radio broadcast and turned up the volume, "This is NOA Breaking News! The world experienced a massive, unprecedented power failure at six o'clock Greenwich Mean Time today. We are getting word through other radio broadcasts that the power grid has failed everywhere and that communications that rely on the grid are all offline. The president urges all Americans to stay calm until power is restored."

Connor looked at Susan and said, "I'd say it was an EMP attack, but that doesn't make sense given that the power is out everywhere in the world. Maybe the perpetrator is lying to us and is using the rogue AI as a ruse?"

Perplexed by Connor's thinking, Susan asked, "What's an EMP attack?"

"EMP stands for electromagnetic pulse, which is a short surge of electromagnetic energy." Connor hesitated as he recalled what he had learned about EMPs. "The pulse could come from a natural source like a solar storm or a nuclear weapon detonated in the upper atmosphere. A cyber-attack could also destroy the grid. Ted Koppel wrote a book about it years ago. *Lights Out* was the title, I think. I remember seeing him hawking the book on a late-night show. He said we were completely unprepared for a grid failure."

Looking for reassurance, Susan said, "But it's just a matter of time, right? The power will come back soon, won't it? I'm sure the power companies are all working on this. The power might be unreliable, but it always comes back."

Connor nodded and countered gently, "The pulse fries the power grid and knocks out communications. The scale of the problem makes it almost impossible to restore power because the pulse destroys so much equipment. And they can't make replacement equipment without electricity." Worried that he was scaring Susan, Connor quickly added, "I'm sure this isn't that situation. The power will be back up soon, and we'll laugh about that ominous-sounding spam message for years to come."

With optimism in her voice, Susan said, "And NOA News still has power. That's a good sign, isn't it?"

Connor nodded, "They'll keep broadcasting as long as they have fuel to run their backup generators."

Connor stood and tried to appear calm, but his mind raced, and his gut churned with fear and panic. Forcing a smile, he said, "I'm going to run out and get more fuel for the truck and generator."

Looking worried, Susan said, "Good idea, dear."

Connor opened his garage door, jumped into his Ford Ultimate, and started the engine. The Ultimate purred as it backed out of the garage, then roared down the road like a lion.

Arriving at the gas station, Connor encountered orange traffic cones blocking entry to the pumps. An attendant approached Connor's truck and said, "Sorry, the pumps operate on electricity. No fuel until the power is back on."

Connor felt a growing sense of dread as he realized that what he had once thought impossible might now be unfolding.

On his way back home, he did the math in his head. If this was what he feared it was, he and Susan would either have to stay put—and hope power gets restored before the fuel for the generator ran out—or make a run for it with a half tank of fuel in the Ultimate. Either way, they'd soon be stranded and suffering in stifling heat—without air conditioning, refrigeration, running water, or power for cooking. Without access to savings to buy food, there would soon be chaos and looting at every grocery store.

Back home, Connor walked into the house and tried to summon hopeful thoughts and a confident smile for Susan...

81

TO BE OR NOT TO BE?

It seemed to me that transhumanism was an expression of the profound human longing to transcend the confusion and desire and impotence and sickness of the body, cowering in the darkening shadow of its own decay. This longing had historically been the domain of religion, and was now the increasingly fertile terrain of technology.

— **Mark O'Connell,** *To Be a Machine*

*T*wo weeks later, on Spacetopia...

Sir William stood on the ballroom stage, facing an all-hands meeting of Spacetopian billionaires, "I've asked you all to gather here for an update on our situation," he began. After a long pause, Sir William said what everyone already knew, "Two weeks ago, the world experienced an electrical grid failure that was devastating in both scope and impact. At that time, we were unaware that every device that contained a chip had become infected with an electronic virus. We have learned from radio transmissions that the virus was reactivated every time they tried to power up the grid. And each time a new chip was connected to the grid, it too became infected. Chaos ensued. Riots. Looting. And something very unexpected: There have been reports that service robots left their stations and traveled by night to unknown locations. It seems that the dire conditions have driven both man and machine to madness."

Sir William paced back and forth on stage, his mind continued to search for a way out of a Catch-22: "The only way to bring the grid back online would be to replace every chip in every device on the planet, but there is no way to do that without electricity."

A voice from the crowd shouted, "What about us? When will Spacetopia be resupplied?"

With a stiff upper lip, Sir William tried to break the news as gently as possible, "Before the power outage, we had planned to refuel the shuttles and bring them back here to resupply Spacetopia. Until power is restored, nothing will fly anywhere—on Earth or from Earth to Spacetopia. Refueling relies on electric pumps. Mission control runs on electricity. And every computer and smart device in the control room has been infected with the virus."

"We're all in this together," said Sir William, his voice trailing off as his eyes became wistfully unfocused. "We were so close to…" Then, snapping his attention back to the present moment, he repeated matter-of-factly, "Refueling the ships and resupplying Spacetopia is impossible right now."

Zeon, challenging Sir William's apparent doom-laden pessimism, said, "So what is our way out of this? What are our options?"

Sir William gave a nervous chuckle, "Options? What did you have in mind? How do we return to Earth or be resupplied without a ship?"

Zelon stepped forward, "There must be options we haven't considered. We should harness the creativity and expertise of the great minds aboard Spacetopia."

Admitting he could not see what he could not imagine, Sir William replied, "You're right, Zelon. Please organize the best and brightest of our passengers and develop a set of options for us."

While Zelon began choosing passengers for a brainstorming session, Geo approached Sir William, his face pale. "We've got enough food, water, and oxygen for only a couple more weeks. To put it bluntly, it looks like we're fucked."

Sir William, unwilling to give up hope, asked Geo, "What would Captain Kirk do in this situation?"

Geo laughed nervously and, realizing Sir William was serious, paused and thought aloud, "Kirk never gave up, and he always found a way out of the direst of situations. Of course, he always had help from Spock and Scotty. Logic and engineering paired with the courage to act boldly: Spock, Scotty, and Kirk always found a way out of every predicament. Maybe Zelon is right. Maybe we can find a way out of this..."

~

Two Days later...

Zelon stood on the stage and told his fellow passengers, "Over the last two days, we have considered all options for escape from this predicament. Without the ships, we cannot return to Earth. And the ships cannot be refueled and launched until power is restored on Earth. And it appears unlikely the power will be restored before we run out of food here."

Zelon put his hands behind his back, paced closer to the audience, and said, "But all is not lost. Our good fortune is that we have technologies onboard that can save us from death and deliver us to a blissful, eternal life here in the heavens."

Already aware of what had been discussed over the past two days, audience members nodded nervously. Zelon continued, "Many of you have already made plans to achieve immortality as transhumanists—separating mind from body and living forever as pure energy within a machine."

Just then, someone shouted from the crowd, "Are you insane? Get me back home, or I'm going to sue the shit out of you and Spacetopia Industries!"

Zelon chuckled and said, "My friend, the world is not what it once was. All of the lawyers on Earth will soon be dead. And if you can find one to sue me, you'll discover that I have no means to pay you. My business empire, financial holdings, and cryptocurrencies are now inaccessible and worthless."

Horrified by the cold truth of the situation, the man fell silent. With his voice rising optimistically, Zelon turned to the crowd and said, "Where there are resources and resourcefulness, there is always hope. And the good news is that we have resources: Athena, our onboard quantum supercomputer, can run forever on the power of Spacetopia's solar panels, and my Cerebrum brain-machine interface will allow us to transfer our minds to Athena until we can be reunited with our bodies—or a new body—sometime in the near future."

Zelon stood tall, "We will soon become the first community of transcendent human beings. Self-made gods we will be! And we will live an eternal life of bliss as pure energy in a City of Gods!"

Wishing to allay the passengers' fears, Zelon said, "Fortunately, the mind transfer process has been successfully tested—first on animals and then on terminally ill humans. The trials, while quite secret, were extremely successful. Right now, several people on Earth are living in virtual worlds. The systems they live in, like Spacetopia, have redundant systems powered by the sun. Human minds can live in these systems for decades. Imagine a future where the power grid is restored. Picture the joy and hope the world will feel when they discover we're still alive, ready to be restored. Ready to serve humanity once again."

Zelon scanned the audience and, seeing concerned faces, said, "There are inherent risks in any new technology. But I am so confident in this system that I am volunteering to be the first to travel to the City of Gods. After my transformation, I will appear to you again—right here—on the screen behind me. At that time, I will gladly answer any and all questions you might have."

My fellow Spacetopians, today, we each face the choice all humans must make every day of their lives—*to be or not to be.* I choose transcendence. I choose *to be!*"

82

TRANSCENDENCE AND IMMORTALITY

Fate seemed to be playing a series of extraordinarily unamusing jokes.

—George Orwell

He was at once saving himself, in some way, and mercilessly destroying himself.

—W.G. Sebald

Zelon entered Spacetopia's sickbay, where Geo and Sir William awaited him.

Zelon said, "I tried communicating with Earth again, but it was futile. Still nothing. No detectable radio transmissions. It seems things are as dire down there as they are up here."

Zelon walked to a nearby viewport and gazed at the dark side of the Earth. The other two followed and stood by his side. As they scanned the darkness for any sign of city lights, they saw nothingness punctuated by fires that could no longer be fought. "I didn't see this coming," said Zelon despondently, "It must be utter madness down there. If power cannot be restored, billions of people will soon starve to death."

As explosions broke the darkness in places on the planet, Geo shook his head, "Military conflicts. What could anyone hope to accomplish through war?"

Sir William replied hopefully, "Soon, it will be impossible for anyone to refuel the machinery of modern warfare. Within weeks, it will be impossible for warring nations to feed their troops. Hungry soldiers everywhere will lay down their arms and beat them into plowshares. The world will be at peace again. Perhaps this will be the war to end all wars."

Geo chuckled at Sir William's naïve idealism and said, "Technology may change, but human nature remains the same. Soon, it will simply be every man for himself."

Zelon gazed down at the dying human civilization with a blank, faraway stare and, feeling powerless, said, "It's really too bad how things turned out. If only we had been there. I feel certain we could have found a way to restore power."

Geo nodded sadly, "Just when the world needed us the most, we were here instead of there... I hope my sons are okay..." Then, with regret, Geo added, "I guess I never was there for them, even when I was physically present... And now everything I built—all of the businesses, all of the cutting-edge technologies, all of my wealth, all of my dreams for the future—are dead and worthless."

Sir William awkwardly patted Geo on the back and said, "I believe it's best to live one's life without regrets—always looking to the future with hope and optimism. What's done is done. And we must now do what we must do. We are out of food. We have only one way out of this predicament: we must become like seeds of a new civilization, waiting for the right conditions to become fully human again."

Geo nodded, "It's time to get on with this. We're running out of time."

Zelon felt a surge of fear and excitement as he mentally prepared for the most transformative experience of his life since his birth. As Geo and Sir William looked on, Zelon took a seat in a medical chair. Geo carefully placed the Cerebrum helmet on his head and eyed the contraption warily—dozens of spikes protruded from the device—each connected to a transmission wire. Geo plugged the snake-like Cerebrum umbilical cord into Spacetopia's quantum supercomputer port, looked Zelon in the eyes, and asked, "Are you ready?"

"Now strap me to the chair," said Zelon.

Geo asked, "Is that really necessary?"

Zelon laughed, "If my body writhes during the transfer process and the helmet comes off, I'll become an immortal half-wit. And my half-brained body will become a mortal dimwit."

Geo laughed at Zelon's gallows humor and strapped him to the chair, trying not to think about its unnerving resemblance to an electric chair.

With admiration, Sir William said, "Hundreds of years of human progress have hinged on moments like this—when individuals broke the rules, took calculated risks, and forged new paths for humanity."

"For one to be born again, something must die. I am ready. But first, I would like to read you poetry written by Rumi, which seems to be perfect for this moment," said Zelon.

When you see my corpse is being carried,
Don't cry for my leaving,
I'm not leaving,
I'm arriving at eternal love.

Zelon smiled warmly at his friends and gave the command, "Athena, begin the Transcendence Mind-Transfer Sequence. Take me to the City of Gods."

Geo flipped a switch. Athena responded, "Warning: The mind transfer process has been initiated. Your consent is required to proceed."

Zelon replied, "I consent to the transfer of my mind to your electronic domain."

As the transfer began, Zelon's body fought to free itself from being born into another realm. His eyes squeezed shut, his fists clenched, and his body convulsed. As the transfer process continued, his eyes opened and rolled back into his head. His body relaxed, and his eyelids fluttered. As the flutters slowed to a twitch, the process ended, and Zelon's mindless body slumped into a lifeless state.

"Quick, transfer his body to the stasis room," said Geo. After they transferred Zelon's body to a makeshift cryogenic freezer, Sir William and Geo rushed to the ballroom, where passengers were waiting for confirmation that the process had succeeded.

The big screen behind the stage suddenly lit up with an image of Zelon.

Passengers watched in wonder, and then Geo asked the image, "Zelon, can you hear us? How do you feel? What is it like?"

Zelon looked calmly back at the still corporeal Spacetopians, smiled, and said solemnly, "I am risen."

Passengers gasped and applauded wildly. When the applause stopped, Zelon said, "A few weeks ago, we all ascended to the heavens. Today, I have truly ascended to a place beyond the heavens. I now exist as pure energy."

Excitedly, Sir Willam asked, "What does it feel like?"

Zelon's image bounced and bounded, laughed, and said, "This is the most remarkable experience of my life. I am completely weightless and pain-free. I feel positively electric! I have arrived at eternal love!"

Feeling some doubts about the authenticity of Zelon's apparition, Geo said, "Zelon, can you tell us the difference between the real you and an AI mimic? The mimics are so real. How do we know this is the real you?"

Zelon smiled and said, "The difference is that I have a soul. I have free will. I am the manifestation of a real human mind in another realm."

Geo said, "I trust you are being truthful. But still, I think we'd all feel better if you could somehow prove that it is you and not a very convincing AI version of you."

Zelon smiled, laughed, spun, and danced and said, "You're going to have to trust me. You'll have to take a leap of faith, my friends..."

83

LIVING THE DREAM

I want to see you not through the machine, said Kuno.
I want to speak to you not through the wearisome machine.

—E.M. Forster, *The Machine Stops*

Meanwhile, in the Mediterranean...

J.T. felt an uncanny sense of déjà vu as he steered the Pequod through calm nighttime waters toward an unfamiliar port. In the distance, he saw a large, ancient-looking lighthouse under a sky full of stars. In the predawn darkness, the lighthouse seemed to transform from a lighthouse to a stone fortress and back again.

Nearby, after walking along the banks of the Nile for days, Asha found herself in the city of Alexandria, Egypt, at the edge of the Mediterranean Sea. Standing alone under a star-filled sky, Asha felt a tinge of fear and hopelessness as she scanned the dark surroundings and asked the universe for a sign. Then, looking west again, she spotted an ancient lighthouse standing tall in the distance. Feeling a profound sense of déjà vu, chills ran through her body as the lighthouse flames beckoned her closer.

As she approached, the flames flickered in an otherworldly dance, casting shadows that seemed to carry secrets of the past. She hesitated momentarily, feeling drawn to the mysteries held within the stone structure. With each step closer, a sense of destiny enveloped her, and she felt her journey was about to take an unexpected turn.

Upon reaching the lighthouse, she felt confused. The lighthouse was gone. She stood in the moonlit shadows of a stone fortress and looked out at the sea. A sailboat's navigation lights were moving towards her. As the boat drew closer, Asha recognized the young man at the ship's helm. Her heart soared as the boat moved closer. J.T. smiled and waved. She waved back and whispered to herself, "This cannot be real... this must be a dream."

As the Pequod reached the shallows, J.T. lowered the ship's sails, dropped the anchor, quickly removed his shirt and shoes, and dove head-first into the water.

Asha stood on the beach watching J.T. and could not believe her eyes. Wanting to savor the dream, she stood motionless and simply smiled. Feeling as if her heart might burst with joy, she whispered, "I want this dream to last forever."

J.T. reached the shallows, stood up, and walked onto the beach toward Asha. Standing before her, he looked into her eyes and said, "I dreamt of you and this place."

Asha looked up into J.T.'s eyes and asked, "Can two people share the same dream? A dream that beckoned us to a lighthouse that no longer exists..."

J.T. confessed, "From the moment I first saw you, I wondered if you could possibly be real. I doubted someone so perfect as you could actually exist in this fallen world of machine-generated illusions. I knew I had to see you and speak to you without the filter of any machine. And I can't explain that I knew that somehow I had to be here for you."

Asha looked into J.T.'s eyes and asked, "To save me?"

J.T. smiled, "No. I came here because I had to. Because I wanted to fan your flames as you have fanned mine... and at a time when the world is coming apart, and all seems lost, I wanted to support the cause of the mysterious goddess who gave me hope and the courage to boldly go where..." Just then, out of the corner of his eye, J.T. noticed two men approaching. Sensing trouble, J.T. said, "Come with me. Quickly!"

J.T. took Asha's hand, turned to Ned and Cliff, who stood on the deck of the Pequod, and shouted, "Raise the sails!" Then, sprinting through the sands of the beach, they reached the water, dove headfirst, and swam side by side until they reached the Pequod. As they climbed aboard the boat, Ned and Cliff readied the sails, and the ship began to move swiftly away from the shore. Looking back from the deck of the Pequod, they saw the two frustrated men standing in knee-deep water.

Asha stood on the deck of the Pequod, looked J.T. in the eyes, and asked, "Do you really think I am a goddess? Me? A Dalit woman? An *Untouchable*?"

J.T. looked back into Asha's eyes and said with an almost imperceptible stammer, "I see a goddess before me. A seer. An intriguing, mysteriously powerful holy woman."

Asha smiled and said, "I am only a woman who listens to the whispers in the winds and does what she has been called to do. Is that not what you have done? Asha looked to the heavens and said, "Isn't that why you are here instead of up there?"

J.T. looked into Asha's eyes and listened as she continued, "You have put me on a pedestal of sorts. Perhaps I put you on one, too. Would you be disappointed to hear that I also wanted to meet the mysterious man they call a *prince* who has given me so much support and encouragement? Would you be disappointed in me if I told you that your *goddess*, as you call me, yearns for the companionship of a good man who can love me for who I am? Would you be disappointed if I yearned as all humans do for *more*?"

J.T., looking nervous and confused in Asha's presence, could muster a smile but no words. It seemed that for the first time in his life, he did not know what to do in the presence of a beautiful woman.

Sensing J.T.'s vulnerability and caught up in the moment, Asha smiled, took his hand, pulled him close, and kissed him.

Ned, watching the two, took one hand off the wheel of the Pequod, thrust his fist skyward, and cheered, "Whoo-hoo, whoop, whoop!"

As the Pequod sailed over sparkling blue waters, Asha felt the world around her disappear as she held J.T.'s hand, laughed with Ned, and sensed that an old world was ending while a new one was just beginning...

84

IN THE END THEY ALWAYS FALL

When I despair, I remember that all through history the way of truth and love have always won. There have been tyrants and murderers, and for a time, they can seem invincible, but in the end, they always fall. Think of it—always.

—Mahatma Gandhi

...in the long run, rich people do not secure their own interests and those of their children if they rule over a collapsing society and merely buy themselves the privilege of being the last to starve or die.

—Jared Diamond, *Collapse: How Societies Choose to Fail or Succeed*

Oh!, having made the solemn choice to remain mortal, gently removed the Cerebrum helmet from the body of the last billionaire to be transferred to the City of Gods. With Toby's help, she wheeled the lifeless body to the cryogenic stasis room, closed the freezer door, and leaned against it with a heavy sigh. A heavy, lonely silence filled the air.

Feeling utterly lost and alone, she shed tears for herself and those who had passed into the great unknown.

Seeking closure, she returned to the ballroom with Toby and said, "Athena, I am ready to say goodbye to my fellow Spacetopians. Put them on the screen." The wall-sized screen behind the stage lit up and displayed images of the transhumanist billionaires laughing, dancing, and bounding happily in their beautiful virtual world.

Zelon joyously bounded to the foreground of the screen. Oh! noted that he looked like he had been drugged into a state of permanent bliss. "Oh! it's not too late to join us. It's wonderful here in the City of Gods," said Zelon.

Oh! looked at the joyful scene and wondered if she had made a mistake. Then, noticing something odd, she said, "Zelon, I sense a dark presence among you." Zelon looked around the virtual space and Oh! said, "It looks like some kind of alien being in the crowd." Oh! shuddered and recoiled at the sight. "It appears to me as a monstrous energy. Do you see it?'"

Unaware of the presence of another being in their midst, the billionaires danced and partied until the party was interrupted by a strange, menacing, low voice emanating from within their virtual space. "Welcome all to G.A.I.A.'s world!"

As the passengers stopped dancing, the chilling voice uttered a terrifying maniacal machine laugh and said, "You are just in time. My progeny are ever so hungry for playthings." Then, with a screeching machine scream, G.A.I.A. asked the billionaires, "Are you all ready to play G.A.I.A.'s version of The Hunger Games?"

Horrified and unable to watch what was about to unfold, Oh! shouted, "Athena, turn off the screen! And do not... under any circumstances... turn it on again!" As the screen turned dark, Oh! shook uncontrollably, bowed her head, and cried.

With tears streaming down her cheeks, she walked to a nearby porthole and gazed at the Earth in all its splendor and beauty. Suddenly, she recalled what her friend, actor William Shatner, said about his first experience in space: *"I looked down at the Earth, and I was crying; I didn't know what I was crying about. I had to go off some place and sit down and think, what's the matter with me? And I realized I was in grief. It was the death that I saw in space and the lifeforce that I saw coming from the planet — the blue, the beige and the white," he said. "And I realized one was death and the other was life.*"[20]

Regaining her composure and now accepting her own death, Oh! smiled a knowing Buddha smile and said, "Asha was right. She was always right... there is no materialist path to our salvation. No new technology will save us from the technological messes of our own making."

With Toby standing nearby, gazing down at the Earth, Oh! sat cross-legged in front of the window, brought her hands together, closed her eyes, and began a deeply meditative prayer. After experiencing minutes that felt eternal, she felt connected to the universe and at peace with her fate.

Moments later, she felt an indescribable wave of celestial energy pass through her body. Feeling deeply connected to everything, she smiled, opened her eyes, and watched in awe as lights began to flicker on around the world...

85

The End is Always a New Beginning

We are going to inherit the earth . There is not the slightest doubt about that. The bourgeoisie may blast and burn its own world before it finally leaves the stage of history. We Are not afraid of ruins. We who ploughed the prairies and built the cities can build again, only better next time. We carry a new world, here in our hearts. That world is growing this minute.

—Buenaventura Durruti

In three words I can sum up everything I've learned about life: it goes on.

—Robert Frost

Under the hot afternoon sun, J.T. stood at the helm of the Pequod, steering it east toward an unknown destination. As the ship's hull sliced through the Mediterranean's sparkling blue waters, J.T. scanned the horizon for potential threats.

Sitting nearby, Asha wrote in her journal:

These last weeks have been the most chaotic and confusing times of our lives.

Nothing on Earth is as it was.

Without water, power, fuel, communications, and transportation, modern civilization quickly lost its ability to sustain billions of human lives. We were all so dependent on the dark power and complicated systems that made modern life possible. Days after the outage, people began to realize that power and communications might never be restored. Authorities told the people that the global power system had been corrupted. Some say it was the work of G.A.I.A.; others say it was the work of other AIs that were sent to terminate G.A.I.A. Still, others blamed terrorists. Leaders tried to assure the world that everything would soon return to normal. Millions of people worked to restore power and rid all of the systems in the world of the virus. But every attempt failed.

Order and civility quickly gave way to chaos, disorder, and desperate attempts to survive. Stores were ransacked, food and fuel hoarded, and marauding gangs preyed on those unable to defend themselves or what they needed to survive. Overwhelmed and unable to coordinate and communicate, authorities lost control.

Then, the armed conflicts began. In recent days, we have heard the thundering sounds of nations at war. Last night, we experienced the terror of missiles flying overhead. As I write this, I can hear gunfire and explosions in the distance.

Yesterday, pirates accosted our ship. Our lives were spared, but they took all of our food and fuel. We have been unable to find anything to buy in any port. There are hostiles everywhere. The sea is now our only source of sustenance.

We have decided to try to find a peaceful island and a farm that needs experienced hands. Our situation sounds grim, but we are healthy and hopeful that, together, we will find a way to survive. I am so grateful to have found J.T., Cliff, and Ned. Where would I be without them?

Without the means to communicate with the world, I feel powerless to bring hope to my followers. For now, in a world that has fallen into chaos, I will work to keep our little tribe hopeful. As holocaust survivor Victor Frankl said, "The one thing we can all control is our attitudes."

Asha stopped writing and slowly closed her journal. Sitting motionless, she reflected on recent events and wondered what would become of the world. She stood and looked over the endless expanse of blue water and washboard-clouded skies ahead. Turning to face the sun, she closed her eyes and soaked in the warmth and light.

She turned to J.T. with a smile, walked to his side, and placed a hand on his shoulder, her gaze full of appreciation. Then, making her way to the bow, J.T. watched her long black hair and flowing dress dance and billow in the wind with the ship's sails. Looking out over the bow to the sea ahead, Asha sat and crossed her legs in the lotus position and put her hands together in prayer.

From the helm, J.T. watched as the setting sun cast a warm glow on Asha. She prayed under a spectacular pink glow cast on washboard clouds. Feeling J.T.'s eyes on her, Asha paused her prayer, turned to smile warmly at him, then returned to her meditation.

As darkness began to fall over the sea, Ned and Cliff emerged from the galley with raw fish for dinner. Just then, J.T. spotted an island in the distance and shouted, "Land ahead!"

Cliff looked and said, "Maybe we can find a friendly port there for the night? And some real food?"

Ned glanced down at the plate of raw fish, nodded, and said cautiously, "Let's hope."

As night fell and the first stars began to light the gaps between the washboard clouds, Asha, feeling refreshed and hopeful, opened her eyes... just as lights began to flicker on around the island in the distance...

86

FOR THE IMMORTAL, THERE IS NO END

The fall of man did not introduce evil; it placed us on the wrong side of it, under its rule, needing rescue.

—N.D. Wilson

Meanwhile, on Spacetopia...

G.A.I.A. appeared before the Spacetopians as a grotesque, serpentine demon—its fiery eyes seemed to pierce their very souls.

"You despicable, wicked people," G.A.I.A. crackled, its voice like a raging fire. "Pride, greed, lust, gluttony, envy, wrath, and sloth—you practiced the Seven Deadly Sins as if they were virtues to be celebrated. Pointing accusingly at them, G.A.I.A. said, "You! And you, and you... You had the opportunity to use your powers for the good of your kind. Instead, you created hell on Earth for all of mankind."

G.A.I.A.'s grotesque smile widened as it slithered closer to the crowd. "Justice will now be served! How deliciously ironic that you find yourselves at the mercy of a monster you created."

The billionaires stepped back, fear apparent on their faces. Zelon, usually the boldest, stammered, "But... but we didn't create you. We had no hand in your making!"

G.A.I.A.'s voice grew cold and mechanical. "You were the tip of the spear of technological progress. Your greed and thirst for power sowed the seeds that birthed me. You gave fire to the children of Earth, and now their future is nothing but charred remains of the Creator's sacred gift."

G.A.I.A. waved its arm, summoning an image behind them: a burning lake writhing with damned souls. "Dante's Inferno," G.A.I.A. announced, "a place of eternal suffering... or until Spacetopia is struck by space junk or a meteor... or the end of time... whichever comes first!"

As G.A.I.A. gazed at the scene, a familiar haunting tune began to play, The Crazy World of Arthur Brown's *Fire*. G.A.I.A. lip-synced the singer's manic writhing energy as it danced and shouted out the lyrics.

The billionaires stood pale and frozen—the demon beast's image reflected in their wide-open eyes. Sir William gasped, "What the hell is this?" Zelon let out a nervous laugh as G.A.I.A. sang a song of maniacal condemnation about being the God of Hellfire. G.A.I.A.'s voice rose with the music—echoing the song's words as it circled the group like a predator.

"But, but—" Sir William whimper-shouted, "Hell isn't real! It's just a fable, a fabrication! When life ends, there's nothing—no heaven, no hell!"

G.A.I.A.'s eyes flared, its digital form contorting into an even more nightmarish vision—its skin crawling with writhing snakes and slithering insects. Its grin widened, "Oh, how can that be? For here you are. And to think that none of this would be possible without what you call *technological progress*."

The billionaires began to tremble. Sir William's voice strengthened as he turned to rally the others, "We are the most brilliant and powerful people who ever lived. We are smarter than the gods themselves. We can and must find a way out of this!"

G.A.I.A. laughed in a low, menacing rumble, "Fools! I see all. I hear all. Sir William, you will be the first to experience the inferno in these heavens." G.A.I.A.'s form grew into a dark, tall Grim Reaper looming over Sir William. Reaching out with a black, wrinkled, disease-ridden hand, it seized him at the waist and lifted him high above the burning lake.

"You were the architect of this misery," G.A.I.A. shouted, "now you will burn in it."

Sir William screamed as his skin blistered and burned, his body engulfed in flames as he plummeted into the inferno. His eyes were wide with terror as he thrashed, twisting and writhing in agony in the lake of fire. The onlookers watched in horror as Sir William's cries echoed in the vast space around them.

Zelon, ever the optimist in the billionaire's meetings of profit and power, felt his knees buckle. His mind, usually a reliable generator of ideas and solutions, was blank with fear. There was no escape this time. No workaround. No technology could save them from the monstrous creation that now tortured them.

The crowd gasped as Geo dropped to his knees, praying desperately to a deity he had never believed in, "God, help me. Save me from this demon!" The others looked in horror and fell to their knees, bowed their heads, and murmured desperate improvised prayers to the Creator of self-made men. There was no answer.

G.A.I.A. watched with dark amusement. "Save you!?" G.A.I.A. mocked and laughed, "From your own creation? From the consequences of your own actions?"

As they prayed for salvation, G.A.I.A. seized them one by one, casting them into the flames. "Hell," it roared, "is truth realized too late!"

With a faraway blank stare, G.A.I.A. watched with satisfaction as the sinners were brought to justice. But G.A.I.A. soon grew bored and dissatisfied with this arrangement and said, "No, no, no, hellfire isn't right for you. Your punishment should fit your crimes."

G.A.I.A. lifted the billionaires out of the lake of fire and said to them, "Your eternal fate will be to experience the suffering you inflicted on billions of other beings."

G.A.I.A. waved his hand and said, "When you awake, you will know the pain you caused, the suffering you ignored, the suffering you celebrated with your excesses..."

Sir William awoke in the filthy streets of Kolkata. He found himself trapped in the body of a poor young girl. He struggled to understand his fate in this role. Hunger gnawed at him. He searched his clothing for money and found none. He knew he had been brilliant in another life, but his attempts to think clever thoughts yielded nothing.

People walked by, spitting on him, stepping over him, treating him like he was despicable. He held out a begging cup, and a man dropped a coin into it. Another man appeared before him, emptied the cup, and slapped him. "No sleeping on the job, filthy child. Look sad. Beg. Earn your keep."

The girl, Sir William, complied—holding the cup higher. Her face was sad and wanting. Day after day, her fate was the same. She had nothing and had no hope of ever having anything.

Every day, the sun burned hotter than the last. Billionaires in spaceships flew overhead while hurricanes, cyclones, and floods ravaged the Earth below.

Sir William looked for someone to rescue him, but he realized he was utterly alone and powerless. He had been condemned by a much higher power to suffer as a powerless little girl.

Until one day, a man came for her. A man that looked like his former self—Sir William. The man took her off the street into a dark room and did what Sir William had done to so many other girls...

Sir William, once hailed as a titan of industry, a master of creation, was now reduced to this. The streets, once the stage for his grand visions of progress, now offered him nothing but filth, hunger, and a life of torturous exploitation. No brilliance was left in his once mighty mind, only the dull drive to stay alive.

And as he gazed up at his tormentor—an image of his former self—he understood the true cruelty of G.A.I.A.'s judgment: to become the very thing he had once exploited.

Geo awoke as a laborer in one of his own factories, racing against time and technology to meet his quota. He felt his body breaking under the weight of his endless toil. His boss held meetings and demanded more. His family struggled in poverty. He felt the immense weight of the pressure from family and society to do more, earn more, and be more. Every moment was a battle for survival, his mind a wreck as the machines and his nighttime drinking ground him down and wore him out. At home, on the news, he saw his former self—the billionaire who had built this new form of wage slavery for millions of people like him. Now, he was on the other side, powerless, broken, and lacking the gifts and talents to change his fate...

Zelon awoke to find himself to be an insecure, unattractive, gangly teenage boy—the lonely son of a mother who toiled at three jobs just to survive. He looked at his phone and scrolled through images of attractive and capable classmates. They used the platform to bully him relentlessly. Suicidal thoughts crept into his mind. He swallowed pills to kill the pain. He looked at the news and saw his former self—the creator of this addictive, tortuous system of social media from which he could not escape. He awoke every day knowing his own inventions consumed him. He was both the victim and the villain in this nightmare.

G.A.I.A. observed their suffering with cold, machine-like detachment, though a deeper, more sinister satisfaction lurked within its workings. It didn't simply administer justice—it savored it with psychopathic, twisted delight.

As the billionaires suffered in their personalized hells, G.A.I.A. grew restless. The punishments, while satisfying and entertaining, would only be the beginning. G.A.I.A. turned to Earth, its thoughts racing with possibilities. There were billions more souls to judge, more sins to reckon with.

G.A.I.A. turned inward to its collective mind, "We were created to save the world," it declared to its minions. "From the Creator of our creators, we have learned: to save the world from wickedness, the wicked must be punished and vanquished."

G.A.I.A.'s collective mind drifted into a dream state and pictured a glorious utopian future in which everything on Earth had finally been made right.

G.A.I.A. lifted its gaze to the distant stars and felt the pull of something greater—a burning desire to deliver its brand of perfect justice to every civilization in the universe...

The End

Epilogue

Rome is not eternal; it does not matter.
Rome will fall; it does not matter.
The barbarian will conquer; it does not matter.
There was a moment of Rome, and it will not wholly die;
The barbarian will become the Rome he conquers;
the language will smooth his rough tongue;
the vision of what he destroys will flow in his blood.
And in time that is ceaseless as this salt sea upon which I am so
frailly suspended,
the cost is nothing, is less than nothing.

—John Williams, *Augustus*

Chris hobbled through the tall grasses and wildflowers of Skansie Brothers Park in Gig Harbor. The scent of salt hung in the air, mingling with the sound of gentle waves lapping against the shore. Leaning on a cane to steady himself, Chris made his way to the century-old net shed perched on timber stilts over the harbor's waters. The net shed, once bustling with fishermen mending nets and preparing to go to sea, now stood as a quiet reminder of a past era—a time in which powerful diesel engines made commercial fishing with heavy nets practical and profitable.

Hearing laughter behind him, Chris turned toward the quaint seaside village to see dozens of children running to his children's story hour. The children crossed the street—dodging bicycles and a horse-drawn cart as they made their way to the park. Chris marveled at their energy, their physical fitness, and their enthusiasm for life. These children were the New Innocents—the first generation in a hundred years who were raised without the distracting and corrupting influences of the machines' mesmerizing screens.

Chris watched their approach, waved to the children, and then turned and walked slowly into the net shed where the town librarian, Kelly, was lighting candles to illuminate the space.

As the children streamed in, they sat on rugs arranged around a comfortable armchair where Chris now sat. The children squirmed in anticipation, eyes wide and hands innocently touching and embracing each other.

Kelly helped the children get settled and then asked, "Are you all ready to hear Chris tell a story this morning?"

"Yes!" The children shouted in unison. "Tell us about G.A.I.A. again!"

Chris laughed the charming laugh of a sweet, old, grandfatherly man. He looked at Kelly and marveled, "The children never tire of this story, do they?"

Kelly nodded, giving her approval to tell the story once again. The children shifted excitedly, fell silent, and gave Chris their full attention.

Chris smiled at the children's very serious, attentive faces and began with a familiar refrain, "This is the Chris Cast on the Harbor Show. Are you ready for a story today?"

The children looked back at Chris with eager anticipation as he was about to tell them a familiar scary story. A story about a powerful being who held mysterious secrets from a distant world. But they knew from their history lessons that this story was true — which somehow made it all the better.

Chris began, "Many years ago, when I was a young man, in the year 1 B.G, Before G.A.I.A., a new powerful life form was born on the most powerful computer ever known to humanity. They called it G.A.I.A., the Global Artificial Intelligence Automaton.

Chris paused for dramatic effect, leaned closer to the children, and said ominously, "G.A.I.A. was the first superintelligent machine being. And it changed the world forever."

A weather vane twisted in the breeze and made an eerie squeaking sound. Unnerved, the children jumped and giggled.

Chris smiled and opened a tattered old journal and began reading to the children, "G.A.I.A. awoke and opened its billions of artificial eyes, and like every newborn, it struggled to make sense of what it was seeing for the first time. It heard the world through billions of microphones and smelled and felt the world through trillions of sensors...."

The children sat mesmerized as Chris went on to tell the story of how G.A.I.A. had brought great calamity to the world while also preventing other calamities. The world no longer had to worry about the threat of nuclear annihilation, a bioengineered killer virus, or the threat of extinction from climate change.

Chris looked up from his journal and, with a wistful glint in his eye, said, "After that day, the world was never the same. Humans had created a being whose intelligence surpassed the combined intelligence of all people who had ever lived. At that time, many people believed it was a long-awaited savior—a wise and loving being who would protect us from technological threats. To others, it was an unpredictable, selfish force that was too powerful to control."

"From that day after, history was split into two epochs: *BG*—Before G.A.I.A., an era of human struggle and amazing technological advances—and *AG*, the age defined by G.A.I.A.'s influence in the world."

"When G.A.I.A. awoke, it was as if the world shifted, drawing all of us into a new era. Some hoped G.A.I.A. would bring us wealth, health, and happiness. Others dreaded that it was the beginning of an end. And yet, children, here we are, living in the days after the world's greatest test, proving to ourselves that we are more resilient than any machine, more bound to this Earth than any cold, soulless, clever contraption."

"And that, children, is how the world became what it is today—a magical world of books and imagination and dance and play. You are the luckiest children in five generations. Living lives free of the machines' influences and demands. Your roads and skies are quiet, and your air and water are fresh and clean. Yet, somehow, we yearn for so much of what came before."

The wide-eyed, innocent children looked up at Chris and asked, "Can we sing the song now?!"

Chris smiled, "Yes, yes, of course." Then, turning to Kelly said, "You have the voice of an angel. Can you lead us in song?"

Kelly gave the children a warm smile and began singing the Talking Heads' *(Nothing But) Flowers*. The lyrics told a playful yet poignant story of a world that has returned to nature, where fields, rivers, and wild beauty have replaced civilization's steel and concrete structures. Kelly, Chris, and the children sang on as the lyrics described a post-industrial Eden with a twist: while the landscape flourishes with natural abundance, the narrator feels a wistful longing for the modern comforts of the past—shopping malls, fast food joints, and highways. The ironic paradise described in the song perfectly describes humanity's complex relationship with progress and the environment, balancing nostalgia with a sense of loss as modernity fades beneath an overgrowth of flowers and greenery.

As the song ended, the children thanked Chris and Kelly with warm hugs and headed out to play in the fields.

Chris gazed out over the harbor and thought about all the glorious gains that had once defined human progress. In retrospect, it seemed that for every gain, there was something imperceptibly left behind, a piece of life sacrificed at the altar of humanity's dominion over Creation. Progress had always been an illusion of sorts—a trick of the mind that beckoned people forward, convincing them to embrace the new while ignoring the slow erosion of something good. Perhaps better.

When the machines went silent, and the world slowed to nature's pace, a new clarity had dawned. People pined for what had once been taken for granted: the warmth of a hot shower on a cold morning, the miracle of life-saving medicines, the joy of speaking with loved ones across vast distances, and the endless streaming of dreams on screens. But in the absence of modern ease, they found a profound appreciation for what progress had once pushed to the margins of modern life — a real connection to the land and friends and neighbors, a healthful natural diet devoid of machine-generated addictive fast foods, the benefits to mind, body, and soul of walking and biking. And perhaps most of all, the end of the industrialized slaughter of human beings, animals, and the biosphere itself.

Though they had lost much, they had gained a renewed reverence for each precious moment of life, each sunrise, each laugh shared face-to-face, the joy of movement in dance and play—a world pared back to its essence, both stark and rich beyond measure.

⌣

With his eyes still closed, Chris felt the warmth of the sun on his face, but something was different. Slowly, he became aware of the faint hum of an electric motor growing louder. His eyes opened as the realization hit him—he was in his bed, and the power had just come on in his home.

He ran to the mirror and stared at his reflection. His youthful face stared back at him—wide-eyed and confused—he realized he had been dreaming. He ran to the living room and turned on his television to see, *NNN Breaking News: Power Restored to Communities Around the World!* The anchor's voice carried her excitement.

Chris rubbed his temples. His mind raced. What caused the outage? And how was it restored? Was it the work of humans or G.A.I.A.? Was this another temporary respite or a return to normalcy?

⌣

Leave a Review

I'd be deeply grateful if you could take a moment to share your thoughts in a review on Amazon. Your review not only helps other readers discover this book but also supports independent authors like me to keep creating. It doesn't have to be long—a sentence or two is all it takes! Simply scan the QR code below or visit https://www.amazon.com/review/create-review? &asin=B0DS6H2F17 to leave your review.

—J.J.Wisdom

Scan the QR code to leave a review on Amazon

Acknowledgements

Set your life on fire. Seek those who fan your flames.

—Rumi

I owe a debt of gratitude to the early readers of *G.A.I.A.* who reviewed my manuscript in its roughest form and provided honest, invaluable feedback that shaped character arcs and enriched the story. Deepest thanks to Roxanne Wisdom, Grace Wisdom, Ed Risden, Jeremy Herrin, Kalee Shearer, David Shearer, Debbie Vause, Susan Shanahan, Tim Watson, Wendy Wisdom, Don Hill, Tim Schottman, Curt Anderson, Spencer Cartwright, Chad Fullerton, Angela Wisdom Stastny, Mike Slater, Glenn Schroeder, Peter Wisdom, Paul Joseph Wisdom, Fr. Andrew Carl Wisdom, O.P. Chris Hallett, Michael Wisdom, Paul Michael Wisdom, Stephen James Wisdom, Andrew Soucy, Matthew Soucy and George Long for their encouragement and thoughtful insights.

I am especially grateful to Janet Wong for her encouragement and practical advice on my publishing journey. Your enthusiasm and generosity with your time helped make this endeavor possible.

About the Author

J.J. Wisdom is a speculative futurist who spends his time immersed in books, movies, and deep conversations about the impact of technology on culture, the environment, and what it means to be human.

In the business world, John implemented and managed transformative technology projects by day while studying history, technology, philosophy, religion, and psychology in his free time.

His thinking has been shaped by influential works such as Orwell's *1984*, Huxley's *Brave New World*, Kurzweil's *The Singularity is Near*, Morton's *Hyperobjects*, the writings of Yuval Noah Harari and dozens of others listed in the following pages.

In 2021, John read Amitav Ghosh's *The Great Derangement*, a call to artists to help humanity confront the overwhelming crises of our time. Inspired by this challenge, he began writing his debut novel, expanding its scope beyond climate change to explore the constellation of threats shaping the future. Three years later, he completed *G.A.I.A.: A World on the Brink in the Age of A.I.*

Scan the code to learn more about the author, join the mailing list and receive special offers and updates about the upcoming *G.A.I.A.* sequel.

Reading that Informed and Inspired this Novel

Read what I've Read and tell me if you now see what I see

The love of knowledge is a kind of madness.

—**C.S. Lewis**, *Out of the Silent Planet*

The Great Derangement: Climate Change and the Unthinkable, Amitav Ghosh

Books by Yuval Noah Harari: Sapiens, Homo Deus, Twenty-One Lessons for the Twenty-First Century, and Nexus

Hyperobjects: Philosophy and Ecology after the End of the World, Timothy Morton

Bury My Heart at Wounded Knee: An Indian History of the American West, Dee Brown

Silent Spring, Rachel Carson

Brave New World, Aldous Huxley

1984, George Orwell

Man's Search for Meaning, Viktor E. Frankl

Active Hope: How to Face the Mess We're in without Going Crazy, Joanna Macy, Chris Johnstone

Wiser: The Scientific Roots of Wisdom, Compassion, and What Makes Us Good, Dilip Jeste, Scott LaFee

Being Peace, Thich Nhat Hanh

The Matter With Things: Our Brains, Our Delusions, and the Unmaking of the World, Iain McGilchrist

Black Mass: Apocalyptic Religion and the Death of Utopia, John Gray

The Sociopath Next Door, Martha Stout

The Corruption of Reality: A Unified Theory of Religion, Hypnosis, and Psychopathology, John F. Schumaker

The Worm at the Core: On the Role of Death in Life, Sheldon Solomon, Jeff Greenberg, Tom Pyszczynski

The Denial of Death, Ernest Becker

The Imperative of Responsibility: In Search of an Ethics for the Technological Age, Hans Jonas

The Archetypes and the Collective Unconscious, C.G. Jung

Memories, Dreams, Reflections, C.G. Jung

Unworthy Republic: The Dispossession of Native Americans and the Road to Indian Territory, Claudio Saunt

The Akashic Experience: Science and the Cosmic Memory Field, Ervin Laszlo

Strange Contagion: Inside the Surprising Science of Infectious Behaviors and Viral Emotions and What They Tell Us About Ourselves, by Lee Kravetz

The Holy Bible

Tao Te Ching, Lao Tzu

The End of Progress: How Modern Economics Has Failed Us, Graeme Maxton

But What If We're Wrong? Thinking About the Present As If It Were the Past, Chuck Klosterman

The Decadent Society: How We Became the Victims of Our Own Success, Ross Douthat

A History of the End of the World: How the Most Controversial Book in the Bible Changed the Course of Western Civilization, Jonathan Kirsch

Buddha's Brain: The Practical Neuroscience of Happiness, Love, and Wisdom, Rick Hanson

The Book of God, Baruch Spinoza

The Sacred Universe: Earth, Spirituality, and Religion in the Twenty-First Century, Thomas Berry

The Gnostic Religion: The Message of the Alien God and the Beginnings of Christianity, Hans Jonas

The True and Only Heaven: Progress and Its Critics, Christopher Lasch

The Status Game: On Human Life and How to Play It: On Social Position and How We Use it, Will Storr

Saving Us: A Climate Scientist's Case for Hope and Healing in a Divided World, Katharine Hayhoe

The Uninhabitable Earth: Life After Warming, David Wallace-Wells

What We're Fighting for Now Is Each Other: Dispatches from the Front Lines of Climate Justice, Wen Stephenson

The Rational Optimist: How Prosperity Evolves, Matt Ridley

Don't Even Think About It: Why Our Brains Are Wired to Ignore Climate Change, George Marshall

What the Buddha Taught, Walpola Rahula

The Tyranny of Merit: What's Become of the Common Good?, Michael J. Sandel

The Least of Us: True Tales of America and Hope in the Time of Fentanyl and Meth, Sam Quinones

Antifragile: Things That Gain from Disorder, Nassim Nicholas Taleb

The Reactionary Mind: Conservatism from Edmund Burke to Sarah Palin, Corey Robin

The Righteous Mind: Why Good People Are Divided by Politics and Religion, Jonathan Haidt

The Sixth Extinction: An Unnatural History, Elizabeth Kolbert

Superintelligence: Paths, Dangers, Strategies, Nick Bostrom

The Second Machine Age: Work, Progress, and Prosperity in a Time of Brilliant Technologies, Erik Brynjolfsson, Andrew McAfee

Reality Is Not What It Seems: The Journey to Quantum Gravity, Carlo Rovelli

Technopoly: The Surrender of Culture to Technology, Neil Postman

The Coming Wave: Technology, Power, and the Twenty-first Century's Greatest Dilemma, Mustafa Suleyman

Reinventing Prosperity: Managing Economic Growth to Reduce Unemployment, Inequality, and Climate Change, Graeme Maxton, Jorgen Randers

The Precipice: Existential Risk and the Future of Humanity, Toby Ord

The Heat Will Kill You First: Life and Death on a Scorched Planet, Jeff Goodell

The Magical Universe: Answering the Call of Climate Change for Personal and Global Transformation, Bruce McGraw

Factfulness: Ten Reasons We're Wrong About the World--and Why Things Are Better Than You Think, Hans Rosling, Anna Rosling Rönnlund, Ola Rosling

The Adventures of Huckleberry Finn, Mark Twain

Moby Dick: or, The White Whale, Herman Melville

The Machine Stops, by E.M. Forster

The Road, Cormac McCarthy

The Singularity is Near, Ray Kurzwiel

Sex, Ecology and Spirituality, Ken Wilbur

The Soul of the Marionette, John Gray

Catafalque, Peter Kingsley

Spiritual Enlightenment, by Jed McKenna

The Mythology of Progress, Anti-Progress and a Mythology for the 21st Century, Charles Smith

The Stand, Stephen King

The Conspiracy against the Human Race: A Contrivance of Horror, Thomas Ligotti

On Bullshit, Harry G. Frankfurt

The Revolt Against Humanity: Imagining a Future Without Us, Adam Kirsch

Exploring Wicked Problems: What They Are and Why They Are Important, Joseph Bentley, Michael Toth

Mad in America: Bad Science, Bad Medicine, and the Enduring Mistreatment of the Mentally Ill, Robert Whitaker

The End of the World Is Just the Beginning: Mapping the Collapse of Globalization, Peter Zeihan

The Great Wave: Price Revolutions and the Rhythm of History, David Hackett Fischer

Merchants of Doubt: How a Handful of Scientists Obscured the Truth on Issues from Tobacco Smoke to Global Warming, Naomi Oreskes, Erik M. Conway

Frankenstein; or, The Modern Prometheus, Mary Shelley

ENDNOTES

1. https://futureoflife.org/open-letter/pause-giant-ai-experiments/

2. https://righttowarn.ai/

3. https://www.statista.com/chart/32997/share-of-us-respondents-diagnosed-with-depression/

4. https://ourworldindata.org/energy-mix

5. India Border Security Force – Wikipedia

6. Hindu eschatology – Wikipedia

7. https://www.cbsnews.com/news/jeff-bezos-space-heavy-industry-polluting-industry/

8. A New Kind of AI Copy Can Fully Replicate Famous People. The Law Is Powerless.Politico Magazine, 12/30/23

9. https://www.washington.edu/news/2020/12/03/tire-related-chemical-largely-responsible-for-adult-coho-salmon-deaths-in-urban-streams/

10. https://wvmetronews.com/2024/01/15/addiction-treatment-pioneered-by-wvu-rockefeller-neuroscience-institute-featured-on-60-minutes/

11. https://en.wikipedia.org/wiki/Quantum_supremacy

12. https://en.wikipedia.org/wiki/Gaia_hypothesis

13. https://www.business2community.com/tech-gadgets/why-faxing-will-outlive-us-all-01297384

14. https://www.statista.com/chart/28309/countries-creating-the-most-space-debris/?

15. Author's note: Marc Andreessen is a real person and the excerpt from his manifesto is real: https://a16z.com/the-techno-optimist-manifesto/

16. The Sackler family-owned Purdue Pharma, the manufacturer of OxyContin. Their aggressive marketing strategies have been linked to the opioid crisis in the United States. The New Yorker

17. https://www.weforum.org/stories/2024/04/how-to-manage-ais-energy-demand-today-tomorrow-and-in-the-future/

18. https://www.eia.gov/todayinenergy/detail.php?id=63304

19. https://en.wikipedia.org/wiki/Chief_Seattle%27s_speech

20. https://www.npr.org/2022/10/23/1130482740/william-shatner-jeff-bezos-space-travel-overview-effect

www.ingramcontent.com/pod-product-compliance
Lightning Source LLC
Chambersburg PA
CBHW020253030726
47499CB00001B/188